"Three months is all I'm committing to."

"Agreed," Dash said. "You'll live in Gilbert Manor and we'll move Rory home this weekend."

"I'm not living there," Elle insisted. "Rory needs to stay in the hospital until she understands we aren't married and is more secure."

"No. I want her home and you are living there."

"I'll have to rethink this."

"You already have. You want a new wing for the hospital. What is three months of your life in return for that?"

"Okay, but no more kissing."

"We're supposed to be married."

"We can hold hands."

"No one is going to buy we're married."

"Only Rory has to buy it. Do we have an agreement?"

An excerpt from *Trapped with Temptation* by Cynthia St. Aubin

Shelby Llewellyn was an angel.

But not one of the glowing, ethereal beings featured in paintings of the nativity.

An *earth* angel.

Rosebud lips, wide fawn-brown eyes and a halo of golden curls. As far from the sleek, severe-looking picture of her on the gallery's website he could possibly imagine.

"I want to do a solo show of your work at the Llewellyn Gallery in San Francisco."

He turned to fully face her. "You came all this way just to say the exact same thing that's in your voice mails?"

She cocked her head and studied him below half-lowered lids. "You mean you actually listened to them?"

"Sometimes," he lied.

Most of them, several times over.

"Do I get an answer now?"

Bastien's brain ticked like a bomb, his senses so full of her he could scarcely manage an intelligent thought. "No."

"No, I don't get an answer, or no, you won't do the gallery show?" Her knee brushed the outside of his thigh at precisely the same moment as her voice dipped into a sultry register. His head swam, light and hollow as a balloon. A sure sign that blood was rushing to regions below the belt.

"Take your pick." Bastien rose from his seat and tossed two twenties down on the bar. He had to get out.

USA TODAY BESTSELLING AUTHOR

KATHERINE GARBERA

&

CYNTHIA ST. AUBIN

IT'S ONLY FAKE 'TIL MIDNIGHT
&
TRAPPED WITH TEMPTATION

HARLEQUIN

DESIRE

HARLEQUIN®
DESIRE™

Recycling programs for this product may not exist in your area.

ISBN-13: 978-1-335-45763-9

It's Only Fake 'Til Midnight & Trapped with Temptation

Copyright © 2023 by Harlequin Enterprises ULC

It's Only Fake 'Til Midnight
Copyright © 2023 by Katherine Garbera

Trapped with Temptation
Copyright © 2023 by Cynthia St. Aubin

For questions and comments about the quality of this book, please contact us at CustomerService@Harlequin.com.

Harlequin Enterprises ULC
22 Adelaide St. West, 41st Floor
Toronto, Ontario M5H 4E3, Canada
www.Harlequin.com

Printed in U.S.A.

CONTENTS

Katherine Garbera is the *USA TODAY* bestselling author of more than 120 books. She lives in the Midlands of the UK with her husband, but in her heart she'll always be a Florida girl who loves sunshine and beaches. Her books are known for their sizzling sensuality and emotional punch. Visit her on the web at katherinegarbera.com and on Instagram, Twitter and Facebook.

Books by Katherine Garbera

Harlequin Desire

The Image Project

Billionaire Makeover
The Billionaire Plan
Billionaire Fake Out

The Gilbert Curse

One Night Wager
It's Only Fake 'Til Midnight

Visit the Author Profile page
at Harlequin.com for more titles.

You can also find Katherine Garbera on Facebook,
along with other Harlequin Desire authors,
at Facebook.com/HarlequinDesireAuthors!

Dear Reader,

I'm so excited to be back in Gilbert Corners with the second book in The Gilbert Curse series. The curse is starting to weaken in the town and businesses are returning to Main Street and Rory Gilbert awakens from her coma, bringing Dr. Elle Monroe—a woman from Dash's past—back into the picture...and into a fake marriage.

After ten years asleep, Rory really isn't sure what is going on, but she is very happy to see her brother and his ex-girlfriend in her room. She assumes they are married, and when they try to dissuade her confusion and her heartbeat spikes, Dash says of course they are married. Elle has seen patients recover more quickly with familiar surroundings and agrees to be Dash's fake wife for a short time.

Except the attraction between the two of them is anything but fake, especially closer to midnight when both of their control is at its weakest.

I hope you enjoy *It's Only Fake 'Til Midnight* and returning to Gilbert Corners.

Happy reading!

Katherine

IT'S ONLY FAKE
'TIL MIDNIGHT

Katherine Garbera

This book is dedicated to Donna and Linda with much love. When I was growing up, I wanted to be an only child as I was the oldest of three girls close in age, but life has shown me how lucky I am to have my sisters and I'm very glad I'm not an only child. Thanks for the childhood adventures on the Swinging Tree, the support when we were young moms raising our kids and the continuous love. I'm so lucky to have you both!

Special thanks to Joss Wood for your friendship, which is a gift I treasure, and for those daily sprints that kept me on track.

One

Dash Gilbert heard the whispers as he walked down the long, sterile hallway at the Gilbert Corners Care Home. Some called him charming and lucky. Others spoke of the curse in town carrying his family name.

He was at the Gilbert Corners Care Home to see his sister. He dreaded Sundays because of the visits yet he never missed one. Rory had a traumatic brain injury sustained after a car crash ten years earlier.

Rory hadn't spoken or moved since that night she'd been crying in the car, just before it had spun out of control. The doctor that he'd arranged to care for his sister had recently retired, and the hospital who staffed the care home, which was on the same campus, had hired a well-qualified replacement—but Dash had yet to meet Dr. Monroe.

He opened the door to Rory's room after checking in at the nurse's desk and noticed that the shades were open. After reading an article about classical music stimulating brain functions, he'd ordered that it be played in the room as often as possible. Instead, "Islands In The Sun" by Weezer was blasting, and a man was leaning low over Rory.

The new doctor? Already Dash knew this man wouldn't do. For one thing, he wasn't following the instructions Dash had left. The man was tall and had dark brown hair and wasn't familiar.

"Excuse me? Are you Dr. Monroe?"

The man stood and turned to face Dash with a smile that faded quickly. "No, I'm not."

"Who are you? What are you doing in this room?" Dash asked, crossing to him and pinning him with a stare that was known to make more than a few men in boardrooms quake in their boots.

"I'm…a friend of Rory's."

"I know all of her friends, and I don't know you," Dash said.

The man stood up taller.

"Well, you don't know me yet," he said, holding out his hand.

"Get out," Dash said in a low tone.

The man looked as if he were going to argue but the bedsheets rustled behind him.

"Dash?"

He turned, unable to believe that he was hearing his sister's voice. It was rusty from disuse, and she looked confused as her gaze moved around the room.

"Here, ladybug," he said around the emotion that was tightening his throat. He never thought she'd talk to him again. He tried to remain calm, sitting down on the edge of the bed and taking her hand.

"Where am I?" she asked.

"In the hospital," he said, turning to the nurse who entered the room. "Turn that music off and get the doctor in here."

He looked back at his little sister and gently took her in his arms and hugged her, careful of the IV in her arm and the feeding tube in her stomach. She hugged him back weakly and rested her head on his shoulder. "I don't remember anything. How did I get here?"

"We were in a car accident," he started.

"What?"

One of the machines hooked up to Rory started to emit an alarm and she was almost shaking in his arms. Dash rubbed her back unsure of what to do, which he fucking hated. He always knew what to do...but with this he had no clue.

"Out of the way, she's in shock," a woman with a doctor's coat on said as she pushed past him.

Dash got up and stepped back. He stood there watching with his heart in his throat hoping he didn't lose Rory again after just getting her back. He took his phone out and texted Conrad that Rory was awake. He didn't want to move from his sister's side but needed to make sure that she got help immediately.

As the doctor and the nurses worked around his sister's bed, Dash turned to find the "friend" who he didn't know. But the man was gone. Focusing on the stranger was a lot easier than standing in the corner of the room like a chump.

One of the nurses asked him to wait in the hall and Dash went out there, leaning against the wall, unable to forget the last time he'd been in the hallway of a hospital. It had been the night of the accident when Rory went into her coma and Conrad had almost died. He felt the panic and grief starting to come back and took a deep breath. He heard heavy bootsteps coming toward and looked up to see his cousin.

"How'd you get here so quick?"

"I live in town now," he reminded Dash as he pulled him into a hug. "What happened?"

"There was a stranger in her room and as I was trying to figure out who he was, she said my name… I got to hold her for a second before alarms started going off—"

"She spoke? That's great. Right?" Conrad asked, pushing his hands through his hair.

"I don't know. The new doctor is with her now, but I'm not sure what her skills are."

"The new doctor is an expert in her field and will speak to you in her office when you're done."

He turned toward the voice and realized as his eyes met hers that he knew her. *Elle Monroe.* The woman who had been his date the night of the winter ball a decade ago. He wondered if she'd remember him. He hadn't forgotten her. How could he? They'd shared an incredible kiss that night, before he'd been pulled away when he heard his sister's scream.

Life had changed for him that night. It was felt like

something out of a fairytale that Rory had somehow brought Elle back into his life.

"Hottie alert."

Dr. Elle Monroe glanced over the rim of her coffee mug to see a tall, broad-shouldered man walking their way. Backlit by the sun, it was hard to make put his features, but he had thick dark hair that was artfully styled. He wore a designer suit that looked as if it had been custom made for him. The other medical professionals at the nursers station were staring at him as he came closer.

Elle did the same—until his features were visible and she quickly turned, heading toward her office in the hall behind the station.

There was no mistaking those piercing blue eyes, the sensual mouth and the stubborn jaw. Dash Gilbert.

They had history, and as much as she was all about fresh starts—hence her return to Gilbert Corners after all these years—she wasn't into making the same mistake twice.

Why couldn't he have put on a few extra pounds, or maybe his hair could have started thinning? There was nothing wrong with either of those things, but why oh why did he have to still look…so breathtakingly hot? Out of all of her exes…okay, there were only three, but he was the only one she still let her mind return to. Just Dash. Mr. Charming. Mr. Unforgettable. Mr. Left-You-Standing-Alone-at-Midnight-at-a-Ball.

Yeah, there was that.

She put the coffee mug on her desk and took a deep

breath. She was here to work, not stroll down memory lane, she reminded herself. She stretched and reached for the stack of patient folders that were on her desk. A lot of the information was also digitally available to her on her laptop, but she liked to see the physical copies of X-rays and lab results. Her mind processed things better on paper.

She was a trauma specialist who concentrated on long-term effects of head and spine injuries. She'd been offered this job in Gilbert Corners when their previous specialist had retired. She'd taken the job because…well, she was turning thirty in six months and she needed some closure, and Gilbert Corners was the source of most of her issues.

An alarm went off and she rushed back toward the nurses' station, glancing at the on-duty nurse.

"Rory Gilbert is awake," she said. "Room 323."

Elle dashed down the hall. She hadn't reviewed the charts yet, so she had no idea what the situation was going to be when she walked in, but she focused on her patient and not the man who she'd spent too much time thinking about.

She had been the one to tell the nurse to order him from the room as she and her nurse worked to stabilize the patient. It seemed to be a spiking pulse, no doubt due to stress.

"Hi, Rory. I'm Dr. Monroe," Elle said once Rory was stable and had a glass of water to drink. She'd been fed via a stomach tube, so they were monitoring her to see how her body handled the water.

"Elle, right? You and my brother are dating," Rory said.

Elle knew from her experience dealing with brain trauma patients that they often spoke of everything in the present. So perhaps her mind was just taking a few beats to catch up. "We were. What do you remember?" Elle asked her.

Rory's hand started to tremble from holding the cup and Elle took it from her.

"Not much really. I mean, Dash of course, and you. How long have I been out?" she asked.

"Almost ten years."

"What? How could that happen?"

Elle explained some of the medical reasons, but her last doctor had speculated that the trauma Rory had experienced that night played a big part in why she hadn't come out of the coma. Her mind had been protecting her, not wanting to go back to the world of pain that she'd left. "The brain works to protect the body and sometimes it shuts down for repairs."

"My brain thought I needed ten years…"

Elle smiled reassuringly at her. "Your body needed time too. Dash can probably tell you more," she said.

"Where is he?" she asked, looking around for him.

"We had to send him out of the room to make sure you were okay. Are you ready to see him again?" Elle asked. Personally, she wasn't sure she was ready for Dash to be back in the room.

"I think so. Ten years is a long time," she said.

"It is. Let me go get your brother and he can catch you up," Elle said.

She looked over at the nurse who nodded that she'd

keep an eye on the patient. Elle took a moment at the door to compose herself before opening it.

She was an expert in the field of head trauma. She wasn't the same girl she'd been at twenty who had thought that, after dating Dash for the entire fall semester, he was inviting her home to ask her to marry him. She was stronger today and more confident than she'd ever been.

And she totally wasn't interested in Mr. Dash Gilbert.

She opened the door and heard the low rumble of his voice. The scent of his spicy cologne wafted toward her, and she shook her head against the memory of how it had felt to be in his arms.

He was saying something about her skills. She knew that he'd fought to have an expert brought in from somewhere in Europe instead of her.

He was so arrogant. How had she never noticed it before?

Probably because she'd been so busy kissing him. They hadn't been able to keep their hands off each other in college. Which just made her more determined to deliver the news that his sister was better and never have to see him again.

She cleared her throat and he turned toward her.

"Elle Monroe."

"Dash Gilbert, still not quite as charming as rumor would have everyone believe you are."

"Oh, I have my moments. They just don't come when I'm worrying about my sister. How is she?"

"She's stable. You can go and visit with her. We'll

run some more tests after you two talk. I told her it's been ten years. She has a lot of questions, I'm sure."

"Thank you, Elle."

"That's my job, and it's Dr. Monroe," she said, turning on her heel and walking away from him.

She did a good job of pretending she wasn't aware of him watching her until she rounded the corner and entered her office. She collapsed into her chair and shook her head. Gilbert Corners didn't disappoint. She'd come back here to get closure on her past and it seemed that on her first day at work, she was getting her wish.

Now if only she could stop thinking about how Dash hadn't really changed much in the last ten years…except becoming even better looking, and definitely more arrogant.

Sitting in the hospital room and hearing Rory laugh at Conrad almost overwhelmed Dash. Dash had to turn away, feeling the sting of tears in his eyes. He had never thought he'd hear these two laughing again. Emotions weren't something he ever allowed himself to indulge in, but seeing the two people he almost lost talking was a good reason to feel. He knew that.

Con looked over at him and arched one eyebrow, asking silently if he was okay. Dash nodded. He'd been the one behind the wheel that night when they'd left the party. He hadn't anticipated being pursued and rammed by the other driver as they'd gotten to the icy bridge in the middle of town. And then everything had spiraled out of his control.

"You're a famous chef?" Rory was asking Conrad after he told her about his cooking show.

"Yeah, and I've got a girl now."

"I bet you have tons of girls. You always did," she said.

"Just one, she's special. You'll like her," Conrad said.

"So much has changed," Rory said. "It's a bit overwhelming."

"I know," Dash said, taking his sister's hand. "But we will take it slowly. What's the last thing you remember?"

"It was summer, and we were all home before college," she said.

"That was a fun one," Dash said. "All those late nights on the yacht."

"Yes. Elle taught me how to do a flip off the bow," Rory said.

Dash had forgotten that. He hadn't allowed his thoughts to dwell on her in the last ten years. He'd been too busy running the company and trying to ignore the fact that his sister was in a coma. But Elle had been so much fun that summer, which was why he'd invited her to the winter ball, though he knew that she didn't have the right connections for a serious relationship. His grandfather had been pushing for him to date the daughter of the CEO of a company he wanted to merge with.

"She did? How did I miss that?" Conrad asked.

"You were busy," Dash said dryly.

"No doubt. So, when can Rory leave the hospital?" Conrad asked.

"I don't know. I think I need to talk to Dr. Monroe," Dash said.

"Go on, I'll keep Rory company," Conrad said.

He left the room and one of the nurses rang for the doctor. He had to admit that Elle scarcely resembled that long ago summer girl he'd met. She had worn her hair down around her shoulders; it was always curling around her face. Her eyes had been full of energy back then. Now she seemed…well, like he felt inside. Like the last ten years had been long for her.

"Mr. Gilbert, how can I help you?"

"Call me Dash for starters," he said. "When can Elle go home? I'm sure she has to be able to do certain things like hold her arm up. She's still weak."

"Yes. I'll have my nurse provide you with a list of things she'll need to be able to do through physical therapy before she can be discharged."

"Thank you," he said, then shook his head. He was having a hard time dealing with the fact that his sister was awake and might be coming home soon. He'd been in therapy since the accident and survivor's guilt had weighed on him, and now, he wasn't sure he could believe that Rory was actually awake.

"Are you okay?"

"No," he answered honestly. "I can't believe everything that's happened today."

"That's understandable. Traumatic brain injuries are so unpredictable. Take some time to just enjoy her recovery. There will be a long list of things that you are both going to have to deal with as she recovers."

She was treating him like a stranger, he realized.

He was one, but at the same time he knew the way she felt in his arms, knew the taste of her mouth under his, knew that she wasn't a stranger. Not exactly.

But it was clear she didn't want to be on intimate terms with him, so he changed the subject. "There was a man in Rory's room when I arrived today. He said that he was a friend of hers. But I don't know the man and I didn't authorize him to be in there."

"Okay. I'll look into our records and see what I can find out," she said. "Is that all for now?"

"No, I owe you an apology. I shouldn't have said anything about your skills. I am sorry that I did. I want the best for my sister."

She gave him a half-smile. "I understand. Rest assured the hospital board wouldn't have hired me if they didn't believe I was qualified."

"I know you are," he said, then gave her that smile… the charming one she had a hard time resisting. "I'm used to being in control and just wanted to pick the candidate."

"You know you're not in charge of everything right?"

"Unfortunately yes."

"Let's go see Rory and tell her what's needed to be discharged. I find that patients in her condition need a list to keep them grounded in the present, otherwise she might dwell on the time and memories she's lost. That's very stressful and can trigger a relapse."

They had gotten to the door of Rory's room when Elle said this. She opened the door and he reached for her arm. Was she saying that Elle might go back into a coma?

"What do you mean by that?"

She looked up at him and put her hand on his chest. Her touch sent a pulse of blazing heat through him. This close, he could feel the exhalation of her breath against his neck. Their eyes met and he forgot about everything but the fact that his sister had woken up today and that he was reunited with the one woman who had seen him as a man, not just a Gilbert. He leaned down slowly to see if she'd react.

She shifted slightly closer to him. She smelled of summer and sunshine reminding him of that long ago time when he'd held her in his arms. He closed the gap between them, brushing his lips against hers.

Two

Kissing Dash Gilbert was a dumb idea, but he was so close, so vulnerable with his emotions for his sister, and she hadn't forgotten that long-ago passion. Maybe a part of her wanted to believe that her memories had exaggerated what it had been like to be held by him. How no other man had measured up to the fantasy of Dash.

But as his arms closed around her and his mouth moved overs hers, his tongue rubbing against hers, she knew that was a lie she'd been telling herself. He tasted so damned good and right. No other kiss had ever affected her the way this one was.

Someone cleared their throat and Dash lifted his head, looking down at her with an unreadable expression on his face.

Idiot, she thought.

"Excuse me," she said.

"No excuses needed, Elle," he said.

She brushed past him, avoiding the gaze of his cousin Conrad, who she recognized from his televised cooking show. It was hard to believe that she had come to the point in her life where she was back in Gilbert Corners, orbiting this family. She moved toward her patient.

Rory smiled at her as Elle got closer to the bed. "Elle, I'm so happy that you and Dash are still together. Were you worried that I'd be upset if I knew about it?"

What? "No, not at all. You have a lot to process. Ten years is a long time and you'll have a lot to catch up on."

"That's right, ladybug. I asked Dr. Monroe to come back in here to go over the steps before you can be discharged so we know what to do," Dash said, coming up behind her and putting his hand on her shoulder. A small shiver went through her. She shook her head. Snap out of it, she thought. That touch was purely platonic.

Yeah, but the kiss wasn't.

Which was why she was planning to ignore it.

"I'm going to have a physical therapist come in so we can get a good read on where you are physically," Elle said, deciding to just concentrate on her patient. She continued laying out a plan for Elle and told her they'd have milestones for her to achieve.

"I understand that you can't just let me go home alone. But if I came home with you and Dash, then that would be fine, wouldn't it?"

Her and Dash?

"Uh, no. You need a medial professional with you 24/7 I'm afraid."

"I am willing to hire whomever you think we need," Dash said.

She understood that he might want to get Elle out of the hospital. There wasn't a person she knew who wanted to spend more time in one, but Rory's medical condition was still in flux. Elle needed time before she'd feel safe signing her over to in-home care.

"Let's talk about that in a few weeks or so," Elle said.

"I don't want to stay here for weeks," Rory said. "Surely, I can come and live with you two. Dr. Monroe—Elle—you're my sister-in-law and my primary care doctor right now. I would be safe in that environment."

Elle leaned over Rory checking her pupils and her pulse at the same time. "Why do you think I'm your sister-in-law?"

"I saw you two kissing and I know you were hoping that Dash would propose at the winter ball," Rory said.

Elle blushed. She'd forgotten that Rory had been in the room with her and her stepsisters when they'd been teasing her about expecting a proposal. "That's not entirely true. I think you're confused."

Rory's pulse started racing and the machine monitoring her heart let out an alarm. Dash tried to reach around her but as the nurse rushed in, Elle turned to him.

"Please wait in the hall with your cousin."

They needed to be alone to figure out what was

causing this reaction in Rory. Elle kept looking at her and then at Dash. She nearly cried when she saw her brother leaving, and Elle realized that Dash was Rory's lifeline at this moment. She waved him back over and he took his sister's hand, staying out of the way of the nurse who was checking the IV drip. Rory was responding positively to Dash and Conrad, who had come into the room and was holding her other hand.

Having her family with her seemed to calm her. Once Elle was satisfied that her heartbeat was steady and her breathing back to normal, the nurse stepped out of the room and Elle got ready to leave as well. Based on her past experiences with patients who had recovered from prolonged comas, she knew that it took a while to start to feel normal again. And the patients often focused on one person or one moment from the past as they recovered. As a touchstone of sorts.

It seemed that Dash was Rory's touchstone. Of course, the last thing she remembered was that winter ball at Gilbert Manor. Dash and Conrad were talking quietly to her, and Elle wanted to contact Rory's previous doctor who had retired and find out if her charts had shown her reacting to Dash even while in the coma.

"I'll leave you all for now. Rory, you will be here for the foreseeable future," Elle said. "But don't worry, my goal is to get you home as soon as we can."

"Thanks, Elle," Dash said.

"No problem."

"But it is a problem," Rory said. "If you and Dash are married, why can't I go home and live with you?"

"We aren't—" Elle began but Dash cut her off.

"We don't have a room for you yet. I need to get things sorted with Elle, and then we can figure it out."

"Figure what out?" Rory asked.

"Which room will work best for you at Gilbert Manor," Dash said.

"Uh, Dash, we need to talk. Now," Elle insisted.

Dash had never been a man to deny his sister anything she wanted. This was a bit more than indulging her when she wanted a new convertible or covering for her with their grandfather. He knew he was pushing Elle into an awkward position, but his sister had been in a coma for ten years. And she was awake.

Awake. Finally.

He couldn't leave her in the hospital a minute longer. If the long hours he'd put into making Gilbert International a Fortune 100 company had been for anything, it had to be to use his money and influence to get his sister home. And if it meant begging Elle to pretend to be his wife, then so be it.

Their upbringing had been marked with tragedy and seeing her awake and talking—he was determined to do whatever was necessary to keep her on the path to recovery. He'd noticed that she seemed fixated on he and Elle, maybe believing that they were together was what she needed to recover. Dash had no idea, but whatever his sister needed from him, he would do. So if that meant pretending they were married then that's what they were both going to do.

He would do anything to protect his family and to make sure Rory made a full recovery.

"What are you saying in there? Lying to her isn't a good idea," Elle said as soon as they were in the hallway and the door to Rory's room had closed behind them.

"You saw how she reacted when you said we weren't a couple. I'm not losing her again," Dash said. "If we have to pretend we're married then that's what we are going to do."

"I don't know. We haven't even seen each other since that night of your crash," Elle said.

"We seemed to be catching up pretty well," he said, remembering that kiss. But he had a feeling that if he was going to get Elle to agree to this charade it wasn't going to be because he'd kissed her. "Also, tell me that you didn't notice the way she reacted when you corrected her on us being together."

"I did. And in the past, I have seen some of my patients with traumatic brain disorders need to feel like the world they remember is still there in order to heal more quickly."

"So…yes to being my fake wife?" he asked.

"No."

"Even if that means she'll recover more quickly?"

"This isn't something I'm prepared to do, Dash. There is no guarantee that this will help Rory remember anything."

"But there is a chance, right?" Dash asked.

"Sure. There is also the fact that I don't know you," she pointed out. "I remember Elle and I know you have always been a devoted older brother. But I don't know the man you've become."

"I still am that man. And speaking of the past, Rory remembers you wanting to be my bride. What's that about?"

She shook her head. "Nothing. I don't remember that."

But the flush of color on her neck told him she did. Interesting. But it wasn't what he needed to focus on. "Gilbert Manor is huge; you could have your own bedroom, and of course you'd be able to work and see—"

"Wow, I'd be able to work? You know it's the twenty-first century, right?"

"Of course, that's what I was reassuring you. What's your objection to coming to live with me until she recovers? You want what's best for your patients. I read the report that the board had done on you before you were hired. I just never connected it to you. You're known for going above and beyond in treatment. And you're not married, so how will pretending to be my wife be any different than the things you've done in the past?"

"Well for one, I never pretended to be married. Also, I'm not sure I like you," she said with more honesty than he'd expected.

"You don't? Why'd you kiss me?"

"Curiosity. Shocking as this might be, not everyone in the world loves you."

"I am not shocked. As you said, you don't know me. Give me a chance to prove I'm not the jerk you think I am," he said. If he thought there was any other way to speed up Rory's recovery he'd take it, but he'd seen twice when he or Elle had corrected her about the past that she had a physical reaction.

He wanted his sister healthy again. He needed her to be, so that maybe he could believe there was some redemption for him for that night. "I'm willing to give you whatever you might want in exchange."

"What do you mean whatever I want?" she asked, tucking a strand of hair behind her ear.

"A new house, a small fortune, just name it," he said.

"A new hospital wing here. This care home is outdated and needs modernization," she said.

"Done."

Elle tipped her head to the side, studying him.

"Wish you'd asked for more?"

"No. That's really all I need."

"Good. So we'll do this for six months—"

"Three months."

"Is that long enough for Rory?"

"It will have to be. Three months is all I'm committing to."

She was stubborn, something he didn't remember about her. But he'd known the girl she'd been—not this woman who she'd become. He wondered what other things had changed in the last ten years.

"Agreed. You'll live in Gilbert Manor, and I want Rory ready to move home this weekend. Just tell me what she needs in her room. Also send me the names of some in-home caregivers you would recommend."

"I'm not living there, and neither is Rory yet. She needs to stay in the hospital until she understands we aren't married and she's more secure."

Dash understood rationally what Elle was suggesting. Any other doctor would probably recommend the same thing, but Dash had been waiting for this moment, and if he were totally honest, had almost felt like this day would never come. A part of him wasn't going to believe that Rory was awake unless she was at home.

Then there was Elle. There were no two ways about it—he wanted her in his home. He didn't even pretend he was going to try to unpack all of those emotions in this moment.

"No. I want her home, and you are living there."

"I'll have to rethink this," she said.

"You already have. You want a new wing for the hospital. What is three months of your life in return for that?"

She narrowed her eyes. "What's in this for you?"

"Rory. Whole and happy," he said.

That was the simple truth.

"Okay. But no more kissing."

He arched one eyebrow at her. "We're supposed to be married."

She shook her head. "We can hold hands."

"No one is going to buy we're married if we just hold hands," he pointed out.

"Only Rory has to buy it. Conrad knows we aren't, as does everyone else in town. Is this even going to work?"

"All the more reason to get Rory to Gilbert Manor. We can control her surroundings until she is strong enough." He paused. "Do you think her memories will return?" he asked.

His mind was flooded with questions as he tried to

focus on nothing but his sister…and an image of Elle in his arms, in his bed. That wasn't the reason he was inviting her to be his fake wife. But he couldn't allow himself to think about her. Having tasted her lips again, he knew he was hungry for more.

They'd been young when they'd been together before. He'd been a different man, but the truth was they wouldn't have lasted together. He wasn't ready to marry any woman. Least of all one like Elle.

"I don't know when or if her memories will return," she confessed.

That wasn't what he had hoped to hear, but the truth seldom was. "Do we have an agreement?"

Did they have an agreement?

The answer should be hell no. Not only because of the kiss. She'd pretended in the past to be someone her patients remembered, to help them ease back into the world that felt foreign to them. It wasn't something she'd had to do long-term, and three months of pretending to be Dash's wife seemed like an eternity. And when Rory found out the truth…

She took a deep breath, trying to find an easy answer, but there wasn't one. She knew that she was going to have to review Rory's records. "Let me have some time to review her records before we commit to this, okay?"

"Yes. If there's another way then I'm all for it," he said.

"For now, I will tell her that I need to review her records and that we need to figure out her rooms at the

Manor. I know you want her home and I believe she'll recover her memory faster there. I just don't want to be a hindrance in any way."

"You won't be. Take the day to think it over. Why don't we have dinner tonight? That way we can get to know each other," he said. "I'll send a car for you around eight?"

Dinner. Of course they needed to talk, whatever she decided. "Dinner sounds fine, but I'll drive myself. Why don't we meet at Two If By Sea on the outskirts of town?"

She suggested the old coaching inn that had been modernized in the last decade. She'd eaten there with some of the staff at a welcoming dinner when she'd agreed to take her job.

"Sure. Will eight work for you?" he asked.

She nodded. "That should give me enough time to review everything. I'll send you a list of requirements for Rory's room. Regardless of what you and I decide, you'll still need to get it ready for her."

They exchanged phone numbers, and as he answered a text on his phone she looked at him from under her eyelashes. There was more to Dash than she remembered from their college romance. He had matured into the man she'd always known he would be. That arrogance and the confidence he'd had back then had been honed, in a way to make him seem more agreeable. But she knew that she was going to have to bring some solid proof to dissuade him from this fake marriage idea.

And did she want to dissuade him? Not just for Ro-

ry's sake but also for her own. She'd come back for closure and not just about being left alone on the dance
floor at midnight. In fact, in the scheme of her life that
was such a small part of her issues. And she had them.

She was reluctant to commit, afraid of attachments.
She ended relationships before they had a chance to be
serious. Part of her thought that was due to her mom's
death when she'd been eight, but another part knew
that it was tied to her father's remarriage. Love wasn't
always the path to happy-ever-after. Sometimes love
was a trap between two toxic people and Elle had always been afraid to risk it.

And this fake relationship with Dash might seem to
be safe on the surface, but if she was brutally honest
with herself, she had to admit her mouth still tingled
slightly from that kiss. That ill-advised, spur-of-the-
moment kiss that had made her feel alive in a way that
nothing had in a long time.

"Sorry about that. I pushed back several meetings
to stay here with Rory but there are some things that
only I can handle," he said.

"That's fine. I'll see you later. I trust you to handle
things with Rory," she said.

"I will. I'll let her know that you have other patients
and need to get up to speed on her recovery plan,"
Dash said.

"Okay well goodbye then," she said.

"Bye," he said.

She turned and walked away from him again. This
time though, she admitted to herself she was keenly
aware of him watching her. Keenly aware that she

wanted his attention. Keenly aware that she should not be entering into a pretend relationship with a man she wanted.

She wasn't a highly sexual person. She knew that about herself. But there was something about Dash that made her feel very feminine and very turned-on. She shook her head as soon as she was in her office and closed the door behind her.

"I heard you're married to Dash Gilbert," Becky Rodriquez said as she entered Elle's office ten minutes later.

"His sister thinks we are." Becky was her assistant and had moved with Elle to take this job.

"How is that a thing?" Becky asked. "I remember when Larry thought you were his sister."

"Yeah, it's like that."

"Except not. Do you even know Dash Gilbert?" Becky asked.

Elle didn't want to get into that. "We knew each other in college. I think Rory just made a connection seeing us both together. And she's really fragile right now."

"I know. I'm surprised she's doing as well as she is," Becky said.

"She and Dash are very close. I think it's helping that he is in there with her," Elle said.

"That makes sense. What a tragic family they are," Becky said. "Mona caught me up on the accident but also on their grandfather closing the factory and all the bad luck that came from it—they say the Gilberts are cursed."

"Do they?"

"Well, sort of, I guess Conrad Gilbert came back to town and fell in love so now the curse is starting to break."

Becky shook her head and they both started laughing. Becky left a few minutes later and Elle got to work reviewing Rory's medical files, and as she did so, she couldn't help but empathize with Dash wanting to do whatever he could for his sister. The last ten years must have been torture for him. He was a man used to getting what he wanted. His money ensured he always got results, but Rory had been the one thing he couldn't fix with his arrogance or fortune.

Had that changed him?

Three

Elle dodged a few more questions from the well-meaning staff on her way out of the hospital at the end of the day. She stopped to check in on Rory, who was sleeping. She looked down on her patient and had the same stirring she always did when she saw a woman in a hospital bed. It reminded her so much of her mom. The sole reason why she'd gone into medicine was her mom's long illness as a child.

She would have done anything to help her mom recover, which was why she was entertaining Dash's idea of a fake marriage even though for her personally, it might not be the best idea. It was one thing to say she wanted closure. One thing to say that this might bring her some, but she hadn't come back to Gilbert Corners because of Dash. Her baggage from the past was that house that she'd lived in with her mom and dad and all the happy memories she'd had there.

That almost-fairytale existence that had been hers until she turned eight. That was what she was trying to sort out. She'd been to therapy, and she knew what she was supposed to do, but somehow, she couldn't get there. Every time she thought she'd figured it out, she hadn't. She had a track record of short-term relationships with decent men. Which, no matter how she tried to frame it, didn't seem that healthy. It would be different if they were all bad guys, but they weren't. She was hurting men for no other reason than she couldn't trust a relationship not to end.

She checked Rory's vitals and left her room. She'd started to touch up her makeup but then reminded herself that this was a business deal, not a date. Which she could almost convince herself of if she forgot that kiss.

Why had she kissed him?

She had no idea. He was close, he'd smelled good, he looked good. And the last time she'd felt any kind of fun in a relationship had been with Dash. So for a second, she'd just taken what she wanted.

And it had backfired. Big time.

She got to the restaurant and went in to get a table. The crowd was light. Most people were back at home getting ready for the work week. She ordered a glass of sparkling water with a twist of lime and then pulled out her tablet and the notes she'd made earlier.

Given her emotional state and the fact that she had so little control around Dash, she had thought she'd try to negotiate him down to one month instead of the time she had agreed to.

"Sorry I'm late," Dash said as he approached the table. She looked up noticing he'd taken time to change into a pair of dress trousers and a button-down shirt.

"You're not. I'm chronically early," she said.

He sat down across from her and the waiter took his drink order. Dash let the man know that they'd need some time before ordering and he'd signal him when they were ready.

"I got the list of the equipment you sent. My assistant is taking care of everything and it should be here by Wednesday. Where do we stand with Rory being discharged?"

She smiled gently at him. He was trying to control the pace at which things would happen, but with medicine it didn't work that way. "We're in the exact same place. Nothing has changed."

"Why not?"

"You know that she just woke up. I'll need more than six hours to diagnose what's changed. We'll be running a whole battery of tests starting tomorrow. I'll let you know when things change."

Dash leaned forward. "You'll update me tomorrow. I have to be in Boston for a meeting from ten to six. So we can talk at seven if that works for you."

She shook her head.

"Why not?"

"Because I don't work for you," she reminded him.

"But you are my wife, don't forget. I'll try to accommodate you, after all happy wife, happy life, right?" he said with a wink.

Would he really put his wife first? What was she even contemplating that for? She didn't come back her to be married to Dash—fake or not. "I'm not your wife. I haven't completely agreed to this fake relationship."

"You're not a wishy-washy person, Elle. I know you wouldn't be here if you hadn't decided to do it," he said.

She hated that he was right and charming. He wasn't arguing with her or bossing her which would have made her turn him down and walk away. "How can you be sure?"

"Because I saw you start to text me and stop several times this afternoon. I can only guess you thought about backing out but decided not to."

She shrugged. "Yeah, I did."

"So why are you here? I'm getting the feeling it's not because of my charm."

She smiled at the self-deprecating way he grinned at her.

"I want Rory back to full health too. I think that giving her a gateway to those lost memories might help. I've looked at her most recent scans and medical reports. I do believe that she'll make a full memory recovery."

Also the chance to help Dash have his sister back—the sister he remembered fully healthy—was something that Elle couldn't resist helping him with. She would give anything for one more day with her mom.

She saw the relief on Dash's face and wondered if his confidence wasn't in a small way bravado. Oh, she knew he had arrogance in spades, but this situation with Rory was different. And she noticed a different side to him where his little sister was concerned.

"That's good to hear. What do you mean by gateway?" he asked.

Her stomach growled. She put her hand on it and took a sip of her sparkling water but Dash summoned their waiter and they placed their dinner order.

"Sorry about that," she said after the server had gone. "I skipped lunch."

"Does that happen often?"

"I try not to let it. But when I get a new patient, I do sometimes get lost trying to put the pieces of the puzzle together. Trying to figure out what course of action will lead to their recovery."

"You like your work then?"

"I love it," she replied earnestly.

"You weren't premed when we were dating, were you?"

"No, I wasn't," she said, unwilling to talk too much about everything that had happened in her life during that post-Dash dating period. She'd gone from having everything to…well, reality, right? No one had a perfect life, so she'd probably been deluding herself when she'd thought she had one.

Their food arrived, and after the waiter left, he gave her a quizzical look. "So tell me more about how you thought I was going to propose."

Of course he'd remember that. The one thing she'd really wished he'd forget. She took a large bite of her salmon to avoid answering him, but she knew she had to eventually.

* * *

Dash hadn't been sure when he'd bring up that bit of awkwardness, but he needed to find out more about Elle than his memory. Had she been in love with him? He remembered their fall semester of college but hadn't remembered her major. She'd been pretty, fun, sexy, but that was it. It had felt like a college fling to him, though that may have had more to do with the pressure to marry an heiress and the trauma of the accident than anything else.

But if she thought he was going to propose, he needed more context on that before he invited her to live at Gilbert Manor.

"Uh, God. So I never said you were going to propose," she said, after swallowing a large bite of salmon.

"Then how did Rory hear that? Or is that something she's imagining?" he asked. Dash still wasn't sure how much of Rory's "memories" were real and how much was her filling in blanks. There had been times during the afternoon when his sister had been very lucid and then times when she'd been sort of foggy and had said things that didn't make sense. "I know this is uncomfortable but I just want to know how things were left in the past."

She put her hand on the table and turned her fork over in her fingers. "Do you remember Dru and Ana? My stepsisters?"

He vaguely recalled that Elle had been living at home that semester and she had two older sisters—he hadn't realized they were stepsisters as they'd seemed so close when he'd been dating Elle. "Sort of. We didn't spend any time with your family."

"They aren't my family—not really. Anyway, Rory offered for me to bring them along to the winter ball your family was hosting and we were all getting changed in the room you'd provided. When my step-sisters were just teasing me and saying that I must be important to you for you to have given us a room and all that stuff. I said we were just dating and then Dru said, 'But hoping for a proposal.' And I replied sar-castically, 'Yes, that's why I'm here, he's going to pro-pose tonight.' I had no idea Rory had overheard that. But that's it."

Her feelings toward her stepmother and stepsisters were complicated, they always had been. She'd felt close to them. Had wanted to have that sisterly bond that she'd never had before. Elle had embraced that feeling that she'd thought was her own until the mo-ment her father died. Everything had changed in that moment. Things that Elle had always believed were truth had been proven lies.

Dash leaned back and studied her. He could see signs of stress around her mouth as she spoke of her stepsisters and refused to call them her family. Elle had always been honest and a little lost, which might have been what drew him to her in the beginning. But this new version had hidden depths that he was starting to get to know. "That makes a bit of sense."

"Were you worried I was a creepy stalker and you had just invited me into your home?"

"A little bit."

"I'm happy to call it off."

"Yeah, that was the other part that made me doubt you were a stalker. You keep trying to get out of being my fake wife."

She raised both eyebrows at him and the made a funny face at him. "So as long as I'm not harboring real marriage vibes, you're good with me?"

"Yes."

"Is it an aversion to marriage to me or marriage in general?" she asked.

"That's a bit personal," he said in a brusque manner that normally shut down lines of conversation he didn't want to have.

"You just asked me something very personal," she pointed out.

He realized that she wasn't intimidated by him. If he thought sitting taller and glowering at her would work, he'd have done it but he knew it wouldn't. "I was involved in that."

"And I'm involved in this. Is it me?" she asked.

"Any man would be lucky to call you his wife," he said. She was pretty, smart, feisty and had an innate sexiness that he thought she probably wasn't aware of. If he were a different man. maybe he'd even consider a real relationship with her.

But he wasn't. He never had been. He had been engaged once and had tried to make both business and a relationship work but it hadn't. He was so mono-focused, more than likely why he'd been thriving as the CEO of Gilbert International. No woman could ever compete with the company, probably because he didn't have to discuss anything and could do what he wanted.

"But not you?"

"Marriage isn't for me," he said, hoping to leave it at that.

"Why not?"

He tipped his head to the side and gave her a hard stare.

"Is it the curse?"

"Yes."

"But your cousin broke it. I heard all about it at the nurses' station."

"If only a curse was that easy to break," he said. "Con coming back to GC just made us both realize we should invest a little in the town."

"So then what is the real curse?"

He remembered their kiss earlier and the way he was getting turned on tonight sitting across from her and talking. She affected him. He couldn't stop staring at the strand of hair that had escaped her updo and how it curled against her cheek, until she realized it and tucked it behind her ear. He remembered that from college, too. The white-hot energy that seemed to arch between the two of them whenever they were together. It was probably better to tell her right now so when they fell into bed—and he was pretty damned sure they would—she wouldn't get the wrong idea.

"The Gilberts have a curse that has nothing to do with the town, or maybe indirectly affects the town," he started, took a healthy slip of his Jack and Coke. "We seem to have the Midas touch."

"That's not exactly a curse. I know a lot of people who would like to have everything they touch turn to gold."

"Possibly, until that quest for gold—or in our case, fortune—takes complete control," he said. "No Gilbert wife has outlived her husband. Most of them have died alone while their husbands were out working to increase the Gilbert legacy. I have decided it ends with me."

"What now? You think if you get married, your wife will die?"

He did believe that, but he'd said as much as he was going to say about it. "That's why our marriage is the perfect one for me."

"Are you afraid of love?"

"I'm not afraid of anything. Plus I'm not really sure that romantic love exists. I mean, I've been in some intense relationships, but I was fine when they ended. What about you?'

"Me?"

"Are you looking for love?"

She shook her head. "I don't want to find love. I know that it can be very hard to tell the difference between the real thing and something that merely looks like it."

"I'm not going to lie to you, Elle," he said.

"Says my fake husband."

Fake husband. The only time he was going to have a wife and it wasn't real. He got why she was reluctant to trust him but he wanted her to. Knowing he had no right to ask for that didn't make him not want it or her.

* * *

Maybe it was the fact that she was tired, or maybe it was the fact that Dash had been so frank about not believing he'd find love because he had the Midas touch. She didn't know. But the truth was Gilbert Corners was that one place in the world where, at one point in time, she'd been truly happy. She'd seen love between her mom and dad and knew that it existed in the world.

The waiter had cleared away their dinner dishes and they'd both declined dessert. She realized she wasn't looking forward to going home. She'd been working longer hours at the care home and hospital because her childhood home was a little rundown and made her a bit sad.

Living at Gilbert Manor would give her a reason to stay away, so she had to be careful she wasn't running away from the past since allegedly she'd come back to confront it.

However, Dash *was* part of her past. She would reckon he didn't remember leaving her alone the night of the ball.

Given the situation with his sister… Rumor had it she'd had an incident with a man and then the car accident came directly after. She didn't hold that moment against Dash. There were other things going on and he had called her the following morning. So that wasn't an issue.

Dash had disconnected from everything and everyone after the car crash, focusing on taking care of his family. Something that Elle knew she would have done for her mom and dad. So she got that part of Dash, too. She had no issues with him in the past, which just left the present.

Living with him might cause issues.

She'd seen her mother's death and how that had devastated her father but not broken him. He'd still been the kind, loving man he'd always been toward her. When he'd remarried…that had broken them. She'd seen another side of love and it was toxic. The thing was, at thirteen, Elle had thought her stepmom and her father were a good match. It was only over time that the truth had come out.

"Then it's good to know that we both won't let emotions get in our way," Dash said.

"No, we won't. Why is it good?"

He reached across the table and took her hand in his. A shiver of sensual awareness went up her arm and straight to her center. She had tried to keep this all business, but there had been times when her gaze had strayed to his mouth, remembering how it felt pressed against hers. One impulsive kiss had lit a fire inside of her.

She could pretend that she had it under control and that her desires for him had been quenched but she knew they hadn't. She knew that if they lived under the same roof, it would be hard to keep her distance.

But she also realized that for her own sanity, she had to. For Rory's sake, they couldn't fall into an affair.

She pulled her hand back, balling it into a fist on her lap.

"Are we pretending there isn't something between us?"

"I am. I don't know what you are going to do," she

said. "But this marriage between us will be for Rory's sake. That means we have to keep her front of mind. I don't want to do something impulsively that will have a negative impact on my patient."

"Why would it be negative?" he asked. "We've both agreed that love doesn't exist and we aren't interested in that. So we can enjoy each other without any strings."

No strings.

As if that ever worked out, she thought. But she was tempted. It had been a long time since she'd really just enjoyed hooking up with a guy. There was always the worry that she'd start to feel something for him and then…her conundrum. Would those feelings be real or not?

She couldn't take a chance normally but as he said… he wasn't going to fall in love with her. "You really love money more than people."

"I didn't say that."

"What did you say?"

"That any woman I love will be sacrificed," he said. "Even Rory, who is only my sister and a Gilbert, was."

"I don't see the logic—"

"It's a curse, Elle."

A curse. She had grown up in town and there were lots of legends and curses that were talked about. The town of Gilbert Corners had seen its fortunes rise and fall with the Gilbert family. And the Gilbert family had abandoned the town more than once and when they returned, so did the good times. So she wasn't just going to dismiss his thoughts on the curse.

She'd seen the power of thought and belief on enough of her patients to know that even if there wasn't something magical at play in Gilbert Corners, the people and it seemed Dash believed in this curse. That was enough for her to treat it with respect.

"I'm not sure about a physical relationship with you," she said.

"I'm remembering that kiss…"

She groaned.

He smiled.

"Me too. I don't even know why I kissed you."

"I'm glad you did," he said. "Whys don't matter if we are just having fun. When was the last time you just did something because you enjoyed it?"

Honestly, she wasn't sure she ever had. She'd always been too worried about her mom and getting back to take care of her to let herself just enjoy the moment. But that made her feel sad, so she shook her head. "Okay."

"Okay?"

"Let's enjoy the ride," she said. "But Rory comes first."

"Of course. I'm not going to put my own needs over my sister's health," he said.

She turned the conversation to the town of Gilbert Corners, asking Dash to catch up on everything that had been going on. But she found it hard to concentrate on his words. Instead, she listened to the cadence of his voice and wondered if this was the road to closure or if she'd somehow stumbled into something else.

But it was different, and she was back home again. She was hoping to recapture some of the girl she'd been and find some peace with the woman she was. She had never been afraid to be alone but she knew a part of her mourned for the family she'd had before her mother's death. Maybe this thing with Dash would bring her some answers.

Four

Dash wasn't really in the mood to go back to his place in the city. He never stayed overnight in Gilbert Corners, and honestly, it was only that he thought Rory would be more comfortable there that had made him suggest Gilbert Manor. "Do you have to get home?"

He'd always been a bit of a night owl, but he knew that not everyone was. His assistant, for one, who didn't respond to his texts in middle of the night.

"I don't, why?"

"I'm restless and don't want to be alone," he admitted. "I could work but…the thought of spending hours at my computer when I could be alone with you…"

"What do you have in mind?" she asked.

"There's a secret bar in town."

"The speakeasy?"

"Yes. Have you been?"

"No, but there was a flyer in my mailbox about it yesterday," she said. "Want to try to find it?"

"Yes," he said. He thought there was something intriguing about Elle. The truth was, lust—if it was lust alone—wasn't all that rare. It had been a while since he'd felt an attraction this strong, but at the same time, he wasn't sure it was wise to pursue. He was waffling around Elle, and that wasn't like him.

So he wanted to figure it out. Was it just relief that Rory was awake? Or was he just lonely? Now that Conrad was with Indy he couldn't just show up at his cousin's place whenever he felt like it. And Rory was stuck in some weird ten-years-ago world that freaked him out and also made him angry at the time for the time his sister had lost.

Rory thought he and Elle were married. For ten years.

It was odd to think that he and Elle might have had a different life but for the car crash. Rory's belief that they would have married was so solid that Dash was looking at her and trying to see what his sister had. Would they still have been together? Would he have dodged the curse? Or would she still be an ex?

His life had been defined by the car crash. He'd been behind the wheel, and he'd been the only one to walk away from it. He felt that it was right that it should define him, but if he were being totally honest, he scarcely remembered the man he'd been before that night.

The past decade had shaped him and honed him into

the man he was. A man without any close connections except to Con and Rory.

That meant unless his sister had lost her edge while she'd been in the coma, she was going to notice if they weren't comfortable with each other.

Oh, damn. Was he justifying spending more time with her?

"I live close to town center," Elle said. "I'll meet you in town square under the revolutionary war statue."

"Sounds good," he said.

He waited until she was in her car and drove away before turning to his driver who stood by the Rolls Royce Silver Wraith. Dash had hired Hamm eight years earlier so that he could work when they made trips to Gilbert Corners to check on Rory. Hamm was strictly his driver. He had an assistant at the office and a housekeeper at his place in Boston but kept his staff small.

"Where to, sir?"

"Town center, Hamm. Then you can head back to Boston to get whatever you need for our extended stay here. I've alerted the staff to ready the garage apartment for you. Take your time. I can make do with Ubers or drive myself until you are back."

"Very well," he said. "I am glad to hear Miss Rory is awake."

"Thank you," he said as he got in the back seat of the car.

He pulled out his phone to answer emails and texts that came in at all hours because of the international nature of his business. But he realized that he was just staring at the phone and thinking of Elle's face. Her mouth especially. The way that it had felt under his and how it had looked full and luscious when she'd sassed him.

There was something about her… He knew he couldn't let her get under his skin. He wouldn't. He'd always been very good at keeping his heart locked away. Of course it had been easier with Rory in a coma. He'd been frozen all of those years. But now he…hell, he wanted to celebrate, and he wanted to let loose and have fun.

He knew that if Conrad were here, his cousin would tell him to pick up someone and get laid. And Dash wanted that, but not with someone anonymous. He wanted it with Elle.

His mind was telling him that was a dumb idea. They had to maintain a facade of being married for Rory's sake. She was in essence working for him, but she wasn't. She'd agreed to the charade. All he had to do was be a gentleman. He could do that.

She'd been open to seeing where this path took them. He would be too. He remembered what she said about love. That made him sad. She'd used to be so easy to share her feelings and open to love when they'd dated. Of course her opinion on love meant that they were both suited for an affair. Neither of them was hoping to find true love. He pocketed his phone as Hamm dropped him off in the town square, then he walked over to the statue.

It was a hot summer evening, making his skin feel too tight. He glanced around and saw signs of the town coming back to life. The storefronts that were no longer vacant, and couples and groups of friends out searching for the speakeasy that moved locations every couple of weeks. He was glad to see it.

He and Conrad had decided to start putting more money into the town and undoing the economic downfall that had occurred when his grandfather had shut down the factory on the outskirts of Gilbert Corners. Dash had looked at the numbers and knew that his grandfather had made a sound financial decision, but seeing this place get so rundown had made Dash realize that there were more things to consider than the bottom line.

Which wasn't like him normally.

"Ready to go find this bar?"

He turned to see Elle standing beside him. She had the flyer in one hand and her phone with a map app open on it in the other. He looked down into her upturned face and knew he was ready for more than that.

"As ever."

"It was your idea," she reminded him. "You don't sound excited.

His path had always been so easy to follow. His duty to Rory and Conrad had been a hair shirt he'd donned every day as some sort of odd penance for not being injured. He'd ignored Gilbert Corners except through the odd glance through the window as he'd driven through to visit Rory.

Everything was starting to change around him. His sister was awake, thank God. It was a prayer he wasn't sure he deserved to have answered. His cousin had found love and had returned to GC and wanted to see it become a home. These were things that Dash had no control over.

There was nothing that was the same as it had been.

Except when he was with Elle, he had a glimpse of something that he might be able to control. A place where he could let himself just be. She wasn't expecting love from him and in that unexpectedly came a freedom he'd never had before.

If only he could let himself reach out and take it. He wanted to, but he was very good at stopping himself from taking what he wanted in his personal life. Could he do it this one time?

There was something very similar to a caged animal about Dash as they walked through town, following the clues to the secret bar. The night sky and the heat of the city were making her feel restless too. This close to the coast she could see lightning in the distance but there was no thunder. She remembered the lightning storms from when she was child.

"I used to love lightning. My mom told me it was ideas and energy spreading over the world."

He turned to look at her. She had forgotten how tall he was compared to her. She had been dating men who were closer to her height. At five foot seven inches tall, most men weren't that much taller than she was.

"My mom said stay away from the windows. She used to pull me and Rory into her bed and she'd read us stories from this old book she had."

"Were you afraid of the storms?" she asked.

He shook his head. "No. Mom was. But holding Rory and I close…it soothed her."

She realized how much she hadn't really known Dash when they'd dated in college. This man was a protector, but she'd never seen it. To be fair, they'd only been on a handful of actual dates before the accident that had changed the course of his life. They'd met at the end of summer and then her coursework had limited the dates they went on. And the ball that had changed hers.

"That's sweet. My mom was a scientist. She died when I was eight, so I wasn't aware of that when she was alive. When I was little, she was always taking me outside to look at the sky and watch the weather patterns. And she always just made up little stories to go with them."

"I'm sorry your mom died when you were little," he said, a hitch in his voice as he put his hand on the small of her back. "My parents died when I was ten."

"Everyone who grew up here knows that story," she said.

"You grew up here? I somehow forgot that, but given that we met at Harvard, maybe you can overlook that."

"I was living in Boston when we met, I probably didn't mention it," she said.

"Why not?"

Yeah, why not, Elle? The favored son of her hometown had asked her out and she'd never mentioned this place. "It's complicated."

He gave a dry laugh. "I say that when I don't want to discuss something."

"Bingo," she answered.

"I'll allow it," he replied jokingly.

"Oh, jeez, thanks. What about you? Have you been living here since the accident?" she asked.

"No. I left to take over running the global corporation after Grandfather's health declined. The years while Conrad was recovering and then 'finding' himself took a toll, and after Grandfather's death, I was sort of sick of Gilbert Corners."

She slipped her hand into his as they stopped to look for the next clue and squeezed it. "I'm sorry for your loss. It must have been hard to be the only one unscathed by the accident."

He turned so that he blocked them from the sidewalk and created a pocket of intimacy. She looked up at him.

"You're the first person not to tell me how lucky I am."

"That doesn't seem like luck to me," she said. People had often told her she was lucky her father had found a new wife with two daughters her age—and after her father's death, she'd realized just how wrong they were. Luck hadn't made her and Dru and Ana sisters. Something that she had realized after that winter ball.

"Elle….what am I going to do about you?"

It sounded rhetorical but she shrugged all the same. "What do you want to do with me?"

He groaned. His hand fell to her shoulder and she felt his finger on the side of her face. He'd captured the strand of hair that had stubbornly refused to stay back in her ponytail and twirled it around his finger. "I'm not sure I should answer that."

"Why not?"

"Because I'm trying to be a gentleman. Trying to give you time to get to know me," he said.

"I think we are getting to know each other," she replied. On the drive back to her place, she'd thought about just how much she'd been hiding from life by burying herself in her work. She'd also hidden away in fear. Almost as if she hadn't wanted to allow herself to have fun. And Dash...well he'd be different. Intense, and she had the feeling, very satisfying.

Tonight, with the lightning dancing in the distance and him so close and so tempting, it seemed like that energy her mom had spoken of was surrounding her. She hadn't felt like this in a long time. She knew that she had to be sensible for the sake of Rory and her long path of recovery, one that would bind Elle to Dash for the foreseeable future. But another part of her just wanted to take this chance.

She put her hand on the side of his face, caressing his mouth with her thumb before she went up on tiptoe and kissed him. He tasted as good as she remembered, and this time, away from the hospital and away from his family, it seemed like they weren't rushed. She felt his arm come around her waist as he lifted her off her feet and more fully into his body.

His tongue rubbed over hers and she tipped her head to the side to deepen the kiss. She put her arms around his shoulders, pressing her chest against his and felt the stirring of his erection against her.

She knew he wanted her.

That was such a heady feeling.

She wanted him too.

She was afraid of that. Afraid that if she lifted her head, reality would set back in and she'd push him away. For just once in her adult life, she wanted to be carefree and not sensible. And if ever there was a moment, it was this one.

He set her slowly back on her feet and lifted his head.

"Talk about complicated."

She had a point. This wasn't something that needed talking through, whatever was between them required action. He rubbed his thumb over her bottom lip which was swollen from his kisses.

The sidewalk was busy, no doubt because it was summer and school was out. He stepped closer to Elle and noticed they were standing in front of Indy's bookstore. He looked at the display in the window that she'd created with summer-themed books on a picnic blanket.

They could keep following the path and go to a bar where they would have drinks and make small talk. But he wasn't in the mood for that. He wanted Elle, and if that kiss was any indication, she wanted him too.

"Want to skip the bar and go somewhere we can be alone?" he asked. He had never been someone to deny himself. And there was still so much about her that he didn't know.

She took a deep breath. He could see her mind working quickly to try to decide if sleeping with him tonight was a smart choice. He wanted to reassure her that she'd have no regrets after being in his bed. But this had to be her decision.

The spark between them was too hot to go out. If they had to wait a few more days or even a week, he could. But he knew eventually they were going to end up in each other's arms.

"Yes. But tomorrow things go back to the way they were." She reached up and tucked that strand of hair behind her ear.

"How were they?" he asked lifting the strand from behind her ear and twirling it around his finger. Her hair was soft and springy. He pulled his finger away and then stepped back to give her room.

"Strangers being fake married for your sister," she said with a faint smile. "Something that will hopefully help her regain her stability. And *that* we won't have to do for too long."

One night. They'd said they'd see where the path took them, but he knew that would be complicated and it seemed that Elle did too. Something short and sweet. This kind of heat, like the summer lightning, wasn't meant to last forever.

"Agreed. I will send for a car," he said.

"Or we could go to my place," she said. "It's just a few blocks from here."

A few blocks sounded good to him. "Lead the way."

She took his hand in hers. She'd done it earlier when she'd been talking about the storms. She was a tactile person and after years of living alone and not really touching anyone, it was…odd to him. He dropped her hand and continued walking next to her, taking out his phone as if he'd gotten a text.

"Work?" she asked.

"I needed to check on the markets in Japan," he said, which was sort of true. He'd sent an email earlier but he needed to find his equilibrium and work always was the way he did that.

The fact was his hand still tingled from touching hers. She was so much more tactile than he was used to. Frankly, he was used to moving through life as if he had a protective wrap on his body. Unless he was shaking someone's hand at a business meeting or having sex, he rarely touched anyone.

"I'm not on call, but if there is an emergency with one of my patients, I'll have to respond too. It's funny, but I never think of businessmen as being needed at all hours," she said. "I guess it depends on the business."

She was talking a lot, which she normally didn't do, not like this. She had to be nervous. "The Gilbert Corporation is global so we have offices all over the world. Most of the time I'm not needed, but there are some decisions that I have to be a part of."

"Why? Because of your expertise."

"You could say that, but its more that most of the time no one else wants the heat if a deal goes sour. And sometimes I have to step in to close it," he said. He had no tolerance for mistakes, and he knew that meant some staff wouldn't make a final decision until he'd signed off on it.

"I don't think I'd like working for you."

"Ouch. Why not?"

She lifted both of her eyebrows at him. "You sound like you are very demanding."

"I am. And technically you will be working for me," he said.

"Not technically. I'm still an employee of the Gilbert Corners Medical Center and Hospital, and Rory isn't my only patient."

He hadn't considered that. "Should you take a leave from the hospital so you can concentrate on Rory?"

"No," Elle said. "I'm not doing that. She'll be fine with the private nurse you hire her and her regular checkups with me."

She wouldn't let herself be bullied into doing what he wanted, which he respected. He would see how the private nurse went. She led them off Main Street on to Briar Wood Run and he noticed the houses here were in good shape with large lawns. He saw her car in the driveway of the last house on the street backing up to a field that he knew lead to the river that also ran through the center of town.

"This is my place. I'm only partially moved in, so excuse the boxes," she said as she unlocked the front door.

"I'm not here for the house tour," he said to her as they stepped inside and he closed the door behind him. She put her keys on a table near the door and then turned to him.

Now that they were alone, he reached for her and pulled her back into his arms. She fit perfectly in them, coming closer until her breasts brushed his chest and he felt himself getting hard. He brought his mouth down on hers and unlike the kiss she'd initiated, his was deep and demanding. He wanted everything she had to give.

If this was to be their only night together, and he was enough of a fatalist to think it probably would be, then he would learn all of her secrets and take his time with her. He wanted to solve the mystery that was Elle Monroe.

Five

Turning off her brain had never been easy for Elle—she lived to overthink so many things—but tonight it wasn't hard. Saying that Dash felt right pressed against her was nothing less than the truth. They hadn't hooked up in college, though they had one heavy make out session before that winter ball and the night the world changed for both of them.

But having Dash Gilbert in her hallway, his hands roaming up and down her back, the heat from his body against her, was hard to actually believe. He turned so that her back was against the wall, and she arched against it putting her hands around his torso, pulling him closer.

Passion was a liquid fire in her veins making every inch of skin feel more sensitive than it had before.

She found the buttons on his shirt and started undoing them. Starting in the center because that's where her hands were. He lifted his head, breaking their kiss and she couldn't help but stare up into his eyes.

There was a surety and confidence to Dash that had always been there, but also simmering passion. She felt the thick shaft of his erection against her stomach. God, she wanted him. More than she had expected to. Her fingers moved more quickly on his buttons because she wanted to put her hands on his skin.

To wrap him in her arms and make him hers, even if she knew there was no future in it. In fact, she could let down her guard precisely because there was no future in this. This night had no consequences—

"I'm on the pill," she blurted out.

"Thank God. I don't carry around condoms," he confessed.

"That's okay, I have some," she said. No way was she ever taking a chance on getting pregnant. She wasn't sure enough of herself and what she wanted from life to bring a child into the mix.

He arched one eyebrow at her. "Want me to wear one?"

"Would you mind? I mean, we're strangers and—"

He leaned down and kissed her not with the intense passion of a moment earlier but something tamer and gentler. "I don't mind. Where are they?"

"Uh, actually. I think in a box in the powder room."

She hadn't finished unpacking yet so everything had been stored out of the way.

"Perfect," he said, stepping back from her.

She ran into the bathroom and found the box, grabbed it and went back in the hallway. Dash had removed his shirt while she was gone and was leaning against the turned spindle banister. He had his legs stretched out and she noticed he'd undone the top button of his pants. She just stared at him, catching her breath at the beauty of his body.

He noticed her and started to straighten up, but she shook her head, crossing the short distance to him. She put her hand in the center of his chest. There was a light dusting of hair that covered his torso. She let her fingers move over it lightly. Liking the texture of his hair under her fingers. She leaned down and nipped at his flat nipple. She felt one of his hands on the back of her head, pushing into her hair as she kissed her way across his chest.

He reached lower and took the box of condoms out of her hands, but she wasn't paying attention to that. Instead, she was moving lower, breathing in the scent of him. It was a faintly intoxicating mix of expensive spicy aftershave and the essence of Dash.

She ran her tongue around his belly button and then glanced down at the bulge of his cock against the zipper of his pants. She reached for the tab of the zipper and drew it slowly down, pushing her hand into the opening and stroking him through his underwear.

She reached lower, cupping his balls through his underwear, and he cursed under his breath as she did so.

"Am I hurting you?"

"Fuck. No. You're not. I just…"

He pushed his underwear and pants down his legs

and his cock jutted out from his body. She touched him, wrapping her hand around the hot, hard length of him. He groaned again but the sound was different.

"Better," he said. "I like the feel of your skin on mine."

"Me too," she admitted.

He put the box of condoms on one of the steps behind them and arched one eyebrow at her. "How do I get you out of this top?"

She smiled teasingly at him. "You're a smart man… figure it out."

She didn't want to stop touching him, so bent to continuing kissing and licking her way down his body. She was getting closer to his erection when she felt his hands running down both sides of her body until he found the hidden zipper. She smiled against his skin as he undid it.

He pushed his hand through the opening of her dress, running his hands down her exposed back. His hands were hot, which tracked because his body was too. And the evening, this summer night was ripe with tension and heat.

It seemed to have followed them in the front door and filled this hallway. She was on fire for him. There was no denying that her pulse was racing and she was almost holding her breath waiting to see where he was going to touch her next.

He tugged at the hem of her blouse and she stood so he could pull it over her head. He tossed it aside. He put his hands on her waist and just stared at her. She knew she wasn't a pinup or a cover model, but she'd made the decision a long time ago that she couldn't live in a body she hated. So she made her peace with her solid B-cup boobs and that slight paunch of a stomach.

But he might be expecting...

Her, she realized.

He wasn't judging her. If anything, his cock seemed to get even bigger as he looked at her body.

This hallway felt close and intimate as he leaned against the stairwell. He didn't remember hooking up with Elle in college but that didn't mean they hadn't. But this time...this time he wouldn't forget. Her skin was soft under his hands as he squeezed her, loving the feel of skin-on-skin contact. He pulled her close to him, feeling the fabric of her pants brush against his erection. He was so hard he thought he'd explode if he didn't get inside of her soon.

But that was a delicious torture. He enjoyed drawing out his sensual pleasure and exercising control over his body and his partner. Skimming his hand up her back, he felt some rough skin, he turned her in his arms and saw a jagged scar just under bra which he undid with one hand while tracing over the scar tissue.

"How'd you get this?"

"Rescuing my cat, Mittens," she replied, glancing over her shoulder at him.

"Lucky Mittens, poor Elle. Were you an adventurous child?"

"I've never really considered that. I mean, I felt safe so I think that lead me to take more risks than I might have," she said. "Not sure that makes much sense."

"It does. Did you stop feeling safe and adventurous?"

"I did. I think most of us do when we become teens and then other things become important," she said. "Like sex."

A bolt of desire went through him. He liked her bluntness and the frank way she was looking at him as she turned back around. She'd undone the side zipper of her pants and, with a shimmy, let them fall to her feet. She stepped out of her shoes and kicked her pants aside. "It wasn't that bad, I got to be homeschooled and spent all day with my mom…"

Knowing that she'd lost her mom young, he realized that must have meant a lot to her and at any other time he'd want to hear more, but she had shrugged out of her bra and honestly, he couldn't think of anything else but her naked breasts. He reached out to cup them in both hands, rubbing his thumbs against her nipples that hardened to his touch.

Her breasts seemed to swell in his hands and he felt her caress down his stomach before taking his length in her hand. He leaned down and took one of her nipples into his mouth, suckling her. She arched her back, her hand tightening on his cock. Her other hand was at the back of his neck, pulling him closer to her.

She held him to her breast as she stroked him, her fingertip swirling around the tip of his erection the way that his tongue was swirling around her nipple. She shifted her hips and rubbed the tip of his naked cock against her pussy. He groaned.

He reached lower pushing her panties down her legs.

He felt the moist heat between her legs and circled his finger around her opening, loving the feel of her passion on his fingers. Every muscle in his body was tense and driving toward having her. He lifted his head and brought his finger up to his mouth, tasting the essence of Elle. Damn.

She tasted good. He felt his control slipping and turned to get a condom from the box behind him. Ripping it open and putting it on before turning back to her. He put one hand on her waist and the other behind her neck, drawing her into the curve of his body and he lowered his head and kissed her again.

He took a step away from the banister and lifted her slightly off her feet as he walked a few paces until the wall was against her back. He thrust his tongue deeply into her mouth and felt her hips arching against him as she parted her legs and lifted one high on his hip. He used both hands on her butt to sweep her off her feet.

"Wrap your legs around me," he said, his voice gravely and raw to his own ears.

She did as he asked and turned so his back was to the wall. She put her hands on his shoulders as he shifted his hips around. Their eyes met as she shifted until the tip of his cock was at her opening.

He thrust up and into her, and he felt her shiver as he entered her. She was tight around him, and her hands gripped his shoulders as she threw her head back and moved on him. The position was awkward for him, so he turned until she was pressed up against the wall. With better control, he drove into her as he found her mouth and sucked her tongue deep into his.

He felt her hands on him, caressing his back as continued thrusting into her. She was tightening on him and her hips were rotating against him. He reached down and found her clit, rubbing it as he continued to drive into her, going as deep as he could until her nails dug into him and she ripped her mouth from hers, crying out his name.

He felt her tightening around his cock and he continued driving into her, again and again until he came. His entire body shook as he emptied himself. He slumped against the wall, careful to brace himself and not let his full weight crush her.

She hugged him, her arms around his body and her head resting against his chest. He looked down at her. He never really knew what to say in this moment and somehow it was easier when he was in his own home. But she looked up at him and smiled.

"I guess some things are worth the wait."

"You definitely are," he said. Lifting her off her feet and turning.

"Is your bedroom upstairs?"

"Yes. Why?"

"I figured we could have a shower and maybe try out your bed," he said.

She rested her head on his shoulder as he carried her up the stairs. "No one has carried me since I was child."

"Do you want me to put you down?" he asked.

"No. I like it," she admitted. "Makes me feel like a princess."

He arched one eyebrow at her not really following the princess correlation.

"Do they get carried a lot?" he asked.

"Just in movies," she said. "It's so seldom that real life gives me these kinds of moments. I'm going to enjoy every second of this night."

She and Dash used separate showers, and when she came out of the bathroom, he was lying on her bed reading the book she'd left on her nightstand. He was completely naked and looked like every bookish, nerdy sex dream she'd ever had. She stood there in the doorway just watching him.

Her bedroom was dominated by the large four-poster bed in the middle of it. This had been the primary bedroom suite and, when she'd been a child, her parents' bedroom. The wallpaper had been changed and nothing resembled the room she remembered from her childhood except for the window seat and the built-in bookcases on either side of it.

He glanced up, shoving one hand through his dark hair and smiled at her. He held the copy of *The Scarlet Pimpernel*. She'd forgotten she'd left it there. She'd found it in a box that had been in the hall closet. Elle was pretty sure her stepmother had stashed it away, as the box had also contained a picture of her parents that Elle had thought she lost.

"I've never read this."

He looked at home in her room, which unnerved her more than it should. She came farther into the room, blotting her thick, curly hair with a towel and sitting down next to his hips and looking up at him. He set the book aside.

"I'm not surprised—it doesn't seem like your kind of book," she said.

"Not sure if that's entirely accurate," he said. "I mean, the man is a secret agent."

"He is. Do you read spy novels?"

"Normally I read prospectus for companies we are thinking of acquiring and financial papers and magazines. I like to read history books, but there never seems to be time for it. What do you like about this book? It looks well-used and like it's been read many times."

"It has been," she admitted, picking up the book and running her finger over the cover. She wasn't sure she wanted to tell him what she liked about it, because that felt too intimate.

A part of her wanted to shrug and just do it. This was only for one night, but another part of her realized that this was more intimate than sex. So telling him would be showing him a part of herself that she hadn't shared with anyone in a long time.

"Elle?"

Ugh. She'd waited too long and now it was going to be awkward. "I love that it's set in the French Revolution and he's liberating persecuted people."

"I just read about a party and the Prince Regent," Dash pointed out.

"I know, it's got a lot going on. It's…my mom loved this book. She used to read it to me when she was sick. She loved that Percy was in love with Marguerite and she with him, even though they both were on opposite sides of the war. Marguerite is so staunchly for the revolution and making those in power pay and Percy…is complicated, right. He believes in justice but can see that killing women and children isn't that. And in the center of that is this couple who won't let go of their marriage."

The memory was so private and one she rarely expressed, so much that she felt vulnerable talking about it. Yet at the same time if there was one person she felt she could trust with this story, it was Dash. He had experienced that kind of longing sitting next to the bed of his sister and hoping she'd get well.

Fortunately, Rory woke and would recover, unlike Elle's mom. Mentally, she warned herself to be careful around Dash. There was something about him that made it too easy for her to share her most private thoughts. And that made him dangerous.

"I'll have to read it with that in mind. My mom used to read to me," he said, absently. "I had forgotten that until you mentioned it."

She wondered if he had locked away all memories of his parents. For a long time after her dad had remarried, Elle had found it hard to think about the happiness she'd felt when her mom had been alive and to actually remember her mom. "What did she read?"

"Her favorite book from when she'd been a kid it's a story about a girl who runs away with her brother to the—"

"*From the Mixed-Up Files of Mrs. Basil E. Frankweiler.* Love that book," Elle said. "Did you like it?"

"It was okay. Rory loved it, and for about two months she kept trying to pester me into running away."

"What happened?" she asked.

"Mom and Dad were killed and we were sent here to live…that changed everything," Dash said.

He looked down at his lap, hiding a part of himself, and after she'd been so open about her mom, she wanted to push. But he had retreated into that arrogant man who had ordered her around at the hospital.

She sensed it was a defense mechanism and if she let him, he'd keep her at arm's length. Without thinking of the why, she reached over and cupped his jaw. The roughness of his whiskers against her palm were a sweet abrasion. He looked up at her and she knew in an instant he still hadn't fully processed his childhood grief either.

"Oh, Dash," she said. She leaned up and kissed him, just a brushing of her lips against his so he knew he wasn't alone. He opened his mouth under hers and the kiss was so tender that she felt like he got the sympathy she had for him. She lifted her head. "Well…"

"Yeah, well. Climb up here so we can cuddle," he said. "What do you usually do at night?"

"I would like to say that I clean out boxes, which is what I should be doing, but usually I just put on the TV and fall asleep binge-watching something or reading. What about you?"

"I put on ESPN and do work until my eyes get blurry, then I crash," he said. Dash was clearly a workaholic and given that his sister had been in a coma and his cousin was a celebrity, maybe that made sense.

"So, if we were married as Rory thinks, you wouldn't be working all the time, would you?"

He shrugged and looked away, taking extra time putting her book back on the nightstand. That was an answer in itself.

"That's a yes."

"Indeed. I'm single by choice, Elle. I know I wouldn't be a good partner to anyone," he said.

"Why wouldn't you be?" she asked.

"I'm a workaholic. And there is the Gilbert curse," he said.

That again. "What about the curse? I thought that had to do with Gilberts living in Gilbert Corners."

"Partially but it also has a direct effect on the men in my family and the women they love…it never works out," he said. Not really wanting to get too deeply into this with Elle. Not tonight.

"But with the right person would you still be?" she asked.

"Who knows," he said, shifting them on the bed until they were lying side by side.

He started kissing and caressing her and she felt herself getting turned on again. He swept her away with his lovemaking, and after they had both come, she curled against his side and fell asleep. It wasn't until the next morning after he'd left that she realized that he hadn't really told her much about himself.

She knew that was a good thing, that they needed to be strangers to pull off the fake married thing, but she was disappointed because Dash had always struck her as an honest man, and his avoidance of his feelings was almost lying by omission.

Six

Dash had texted her to find out about the man who'd been in Rory's room when she'd awoke from her coma, and Elle was doing her best to figure it out. There were no records of visitors, but the care home didn't track them as they entered since most of the patients in this unit had a lot of family in and out.

Her PA was in the office next to hers and Elle went to see her. Justine had short reddish, blond hair that she habitually wore in a pixie cut.

"Hey, Elle. How's the move going?"

"How much time do you have?" Elle asked. She didn't really want anyone outside of Dash, Conrad and his fiancée, Indy, to know about the fake marriage.

"Our schedule is pretty open this morning," Justine said.

She was enjoying her time with Dash, but there was a part of her that knew just because her feelings might change, didn't mean his would. Perhaps this was why she'd kept her relationships short-term. Love was probably the scariest of the emotions. There was no guarantee that the other person would love her back. So instead of just catching feels and acting like she'd fallen into a Hallmark movie, she needed to remember she lived in the real world.

"Well, I'm staying at Gilbert Manor to oversee Rory's recovery, so I haven't been working too much on my place. I have a contractor coming next week to give me an estimate on how much it will cost to do all of the things I want," Elle said. "I wonder if you could help me with something."

"Maybe," Justine said with a laugh. "I'm not good with construction."

Elle laughed and shook her head. "Not about that. It's a work thing. Dash Gilbert mentioned there was a man visiting his sister when he came in and she awoke from her coma. Dash didn't recognize him, and though I've talked to the nurses up front, no one seems to know who he is. Any clues how I can find out?"

Justine leaned back in her chair. "Well, if he didn't sign in, I guess we'd have to ask the staff who were in her room that morning. I had the afternoon shift. But I'll see if Dan or Marty remember seeing anyone."

"Thanks," Elle said, turning to leave.

It was probably nothing, but she didn't like the fact that someone no one knew had been in her patient's room. Elle made some notes to discuss it further with the head of the hospital. She knew that the care home was on the bottom of the priority list, but Dash had told her he'd pay for improvements, and this seemed like one that he'd find easy to say yes to.

She texted his assistant to ask if Dash had time to speak to her and got a response that he'd let Dash know. Elle went about the rest of her morning, seeing her patients and walking over to the hospital to give a second opinion on a head injury that came into the emergency room. On her way back crossing the quad between buildings, she saw a familiar man coming toward her.

Dash.

He heartbeat sped up and her body got all tingly just seeing him walking toward her in his Hugo Boss suit. If ever there was a man who was built for dress suits it was Dash. It fit him perfectly, accentuating his broad shoulders and slim hips.

Knowing exactly what his body looked like under that suit was probably part of the attraction. He looked so businesslike and professional, but she knew the raw sexuality that he kept leashed.

"Hope you don't mind me dropping by instead of calling," Dash said. "I was in Gilbert Corners talking to the town council on some improvements for the old factory building."

"I don't mind at all," she said. "I spoke to my PA about the man in Rory's room and our conversation made me realize that we need some improvements not only in the facility but also with security and staff. And you know, you said that you'd fund them."

He smiled at her. "I did say I would. What do you need?"

Elle tried not to notice the way his smile changed his face. He was still sort of aloof and standoffish, but the smile made him more approachable. Like she needed to be thinking about him being more appealing. She was trying to keep her distance and be smart after she slept with him. Remember that.

"I didn't expect you to say yes so easily. I want to talk to my hospital board at the facility I worked at in Boston and get some recommendations,"

"Perfect. Send me what you need and I'll have one of my staff draft a proposal we can take to the Gilbert Foundation. Is that all?"

She crossed her arms over her chest. "For the care home, yes. For you, no."

He arched both eyebrows. "What else?"

"I know we are supposed to be married in Rory's eyes but I really don't want anyone else to know about this," she said. "I mentioned to my PA. that I'm temporarily residing at Gilbert Manor to oversee Rory's recovery. I'd appreciate it if you stick to that story if you're asked about me."

It was a temporary arrangement they had and until they were both in agreement to make it permanent, she didn't want her coworkers to know.

"Don't want anyone to know that you've fallen for my charms?"

She shook her head, unsure how to express what she was feeling without making it seem like she was fishing and trying to find out how he felt. This was an awkward conversation but it was important to her that she at least pretend she was still being sensible where Dash was concerned. "Or that you've fallen for mine. Which isn't true anyway. We hooked up. It was a one-time thing. But I think it will be easier down the line than having to explain our supposed marriage."

He moved closer to her. She wondered if he was trying to use his size to intimidate her, but instead he quirked his head to the side. "What if we hook up again?'

"That's a big what-if," she said, even though a pulse of liquid desire pooled between her legs. She wanted him more than she wanted to want him. But there was no denying that her body craved him. Right now, it felt like if she didn't keep herself on a tight leash, she was going to be creating a mess she didn't want to solve.

"But still," he said.

"If I sleep with you again, Dash, things between us would have changed and I think we'd both know how to handle it," she said. "I'm not being difficult just to make you miserable. I am just…trying to figure myself out and adding you and sex into the mix at this moment is more than I want on my plate."

"Fair enough," he said, then reached out and pushed a strand of hair behind her ear. "For the record, I'm not miserable. I like getting to know you again, Elle."

"You do?" she asked, that old insecurity raising its head, but she had to admit she got a thrill from hearing him say he was enjoying their time together. That secret part of herself that she pretended didn't exist had always wanted someone to call her own.

From the moment her father died, she'd been alone and afraid to take a chance on anyone, and Dash couldn't know, but this fake marriage was something that her secret self had wanted long ago but that sensible-Elle would never have allowed herself to pursue.

"Yes. We didn't really get a chance to know each other in college, did we?"

"No. Two dates and a handful of group dates doesn't really make a relationship."

"Very true. If nothing else comes of our time at Gilbert Manor, I hope we at least can become friends."

"I'd like that too," she said. Her phone pinged and she glanced down to see she needed to be back at her office. "I've got to go."

"Of course. Later."

Work had always been his solace and the one place where he could relax. Part of that was because he'd been away from Gilbert Corners and Rory. In a way, he'd become inured to seeing her in that comatose state. His emotions had run high those first few years when it seemed like the Gilbert Curse was in full effect and taking its toll on anyone with the Gilbert name. To be fair, even the town had been affected, with businesses pulling out and the shops on Main Street closing.

His grandfather's death had been the catalyst for Dash to start making changes. Conrad's recovery had been long once he'd left the hospital and disappeared. Dash had received monthly postcards and Conrad had signed over the power of attorney for his share of their fortune, so Dash had focused on that. Growing his family's wealthy to keep them all safe until that safety had been shattered by one night.

He'd focused on the one thing he had control over, keeping his family's fortunes and growing them. As a solution for dealing with trauma, it hadn't been ideal, but it had served him and allowed him to shove his feelings away and pretend that he was normal.

But he hadn't been. That night had broken something inside of him and until Elle, he hadn't realized that. He'd felt untouched and confident. Like he'd smoothly moved on from the crash and only now he realized he'd been hiding in his success.

Dash never let himself think about what had happened that night with Rory or afterward. He had ruined the Orr family who had once thought to join their business to Gilbert International. He felt no shame in what he'd done after all their eldest son, Declan, had been the man to sexually abuse Rory the night of the ball.

His assistant handed him some papers to sign and Dash was glad for the distraction from his thoughts. As happy as he was that Rory was awake, there was a part of him that was struggling with the changes it was bringing to his life. Most of them were good. Rory was definitely the best part of it, but Elle was a close second. He might be sexually frustrated by the fact that she was keeping them at arm's length now that they were living together, but there were also some good things to come from having her so close.

"Sir?"

"Sorry, Ben. What is this?"

"It's the request from Gilbert Corners Care Home,

annex of the Gilbert Corners Medical Center and Hospital, to fund an upgrade to the main facilities as well as improvements for staff and security services. Dr. Monroe sent it over and I vetted it, changed the wording and added in some numbers," Ben said.

"Thanks. Let me read it and then I'll sign it. Anything else?"

"Yes. I heard back from the investigator about the man who was seen in Ms. Gilbert's room and he's got a lead. We should have more information when we land," Ben reassured.

Good. He knew that Elle had someone on her staff questioning the care home workers, so together with his investigator they should find out who had been in Rory's room that night.

Ben went and sat back down doing more work on his laptop and Dash read over the proposal and signed it. He should have done this years ago. But the guilt he felt when he visited Rory had blinded him to what was going on. He'd seen just the sister he was responsible for putting in that bed.

Maybe if his driving had been better or if his emotions hadn't been so high. Conrad had been raging in the passenger seat and Rory crying in the back seat as they'd driven away from the mansion.

He rubbed the back of his neck as the sound of breaking glass and crumbling metal echoed in his mind. He hated those sounds. He took a moment to do some deep breathing and pushed those thoughts out of his head. No matter the reason, he had ignored Gilbert Corners for too long.

Conrad had been partially responsible for bringing him back to the town and opening his eyes. But really, until Rory awoke, he'd struggled. He still didn't love GC or Gilbert Manor. But with Elle living there, it felt different.

Elle.

What was he going to do about her?

She'd been good to her word about keeping her distance physically and he was pretty sure she was outright avoiding him too. He'd seen her literally running down the grand staircase the other morning when he'd exited his bedroom. He'd caught a glimpse of her in the hallway but hadn't called out.

Her hair had been in a loose ponytail, not the severe tight one she wore when working. She wore a skirt that ended at the top of her knees, and though he knew he shouldn't, he couldn't help staring at her legs and enjoy the view of her as she hurried away from him.

He knew she needed space. She'd been so open in saying she was dealing with her own stuff and he wanted to help her with that. He wasn't the kind of man to ever open up about his own problems, but fixing hers…well maybe that would be enough to show her that he cared. And he did care. But he also knew himself. Connecting with her physically was where he felt safest.

He couldn't write it off as scratching an itch. Not with Elle. She was so much more than a convenient sex partner. The one night he'd spent with Elle had been as powerful as watching his sister wake from her coma.

It had shifted something inside of him, and he might be as unsure of who he was as Elle was.

Not on this front. He was still sure in the boardroom and confident in his place as head of the family. But this interpersonal stuff...hell, it was throwing him for a loop, and he'd be so much happier if he could just take Elle to bed and make love to her again and again so maybe he could figure out why he felt this way.

And what it all meant.

He'd always been so sure that he was doing the noble thing by not getting involved because of the curse, but now it seemed he might have been doing it just to protect himself from feeling anything again.

Two weeks later, Elle was still trying to sort the truth of who Dash was. They had both attempted to tell Rory the truth once again, but it was still as if she needed everything that happened the night of her accident to be true. So they'd both gone ahead with their fake marriage. Because of their jobs and the supposed longevity of them as a couple, it had been fairly easy for Elle to avoid Dash.

But now that Rory was well enough to move into Gilbert Manor and an in-home nurse and physical therapist had been haired along with a therapist, it was downright awkward. Elle had thought she'd have her own room, which she did, but it was part of the primary suite which also had Dash's bedroom.

Rory had started to walk with the assistance of a Zimmer frame so she wanted a tour of all the rooms. Elle had recently moved into Dash's suite of rooms so she'd have her own space, but they would give the illusion of sharing one rooms.

"Do you feel up to walking through all the rooms?" Elle asked. She completely understood Rory's need to not feel trapped, but as her doctor she was concerned about the other woman's stamina.

"I want to at least try to see yours and Dash's. Conrad told me he'd give me a tour of his when he and Indy come for dinner tonight," Rory said.

"I think we can manage that. It'll be nice to see Conrad and Indy," Elle said. "You know Dash and I haven't been living in the manor, so our room isn't too personalized."

Rory frowned. "I'd forgotten. I hate this."

This was one of the first times that she was actually this close to a patient going through recovery. Elle reached out and gently hugged Rory, who hugged her back with one arm. The Rory that Elle remembered had barreled through life with a smile and laughter. This new woman seemed so small in comparison.

It was hard to see Rory this way even though Elle knew that she'd continue getting better medically. Emotionally, it was going to take Rory a lot longer. Elle wished there was something she could do to speed things up.

She guessed being Rory's fake sister-in-law would help. She had some memories of the past that she could share with Rory.

Elle led Rory to a love seat in her own room. Her staff were readying the bed and the room. "I hate it for you. But don't stress about it, these things take time. Remember the night of the winter ball when we were all in that big room at the end of the hall getting ready?"

"I do, sort of. I remember hearing all the voices talking at once. Everyone was so excited…but I don't feel the excitement myself," she said. "I feel like I've already missed so much. My life has been on hold for ten years and a lot of things have changed."

Elle smiled at Rory. "What's one thing you want to do that would make you feel good?"

The therapist had given both herself and Dash some tips on how to ease Rory back into her life that might also help with her memories and doing things that Rory remembered was one of them.

"Making ice cream sundaes," she said.

"Okay. We can do that," Elle said. She'd deliberately taken the day off from work to help Rory transition. Dash had as well, but he had to take a call once they'd arrived at the manor. He'd promised to join them "as soon as possible." "Do you want to try walking there or should I get the wheelchair?"

"Would you be annoyed if I said walking but still wanted to bring the wheelchair just in case?" Rory asked.

She was still physically weak from ten years of being bedridden but was getting stronger every day. "Not at all. In fact, I think that's a great idea."

She got the wheelchair and told the staff they'd be downstairs in the kitchen, which made Rory's physical therapist decide to accompany them on the walk. They passed Dash's study on the way to the kitchen, and Elle heard his voice talking in that firm, low cadence of his. She couldn't help but remember how his voice had sounded when he'd made love to her in the hallway of her home.

A shiver of sensual awareness when through her. She was trying to keep things platonic, but her body didn't seem to be on the same page. In fact, her mind was starting to agree. And it took all of her control not to go and join him in his study. Maybe climb on his lap and kiss him and see where that led.

She shook her head. That was one night. She had to stop these flashes of memory that made her think of possibilities that weren't realistic. Dash had been very plain about how he viewed love and relationships. Falling for him had dumb idea written all over it.

Yet her heart still beat a little faster when he poked his head out and mouthed that he'd be with them shortly. Then he winked at his little sister and Elle had to turn away. He was just playing the part. If Rory wasn't here… Elle wouldn't be. She had to remember that.

She didn't want to fall for an illusion again, the way she had with her stepmother and stepsisters. Though she knew that Dash was nothing like her stepfamily. He might be closed off when it came to sharing his emotions, but he was a man of integrity and honor.

He'd been very careful to make sure that she was cared for and felt safe with him. And she did. She couldn't pretend that he was anything like the last family she'd thought she had.

Her stepfamily had made her feel like they were a

real family and it had only been after her father's death that they'd shown her how wrong she was. They treated her like a burden and an outsider.

She wouldn't let that happen again. Not that it would in this situation, she was an adult and loved the life she'd made for herself. Also, Dash wasn't a man to fake anything. She knew that. It was only her own weaknesses, the ones she knew better than most, that could lead her to ruin. She had always wanted…well, what she'd just exchanged with Dash in the hall.

A sense of belonging that had been ripped away from her first with her mother's death and then almost ten years later with her father's.

"I'll leave you two to get on with your sundaes. Use the app on your phone to let me know when you're ready to go back upstairs, Rory. Okay?" her physical therapist, Monty, said.

"I will. Thanks, Monty."

The housekeeper's office was located in the back of the kitchen and she stepped out to give both women an overview of the space before leaving them alone.

"I'm glad that I'm not the only one who didn't know where everything was," Rory said. "But I think I remember that Grandfather used to forbid us to come in here."

"Do you? I wonder why?" Elle asked as she pulled bowls, spoons and ice cream out and placed them on the table in front of Rory.

The Gilbert kitchen pantry was so fully stocked with all kinds of ice cream toppings, it took Elle two trips to get all of them and assemble in front of Rory.

"Oh, he thought that we shouldn't do menial labor including fixing food for ourselves. Back then we had an intercom system," she said. "Conrad snuck in here a lot. He loved being in the kitchen."

"Makes sense since he became a chef," Elle said. She realized she had a source for learning more about the man who spent too much time in her head. "What about Dash?"

"What about me?" he asked as he entered the kitchen.

"Did you sneak into the kitchen?" Elle asked. Wondering how much he'd heard. But she wasn't going to pretend that she hadn't been talking to Rory about him. Dash kept so much to himself and she needed to know more.

"Yes, he did. And into the liquor cabinet in Grandfather's study," Rory said.

"What else did he do?" Elle asked.

"Stuff that my little sister isn't going to divulge," he said teasingly. "As my wife, you should only see my good qualities."

She shook her head, but in her heart and soul she knew that she did. This feeling of being a part of this feeling and unlike the last time…this family felt real. "That's not realistic after eight years of marriage."

"Just give me the illusion that it is."

Seven

Eight years of marriage. He wondered what their relationship would be like had they been married eight years ago. She'd be sleeping in his bed every night, maybe even joining him in his study after midnight, tempting him into stopping work to make love to her. Which he totally would. Would they have kids? He hadn't ever thought of them before, but looking at Elle, he knew he'd want them with her. A little girl with Elle's keen intelligence and stubbornness and his drive and determination. Then shoved the thought aside as he'd been doing with many of his thoughts about Elle lately.

Of course, it seemed like every night she was in his fevered dreams which had left him on edge. He was tense and he could explain part of it as the fact that his sister's recovery wasn't as straightforward as he'd hoped it would. Or maybe even the fact that one of his business deals kept experiencing setbacks.

But that wasn't the truth, and he tried to never lie to himself.

With Elle, this fake marriage was going to be hard. Because that one hot summer night when they'd talked had changed everything. That one night he'd spent with her in his arms was never fair from his mind. That one night he'd promised himself would be enough, wasn't.

It was that simple and that complicated, he thought. Elle seemed to have no problem ignoring the sexual tension between them and falling into the role of his wife and Rory's big sister-in-law. He was annoyed at how easy it seemed for her, so he pulled her into his arms in the middle of the kitchen and kissed her.

He'd meant for it to be a sort of quick buss on the lips, but her hand went to the side of his neck and his entire body reacted to her touch, which he'd been missing. He deepened the kiss as she tipped her head to the side and his hand slid down her back. She tasted better than he remembered and while she was in his arms, he couldn't remember why one night was all they'd agreed to. Surely, they should be doing this more often.

Someone cleared their throat.

He almost ignored it until Rory did it again.

He lifted his head. Her lips were swollen and wet from his kiss and face flushed with desire. She let her hand drift slowly from his neck and Dash had to adjust his stance as he turned to face his sister.

"Guess she still likes me," he said with a wink at his sister.

"Of course she does, silly. She loves you," Rory said. "I'm glad you two had each other."

"Me too, ladybug. So, sundaes. I seem to recall you liked chocolate ice cream with blueberry compote and sprinkles."

"That's right, and you like rocky road smothered in chocolate syrup."

"I used to," he said, feeling happy and lighter seeing his sister smiling and Elle watching them with a delighted look on her face.

"What about you, Elle?"

"Oh, well, cookies and cream by itself," she said. "Why is the house stocked with every flavor of ice cream?"

"Gilberts like to be prepared."

"Is that your motto?" she asked.

"No, we're not the scouts," Dash said as he went to the freezer and got the ice cream for all of them.

"Do you have a motto?" Rory asked Elle as she sat down across from his sister.

She shrugged. "Not really a motto, but my mom always said to be brave and nice."

"I like that. I don't remember my mom that much, but I don't think that's the amnesia. I was six when she died."

Dash's heart clenched hearing the sadness in his sister's voice that matched some of the emotions he'd locked away a long time ago. Dash came back to the table and set the ice cream containers down next to the scoop that Elle had gotten.

"Mom used to say, 'Go boldly or don't go,'" Dash said. "And you used to do that all the time. As you got older whenever we left each other to go back to boarding school—"

"We used to say, 'Be bold.'"

He nodded at her as he sat down next to his sister. Rory reached over to squeeze his hand. "I'd forgotten."

"You have been busy trying to remember a lot."

"I have been," Rory agreed.

"Being home is going to help you," Elle said. "Here you're not thinking 'I have to remember' but actually seeing familiar places all around. It should stir some memories."

"It already is," Rory said. "Do you think this will help me remember faster?"

Elle took her time answering, something he realized she did a lot with Rory when his sister asked about her recovery. He suspected she did it so that Rory wasn't disappointed by any of the answers. It was one of the many things he respected about Elle in her role as a doctor. It was something she carried across into her personal relationships as well. Probably why he was falling for her. He wanted to pretend he was immune, but he knew he wasn't.

"It will help, but speed isn't the goal here. Healthy is, remember?"

"Ugh. Don't make that your motto," Rory said laughing. "Though I do hear what you're saying, Elle."

"Good. I just don't want to make you think it will

happen magically. It's going to take work and time," she said.

Dash scooped out the ice cream for them.

"So tell me what's good on TV," Rory said. "I used to love *Dancing with the Stars* and *Glee*."

Rory really liked Elle, and though Dash knew that marriage was a no-go for him, he couldn't help wondering if having Elle in their lives permanently might help his sister.

Of course, if she stayed, then they'd have to make a new arrangement. They could be married and have sex without being in love.

Even as the thought formed in his head, he knew that he could never say that to her. That wasn't a relationship that anyone would want…except him. That way he'd be safe from the curse and so would she. He realized that he wanted that to be true. His heart and his mind were at war.

Logically, he had to only look at his own past to see the proof of how love was a curse to himself. But the truth was that a woman with Elle's soft heart would never agree to an emotionless marriage.

And that was all he felt safe offering her. He would die if anything happened to Elle.

His sister, who had only known the adult Elle a few short weeks since she'd woke, was already in love with her. Dash shifted his gaze away from Elle. He wasn't capable of love. He knew that about himself. Didn't he?

Talking about *Dancing with the Stars* with Rory almost made her forget about Dash sitting right across the table from her. Her pulse was still racing from that kiss he'd planted on her, and the truth was, she wished it had lasted longer and maybe ended with him lifting her up on the kitchen island and doing…stuff that had nothing to do with the drama, costumes and backstage gossip of a reality show.

"There's a new musical series that you might like if you liked *Glee*."

"Sounds good. Any other shows I should watch? I tried asking Con and Dash, but they like sports and told me a bunch of stuff that I don't care about," Rory said.

"I think knowing who won the World Series is important," Dash said. "We can have a Netflix night."

"Is that a thing? You said it like it's a thing," Rory said teasingly.

As much as Elle knew she'd been fishing for information on Dash, she realized she didn't need Rory to tell her anything—just seeing the two of them together was giving her insights she wouldn't have found otherwise.

"Yes, it's a thing. Right?"

She smiled and laughed at the way he looked over to her for confirmation. "It is, don't you trust him?"

"I would, except he sometimes tells me things that he thinks is funny," she said.

"Like what?"

"Like nothing. You two aren't going to be ganging up on me," Dash said.

'We totally are," Elle said, smiling at Rory.

"Yeah, we are," Rory agreed. "But not today. I'm so glad to be back home."

"I'm glad to have you back home," Dash said, and that barely controlled emotion was back in his voice as he hugged his sister and Elle turned away.

He had said he was a man who didn't believe in love, and yet she saw that he definitely experienced it. She couldn't help but notice that he and his sister had a very deep bond and spent a lot of time together. Dash loved Rory. As much as he wanted to say he didn't, she saw the proof of it when he was with Rory.

She watched them with longing. That sibling bond was one she'd always wanted for herself; she'd made her peace with being an only child but still felt a twinge of envy seeing their closeness.

"Elle, do you want to?"

"I missed that, sorry," she said.

"Rory suggested we go watch Netflix while we're eating our ice cream," Dash said.

"Yeah, that sounds great," she said. And it was a good distraction. They called Monty, who monitored Rory as she walked to the family room tucked away at the back of the house. It was a large room with French doors on one wall that led out to the large patio and overlooked the manicured gardens.

Dash asked a lot of questions of Monty as they walked over; he was learning what his sister needed. She helped get Rory settled on a large, overstuffed leather chair that was a stand to sit model. Once she was settled, Elle took a seat on the leather sofa, Monty sat down in an armchair near Rory and Dash took a seat right next to her before he hit a button on the remote, which closed the shades on the French doors and turned on some theatre-style lighting.

He talked into the remote and in a few moments, the show was playing on the TV, but Elle couldn't concentrate on anything but his closeness next to her on the couch. Her lips tingled, echoing that kiss that hadn't been long enough and the feel of his body next to hers. She could feel his body heat wondered if she should scoot away from him, but she didn't want to.

She sneaked a glance at him and found him watching her and not the television screen. She licked her suddenly dry lips and then lifted her head to meet his gaze. He took a deep breath and then deliberately lifted a spoon of ice cream to his lips. There was something sensual about the way he ate it. Her breasts felt heavier, and she felt a pulse of moisture between her legs.

She wanted him.

Hell, she'd known that when she'd agreed to move in here and be his wife. She thought…what had she thought? She forced her eyes away from Dash and back to the TV, but it didn't matter where she looked. Her mind and her thoughts were on him. Remembering the way his mouth had traveled all over her that night he'd stayed at her house.

Just the memory made her body tingle and her breasts feel heavy. She recalled the feel of his lips against her neck which sent a pulse of need through her.

It felt like it had been much longer than just two short weeks. That kitchen kiss was simply reminding her that she still wanted him. And there was no way she was going to be able to live in this house close to him for months without giving in.

So she had a decision to make. Was she going to just do the no-strings-attached-hookup? Or was she going to go for broke and try to figure out a way to make this marriage into the real thing?

She wasn't entirely sure she could do that.

But she remembered her mom's motto about being brave. She'd somehow let herself forget it in the years since she'd left medical school. That had been the last brave thing she'd done. She had gotten into a routine of studying and achieving, working hard to get her goals. Never letting anything sway her from her course. Too many years had passed, and she'd fallen into the safety net of routine.

But being with Dash, living at Gilbert Manor, had sparked something inside of her. Reminded her of the woman she'd been. She missed that woman and had only herself to blame for forgetting that part of herself. But tonight…

She was going to for it. She was going to be brave and take the thing she wanted the most. She wanted the happiness she'd found with Dash and Rory to be real.

Dash not as her fake husband and onetime lover but as hers. The risks were high, but she thought that the payoff would be too.

Dash made his excuses after the Netflix session and locked himself in his study for the rest of that evening. If he had to sit next to Elle on the couch and keep his hands to himself, he was going to lose his mind. He couldn't have her pressed against his side and not want to put his arm around her shoulder, let his hand drop to her breast and caress her. He wanted her head to drop back and then he'd lean in and kiss her until she was moaning and demanding he make love to her.

But what he wanted from her wasn't just sexual. He'd had that realization somewhere between her laughter at something on the screen and her touch on his thigh.

Of course the intensity between the two of them was hard to ignore. He wanted her. But he knew that he had to be careful how he moved forward if he did. Elle was important to Rory and to her recovery. Also, quite honestly, he liked Elle and didn't want to hurt her. And when had he ever not hurt a woman in a relationship?

No one knew about Candace. But Dash did, and he had to keep his guard up and make the hard choices to ensure that Elle didn't end up in the same situation...

He worked until midnight and then went through the large empty hallways toward the primary bedroom suite. He had no choice but to put Elle in his suite. Rory would question why they weren't sharing it otherwise. But there were technically two rooms so they both had their own space. The second room was meant to serve as a nursery but hadn't in years.

A soft light shone under Elle's door. Dash took one step toward it before cursing succinctly under his breath and going instead to the adjoining bathroom, taking a very cold shower and masturbating to relieve himself—and maybe give himself a chance of staying away from Elle. He walked back into the bedroom, towel drying his hair.

"Oh."

"Fuck."

He moved to wrap the towel around his hips, but just the fact that Elle was in his room was undoing all of his work in the bathroom. She stood there with her hair hanging around her shoulders and a robe that was cinched tight at her waist, her bare feet on display with a pretty coral color on her toenails. It felt intimate, and he wanted to slowly undo the knot that held her robe together. He tried to school his features into an implacable stare. That seemed the right attitude to take.

Be chill.

But he wasn't chill. What was she wearing under her robe? Could he have her naked and in his bed with just one tug of the cloth belt around her waist?

Did she even want to be there with him?

"Sorry. Um… I need to talk to you about schedules. I'll give you a minute to get presentable," she said turning her back.

He opened his dresser and took out a pair of basketball shorts and grabbed the first T-shirt his fingers touched. As he pulled them on and looked down, he almost groaned. It was for a beer company that he'd invested in with the logo of Inferno Brewing and the slogan "Own your vices."

He didn't want to be dwelling on his vices while Elle stood in his bedroom. It wasn't lost on him that he was known in the business world for his stoicism and being unflappable. But with Elle, none of that seemed to hold true.

"I'm good."

She turned, her eyes drifting slowly down his body. Because her hands had caressed that same path the night they'd spent together, he felt a sizzle just from being close to her. He glanced up to see if she was affected and noticed that her gaze lingered on his chest, and she chewed her lower lip between her teeth as if she was holding her emotions in.

"I like the tee. So… I am on call next week which means I'll need to be available all hours. I'm sure you're not going to be able to work from home all the time. Do you think we should have a shared calendar to keep track of things so one of us is here for Rory?"

"Great idea. I'll hire someone to be our assistant. But until then, just use my assistant at the office who keeps my calendar, Ben," Dash said, grateful to have something to focus on other than the fact that he could see the faint outline of her nipples through the fabric of her robe.

He walked to the dresser, retrieved his phone and set up a group for messages with Ben and Elle and added Conrad as well. He introduced everyone in the chat and asked Ben if he'd start a new calendar with all of their schedules on it.

"I talked to Conrad earlier this evening and he'll pick up the slack when I'm gone, but there is no reason he can't do the same for you. I think between the three of us, we can make sure Rory has a family member with her at all times," Dash said. He'd video chatted with Conrad earlier to mention the fake marriage. His cousin hadn't said a word about it, just shook his head and wished him luck. "I mentioned Rory thought we were married and that we were doing our best to pretend to be."

"Oh, good, I guess," she said, but the expression on her face seemed at odds with her agreement. "I'll send Ben my rotation schedule so he can keep track of it," she said.

"Sounds good," he said.

Elle put her phone in the pocket of her robe and stood there, as if waiting for something, as she stared at him.

"Is there something else?"

"Yes. Why did you disappear after we did ice cream this afternoon?" she asked.

Dash took a deep breath. Truths or half truths. His grandfather had once said to him that life was made up of those two things and money. Money was always the groundwork for any conversation with the old man. Dash knew in this moment what he said next would influence how his relationship with Elle would play out.

He thought back to Candace. A half truth now would be kinder than the full truth later. He knew it. But there was something about Elle that made him want to just admit to the aches in his gut. Tell her that he'd left because he hadn't been thinking about his sister, that instead he'd been thinking about carrying her upstairs and making love to her.

"I had a meeting," he said.

"A meeting that went until midnight."

"What do you want me to say, Elle?" he asked her.

"The truth."

He moved closer to her and stopped when there was just an inch of space between them. "What do you think I'm hiding?"

Eight

Elle was playing with fire, but that was her plan. As if she could call this any sort of a plan. It was more a game of chance to see where this passion led, and if there was more between them than magnetic chemistry. But at the moment, after seeing him naked from the shower, she honestly wasn't too sure that she cared about anything other than the physical.

She'd thought over the last two weeks that she'd remembered every detail of his body, but it was clear to her now she hadn't. Like the tattoo on his forearm of some sort of Celtic-looking symbol. How hadn't she noticed it?

It was on his inner forearm, going from the bend in his elbow down to just above his wrist. It was thick, black lines that created a scroll and a symbol. That much black ink must have taken a long time to be completed and would require touching up.

That tattoo meant something to Dash. The man who was so convinced he didn't have emotions…it was another thing that just made it harder for her not to care for him. He had all these markings of a man who struggled with his feelings.

But then she had been more entranced with other parts of him. She licked her lips, now that he was so close, she just wanted to touch him. But this had to be about more than hooking up. She couldn't risk another sexual encounter without knowing if there was the potential for more between them. Because she knew herself.

She wasn't going to pretend after this afternoon in the kitchen that she wanted anything less than a real relationship. And her mind was already halfway there, finding little connections that, over time, Elle would make into something real. But that didn't mean they would be.

That was one of the reasons she'd kept most of her relationship short term. She'd been afraid to fall into thinking something was real when it was just born from her own secret need to find a family. She spent all of her time looking for signs that the other person cared for her instead of just letting herself be in the relationship.

"I'm not entirely sure. But I think…there's a spark between us, Dash, right?" she asked.

He lifted both eyebrows at her and gave her a grin

that made her heart beat faster. "Uh, yes. Did you think I was lying about that?"

"No. I just… I think we had a moment today and then you left and…" Ugh. Why was it so hard to just say this out loud? How was she going to have any relationship with him if she couldn't speak her mind?

She closed her eyes because when she looked at him, all she could see was that strong jaw and those firm masculine lips that she wanted to feel on her skin. His warm mouth moving down the side of her neck to her shoulder and then down lower to her breasts. But closing her eyes was a mistake, because the scent of his aftershave was strong and stirred memories of how intoxicating that night in her hallway had been. "I think you like me for more than sex."

The words kind of came blurting out in a rush and she shook her head as she opened her eyes. *Really, Elle. You've been to freaking medical school and most people consider you intelligent.* Not that the previous statement reflected that.

"I do," he said.

"So."

"So?" he returned, his face closed and icy.

"Never mind. Forget it," she said, turning on her heel but he caught her arm midspin and stopped her.

"I was being a jerk. I like you. I think it's dangerous, and not just because of my sister's health."

His hand was hot on her arm and the backs of his fingers brushed the side of her breast; she tipped her head as he looked up tat him. "Dangerous how?"

He let go of her arm and pushed his hand through

his thick hair as he turned and walked to the large bay window where he'd left the curtains open.

She stayed where she was watching him. His body language which had been open and teasing earlier now seemed closed, tense. What was on his mind?

"Dash?"

"I told you earlier that the Gilbert men were cursed, do you remember that?" he asked her.

She walked carefully toward him but as he hadn't turned to face her, she suspected he might be unaware of how close she was. But he wasn't. He turned as she approached and gestured to the love seat.

"You'll want to sit down for this," he said.

"I will?" she asked. It was hard to discern if he simply didn't feel anything for her or if, as she had hoped, that he struggled to express his feelings. She saw him wrestling with wanting to show her how he felt, but was she making him into the man she wanted him to be? Just as she had with her stepfamily?

"I think so."

"I don't really buy the curse; I know you and the town are really into it—"

"I'm not into it. Elle, things have happened that have shaped me into the man I am today," he said.

"Like what?"

"I told you about my mom."

"Yes. But your dad died, too. That doesn't mean it was the curse," she reminded him gently.

"Believe me, I know," Dash said. "He took a risk and paid the price. Love and the Gilbert men don't mix."

"I thought you didn't believe in love," she pointed out.

"I do. Just not for me."

"So tell me about how you don't mix with love. I mean, you were in a car accident and I read the report. The other driver was chasing you and rammed the car. It's not your fault Rory was injured and put in a coma," Elle insisted.

He sat down next to her and took her hands in his. "You're right. But after that. When Rory was in a coma, they had put Conrad in a medically induced one to help his healing. I was…alone."

She put her hand on the side of his face. Whatever he felt about this curse, the pain in him was real. She could feel it and it was making her heart ache. There was something about this man that made her want to wrap him in her arms. "When my dad died, I was alone too. I thought I trusted my stepmother and believed we were a real family, but as soon as the will was read and nothing was left to her but the house they'd lived in, she kicked me out."

"Oh, Elle, I had no idea."

"Why would you? I'm just saying I understand that feeling of being totally alone and realizing that you have to figure out everything from that moment on," she said, quietly. "It's not easy, but I think those are the moments that make us."

"They are," he said, sitting up a bit straighter and taking her hand in his. "They made me into the man I am today. I can't deny that that time changed me."

"We have that in common. You do seem very different from the boy-man I knew in college," she said.

"Boy-man?" he asked.

He seemed to be having a hard time not just pouring everything out to her. She sensed he didn't want to complain about his circumstances. She could see he'd been blessed with so much since his birth. But, he'd also seen.

"Well, you did party all the time," she pointed out.

"I did."

"So what happened?" she asked.

This.

This right here was exactly what she'd wanted, and it seemed her gamble had paid off. Her desire to have a family with Dash and Rory was becoming more real each day she spent with them. Dash's honesty with her was a confirmation for her gut. She knew that she couldn't be too dismissive of his curse claims. She got it. She felt for a number of years that she'd never have a family again.

But today in the kitchen, she'd seen something that she'd forgotten she wanted. And tonight, she was inching closer to it. She wasn't pinning all her dreams—oh, who was she kidding—she *was* pinning them on Dash. She liked him and could easily see spending the rest of her life with him. He was so kind and caring with Rory. It made her think that if they did get together and things worked out, he'd be a good husband, a good father.

And that was a nonnegotiable for her since her father had been the best.

"I started an affair with a woman I met at the hospital."

"Oh. I thought you said—"

"I'm not in a relationship. No matter what you may have read about me online, I'm not a douchebag."

"I didn't think you were," she said. "So what happened?"

"Um, Conrad got well first physically, but mentally, he had a lot of anger and he had to get out of here. He had a huge fight with Grandfather, and after Con left, Grandfather wasn't the same. He died a year later."

"And the woman?"

"Candace was by my side through it all. I started working more hours. I had to because Grandfather had let the company sort of go wild and there was a lot that needed attention. Candace was fine with it at first, but as trips took me overseas for weeks and then months, she had enough. I came home in the middle of the night and she was gone."

Elle wasn't sure how that was caused by the curse, but she put her hand on his knee. "That was not a great thing to do."

He stood up and walked to the window looking out into the night. "I thought so too, until the next morning I found a note from her. The gist of it was that I wanted the company more than her and she wasn't going to try to compete with it. She said I couldn't love two things at once, and I'd always choose Gilbert International."

Elle went over to him, put her arms around him from the back and hugged him. She knew this still hurt him because of the lack of emotion in his voice. He was stiff in her arms as she rested her head between his shoulder blades. "I'm sorry."

"Don't be. She was the first to point it out, but after a few bottles of whiskey and some time to think, I realized she was right. I'm always going to be a Gilbert, and Gilbert International is the most important thing to me aside from Rory and Con."

He turned in her arms, putting his around her. She tipped her head back to look up at him. "I think if you wanted a woman to matter to you, she would."

"Perhaps. Or maybe I'd be like my dad and think I could have it all and end up dead with my wife."

"Dash—"

She had more to say but he brought his mouth down on hers, those firm lips moving over hers until she stopped thinking about anything but the way his torso felt pressed against her breasts. She went up on tiptoe, deepening the kiss and sucking on his tongue as he undid the belt of her robe and shoved it off of her.

He lifted his head and looked down at the Pikachu nightshirt she had on.

"Damn, I'd hoped you were naked under there."

She smiled and then stepped back. "I want you, but you can't end a conversation with sex."

"Why not?"

She picked her robe up from the floor and walked to her bedroom. "It's called avoidance. And it's not very respectful to either one of us. I like you, Dash, but if all you can offer me is sex, then I'd rather stick to the fake marriage."

He put his hands on his hips. "I hate digging these feelings up again."

"I get it—it's hard and it makes you feel vulnerable.

I had to close my eyes to ask you if you liked me…
so believe me, I know how it feels. But if I'm going
to take a chance on believing I could have a family
again, then I need to know that I'm not the only one
on the precipice."

"A family," he asked arching on eyebrow at her.

"Don't panic. I wasn't talking about a baby. I was
talking about people to call my own."

"Like Rory and me?"

"And Conrad. You are asking me to play a part that
makes me very exposed—before you say it, I know I
agreed to it. But if you and I are lovers, the lines will
start to blur, and I'll see this as something other than
a fake relationship. I can't take that chance if you're
not with me."

"Even if I said I would, it still might not work out,"
he said.

She shook her head and tried to smile at him. What
could she say to make him see what she meant? She
felt as if there were no words that could break through
to him right now. And she'd ruled out sex as a means
to communicate.

"I know. But if you were to let down your guard and
just show me who you are, that might help," she said.

"And we can f—"

"I know you're being crude as a defense mechanism," she said.

He shoved his hands in his hair again.

"I was. Sorry."

"It's okay. Like I said, scary." She couldn't be of-
fended by his words when she knew he was trying. He

hadn't turned around and left when she'd pushed him into a conversation she knew they needed to have but that he'd rather avoid. It was enough for her at this moment that he was staying. That he was trying.

It made her heart feel hopeful in a way that helped justify her determination to put herself out there with Dash.

"So how would I do this?"

"Just one date a week where we talk and get to know each other, and then f—"

He crossed the room to her and pulled her into his arms again. "You already know how to reel me in with the dirty talk."

She laughed, but she knew this was a fragile agreement and she could only hope they'd both stay true to their word.

It had been two weeks since that moment in his bedroom and he had agreed to a weekly date. The first one had been canceled by Elle, who had been called into an emergency at the hospital for a traumatic brain injury. They'd rescheduled, but this time, he'd had a deal put in jeopardy and had to fly to London to save it.

So here it was, week two, he was still horny as hell, still unsure of what she wanted on these "dates" and their schedules still weren't lining up to allow time together. This was very much on his mind when he showed up in the solarium to spend the afternoon with Rory. Conrad was there with his fiancée, Indy, and when Dash walked in with his phone in hand, they all started laughing.

"I'm guessing the joke is on me?" he asked as he kissed his sister's cheek and sat down next to her on one of the overstuffed loveseats.

"Not really, we just had a bet that you'd either be on your phone when you came in or text to cancel," Conrad said. "Sorry, I started it."

"Fair enough," he said. "But I'm putting it away for the next three hours as I promised Rory."

"Good for you," Conrad said, getting to his feet, and when Indy stood up next to him, he draped his arm around her shoulder. "I'm taking this one for a ride on my bike. We'll see you in a couple of days, Rory. Be good."

"I'm always good," Rory said. "And I know Indy will keep you in line."

"I try," Indy said. "But it's a full-time job."

"I'm just glad I'm not the one who has to do it," Dash joked with a smile.

He was happy his cousin had found love after so many years on his own. He and Conrad were close. They both had the Celtic word for "brother" tattooed on their bodies because that bond they had was one of brotherhood. Conrad had already covered his body with thorny branches, so his brotherhood tattoo was interwoven on his inner forearm similarly to Dash's For many years they'd simply had each other to lean on.

"She's a hell of a lot prettier than you," Conrad said.

"Oh, I don't know, Dash is very pretty," Rory said.

"Ugh," Dash said.

"Double ugh," Conrad added. "Let's get out of here before I hear anything else like that."

Indy gave Rory a hug and Conrad did too before they left. Rory was sitting in the specialized chair they'd gotten for her that could be raised to help her stand. "Do you feel up for a walk?"

"I do. Should we call Monty?"

"If you feel safer with him, but I stopped to talk to him before I came in here. He said with the Zimmer frame you should be fine on the stone pathway," Dash said.

"Good. I want to hear all about London. Wait, did you bring back my tea from Fortnum's?"

"Yes, and I gave it to Mrs. J. After our walk, she's preparing afternoon tea. I brought more than your favorite blend back. I figured we'd have high tea in the library if you want to."

"You're the best. Of course I want to," Rory said. "You spoil me, Dash."

"I don't think tea is spoiling you, but if I do, I think I'm entitled. I have ten years to make up for," he said. He loved seeing the joy on Rory's face at the thought of having a proper tea.

He still struggled with believing she was out of her coma and back home again. His love for his little sister was strong and deep. He had spent so many years sitting by her quiet bedside making promises and deals with the universe.

If Rory wakes up, I'll show her how much I love her.

But the reality was harder. He had fallen to spoiling her because emotions fucked him up. They made him feel weak in a way that he couldn't deal with. He was the charmed Gilbert. So many times he'd struggled to make sure he portrayed that image. But inside he wanted to take Rory and Conrad and Elle and hide them away from the world. Put them someplace where he could protect them.

Even though he'd failed to protect all three of them.

Rory tried to hide it, but he had caught glimpses of melancholy on her face. The lack of certain memories was clearly frustrating her. Monty had also confided that Rory was disheartened with her physical abilities and the time it was taking for her regain her strength. So Dash cherished these moments of happiness.

"So how was London?"

"Sunny for about thirty minutes and then rainy and cold," he said. "You would have loved it."

She smiled up at him as he helped her down the ramp to the garden path. The manicured gardens were modeled off the large estate gardens of palaces in France and manor houses in England. There was topiary in traditional shapes and then a hedge maze in the back, but for today's walk, Dash thought they'd stroll through the roses as the gardener had mentioned they were in bloom.

"I would have. But now I'd probably be afraid of slipping and falling and just sit inside," she said.

"I wouldn't let you fall," he said.

"I know. But I want to be able to do things on my own. I'm sick of always having people around me," she said.

"I can arrange for you to have some alone time," he said. "You should have mentioned this earlier."

"It's okay. I do have alone time in the afternoon.

Monty and Frida help me to the library, and I've been spending two hours reading on the window seat. It's nice. But I want to be able to walk by myself." She'd mentioned her physical therapist and the private nurse that had been hired to help her out.

He understood where she was coming from. But she wasn't there it. He suspected this was the underlying frustration that Monty had been indicating. "Well, the more you walk with me and Monty and everyone, the sooner that will happen. In fact, I bet you'll be running circles around me in no time at all. And each day you are getting so much stronger."

"Monty keeps pointing out that I was in a bed for ten years, and I do understand where he's coming from. But I'm awake, Dash, and I can't help but feel like I'm not really living."

"What can I do?"

"Nothing. That's the thing. I see how desperate you are to help me. And I realize how my coma and Conrad's accident…it changed you. I'm trying to get myself well so that I'm not just one more thing for you to worry about."

"I'm always going to worry about you, ladybug."

"And I worry about you too. You don't spend any time with Elle. I know the both of you are working demanding jobs and now your alone time is all with me," she said.

"That's not entirely true, and neither of us really minds."

But he knew that wasn't true. He missed Elle when he wasn't with her, and he knew a part of him was managing his expectation that he might not be able to keep her. Because every day he spent with Elle was making him realize that he might be able to find a life with her.

Nine

Elle was tired when she got back to Gilbert Manor close to 11:00 p.m. Dash had texted her that he was back in town and they were attempting to reschedule their date. Elle was beginning to realize how hard a relationship would be between the two of them. They both had demanding careers and she could respect that, but with his family and his obligations, she had to be realistic.

A marriage to Dash wasn't going to be like her parents' marriage had been. And a part of her had been trying to replicate that. She wanted that same dynamic she'd had growing up. Just the three of them in the house together, spending time together. As an adult, she realized that her memories were skewed and that her parents weren't always together, but her father had been a CPA and was home on the weekends. Her mom had been a bookkeeper in his business. They spent a lot of time with each other.

Was that the only way to have a successful marriage? She wasn't sure. A lot of the doctors she knew in her business were divorced or married to other doctors or surgeons, so that didn't help.

"Do you mind some company?"

Elle glanced up from the salad she was eating to see Rory standing in the doorway with her Zimmer frame to support her. In the shadows behind her was Monty, who smiled back at Elle.

"I don't mind at all. Just eating and trying to unwind before bed," she said.

Monty waited until Rory was seated and then stepped back.

"I've got Rory for the rest of the night, Monty."

"Good night, ladies," he said before leaving.

Rory sighed and Elle glanced over at her patient. Her hair was starting to regain some of its luster. She'd had it cut and now it curled around her shoulders. Her skin had a healthy glow to it, but it didn't take a genius to figure out she wasn't happy.

"What's up?"

"I hate that you and Dash are always having to watch over me," Rory said.

"We don't mind. That is why we all moved in here," Elle pointed out. "Actually, I'm glad for your company tonight."

"You are?"

"Yes, and pretty much all the time. I just moved

back here and I don't really know that many people," Elle said. "It's nice to have a friend."

This renewed friendship with Rory was a bonus that Elle hadn't expected when she'd returned to Gilbert Corners. There was a part of her that had spent so much time alone, she'd sort of forgotten what it was like to have friends and how much she'd missed it.

"For me too," she said. "I want to know more about you and Dash. My memories of you two…might have been foggier than I realized at first. I mean, you had just been on one date when I met you that summer."

"That's true. But we had a few more dates after that, and I came to the winter ball. Do you remember that night?"

"Not all of it. I remember you and your friends getting ready. They were the ones that said Dash was going to propose," Rory said.

"That's right. You were supposed to go with a man your grandfather had asked you to date. I think he was the son of a businessman whose company he wanted to merge with. Do you remember that?" Elle asked.

Rory just shook her head. "I mean, that doesn't sound impossible, but I don't remember it. Grandfather was forever trying to get me to date someone who would provide an advantageous merger with Gilbert International. I kept reminding him it's the twenty-first century, not the Dark Ages when he grew up."

Elle laughed at Rory's comments. "Did he have an arranged marriage?"

"He did. I never met my grandmother, but she came from the Fairchild fortune. I wasn't old enough to ever ask my dad about his mom, so I don't know if she was happy or not. I mean, I don't think I would be, but who's to say that I wouldn't fall in love with someone in an arranged marriage."

"I know it's odd, isn't it, to think of arranged marriages. But how is it any different than dating and getting to know someone? I mean I know you can back out, but back then people sort of got to know each other after they were married." Elle said, thinking of her current relationship with Dash. They might fall in love… but they might not. Was an arranged marriage any different than what they had? She wasn't entirely sure.

"It is odd. If Dash comes at me with a man he thinks I should date because of business reasons, I'm going to tell him no."

"I've got your back," Elle said, but she knew that Dash would never do that to Rory. Over the last few weeks, she might not have seen him much, but she had noticed his little touches everywhere. He'd gone out of his way to make sure the house was full of things that Rory loved. He doted on his little sister so she didn't have to worry about anything but her recovery.

"I know you do. One thing I always wanted was a sister. Now I have two," Rory said. "Are you close with Indy?"

"I'm not, but she and Conrad haven't known each other long and I did just move back," Elle said.

"We should have a girls' night with her."

"That sounds good to me," Elle said.

She noticed that Rory seemed lighter than she had been when she'd come downstairs. But something still seemed a bit off with her. She hoped she wasn't getting frustrated by how slowly her progress was going. Her physical therapy was going to take a lot of time. "How are your therapy sessions going?"

"Good."

Her answer didn't invite more questions, so Elle let it go, finished her salad and then cleaned everything up before placing it into the dishwasher. "Ready to go up?"

"I guess."

"Want to watch a few old episodes of *Glee*?"

"Aren't you tired?" Rory asked.

She was, but she also could tell that Rory needed something more. Elle wasn't entirely sure what, but she didn't want to leave her alone. "I'm still wound up from my evening."

"Good. We can watch TV in the upstairs family room, that way we don't disturb Dash and we can be alone."

"Sounds good."

She helped her upstairs and when they got to the family room, Rory frowned at her chair. "I don't want to sit in that."

"Okay. Well, if I help you, I think you could sit by me on the couch."

"I'd love that."

Dash heard the door to Elle's bedroom open. He was seated at the desk in the corner of his room and watched the light under the door of her bedroom as he finished typing an email and hit Send. He'd spent most of the evening with Rory playing Mario Kart, then working when she'd gone up to bed—but a part of him knew he'd been waiting for Elle to come upstairs.

He'd heard her come home about an hour and a half ago and had gone downstairs, but then he overheard her and Rory talking. He'd left the women alone, sensing his sister needed some girl time.

But he had missed Elle while he'd been away, and he wanted to get something like a date between them. He wanted her, true, but it wasn't just lust driving him. The odd thing about his relationship with Elle was that it was *more* than lust. He'd thought of her in his bed and naked under him more than a dozen times since he'd last seen her. But he also had wanted to share London with her when he'd been there.

He thought she'd love the British Library with its collection of old illuminated manuscripts and then high tea at the Ritz. Hopefully she'd be better by the holiday season, then he'd take her to his favorite pub in Covent Garden at Christmastime before going for a stroll through the lights.

It was odd because he travelled alone for most of his adult life. But during this trip, he couldn't help but think of how he wanted to show his favorite spots to Elle. Which brought him right back to the conversation they'd had in this bedroom about a relationship.

He hadn't thought he'd want one with her. Hadn't wanted to let himself be vulnerable to her or the curse. But in London, he'd realized that he might already be.

He couldn't imagine his life without her. She made him feel really alive in a way that nothing else ever had.

Even before the accident when he'd been partying and living up to his grandfather's version of what a Gilbert should be, he'd been pretending.

With Elle he didn't have to.

He walked over to her door and knocked on it.

"Come in."

He entered her bedroom and found her sitting on the edge of her bed rubbing her feet. "Want me to massage your feet?"

"Thanks but I'm just putting lotion on. What's up?" she asked.

He came farther into her room, which was smaller than his but still large by anyone's standards. "I wanted to see if you'd consider a late-night date—maybe at midnight. I think we're never going to have a day off together."

"I agree to the day off together. What do you mean by late-night date?"

"Well, I know you have the late shift again tomorrow night and I'm going to be in Boston all day, so I thought we could have an evening picnic in the solarium."

"I like the idea of that," she said.

"Good. I'll take care of everything. See you after work tomorrow," he said, turning to leave before he gave into the temptation to take her in his arms again.

She'd been clear that dates were required before she was letting him back in her bed, and he respected her wishes and understood them. But if he stayed in her bedroom, he wasn't as confident in his self-control.

It didn't help that she was wearing that damned

Pokémon nightshirt again. He could see the shape of her breasts right above Pikachu's ears and her long legs were bare under the hem. She had been rubbing lotion on her feet, drawing his attention to her shapely calves, which had then made him keenly aware of how those legs had felt wrapped around his hips.

His cock stirred and he turned away, knowing he had to get out of that room before he did something that would destroy this fragile peace they had. "Good night."

He walked quickly toward his room and the door and heard her behind him, moving around. "Good night, Dash."

He hurried into his room and closed the door behind him. He wanted to punch something. He had too much tension in his body. He grabbed his running shoes, went down to the gym and got on the treadmill, running for forty-five minutes hoping to force his body into exhaustion, but he couldn't.

Images of Elle kept playing in his head. He had to have her again. Living in the same house, not sleeping together—that had to be why he'd thought of her in London. There couldn't be more to it than that otherwise he was in deep trouble.

After tomorrow night when they had their date, he'd feel comfortable kissing and touching her and making love to her. Then he'd be able to assess what the hell was going on. Was this just him being denied a woman who was so close and so tempting? Or was it the start of something more?

In the old days, he would have texted Conrad, who

was an insomniac and up most nights, but since his cousin had started living with Indy, Dash hadn't wanted to intrude on his time.

His cousin deserved all the happiness he had found with Indy. Dash wasn't going to disrupt it and come off as needy.

That was the one thing he'd never been. He was the strong one. He took care of everyone and made sure that the Gilbert name and the Gilbert businesses kept improving and growing. That was his job.

But there were moments, he thought as he punished his body by running harder on the treadmill, when he wanted to walk away. When he longed to say fuck it and just pretend he'd been born an ordinary man.

A man who had choices that weren't tempered by thoughts of heritage or legacy.

But he wasn't.

He was responsible, and his shoulders, though tired from the burden, weren't bowed by it. He would do the right thing for his family and for Elle. Regardless of how he felt about her and how the next night turned out, if it seemed there was any chance he'd hurt her, he'd have to walk away to protect her.

His honor would demand nothing less. But his heart…his heart. He wasn't even sure he had room for romantic love. But if he did, there was something about Elle that warned him it might shatter into a million pieces.

Elle was glad that she had a light workload that day. Aside from a text message from Rory confirming a girls' night with Indy at her bookstore—which had been approved by her private care nurse, Frida, and Monty—Elle spent most of the day thinking about her upcoming late-night date. For a moment, it felt like she could touch the girl she'd been when she was eighteen.

As much as Dash leaving her at the ball had been traumatic for her, the real event that had hit her hard was realizing the family she'd thought she'd had with her stepmother and stepsisters wasn't real. It had changed the woman she might have become.

She tucked a strand of hair back behind her ear as it had escaped once again from her ponytail. She got an alert on her phone and pushed the notification up to ignore it, but her finger must have lingered too long because the notification opened.

She glanced at it, intending to clear it immediately until she saw it was from Dru. It had come through on a professional network sharing app that she had. Elle wasn't on social media as there were only a handful of people she wanted to connect to outside of work and she kept in touch with them via email.

Private Message from Dru Miller.

Elle, hey, I think it's been almost ten years since we spoke. Mom is moving out of the house and we found a box of your things stowed away in the attic. You can come and get them at the house before Saturday. We're having an estate sale on Saturday and will sell them if you haven't collected them. I'm enclosing the address in case you no longer have it.

Shocked, she glanced at her watch and then back at her schedule. As it was Wednesday, she really didn't have a lot of time to go and get the box. What was in it? Surely nothing of monetary value or Dru would have sold it. But it might be more pictures of her parents or some of her mom's stuff.

She hadn't allowed herself to think of Dru in years. It wasn't like Dru was trying to reconnect, more like she was trying to get rid of the last vestiges of their connection to her.

She definitely wanted to go and get the box. But she'd promised Dash a date after work. And he said midnight, but they were both off at seven tonight, which could mean…

She hesitated, and then texted him.

Hey, um, how would you like to take a road trip instead of having a picnic tonight? My stepsister found a box of my stuff and if I don't collect by Saturday she's going to sell it.

Sure. Where are we going?

Cockell Shores. It's about forty-five minutes from here.

Dash called instead of texting back.

"Thought this would be easier. There's a yacht club in Cockell Shores. I can have my yacht moved there and we can have our date on the water after you pick up your box."

She loved the idea of going out on his yacht that

she'd been on once before when they'd been dating in college. Was it even the same one? She knew it didn't matter and was using that distraction not to think about the unexpected message from Dru and all the past hurt it stirred up.

"Sounds great. I might try to leave early. I have to check with Dru. She might not be available tonight."

"Either way I like the idea of our date on the yacht. I'm still game if you are," he said.

"I am. Let me message her back and I'll let you know what she says."

"Good. I've got to get back in a meeting," he said.

"Did you leave to call me?" she asked.

"I did," he said.

"Oh. Thanks," she said as a warm feeling spread through her like a scarf on a cold day. She knew that he rarely stepped away from his business so that meant more to her than maybe it should.

But right now, when she felt so raw thanks to Dru's message, it was something she needed.

"No problem. Text me about tonight. Bye."

"Bye."

She clicked back on the message from Dru and replied, asking if she'd be available that evening. Elle worried that her stepsister might not be. Dru texted back that she wasn't but could leave the box on the back porch. The side gate would be unlocked.

Elle texted her thanks. But inside she felt that old sadness that came from remembering the supposed close bond she'd had with her stepsisters when her dad was alive.

She shook it off. She was older now; she had the strength to know that family didn't only mean those who were legally bound to her. She was finding her own way. She went back to analyzing the tests of her patient and put on Beyoncé while she worked just get herself back in a better mood.

She'd come too far to let Dru bother her now. She'd get her box and then go on her date with Dash, and that would be it. This was the last time she'd have to deal with them.

She texted Dash they were good to meet at the yacht club, which he thumbs-upped. She smiled at it because she knew he must be needed in his meeting. That made the fact that he stepped out to call her mean that much more.

There was something about him taking that moment that made her feel cared for, and not so alone. Indy texted her a few minutes later asking if she was free soon, that she was out at the hospital visiting her teenage assistant who had been injured at school.

Elle mentioned she could take a break, she needed to get up from her desk and walk around to clear her head. As she headed to the walking path and outdoor area where they were going to meet, Elle realized that she wasn't alone anymore. She had this new family and these new connections.

She thought she should be cautious about letting them into her life as everything with Dash was so uncertain, but she couldn't be. She liked the way that she was in this new dynamic. She liked that she had a place where she belonged and people like Rory and Indy, the sisters she'd always wanted.

Ten

Dash knew that Rory would be fine if they weren't at the mansion with her, but he called his sister when he got out of his meeting just to check on her, and she sent his call straight to voice mail. She texted saying she was visiting with a friend and that they could talk later.

The entire board of Gilbert International was going to have to be at the next meeting to vote on some new measures that Dash was introducing, and for the first time in years, all three of the Gilbert heirs were going to attend. He called Con instead of texting. He had to admit he was excited at the thought of having Conrad and Rory at the meeting. It would be nice to hear their input.

"Gilbert here."

"Gilbert here," Dash greeted in return. "I'm going to need you at the next board meeting."

Conrad gave an exaggerated sigh and then said, "When?"

"One month's time, I'm sending you and Rory a calendar invite."

"So why are you calling?" Conrad asked. "Trouble in fake paradise?"

"Maybe, I don't know," Dash said, leaning back in his big leather executive chair and turning it so he could see out the windows that overlooked downtown Boston harbor. "How did you get together with Indy?"

"Dude, I know you've had lovers before."

"Fuck off. I'm talking about the falling for her stuff," Dash said.

"Oh, that. I have no clue. I mean, it was a million little things," he said. "She kind of pushed me to open up and I resisted."

"Because of the curse?"

"I don't like to give that any weight," Conrad said.

"You were in a horrible car crash the same day that Grandfather closed the factory and created economic hardship for GC. Do you really not think there is a correlation?"

"Hell, I don't know. If there is then I think I broke it when I came back," Conrad said.

"If only it were that easy. Anyway, I have some news. I'm not really sure that we're going to be able to move the business into town like we hoped."

"Why not?"

"The board is resistant. I have final say so they'll do it if they have to, but…"

"Your personal curse is stopping you," Conrad said blandly.

Dash knew his cousin put very little stock in Dash's Midas idea. That because everything the Gilbert men touched turned to gold, they couldn't find love and happiness or if they did it never lasted. But the truth was, since Rory had awoken from her coma and he and Elle had started to be fake married, financial opportunities had been pulling him away. He saw a lot of potential in them, and he wanted to endorse them, but they would take more time, take him away from Gilbert Corners. But if he pursued these opportunities, he could potentially convince more businesses to follow their lead and move into the town.

"Yes. Don't be dismissive. You were out of it for three years. You have no idea what my life was like."

"Dash—I know. I'm sorry. You were alone and had to shoulder too much of the burden. I'm sure the old man was no help at all. But I'm here now. You're not alone. What is it you're afraid of?"

"Hurting Rory and Elle. Hurting the town," he said. Spending the rest of his life alone in his office.

He had his own will, and his choice would dictate most of those things, but there was a lot more to it than that. He had a feeling that if he took his eye off Gilbert Corners, the businesses that he'd offered incentives to move to the retail space and park he was renovating from the old factory might not be successful.

"You won't."

"How do you know?"

"I know you, D. Also, you got me here with you now. I've got your back."

"I know you do but you're busy and can't—"

"Can't do the eight million tasks you do for the family and town on top of your job of running a global conglomeration?"

"There aren't eight million tasks."

"You know what I mean. You're busy too. I think that, more than a curse, you're struggling to let go. I get it, I used to do the opposite and let go too easily. I mean, I left and didn't really look back or reach out unless you did it first.

"But you're holding everything inside your grasp. It's like you wrapped your arms around Rory, me and the entire town of Gilbert Corners to protect us and now you're afraid to loosen it."

Dash knew that Conrad was right. He was afraid to let go. He had worked so hard to draw everyone into a place where he could protect them and the thought of failing now…he couldn't let that happen.

"How would I even do that?" he asked.

"Only you know," Conrad said. "I'm not being a dick with that answer. It's just that only you know what caused you to hold on so tightly. I don't."

He wasn't entirely sure, but he figured it had started when Candace had left. That moment when he'd had the choice of love or business taken from him, and he'd decided to never be in that position again.

"Thanks."

"That's it?"

"Yeah. You helped."

"That's what I do," Conrad said dryly. "Want to have drinks while the women are having girls' night?"

"Sure. When is that?"

"I'll text you. Later, Dash, and man?"

"Yes?"

"I love you."

"You too," Dash said and disconnected the call.

He felt slightly—well, better wasn't the word he'd use—but more settled than he had been. Conrad had been as messed up by their childhood and upbringing as Dash was and he'd found love. Was it possible for Dash as well?

And if he did find it, would he be brave enough to take the risk of it? If ever he was going to take a chance it would be with Elle. He knew that. She had awakened something inside of him that he was struggling to keep contained despite his fears.

That was something he wasn't going to answer today. Instead, he made plans to have his yacht moved to Cockell Shores and arranged for a private chef and crew to staff the yacht. He wanted this date to be something that Elle wouldn't forget. He needed this date to be one she couldn't walk away from.

Elle pulled up into the circle drive of the house that her father had bought for them when they'd moved away from Gilbert Corners. Dash had offered to meet her, but she'd wanted to do this on her own. It was a nice house in a good neighborhood that had quality schools. Her stepmother had picked it out and Elle had thought it was a bit much for them, but her father said if it made Maude happy that was all that mattered.

She got out of her car and walked to the side gate which had been unlocked for her, and as she came around to the back of the house, she saw the padded bench that her father had carved all of their names on. She took a moment to go and run her fingers over the back, lingering on his name.

She still missed him.

She saw that Dru had put her box on the table and walked over to pick it up. The house itself was dark and Elle went over to look inside. She didn't know what she expected to feel when she looked into the house that had been her home for almost eight years, but she'd expected to feel *something*.

Normally she only recalled that last year, but time must have given her some buffering, and she remembered sitting in the living room while they did karaoke battles, the sound of her dad's baritone duetting with her on Elton John and Kiki Dee's "Don't Go Breaking My Heart."

It had been her parents' song, and after Elle's mom had died it had become hers and her dad's. She'd forgotten that. Forgotten about how her, Maude and Dad would sing "Picture" by Kid Rock and Sheryl Crow, and how when her dad had looked at Maude, Elle had been able to see a different kind of love. But love all the same.

How had he been brave enough to love again? But also, how had Maude only loved her when her dad was alive? That was a question she'd never been able to answer. And she knew that she probably never would.

She turned back and picked up her box. It was time to leave this part of her past behind for good. She'd been spending so much time at Gilbert Manor that she hadn't had a chance to work in her own home. But she thought she might invite Rory to come down there with her on her next day off.

She got in the car, glancing at her watch. She was early for her 8:00 p.m. meeting time with Dash and she was curious what was in the box but didn't want to linger here. So she drove to the yacht club and parked near the back of the parking lot. She looked over at the box.

What was inside?

Why was she so afraid to open it?

She undid the tucked in flaps at the top and the smell of mothballs and dust wafted up toward her. She sneezed and shook her head as she undid her seat belt and turned more fully toward the box.

She reached inside and the first thing she touched was lace. She drew it out and realized it was a wedding a veil. Was this her mom's? She started to pull more things from the box and confirmed that it was her mother's.

Her parents' wedding album was inside and then farther down, Elle's baby book. She wasn't sure that Dru could have sold these things, except for the veil. She put it on her head and pulled down the sun visor, checking her reflection in the mirror.

She wondered if she resembled her mom. If Elle was being totally honest, there were times when she struggled to remember what her mom looked like. She took out the wedding album and opened it, and the picture on the front page confirmed that they *did* look alike.

She touched the smiling face of her mother. Young and happy. Not knowing that cancer would hit her hard just a few short years into her marriage, and after a relapse, she'd die when her daughter was eight.

Her heart was breaking as she looked at her parents.

There was a knock on the window of her car door and she looked up. Dash. She pulled the veil off her head and closed the album, putting them both back in the box before opening the door.

"Hey," he said. "So it was some good stuff?"

"Yeah," she said, feeling so heavy from the memories of the past and trying to figure out how to be smart about her relationships with Dash that she shook her head. "I was going to wear the veil, but since it's our first date, I thought it might be too much."

"Oh, well, this is awkward. I did pack my tux."

She laughed, relieved that he'd just gone along with her silliness. "Maybe we'll save that for our second date."

"Definitely. I have a driver standing by to take your car. Figured we could drive home together later," he said.

Home.

Gilbert Manor.

It wasn't her home. But it was sometimes starting to feel that way. The same way that house on Oleander had felt like home once upon a time.

"Elle, you okay?"

"Yes. And yes to taking the car back to Gilbert Manor for me. Let me grab my purse and we can be off. Did you really pack a tux? Is what I'm wearing okay?"

"It's perfect," he said, pulling her into his arms and hugging her tightly.

She tipped her head back, trying not to let the feeling of his body against her get to her, but it did. He did. He had some power over her that she was tired of ignoring. Plus, she was feeling battered from her day, so went up on her tiptoes and wrapped her arms around his neck and kissed him.

She took the kiss she wanted and shoved aside that nagging voice in her head that warned it might be unwise. She was tired of being sensible when it came to Dash and to her life.

Elle seemed pensive as they sat under the stars eating the gourmet meal the chef had prepared for them. The discreet staff had all retreated below deck and the captain kept them on a nice, smooth sail around the harbor area.

The summer evening was clear and the sea breeze cool but not cold. Elle's hair was still back in that tight ponytail she favored. She picked at her food and Dash was laboring to keep the conversation going.

"I've been told I'm not really intuitive when it comes to people so if I'm off-guard, apologies, but it seems like something's up with you," he said, after their dinner had been cleared and they were sipping drinks on the cushions at the aft of the boat.

"You're not off base. I think… I still don't understand what happened with my stepfamily," she said. "I mean, I'm over it and I've tried to move on, but I haven't, and being back there today reminded me."

"I'm not sure what happened with them," he said. He had a few vague details that she'd shared about them moving on after her father's death, but he wasn't sure what that meant. He could see that it troubled her. And in a way, he understood where she was coming from. After all, he'd lost everyone in his family in a few short years. Rory to the coma, his autocratic grandfather to death and Conrad to his own pain.

She shrugged.

"When…everything happened, first Rory and Conrad, then Grandfather and Candace, I realized I was on my own. I know how ridiculous that might sound given that I have a full-time live-in staff, a driver and tons of other employees but family-wise, I was alone. It was frankly the most adult moment of my life."

She turned to look at him, her face illuminated by the lights on deck and the moon shining down on them. That strand of hair that always escaped her ponytail danced around the side of her face and he realized that in a way that strand of hair was very indicative of Elle. She tried to be all neat and tidy but there was also something a little wild and uncontrollable that always slipped out…like her wearing that wedding veil in her car.

"It's such a strange thing to go from having a full family one moment to being all alone in the next," he said.

"Yes. That right there. When my dad died, it was

unexpected. I mean, my mom had cancer and it was a long illness, so I had time to try and prepare for losing her. Dad got up to make coffee one morning and had a heart attack in the kitchen. Maude and I found him when we came downstairs to make breakfast."

Her voice broke on the last word and she turned her face away, but not before he saw the glimmer of tears in her eyes. He reached out and pulled her into the curve of his body, hugging her close and hopefully offering her some comfort.

"I'm sorry."

She wiped her eyes and tipped her head back to meet his gaze. "I'm sure your experience with Rory and Conrad was similar in a way. I felt so powerless. I was frantically praying, except I'm not religious and I don't know any prayers, so instead I was just repeating the lyrics of the Smiths song, 'Please let me get what I want.' But I knew I wouldn't.

"I kept praying that Dad would wake up…"

He had never felt more connected to another person than he did to Elle in this moment. "I think that song gets the job done. Like you, I was making frantic deals with God or the universe the entire ambulance ride after the accident. I was transported and checked and released. Not a scratch on me. I punched the wall outside of the emergency room trying to understand why me."

She turned slightly in his arms put her hand on the side of his face. "I hate that for you. It was bad enough finding Dad, but it was a medical condition he didn't know he had. With you… I just can't imagine it."

He swallowed hard, fighting against the unexpected stirring of those emotions from that night. "I hated myself, Elle. At that moment, I, who'd always been so charming and well-liked to everyone, really came to hate the man I was. How could I survive when I'd been the one driving?"

"Don't. Don't do that to yourself. Accidents are just that. And fate sent all of you on a path. As much as you say you weren't harmed that night, you were the one who had to be strong and watch over them both as they recovered. Maybe fate thought you were the only one who could handle it."

He wasn't too sure about that. He saw nothing heroic in himself that night. He'd spent the next years until Rory awoke being the best man he could be. Trying to make sure that he'd walked away unscathed for some reason that could be justified. But inside he'd felt the scales were still out of balance.

"This isn't supposed to be about me," he said. "What happened after with Maude—is that your stepmom?"

"Yeah. Um, she was super nice through the funeral and wake. It happened New Year's Day, the year right after the winter ball and your accident. Dad's will was found and read and he had divided his estate into two parts. One for Maude after their life together and the other to me from his life with Mom. I got the business and their house in Gilbert Corners and a lot of investment accounts. Maude got the house we'd lived in and some spousal benefits. She…changed toward me. Told me I had my own house to go live in it."

"Bitch."

She smiled at him. "Thanks for the support. But I know she was grieving and felt hurt by the way he'd divided his estate. I don't know."

"Have you tried to talk to her?"

"One time, but she told me I wasn't her daughter and she didn't want to see me again."

Dash wasn't sure what to say to that kind of attitude. He wished he'd been there to protect her. He wanted to make promises to Elle that he'd never let her be treated that way again.

Eleven

"I'm sorry you were alone," he said.

She hadn't meant for all of that to come out, but with Dash, she was coming to learn that her words seemed to spill out without thought of the consequences. That story, what Maude had said to her, was her most embarrassing moment. The one time when she'd felt not only on her own but also not good enough. Not worthy of being considered part of her family.

And all those years she'd spent with Maude and her daughters had suddenly become a lie. So she'd shut everyone out. Went back to school and focused on her studies, trying to get through the pain by ignoring it. And one day, she'd woken up numb, and honestly, that hadn't bothered her. She just had found this nice, empty place to exist which she'd been doing until earlier this year.

Until she turned thirty and decided to return to Gilbert Corners. The job had been the jolt she'd been looking for. She almost smiled to herself thinking she hadn't been numb since she'd seen Dash in the hospital.

"Thanks. I'm sorry you were too," she said. "You don't still hate yourself, do you?"

"No. I don't think I do. Definitely not since Rory woke up and we got together," he said.

A thought occurred to her, and she wondered if she should keep it to herself. But things had already been sort of odd tonight, so why not, right? "Were you punishing yourself when Rory was in the coma?"

"What?" he asked, sitting up, shifting his body subtly away from hers.

She turned to face him more fully as he did so. "I'm sorry if I stepped over a line, but I was just thinking that when Candace left and you had no one, if you got into the habit of…."

She trailed off because she realized she was going too far. She couldn't ask him if Rory had been an anchor that had tied him to Gilbert Corners, keeping him from moving on. She wouldn't. Yet hadn't she all but implied that just now?

She'd wanted this first date to be the start of something and, instead, she was ripping off her own scabs and now starting in on his. "Don't answer that. I'm sorry. I didn't realize how vulnerable I felt when I told you what Maude said. I think I wanted to make you feel vulnerable too."

He nodded. "I don't think you did it on purpose. You're not that cutthroat when it comes to people."

He was right. But as soon as she realized where she was pushing him, she had known why. She hated to feel this out of control and unbalanced. After Maude had kicked her out, Elle had promised herself she'd never let anyone have any control over her life like that again. She had her boss at work, of course, but in her personal life, she always kept her guard up.

"I can be pretty cutthroat," she said lightly, wanting to save a little of this date with Dash. She had been looking forward to being alone with him. Learning a little more of the complicated emotions that made him was more than she could have asked for. But she wasn't looking to leave either of them feeling unsure or drained. And as much as a part of her wanted to believe that Dash didn't have any insecurities, another part of her was keenly aware that he did.

He arched both eyebrows at her. "When?"

"Pool," she said. "I can't tell you how much money I made in medical school playing."

"Are you a pool shark?"

"Ha, not really. I am always very up front about the fact that I have skills. Men don't believe me."

"I believe you," he said. "I'm pretty damned sure that if you wanted to, you could beat me at a lot of things."

"Really? Are you good at pool?"

"I'm fair. I've never hustled a game," he said.

"You wouldn't have to, Money Bags. Some of us had to decide between rent and food."

"I thought you inherited the bulk of your father's estate?" he said. "Doesn't sound like you had to either."

She chewed her lip and wrapped one arm around her

waist remembering those days. "Maude contested the will but had already kicked me out, so everything was frozen until it was resolved. I had a scholarship that covered my tuition, but room and board was on me."

"Why didn't you come to me? I know we lost touch, but I would have helped you."

She suspected he would have. Dash was a very generous man.

"You were dealing with enough of your own stuff. You didn't need to take on the problems of a girl you dated a few times. Plus, I needed to do it on my own and not lean on someone else. Just to prove to myself that I was going to be able to do it."

He shifted on the bench and touched the side of her face and a warm tingle went through her entire body.

"You weren't just a girl I dated a few times. I liked you," he said.

"But your life was falling apart and you didn't return to college that year," she pointed out.

"Fuck fate."

"Fuck fate," she agreed. "Actually, I don't regret it. I mean at the time I did, but if I hadn't lived through all that, I might not be here with you tonight."

"And tonight is worth it?" he asked.

The date hadn't been normal, all down to her, but Dash definitely was worth it. The more she got to know the real man—the man behind the legendary charm and legendary family—the more she was falling for him.

Which she'd promised herself she wouldn't do. Except it was hard not to when he was looking at her this way. A way that made her think she saw love in his eyes.

Real love that would last past accidents and upheaval. And once again, she started to pray the only way she knew. That Smiths song. *Please, please, let me get Dash.*

"Was tonight worth it?" he asked again. He wasn't sure it was as far as Elle was concerned. He'd stirred up memories she probably never wanted to live through again and then revealed that he had his own cracks. He hadn't been old enough when his father died to ever have a talk about how to handle things as a man.

His grandfather was gruff and told him to stop being a wuss if he ever let any emotions show. His father had been more open to talking about things when he'd been home. But his dad had been gone. A lot.

There were times when he felt the battle inside of himself to be both like his father and grandfather. His grandfather was autocratic and self-serving, and never questioned himself. Just bulldozed his way through life and made damn sure that everyone knew he wasn't stopping. His father was different. That part of Dash empathized with others and had tried to be aware that he was luckier than most and use his privilege and position to help as many as he could.

But it was hard.

Tonight was no exception. He wanted Elle, but suddenly, seducing her wasn't as straight forward as he'd expected it to be. She'd said she wanted a date before they hooked up again and he'd given her one. But this… well this was more than he'd expected.

"Yes," she said. "You're worth it."

"Me?"

"You. Am I?"

He rubbed the back of his neck. Was she? Maybe, but he could never tell her that, could he?

What if he had to? Hell, he was letting too much time pass wasn't he.

"Yeah, you are."

She shook her head almost sadly at his response and he knew he'd fucked it up. Hell, he'd guessed he would from the very first moment she'd asked him that.

"You don't have to lie. We're in a fake relationship for your sister's health, so if this isn't really developing into more than that, don't pretend with me."

He hated her honesty. Hated that she could just open herself up to him and say things that really made him wish he was a different man. Or the same man but one who could open himself back up to her. But he wasn't even sure there was anything inside of him.

He loved Rory, but for a time part of that was duty and guilt. It had been the same with Conrad. This… whatever it was that was slowly growing between him and Elle, he had no idea what part of him it came from.

"I wasn't pretending. I don't know how you do that. How you open yourself up like that?" He shoved his hand through his hair again. And then realized he was doing all those small ticks that had earned him a back-hand from his grandfather for fidgeting and immediately put his arms at his side one hand in his pocket. The more he dealt with his past, the more it came to the surface.

"I don't know another way to be with you," she ad-mitted. "It's not easy and I'm not doing it to manipulate you, I just… I don't want to fool myself again, Dash. Not with you. I think—I know you're a decent man and that you don't want to hurt me. But that doesn't mean you won't and I'm trying to be as honest with you so maybe that won't happen."

He got it. He knew what she wanted. And until Elle, until this moment, he hadn't realized that this was his worst fear. It wasn't Candace leaving all those years ago, because truth be told he hadn't really missed her but more the idea of her. It was Elle, tempting him. She made him want things that he'd told himself he was good without.

He wanted to be able to love her. He wanted to search out the hollowed-out parts of his soul and figure out if love could exist in there. But what he wasn't sure of was if he was brave enough to do it.

He had never thought of himself as a coward. Never believed there was anything after that horrible December car crash that could shake him. Until her.

"I can't—"

"I know. I shouldn't have come out with you tonight. Getting that box, being back at my old home, seeing my mom's wedding stuff. It's stirring some chaos inside of me and I'm just sort of bumping all around tonight. I'm asking you for these big leaps and you're not ready."

He hated, *hated* the way that sounded. It made him feel less than in her eyes and he couldn't—wouldn't allow that. If she wanted the truth, then he'd give it to her.

"Truth is that all you want from me?"

She nodded.

"Here it is. I don't know what to do with you. I'm

not sure what emotions I actually can feel and I'm not even sure if they are real. Right now, I'm happy my sister is out of her coma and you're back in my life. I'm not sure that I can make this last. Fuck, I haven't made anything last except business deals and upkeep on an old mansion no one had lived in for years. So there it is. I'm not sure I'm the man you'll want me to be, but I'm more than man enough to take this on."

She kind of nodded and swallowed hard.

He hoped she wasn't struggling to believe him. What more could he do to show her how much she meant to him?

"Okay, good. So we're doing this?"

"Yeah, we're doing it," he said, but the words were sort of barked out. Not sexy or romancey at all. Nothing like the Prince Charming he'd always thought of himself to be with the ladies. Nothing like the man he thought Elle should be with in his mind.

But this was who he was. Underneath the charmed life, he was rough, maybe more so than Conrad was, and Dash had finally admitted it.

"Good. Don't pretend with me when we're alone anymore. I want to know the real man."

"What if he's not what you're expecting?"

"What if *I'm* not?" she said. "We both are used to projecting a certain image…maybe it's time we stopped pretending with each other and see what happens."

Not pretending should be easy, but Elle knew it might not be a simple thing for either of them. She had no idea how much of Dash's persona was real and how much was put on. And for herself, it was necessary. She'd been pretending she was cool with being on her own since Maude had kicked her out.

And it had really only been today, when she'd stood on the patio looking into the house and remembering the good times, that she realized she wasn't fine with being alone. She'd spent so many years not letting her mind wander back to that part of her life and now... it seemed cowardly to her, and it was time to let it go.

"Sure," he said.

She laughed at the dry tone. "I know it's a big ask, but maybe it'll work."

"Honestly, you seem very good at putting your mind to something and getting results. I'd have to say tonight didn't turn out as I'd expected but I'm not disappointed."

"You're not?" she asked.

He pulled her into his arms and kissed her. It was the kind of slow, long kiss that stirred to life so much more than sensual heat. It was calling her deepest emotions, and they didn't need any more encouragement from Dash. She knew that she was challenging herself to be the best version of herself for him. Not just for him, but because the life she wanted with him was only going to happen if she was at her best.

His lips against hers were firm and familiar. His tongue rubbed against hers and she put her hands on the sides of his head as she sucked it deeper into her mouth. God, she wanted this man. No one had ever got her hotter quicker than he did.

He lifted his head and they were so close as he

rested his forehead against hers; she felt the warmth of his exhalation as he breathed. His eyes were wide open and in them she fancied that she saw the same confusion she felt inside. That desire for something more, and a little of that fear of what changes it might bring.

His hand moved down her back, finding the hem of the cropped top she'd changed into after work and then slipping underneath it so she felt his hot hand against her spine. He splayed his fingers so that he covered much of the naked flesh under her top and she trembled with desire in his arms.

She swallowed hard and lowered one of her hands, finding the buttons on his shirt and undoing them down the middle of his chest until she could slip her arm underneath it, her hand caressing him. She held him to her.

Her breasts were full and heavy as she breathed. She felt them brushing against his chest, they were so close. His erection grew against her. At times they communicated better without words.

Duh.

She had been looking for some reassurance he wasn't going to abandon her the way that her parents had in death, or her stepmother had out of anger, grief and spite. But life didn't work that way. Was she truly just now realizing, body-to-body with Dash, that the safety net she wanted didn't exist?

Yes, she thought. She most definitely was.

She kissed the side of his neck where he smelled faintly of his cologne and that other essence that she associated only with Dash. When she closed her eyes, his scent immediately stirred memories of the last time she was in his arms. That frantic coupling in the hallway of her home.

Something that had soothed an ache inside of her but had also created a longing for something more. And now she was back in his arms. The craving had returned with double the strength. And the longing... well, it was back too, and even though her gut was pretty darn sure she'd never be fully satisfied and would always want more of Dash, she quieted it.

She wasn't going to find an easy answer to the dilemma she was puzzling over. Love didn't work that way. She could fall in love with him, and he could end up feeling only affection for her. She knew that. She could live with that, she thought, as she felt his mouth on her neck, sucking at that spot where her neck and shoulder met and sending shivers down her body creating wetness between her legs.

The thing she couldn't live without was Dash.

She couldn't live with regret if she walked away from him because she thought it might be safer. When had safer ever been a way she wanted to live her life?

She pushed hand lower down his back, burrowing it under the waistband of his pants, but only a finger could fit. Impatient to reach more of his skin, she loosened the fastening at his waistband with her other hand and then let her hand on his back move lower, sliding over the firm flesh of his butt and cupping one of his cheeks in her hand, drawing him closer to her.

He groaned and his mouth moved lower along the edge of the ruffled neckline of her top. His tongue traced the path where fabric and flesh met. She arched her back and thrust her chest toward him, wanting so much more than these teasing kisses that set fire to her body.

"Dash?"

"Hmm…" The sound vibrated against her skin.

"Are we alone here?"

"Uh, they'll come and check on us," he said, lifting his head. "Unless I tell them we don't want to be disturbed."

"Go tell them," she said. He nodded and walked away quickly.

She reached up under her skirt, took off her panties and stashed them in her handbag that was on the deck next to her. Then she sat down on the padded cushions and laid back against them. The sky seemed so big tonight with no clouds and only stars, satellites and the moon to fill it.

She took a breath and, on the breeze that blew past her, let go of the illusion that she had any control over her life.

Twelve

The crew he had on the yacht were known for their discretion, and after a quiet word with the captain, he headed back up on deck. This had been his main reason for setting up a date, but somehow this felt like more than sex. Hooking up with Elle would give him some kind of relief from the lust that seemed to settle on his body like a heavy cloak whenever he thought about her—and he thought about her way too much.

But their conversation had made him realize how complicated and special sex could be with the right person. He wanted her more than he had wanted anything or anyone before. That scared him. He'd be an idiot to not let it. He got a condom and went back up on deck.

Anyone and anything attached to the Gilbert name was cursed, he knew that. But at the same time, as strong as his desire was to protect Elle, he couldn't fight his need for her. He returned to deck and found her lying on the cushions. One of her legs was bent at the knee and she had her arms spread out to her sides.

He stood in shadows watching her. Remembering the hurt she'd expressed to him about her past made his heart hurt. But seeing her this open, this ready to take a chance on him. It was humbling.

He didn't want to fuck this up. Wouldn't allow himself to. Not the lovemaking. The other stuff. The stuff he'd never considered or tried before. He had to do it now for her. Had to match this openness he observed in her.

He toed off his deck shoes as he got closer to her and lay down next to her on the cushions as she turned her head toward him. She'd undone her hair and it was spread around her head in a riot of curls that caught him by surprise. It was easy to forget what Elle really looked like when she wasn't all buttoned-up.

He caught one of the curls and twirled it around his finger as he leaned over her. He let go of the curl, drawing it down to her bare collarbone and then moved his fingers lower to push the ruffled sleeve down her shoulder until the top of her breast was revealed. He paused, lowering his head and kissing the spot before pushing the stretchy fabric of her top lower, until he saw her naked breast in the moonlight.

Her breasts with their tight nipples beckoned him and he began sucking one nipple into his mouth. She put her hand on his shoulder and stroked him for a moment, and then she fumbled around until she had her hand under his shirt. He lifted his head and sat up, tearing his shirt off and tossing it to the deck. He undid his pants and then went back to her breast.

He caressed his way down her body, stopping at her nipped-in waist and the flesh under the crop top. He moved his hand farther down her body, taking her by the waist and turning her on her side.

Her hands were on his chest caressing him. Her fingernails raking slowly over his skin and sending tremors of lust through him. His cock got even bigger and he lifted his head and closed his eyes for a moment to pull himself back from the edge of coming. That trick might have worked if her hand hadn't slipped lower and started to stroke him through the fabric of his underwear. He reached down with one quick movement and freed his cock and balls.

She moaned her approval against his chest where she was kissing him as her hand wrapped around him and stroked his length. He cupped her butt through her skirt and it felt like she was bare-assed naked underneath, which made his hips jerk just as she reached the top of his cock and ran her finger over the sensitive tip.

Done with pretending this was going to last much longer, he pulled her skirt up and cupped her naked butt, running his finger along the furrow between her cheeks and then lower to her pussy, which was moist and hot. He pushed his finger into her as he lowered his mouth onto hers and kissed her long and keep. He thrust his tongue slowly in and out of her mouth mimicking the motions of his finger on her female flesh.

She groaned and her hand tightened on his cock,

moving up and down on him. He wanted her so much that he felt that tension moving through him. He had to fight himself not to thrust harder into her hand and cum. But he wanted to be inside her.

He pulled his hand from her pussy and lifted his head. "There's a condom in my pocket."

She nodded, got the condom and then shifted around to hand it to him. He tore the packet open and put it on one-handed and pulled her back into his arms. His mouth going back to hers. Her hand going back to his cock, and his hand back on her butt and then lower to her pussy.

He was riding this knife's edge of his desire, turning himself on as much as he could before he took her, because as everything else with Elle, when he had her in his arms, he felt like he needed to make it last. As if this might be the last time he was with her.

She might be open to him and the possibilities of the future but life had shown him that the future wasn't also open back. So he wanted to draw every possible moment out with her. Make it last for as long as it could.

Elle was on fire for Dash. She could tell that he was drawing this out. The way he kept trying to slow them down…but she didn't want that. That wasn't who they were or how she saw them. She put her hands on his shoulders and pushed him flat on his back over the cushions and straddled his waist.

He pushed the fabric of her skirt up high on her waist and his hands were back on her butt as she posi-

tioned herself over him and then took the entire length
of him inside of her. She stopped when he was fully
inside her. Their eyes met and he groaned as he sat up,
pushing him deeper inside her. She wrapped her legs
around his waist as his mouth came down on hers and
his hands tightened on her butt.

He moved her against him, his hips pumping her
under and his hands pulling her down with each of his
upward thrusts. She sucked his tongue deeper into her
mouth wanting him to fill her as completely as possible. She closed her eyes and felt the hardened tips of her
nipples rubbing against his chest. Wrapping her arms
around his neck as she continued to drive her higher
and higher. She felt like every part of her was straining for release. She wanted to be able to touch him
harder, she needed more of him and rode him harder
and harder until he ran his finger along her butt crack
and he pushed the tip of his finger inside her.

She screamed as that tipped her over the edge and
her orgasm ripped through her. Her pussy tightening
on his cock, she sucked his tongue hard as her body
kept clenching on him. He tore his mouth from hers,
buried his face in her neck and rolled them over so she
was underneath him as he drove into her harder and
deeper than before. He cried out her name as his hips
jerked forward and, she suspected, he came.

He thrust a few more times before he lowered his
head to her breast, carefully holding the full weight
of his body off hers. She couldn't stop her body from
clenching around his and thrust her hips upward a few
more times, hugging him to her with her arms and legs.

She tangled her hands in the hair at the back of his head and held him looking up at the sky. She saw the possibilities of a future with Dash. God, she wanted to keep him. Wanted him to want to keep her. Wanted this feeling of belonging to be real and last.

She licked her lips, not liking the path her thoughts were on, so she turned her head downward and found Dash looking up at her. "God, woman."

"Am I supposed to respond to that?" she asked laughing. She pushed her worries away and just let the joy that she felt move through her.

His smiled back and it was the most relaxed, most vulnerable smile she'd seen on his face ever. She hugged him even tighter with her legs and arms and he smiled again. She wanted to protect him. She knew that he was capable of taking care of himself, but there was a part of Dash that was very vulnerable. How had she just noticed it?

But she knew why. It was because he had to be strong for everyone and now, in his arms, he hadn't had to be. She lifted her neck and shoulders so she could kiss him on the jaw, and he turned his head and kissed her tenderly back.

"I'm not sure I can move from these cushions," he said.

"Well, this is awkward. I was hoping you'd carry me like you did the last time,' she teased.

"Oh, I'll carry you in a minute. That was… Thank you, Elle. You gave me everything and it made this… oh hell. I'm going to leave it at that."

She smiled at him, realizing that until this moment

she hadn't allowed herself to be this relaxed with him. But his happiness here in her arms was infectious and she would be content to stay like this for as long as he wanted.

He rolled to his side and pulled her into his arms. She was cuddled close to his side, her head resting on his chest and the reassuring sound of the solid beating of his heart was under her ear. The breeze stirred around them and he stroked her back.

"I don't like to make promises I can't keep, but I will do my best to make a relationship with you work, Elle."

She turned her head to look up at him. "I will do the same."

He nodded. "I feel up to carrying you now. Want to go back home and do this again?"

"Yes," she said. Not even allowing a moment's fear in when she thought of going home with him. To their home. It might be a fake marriage that had brought her this close to him and back into his life, but she knew this was real.

He had made as much of a promise to her as he could and for now that was enough. It had to be because that was where they both were. She had to stop trying to force things into being. She'd realized that when Maude had rejected her attempts at reconciliation, and this was nothing like the relationship with her stepmother.

This was Elle as an adult making a conscious choice to be vulnerable to Dash. To let her emotions out of the locked chest she'd shoved them into all those years ago and finally live again.

He got to his feet and fastened his pants before holding out his hand to help her up as well. He'd said they should leave but he pulled her into his arms and just held for a few more minutes.

Elle was tired when she returned home from work a few weeks later. She had a new patient with a severe traumatic brain injury where the outlook wasn't good and talking to the parents hadn't been easy. She'd spent extra time at her office going over the medical reports and brain scans to see if there was something extra she could glean from them, but nothing stood out.

She put her bag down on the kitchen table and saw that the housekeeper had left her a note telling her that there was a prepared dinner for her in the fridge. Kicking off her shoes, she padded over to open the fridge and as she heard someone behind her, turned and was happy to see it was Dash.

"Rough night?"

"Yeah," she said, taking the plate that had been left for her to the microwave, and after she hit Start, she felt Dash's hands on her neck and shoulders gently massaging away the tension that had settled there. She leaned back against him and closed her eyes. The last few weeks had made her realize how much she needed him in her life.

Not for financial reasons or social standing as her stepmother and stepsisters had once thought, but because of this. These quiet moments when she could let her guard down and know he'd be there for her.

"Oh. I forgot to say that Justine finally got a name

for that guy who was visiting Rory," Elle said, turning in his arms and smiling up at him.

"That's good news. I'll send it to my investigator so we can find out more about him. Who is it?"

"Kit Palmer. He had a friend at the facility, but they were discharged the same day Rory woke. He hasn't been back since," Elle said.

"Why was he in her room?"

"Justine said that he'd mentioned he knew Rory from school and wanted to just talk to her," Elle said.

"From school? That makes no sense to me, and I gave orders that no one be allowed in her room without my permission," Dash said.

Elle gently laughed at the autocratic way he said that. "You know you're not the boss of anyone at the care home, right?"

"Of course, but usually people are afraid of me and do what I say."

She outright laughed at that. "Afraid of you?"

"Darling, you're the only one who teases me like that. Most are afraid that I'll ruin them if they cross me," Dash said.

"Why?"

"Grab your dinner and I'll get some wine and tell you," he said.

She took her dinner from the microwave and went to the table to sit down as Dash returned with two glasses of white wine and sat down across from her. She took her glass and lifted it in a salute to him. As she took a sip, she tried not to dwell on how on how fragile their new relationships remained.

"So?" she asked as she started eating. As much as Dash was a powerful man in the business world, she'd also seen his generosity and kindness to many.

"The man who attacked Rory was the son of a family that Grandfather was intending to merge businesses with. He thought that the match would be advantageous and keep both companies in the family so to speak," Dash said, taking a long swallow of his wine.

"I guess the merger was off after she was assaulted by him. Who was it?"

"Declan Orr. And yes, it was most definitely off," Dash said.

"I know that name. Wasn't he a bit old for Rory? I think he was running the factory, right?"

"Yes to all of it," Dash said. "You know he died in the car accident but…after that night, I couldn't let it go. I ruined the Orr Group financially. Bought up as much stock as I could find and then slowly dismantled all of their holdings until nothing was left. Orr's parents died a few years ago."

She thought about that for a moment. It wasn't like the man she knew Dash to be, but she could see that ruthlessness in him when it came to his sister. "Did it make you feel better?"

"What?"

"Ruining them, did it help?" she asked.

"Not really," he said. "I still feel guilty for the accident."

She reached across the table and took his hand in hers. "You shouldn't. That's why it's called an accident."

"I'm not sure that logical thinking plays a part in guilt," he said dryly.

"It definitely doesn't. It's kind of like hindsight. For me looking back, I can see how obvious it was that Maude didn't really love me like her daughters. She gave me the smallest room and I wore a lot of their hand-me-downs, but because I didn't really care about clothes and I thought she was my new mom… I viewed it differently. It was only when she kicked me out that I started to go back over everything."

He rubbed his thumb along the back of her knuckles sending a shiver of desire through her. "Did it help?"

"No. Just made me feel worse because now the happy memories I had felt like a lie," she said. "And I have to wonder if happiness sometimes isn't a lie."

She tried to stay positive but tonight, she was remembering not only her patient but also her mom. Life had a way of going from happy to unhappy so quickly. Elle knew no matter how "realistic" she was, there was no way to really be prepared for it.

"Woah, that's not what I expected from you, Elle. What's going on?"

"Just a bad night with a patient who I don't think I'm going to be able to save," she said. "And of course I still have that box upstairs from Dru."

"Not everyone can be saved, even by an amazing doctor like you. And that's your box and that family's loss that they didn't love you the way they should have," Dash said. "Happiness isn't a lie, by the way."

"How do you know?"

"Because it's how I feel when I'm with you and we promised each other no lies," he said.

"Yes, we did," she responded.

"Ready to go up?"

She nodded and cleared her plate and wineglasses to the sink and then Dash sweep her up in his arms. "I know you like being carried."

"Only by you."

Thirteen

Dash had spent more time than ever with Elle over the last six weeks, and he knew he was falling for her. There was no denying that everything changed that night they'd made love on his yacht. He had no regrets. Fear, yes, but regrets? Never.

Tonight, they were hosting a gala to raise additional funds for the new hospital wing that the Gilbert Trust had provided the initial funding for. The gala was being held at Gilbert Manor in the ballroom and Elle and Rory had both been pretty excited about the party.

His sister had been improving steadily and was able to walk on her own now. Though she was still doing physical therapy, the in-house nurse was now visiting once a week, which really had made a huge difference to Rory's mental state. His sister, he reflected, seemed happier and more like her old self. Some of her old memories were coming back to her and Dash knew it was time to tell her that he and Elle weren't married before she figured it out on her own.

The night of the accident and the incident leading up to it were still hazy for Rory, and there was a part of Dash that hoped his sister never remembered the sexual attack of her date.

There was a knock on his door, and he glanced at the door to Elle's adjoining room which was open. She was helping Rory with her makeup for the ball, and he had to admit he missed her.

He opened the hall door. Conrad was there wearing a tux and holding two bottles of beer in one hand.

"Should I ask?"

"No," Conrad said.

"Trouble in paradise?" he asked all the same.

"No, not really. I mean, Indy is trying to get me to do some co-op training class at the high school," Conrad said, handing him a beer.

"I don't really see the problem with that."

"They have inferior facilities. I can't work in those conditions," Conrad said.

"You're such a diva."

"Dude, drink your beer so I'm not tempted to punch you."

Dash knew he was safe from his cousin. "Why don't we fund the renovation of the rooms you'd use to teach there?"

"Could we? I mean, then I would oversee it and make sure that everything is state-of-the-art."

"Of course we can. Don't you read the financial statements that are sent out each quarter?"

"No, but I'm glad we can do that. Do I have to do anything or will you take care of it?" Conrad asked.

Dash had a sneaking suspicion his cousin had just played him. He didn't mind it because taking care of the family was what he did. But Dash also knew that if he made it too easy, Conrad would take advantage of it. "You have to fill in the paperwork and show up to the next two meetings."

"Two?"

"Yeah. I might want to take a vacation and you might need to step in," Dash said. "I was thinking about sharing some of the responsibilities."

Conrad nodded a few times and then smiled. "So the fake wife is working out?"

"Yes, she is. I mean, I don't know how she feels but…"

"Dude, I've got your back. I know you have taken care way more than your share of things for the last ten years, I can step up more often," Conrad said.

"I like doing it, I'm a bit of a control freak as you know."

"I do. I guess one of us has to be," Conrad said with a laugh. "So, vacation?"

"Yes. I want to tell Rory the truth about me and Elle and then hopefully take Elle away for a few weeks to Gilbert's Paradise," he said, naming the island they owned near the Bahamas.

"Good idea. I'll be in town for the foreseeable future. Indy's got me volunteering all over the place and

I start filming the next season of my cooking show in the fall."

"Nice. Thanks," Dash said.

"No problem. I'm just happy to see you living and doing things for yourself. It's been a long time."

It had been a long time. And as much as he'd always told himself that it was because of the curse and that he was protecting himself, he knew that wasn't the case. He'd been doing it because he'd been punishing himself. Knowing he'd been behind the wheel that night, walking away without a scratch and then watching the long recover of Rory and Conrad had shaken him. Had left him feeling hollow. It had taken Elle to make him see that. To make him want to live again.

Rory might have been the one in the coma, but in retrospect he'd been in one too. Tonight, Dash was determined to change all of that. He was ready to tell Elle how he felt about her. Ready to commit to something more than the relationship they'd built and the unspoken agreement they'd somehow both made not to talk about their feelings.

Though he felt hers each time she waited up for him to come home from a business trip and sat in the den with him while he ate, just talking about everything and nothing. He felt it in the way she left him little pictures on his desk or texted him in meetings just to show him something that mattered to her. By doing that, he knew that she mattered to her as well.

And there was a part of him that honestly was scared spitless by how much he needed and wanted her in his life. But another, bigger part knew that if he didn't take this chance, didn't tell her how he felt and try to carve a future together, he'd spend the rest of his days back in that emotional coma that he'd existed in for the last ten years.

And he didn't want to go back. Wouldn't go back. Conrad wasn't the only one changing and Dash knew it was time to stop letting fear and guilt rule him.

Elle finished helping Rory with her makeup and Indy put some finishing touches on her hair. Elle's dress was a beautiful soft robin's-egg blue satin sheath that had a large bow on one shoulder, and her other shoulder was bare. Instead of wearing her hair up as she normally did, she'd left it down and curly. She swept one side back behind her ear and used the vintage rhinestone haircomb that she'd found in her mother's stuff to hold it there.

Rory and Indy were talking and Elle moved away for a minute to give herself room to breathe. The last six weeks had given her a glimpse into what life with Dash would be like, and though not perfect, it was everything she could want. The weekly girls' nights that she'd had with Rory and Indy had showed her that the family she'd thought she'd had with her stepsisters had been shallow, in a way that Elle had never realized before.

And not just on their part. Elle had held part of herself back from her stepfamily, and it was only here in Gilbert Manor, while she was living the biggest lie she'd ever told, that she found a true bond with these women. The sisters her heart had always longed for.

She could barely let herself think about Dash. That night on his yacht six weeks earlier she'd taken a risk, told herself she was going to go all in, and she had. But she hadn't known what that would feel like or how quickly and totally she would fall in love with Dash.

It wasn't just the lovemaking, which left her breathless and fulfilled and, as she thought about it now, hungry for Dash. It was the little things like a gardenia on her nightstand after a long night at the hospital, left by him because he knew they were her favorite flowers. Or the quiet way he just held her when she got home and was too exhausted to talk or have sex but just needed the comfort of his body, which he always offered.

There were a million ways that she'd fallen in love with him over the last six weeks and only one reason why she hadn't told him.

Fear.

Which ticked her off because when she'd finally found herself, she'd thought that nothing could scare her. She hadn't realized that finding everything she wanted would make her tremble in good and bad ways. She longed for this family that she had now to be hers for the rest of her life.

But there was still the lie that she and Dash had told to Rory. As she got healthier and healthier and her memories were trickling back in, they both knew it was time to tell her they weren't married. And yet the fake marriage was a safe way for them both to just stay together.

She knew that.

But she also knew that this had to end. It was time to take that next leap and face her fear. If anyone had told her that falling in love would make her afraid, she would have laughed at them. She'd seen movies and maybe that should have been an indication. She had been watching someone else, not falling herself, and now that she was in love with Dash, it was more intense than anything she'd experienced before and she didn't want to lose him.

So she was waiting, but she'd made up her mind that tonight, she'd tell him her feelings. She couldn't keep doing this. She wanted their marriage to be real. She wanted Rory and Indy to be her sisters. And she wanted Gilbert Manor to be her home.

She may have moved back to find a bridge to the past, but instead she'd found her future. Now she just had to be woman enough to take it.

"We look hot, don't we?" Rory asked.

"We do," Elle agreed going back over to the women.

Indy, who was the tallest of the three of them, held her phone out and turned the camera application on as she put her arm around Rory. "Come on, Elle. Selfie time. I'll send this to Conrad and Dash so they know they have the best-looking women in town."

"I think we already know that," Conrad said from the door as he entered.

She glanced over her shoulder and her breath caught in her chest as she saw Dash in his tux. God, he looked so good in formal wear. She couldn't take her eyes off him, moving over his broad shoulders and the suit which was cut to fit him perfectly. Their eyes met and something shifted between the two of them.

She felt like…he had fallen in love with her too. Surely, she wasn't making that up. He came over to her and pulled her into his arms and kissed her, which made everyone else sort of laugh.

"Let's get a photo," Indy said. "Conrad, you take it."

They put Rory in the middle with Indy and Conrad on the left and then Elle next to her on the right with Dash behind her, his arm around her waist. She looked at the camera. But the image staring back at her felt unfamiliar. Until Dash smiled at her in the selfie camera, and she smiled back.

This was real. This was what she'd been waiting for. She hadn't had any idea that returning to Gilbert Corners would have this profound an effect on her and her life.

"Who would have thought that we'd all be here for another ball?" Rory asked. "I've missed so much."

Dash kissed his sister on the top of her head. "But you're here now and that's all that matters."

It *was* all that mattered, Elle thought. That and the love she felt for these people. She'd found the family she'd always wanted.

Dash had forgotten how the house really shone when it was full of people. When Conrad had thrown a ball a few months ago to celebrate the success of the town council and Indy's renovation project, Dash had felt a bit out of place. Almost as if he hadn't belonged in the house or the ballroom.

The same three-piece orchestra was playing in the foyer as guests entered the house, and there was a bubble of excitement in the air as the waitstaff circulated champagne and appetizers prepared by Conrad. Many in town believed the Gilbert curse was truly broken now that Rory had awakened.

But Dash still had his doubts. They hadn't all found love, but for himself, he felt closer to it than he ever had before. Elle came up next to him, slipping her arm around his waist. She looked so beautiful tonight. As she peered up at him, he knew that she had fallen in love with him.

And he knew that she'd never looked more beautiful. Love had done that to her, transformed the woman who had pulled her hair back into a tight ponytail and focused on her work into this glowing woman next to him tonight. He knew that all he had to do was trust in her and in himself and he could see her next to him every day for the rest of his life.

Trusting anyone other than himself had never worked out for him before.

But this was Elle.

The woman that he wanted to protect with the same ferocity that he'd looked after Rory and Conrad.

Except this was sharper. More personal.

Was this love?

He thought it was. Had identified it as such, but now that she was so close and looked so gorgeous and in love with him, he didn't want to mess this up. Didn't want to hurt her in any way. Didn't want to speak it unless he was sure it was the truth.

"Why are you looking at me like that?" she asked.

"I feel like I'm seeing you for the first time tonight," he said.

"Is it my hair? You've seen it down before," she said.

"It's not your hair," he said, pulling her away from the landing and the stairs and into the hallway where they couldn't' be seen. "It's you. There is something... glowing inside of you tonight."

Oh fuck him. He sounded like an idiot. If this was what it meant to be in love, he better keep his mouth shut.

But Elle didn't seem to mind. Instead, she kissed him and then put her hand on his jaw. "It's you that's making me feel like this."

He swallowed hard. He hadn't expected the moment to come now, or here in the hallway that was just off the main sweeping staircase. But it had. He wasn't going to pretend he didn't understand what it was she was saying. He knew it the same way he knew what was in his heart.

"You are doing the same to me," he admitted.

"Oh, I'm glad. It would be a shame if I was the only one to feel this way."

"You're not," he said, turning so that she was between him and the wall so that she was blocked from anyone who might come upstairs, lowering his head kissed her long and deep. It was so much easier to show her how he felt than to tell her. Words weren't easy for him, and he wasn't going to risk another rambling sentence like that one about her glowing.

He wanted her to know what he felt in his heart. He

wondered if this kiss was conveying how lonely he'd been all those years driving Gilbert International up the Fortune 100 list and making billions for his family members who were both wounded. Doing the only thing he knew how to do until Elle had come back into his life.

He kissed her deeper and her hands were on his shoulders. She moaned as she pressed herself more fully into his body and he swept his hands down her back as he felt himself harden. Maybe he should have taken her to their room.

A scream rent the air and he lifted his head from Elle's, turning toward the sound. He saw it was Rory, and she just kept screaming as tears were running down her face. Alarmed and scared for his sister, he raced to her with Elle by his side. He tried to touch her, but she flinched away from him.

Elle reached for her and again Rory flinched. But she stopped screaming.

"Rory? Ladybug, what is it? What's wrong?" he asked her.

Conrad and Indy rushed up the stairs. Dash motioned for Conrad to see to their guests as he and Elle led Rory away from the staircase and back to her room. She was breathing heavily and she just kept muttering to herself. Words that Dash didn't understand.

His heart was breaking for whatever his sister was going through. "What is it, ladybug? Tell me what I can do to fix this?"

"You can't. You tried. You and Con tried, but you can't fix this," she said. "I remember what we were running from the night of the accident. I remember his hands on me, tearing my dress... I remember it all, Dash."

He wanted to hug her, but she'd flinched before when he'd tried to touch her. So this time, he just opened his arms, and she made a small sound that made him want to find the man who'd been dead these ten years and beat him the way Conrad had on the night of the attack. But Rory was his focus. She buried herself into his arms and he held her close to him, stroking her back.

His eyes met Elle's gaze over his sister's head and he saw understanding in her eyes. Neither of them had expected her memories to come back like this. Elle grabbed her phone, texting her staff to alert them they'd need a therapist sent to Gilbert Manor and they paged Rory's nurse, but it took them a long time to get her settled down.

The party had ended, and Conrad and Indy were back upstairs all of them in the room with her when Rory sat up.

"You two aren't married, are you?" Rory asked. "You left Elle on the dance floor to get me out of here that night. Why did you lie like that?"

"We wanted to tell you the truth," Elle said. "But for your mind to recover, it was easier for us to be what you needed."

"Was I so fragile?"

"No," Dash said. "So important. I couldn't risk losing you again."

Fourteen

Elle felt like she was on a roller coaster. The ups of almost confessing her love to Dash—and then this moment when Rory was living with the trauma of date rape and the cascade of her memories returning. Dash was talking to her, but Rory looked horrified and fragile in a way she hadn't since she'd woke from her coma.

"Rory, memories are a tricky thing, and as the mind heals, you need time to adjust to the world around you," Elle said, sitting down next to Rory on her bed and taking her hand. "There was a lot of new stuff coming at you as you awoke and seeing Dash and Conrad calmed you, and then you saw me and remembered the happy times we had together."

"I did," Rory said. "How did I remember only select parts?"

Elle stroked her friend's arm as Dash moved to the other side, watching him. She could tell he wanted to do whatever he had to in order to protect his sister, but he couldn't keep those memories of the night she was attacked from hurting her.

"The trauma of the event before you got in the car. Your mind was protecting you just like Dash and I were, until you were strong enough to deal with what was hidden."

Rory pulled her hand out from under Elle's. "You lied."

"Only about being married. Dash and I have re-kindled our relationship, and you and Indy and I have formed a strong sisterhood. That wasn't a lie."

Rory looked sad as she glanced over at her brother seeming to search for confirmation. "Dash?"

"It's true," he said, but there was a note in his voice that Elle couldn't identify.

"So you two are going to get married?"

"I hope so," Elle said.

"Well…" Dash said at the same time.

Looking up at him, she got the feeling that she had been dropped into some mirror world. What had happened to change his mind other than Rory's memories returning?

"So then it was a lie," Rory said. "Not that it matters to me. Do I have money in my own right, Dash?"

"It does matter. And why do you want to know?"

"Do I?"

"Of course, I've managed your portfolio the same way I did Conrad's. Why?"

"I want to move into my own place. I need to be on my own to figure out what I'm going to do next. I know you both thought you were doing what was best for me, but lying and deceiving me doesn't seem right."

Elle stood up, nodding. "Of course. I'm here for you as a friend if you need me."

"Thank you, Elle. I might switch doctors down the road, but right now…"

"That's fine. We have a treatment plan and we can go forward however you decide," Elle said. Then she looked down at Rory and, for the first time, she noticed that the other woman seemed truly alive. The amnesia had been like a gauzy lens covering her friend. Not anymore. The truth might not be pretty, but it was a missing piece of the woman that Rory was. "As painful as they are, I'm glad your memories are back. Now I think you'll see faster progress in your recovery. I'll leave you and your family to finish talking things through."

Elle turned and walked out of the room. Indy gave her a quick hug and followed her out as well. "I think the three of them need to talk."

"Probably. I'm sorry, Indy, I really need to be alone."

Indy just hugged her. "Dash was probably just trying to say—"

"When has Dash ever not spoken the truth? He meant it when he hesitated. That was all I needed to know about our future together."

"Well then he's an idiot," Indy said.

"Or I am for believing that I saw something that wasn't there," she said. She had been trying to tell herself that she believed in love and that being open to it was all she needed to bring it into her life, but now it felt like a lie. And not the kind of lie that her time with her stepfamily had been. This was a lie she told herself because she'd seen something in Dash that had made her feel seen and accepted. Like he had been on a similar journey and was glad to have finally found someone to share it with.

"You are one of the smartest women I know," Indy said. "Emotions are hard. The Gilberts have dealt with a lot of tragedy, and Dash still believes in that curse."

"I know. And I can see where his belief stems from, but at the same time, that's not a good enough reason to…"

Not love me.

Indy didn't say anything, just looped her arm through Elle's as they walked down the hall toward her room. But she didn't want to sleep so close to Dash tonight. Not now that she finally could admit to herself that the love she felt for Dash wasn't going to be enough for him to take a chance on her.

"I want to go home."

"I'll help you pack some stuff," Indy said. "You can come back later and get the rest."

"I'm not coming back so I'll pack it all. But thank you, Indy. You really are like a sister to me," Elle said.

"You're the same."

With Indy's help, Elle packed up her stuff in a short time. She glanced around the room, saw the single gardenia in the bowl on the nightstand and the note that

Dash had left for her yesterday. Turning away from that, she felt a tinge of anger seeping into her pain.

She couldn't blame him; he hadn't made any promises. If anything, he'd warned her that he wouldn't make any. But she could be mad because he'd made unspoken vows when he'd made love to her and when he'd left her tiny notes and gifts. He'd show her in a hundred different ways he cared, but not to her face, and not when it mattered.

Conrad and Dash left Rory's room an hour later. Dash leaned back against the paneled wall and closed his eyes. He had been so close to having Elle. To taking the risk. But when Rory remembered her past, it had been a stark reminder that just because his sister was awake, she wasn't out of the woods yet. There was still so much he had to do to for her. And her recovery from the sexual violence she'd encountered was going to take time. His chest felt like it was going to explode and tears burned his eyes.

He rubbed the heels of his hands against his eyes until he saw stars and the tears disappeared. He lowered his arms and looked over at Conrad who seemed tense and looked like he was going to punch something.

"You okay?"

"No. That goddamned bastard who hurt her. Makes me want to beat him again, and he's fucking dead so I can't. I thought I'd dealt with this but seeing Rory tonight…it's still there."

"Yeah, me too. Except different."

"I know. If you'd gotten there first, I'm pretty sure

we would have killed him with our bare hands," Conrad said.

"We never talked about that night. Do you think I made a mistake getting us out of there?" Dash asked.

"You had no choice. The old man wanted Rory to apologize and that bastard looked so smug. I was out of control. We had to leave," Conrad said.

Memories of that night flooded his mind, and he couldn't stop them. He remembered the way Declan had looked standing next to Grandfather. Bloodied from Conrad's fists. Rory was clinging to Dash's arm, trembling, her dress torn, her body bruised and her spirit badly damaged. There hadn't been an easy solution, but Dash had known then that they had to leave. They couldn't allow themselves to be pawns in their grandfather's game, so he'd hustled Conrad and Rory to his car, a super-fast Bugatti Veyron that he'd coveted.

The roads had been icy and wet when they got to the car and Declan had followed them out, telling Rory that she'd better get used to his hands on her. Dash had snapped. He'd decked Declan and informed the douchebag that he'd never marry Rory. Then they got in the car.

Rushing down the icy drive, he'd gone fast but he wasn't driving recklessly. It had been Declan speeding up behind them, ramming them hard. Then Dash hit the brakes before Declan tried ramming them again and the impact had caused them to skid, spinning and then careening as they went off the road. Conrad had taken off his seat belt, ready to get out and finishing beating Declan up before they tumbled off the road and down the slope.

He had been thrown from the car and left unconscious. Rory had been jerked around in her seat and hit her head hard on the dashboard as the airbag exploded. Dash had a bruise on his shoulder and some cuts on his hands. And Declan's car was totaled and crushed, the driver dead.

"I never think about that night," Dash said, his voice raw with emotion and grief.

"I can't remember anything after we get in the car," Conrad said.

"I'm glad. You were in a lot of pain, and I thought we were going to lose you," Dash said.

"I'm too ornery to die," Conrad said.

"That's not how death works," Dash said.

"No, it's not," he admitted. "What are you going to do?"

"Honor Rory's wishes of course. I'll set up staff for her and hire a security guard if she insists on living on her own," Dash said.

"Yeah, I figured that. I meant about Elle."

Elle.

He went into her room and saw that she'd taken all of her things. He sat on the bed his head in his hands. Conrad followed him.

She'd texted to say she was going home and he hadn't been able to respond. Just earlier this evening he'd been ready to risk the curse. Had believed that maybe over the last six weeks he'd found his way past his old beliefs. He had something new to believe in. Elle and his love for her.

But Rory's memories were a wake-up call. That night of the accident, he might have come out unscathed, but emotionally he'd been washed up. His grandfather, whom he'd long respected, had shown him the man he really was, and Dash had been left questioning if he wanted to follow in his footsteps.

And then…he was the only functioning Gilbert left. His choice had been taken.

"I don't know."

Conrad clapped his hand on Dash's shoulder. "I've never been one to give advice, but I think you need to go after her."

Dash thought so too. But he was tired and there was the decades old anger stirring inside of him. That wasn't the man he wanted to be for her. "I think so too, but I'm scared."

"Fuck. You love her."

"How do you know that?"

"That's the only thing that has ever scared me. And you're braver than I am," Conrad said.

"I'm really not," Dash responded.

"You have to be. You were all alone and kept us together. That's a strength I've never possessed. So what are you afraid of?"

Dash pushed his hand through his hair and looked his cousin straight in the eyes. "Being too much like Grandfather."

Conrad shook his head. "You're nothing like him. You never have been."

"I am very like him in the boardroom," Dash said. He'd heard that comment more than once from business rivals and board members.

"But not in life. You'd never sacrifice someone you love for a deal," Conrad pointed out. "I think there's more to it than just your fear."

"What else could there be?"

"That you think you aren't good enough for Elle."

"I'm not," Dash said.

"And I'm not good enough for Indy. But here's the thing—she believes I am. And it's okay with her when I'm not perfect. I bet Elle feels the same about you."

Did she? He suspected she did, but he had hurt her when he'd hesitated at Rory's bedside. He could say it was because he wanted to reassure his sister, but he also knew he'd been afraid to really risk it all and let himself admit how much he loved her.

"Thanks, Con. Love you."

"Love you too," Conrad said hugging him, before he walked out of the room.

Dash saw something out of the corner of his eye on the floor. He reached down to pick it up—Elle's rhinestone haircomb. The one that had been her mother's.

Dash looked at his watch. It was almost 2:00 a.m. and too late to call his driver. But he didn't want to wait until morning to see Elle. He went down to the garage and took the keys to his car from the peg on the wall. Ten years ago, he'd left Elle at this house with rage in his heart and anger flowing through him. Tonight, he was going to Elle a different man.

* * *

Elle sat on the sofa in the living room of her child-hood house. It was after two and she should be sleeping, but she couldn't go into her bedroom without remembering the night she'd spent there with Dash. The sheets, which hadn't been washed, still smelled like him, and that was why she'd brought his pillow down to the living room with her.

She had changed into leggings and a faded *NSYNC shirt that she'd found in her dresser. For some reason, it had always felt to her like there was power in leaving. She knew from therapy sessions and some of her own journaling that because her mom and dad had died, she had abandonment issues. But this time…she wasn't sure that leaving had been the right thing to do.

She knew that Dash would have been reeling from having Rory's memories come back. Elle had read the notes in Rory's file and saw that Dash had mentioned his sister had been attacked by her date but hadn't been sure if she'd been raped.

She'd never discussed this with Dash and wondered now if she should have. She was beginning to think that no one had talked about that night. Conrad had been badly injured too, so Dash had been alone dealing with the death of Rory's attacker as well as their injuries.

How much of that made him the man he was today?

All of it, she thought. The two of them were his family and Dash would do anything to protect them. Which wasn't really what was bothering her. When he'd taken her in his arms in the hallway, she'd felt like she'd finally found that home she'd spent too many years searching for. And then when his mouth had touched hers…she had.

It was like fate had looked down on them and put them in that moment. She could understand needing to reassure his sister. But when he'd hesitated…it hadn't just been in his words. When their eyes met, she'd seen that it was something more. He was putting those walls back up and Elle had just felt tired.

Tired and sad. So she'd left. Left before he suggested she leave.

And now she wasn't sure she should have. Dash had been abandoned just like her, and she'd asked him to take a chance on a relationship with her. When things got rough, she'd left. Was that fair? Was she taking too much on herself?

She'd texted him that she was going home and he hadn't responded. She wasn't sure if he was still with Rory or not. She looked at her phone again willing it to buzz with a text message notification, but just like that time in sixth grade when she'd tried to make the door slam closed with her mind a la Matilda, nothing happened.

He wasn't texting her back.

Maybe a good night's sleep would help. But she couldn't sleep her mind was whirling with possibilities and scenarios of what she should have done. Was it too late to go back to Gilbert Manor?

Did she really want to?

She went and got her shoes and a jacket as she heard the heavy fall of summer rain. Then turned to pick up her phone as it rang, seeing it was the on-call service.

"Dr. Monroe."

"It's the emergency room. We have a patient inbound with a head injury."

"On my way."

She grabbed the bag she kept ready for emergency calls and headed to the hospital. She'd have to wait until morning to talk to Dash. Maybe then she'd have figured out what to say. How to put into words that she'd felt like he'd left her hanging in Rory's room. Right or wrong, she needed to know that he'd never do that again.

She pulled into her parking spot and went into the hospital through the doctor's entrance after letting the head of ER know she was here.

Rachel Lewis, the head ER doctor, came into the changing room with X-rays as Elle finished getting into her scrubs and washing her hands and arms.

"Not sure how bad this is, but it looks like some swelling, and given the fact that it's a Gilbert I'm sure it's not good."

A Gilbert. "Conrad?"

"No, Dash," Rachel said.

Elle could see the other's woman mouth still moving and knew she was talking, but stars danced in front of Elle's eyes and there was a buzzing noise in her ears. She started swaying and Rachel caught her arm as she almost collapsed.

"Call Iverson," Elle said shakily. "I can't operate on Dash, he's my…boyfriend."

"Crap. Sorry I didn't know. Sit here. I'll send someone to check on you."

Rachel left the room and Elle sort of stumbled to a bench and leaned forward putting her head between her knees. This was her worst fear. Losing the man she'd loved to death.

Fifteen

Dash woke up to the whirring of machines and a sharp pain in his side. He opened his eyes, not sure where he was. Then he saw Rory and Conrad sitting in chairs staring at the bed. Hospital.

The crash came back to him. He'd lost control of the car when he'd hit the corner heading toward the bridge that went into Gilbert Corners. "What happened?"

His voice sounded dry to his ears and he tried to sit up but the IV in his arms pinched.

"You fucking scared us," Conrad said as he and Rory rushed to his side. "I'll ring for the nurse."

"I'm so glad you're awake, Dash. I was so scared," Rory said.

"Are you okay?" he asked her.

She smiled as tears sparkled in her eyes. "Yes. I'm fine. Don't worry about me. What happened to you?"

"I was going into to town to find Elle," Dash said.

"She's here," Conrad said. "She's been sitting in the hallway by herself."

"Why?"

"She said she wasn't sure where you two stood," Conrad said. "I'll go get her. Rory and I need some coffee."

Rory leaned over him and kissed his forehead. "I think I understand why you lied to me. I was thinking just now that I'd do anything to have you back and healthy. And you've only been in the hospital for sixteen hours."

He nodded. "Watching over you two was the hardest thing I've ever done."

"We know. Now we're going to take care of you at least until you're out of here," Conrad said. "You want to see Elle, right?"

"Yes. I was going...help me sit up, Con."

Rory and Conrad helped him raise the bed once the nurse had been in to check on him and okayed it. Rory also combed his hair and the washed some blood off of his face. He reached up to touch the bandage on his head. "What's wrong with me?"

"Cracked ribs and a concussion," Conrad said.

"They are probably only keeping you overnight," Rory said. "They wanted to make sure you woke up."

"Thanks," he said. "Hey, Con, I have a haircomb in the pocket of my pants wherever they are. Will you get it for me?"

His cousin got it and handed it to him, then Conrad and Rory both hugged him before they left the room. He sat there for a few minutes listening to the sounds of the hospital and then realized that he had no idea what he was going to say to Elle. He'd thought he knew how this would play out, but the accident had changed everything. He been afraid that if he let himself love, he'd lose her, but he almost lost her tonight.

It seemed to Dash that he'd gotten things mixed up in his head, and maybe the Gilberts hadn't been cursed in love but blessed to have it for the years they did. He needed to think on it some more, but for himself, he knew if Elle would have him, he wanted her at his side and in his life.

The door opened and she walked in. She wore scrubs and had her hair pulled back in a ponytail. Her skin looked paler than it had earlier that night when he'd last seen her.

"Hi."

"Hi," he responded.

"How are you feeling?" she asked.

"Like shit," he said.

She laughed. "Yeah. You hit your head pretty hard. I suspected you'd be okay because you're hardheaded."

He started to laugh but it hurt, and he groaned.

"Sorry, I forgot about your ribs. I was so scared for you," she said, coming farther into the room.

When she was by his side, she sort of reached for him and then hesitated and put her hand back to her side. "I was on call tonight. They paged me when you came in and I felt so helpless. I knew I couldn't operate on you if you needed me. Don't worry, we called in another specialist. You weren't in danger."

"I know that. Are you okay?" he asked.

"I'm fine. I was just… Dash, tonight has made me realize what you were saying all this time. I thought if I can just make you see that love exists, if I can just make you realize that loving someone is a good thing, then we'll be okay."

"I know you did," he said. She had made him see that love existed in ways he never would have guessed before this moment.

"But I see now that you were right," she said, tucking that one strand that never seemed to stay in her ponytail behind her ear. She wrapped her arms around her waist and turned to look at the monitor next to his bed.

"What was I right about?" he asked.

"That love is dangerous. I don't think I was mature enough to realize what this pain felt like when my mom died. And when my dad died, Maude gave me something else to focus on. But when I was sitting in the hallway singing that stupid Smiths song and hoping you'd live, I realized what you had meant.

"This kind of pain. That hopeless feeling of not being able to help or save the person you care about. That is something I don't think I want to ever experience again," she said.

"It is the worst feeling in the world," he agreed. "But it doesn't last. People get better. You showed me that."

She shook her head. "Not all the time. You know I see the worst cases when it comes to traumatic brain injury. You got lucky tonight."

"What are you trying to say here, Elle?"

He tried to sit up straighter but his head hurt and his mobility was limited by the IV. But this didn't feel right. Something was off. He saw in Elle's eyes what he'd felt all those years ago. That feeling inability to save Rory and Conrad.

"Just that I think you were right. Love is much too big a gamble to take."

Dash took a deep breath. This had to stem from more than the accident. He shouldn't have hesitated earlier. He'd left room for doubt to grow between them and he knew he had to fix this. But he wasn't sure he could.

Elle had too much time to think when she'd been waiting for Dash to come out of surgery. She'd stood in the observation area usually reserved for training doctors and watched as they examined his head wound while he was unconscious. He'd lost too much blood and had broken ribs, but barely avoided a brain injury.

She kept forgetting to breathe, and for the first time since her dad had died, she'd cared about another person with everything she had. She'd let another person into her life and it scared her.

It scared in ways that she hadn't know she could feel. Dash had been trying to tell her this, she thought. This was what he meant by his curse. It felt like a curse to watch someone you love on the operating table and honestly, she'd never viewed what she did for a living this way before.

Her heart was beating like crazy and her thoughts were spinning in a bunch of different directions, but there was no two ways about it. If she'd stayed at Gilbert Manor, Dash wouldn't have been in his car. She didn't know for sure he'd been coming to see her but given the fact that he had driven himself made it a strong possibility.

She felt guilty. She'd run away and look at the wreckage it had caused. And she knew that rationally those facts weren't true, but she was tired and the man she loved was lying in a hospital bed, and she felt like her heart would never be the same. She would never be the same again.

She wanted to just blindly go back to the woman she'd been before she'd realized that Dash was the ER patient who potentially needed a brain surgeon, but she couldn't. There was no going back to the woman she'd been before she'd realized how it felt to almost lose him.

And she wished it made her want to hold him tighter. Part of it did, but another part was still struggling with the fact that she almost lost him, and she felt like she was going to shatter into a million pieces. She never wanted to experience that again.

How could she?

How could she ever deal with this?

"Elle, come here," he said. His voice was strong and firm.

With her gaze on the ground, she could almost forget the bandage on his head and the fact that he had cracked ribs and they'd had to reinflate one of his lungs. But when she looked up and saw Dash—the charming one who had skated through life unscathed by injuries like this until her—she started to cry.

"Elle, darling, you're breaking my heart. Come over here. Or I'm going to rip out this IV and come and get you."

"Don't you dare," she said. "You have a concussion."

She walked closer to him but that was a kind of torture because she really wanted to run her hands all over his body and make sure he was okay. Except she knew if she touched him…it would be harder to keep the promise she'd made in the hallway to whatever it was in the universe that had been listening to her singing that Smiths song. She'd promised that if he was okay, she'd let him go. She'd give him the space he needed and move on with her life.

She hadn't truly known why he'd hesitated earlier, but she knew she'd been pushing him since she'd moved into the mansion to care for her and commit to her. Now she wished she'd been more patient.

She got to his side and saw the bruising on his hands from where the airbag had gone off when he'd rolled his car off the road and into the ditch. She reached and this time couldn't stop her trembling hands from touching him. Just rubbing lightly over the bruised skin, and her tears fell harder. All those years of being careful and leaving before anyone else could hadn't protected her at all.

Once again, she hurt in a way she hadn't in a long, long time and her gut was telling her to run away. To leave. But Dash had asked her to come closer, so here she was—barely breathing and waiting for him.

"I'm sorry," he said.

"Why?"

"Tonight, when you looked at me over Rory's head... you were reaching out and asking me to take your hand. And I left you hanging."

She shook her head. "I was pushing you. You asked for space and I couldn't give it."

"I didn't need space," he said. "You didn't push me."

"It felt like I did," she said. "I'm sorry. I shouldn't have left. You would still be safe if I hadn't."

"None of this is your fault. I came after you," he said.

"I know you did," she said. "That means a lot to me."

"A lot to you?" he asked.

"Yes," she said, then bent down and kissed him gently on the lips. She needed that kiss more than she'd realized. His mouth was firm and tender under hers. He reached up with his free arm and hugged her. He smelled of his cologne and blood and hospital anesthetic. She lifted her head, looking down at his dear face. Memorizing the laugh lines at the corners of his eyes and the flecks of green in his eyes. Rubbing her finger over his eyebrow and then she straightened.

"Elle?"

"Yes?"

"I found this in your room," he said, taking the hair clip from the spot where he'd tucked it next to his hips.

"Oh, thank you. I didn't realize I'd left it behind. Is this why you were coming to see me?"

"Not the only reason. I love you," he said. "I don't know what's going on in your head, but I think you should know that the accident just reinforced what I know about life."

Her heart had accelerated at his words. Having his love was what she'd been hoping for but the rest of it. Well, she'd known that too. They couldn't live together. They both were afraid and worries and love wasn't enough to overcome them. They'd both been left too many times.

Dash felt like he was losing her. He saw the sadness in her eyes, and it felt like she was going to say goodbye. And this was one time when he truly understood where she was coming from. The pain of seeing someone you loved lying helpless in the hospital. It took a heavy toll, but he wasn't willing to let her walk away again.

She took a deep breath and he felt like she was searching for the words, and he knew then what he had to do.

"I could live my life without you, Elle. I have been on my own for the last decade and if I had to for the rest of my life, I could follow that path. But then I met you. The first time we dated, I don't think I even saw who you truly were, but this time I've learned your heart and your soul. The way you care about your patients and how you can't see that you have made a family for us."

"Dash, I don't want you to be alone. I think I did try to make us a family but that was because I thought I don't know—"

"You do know. You're just afraid. Stop letting fear rule your heart and mind," he said.

She gave him a stubborn look, but he saw the sheen of tears in her eyes and knew that she didn't want to leave. Why was she trying so hard to?

"Don't you love me?" he asked.

"I love you more than that I ever thought I could love anyone," she admitted. "But I almost lost you and it felt as if my heart was ripped right out of my chest. I don't know if I could handle that again."

Good. She loved him. Everything else he could fix. He reached out and took her hand in his. "I know how you feel and that loneliness that you think is protection, it's not. Those long years by myself didn't make me stronger. If anything, they detached me from the world. And I don't see how you could ever manage that."

"No, I'm not sure I can either, but…are you sure? What changed from when I left Gilbert Manor? I'm not doubting you because you're not a man to lie about his feelings. I'm just…scared."

He pulled her even closer, frustrated with the IV. "Will you please climb up here in this bed with me so I can hold you?"

"No. It's against the rules and I might hurt your ribs. What changed?"

"I did. And it happened before the car accident. I have been watching over Conrad and Rory for so long, protecting them and the Gilbert name and trying to take care of everyone else. But tonight, after you texted me that you'd left, I realized that I hadn't taken very good care of myself or of you, the woman I love."

She shook her head. "You are always going to protect the ones you love. I never felt neglected."

"Good, then there is no problem."

"This isn't resolved."

"Yes, it is," he said. "I love you. You love me. I know we still have a lot to talk about. I'm going to stumble and you are too, but as long as I know that you're at my side, I think we'll be okay. Don't you agree?"

He held his breath while she thought it over. It was a big ask. He knew that his accident had scared her and she'd told him that she had scarce few people in her life she had loved. He got it. He was the same. He didn't collect people the way some did; he had walled himself off to them until this woman had come back into his life and kissed him on the spur of the moment.

Everything had changed and he couldn't go back to a life without her. If she needed time, he'd give it to her. But he knew that he wasn't ever going to let Elle go.

"I'm still scared," she said. "I didn't realize how much loving you could hurt."

"I'm sorry I hurt you," he said.

She leaned down on his good side, carefully kissing him again. "You didn't hurt me. My own fears did. And yours too, I guess. I think we're going to have to just take this slow."

"I'd say we have. It's been over ten years since we first started dating," he said.

"But I've only just started to get to know you," she pointed out.

"And I you. I'm not in a rush as long as I have you in my life," he said.

"Same. Oh, Dash, I love you," she said.

"I love you too," he said, kissing her again. She lifted her head after a long moment had passed.

"Do you think your curse is finally broken?"

"Yes, you showed me how to break it."

She laughed at the way he said it. Conrad and Rory came back in a few minutes later and looked at the both of them.

"Did you two get everything settled?" Conrad asked.

"We did."

"Am I getting another sister?" Rory asked.

Dash looked up at Elle. He hadn't asked her to marry him with words, but he knew in his heart that he wanted her to be his wife. Not by pretending to help his sister or for any other reason other than that he loved her and he wanted to share the rest of their lives together. "Will you marry me, Elle?"

She looked down at him and smiled that secret smile she only showed him and nodded. "Yes. But you promised me time."

"We can get married at Christmas…is that enough time?" he asked in a whisper.

"Yes," she whispered back. "That sounds perfect to me."

"I'll take that as a yes," Rory said with a sweet laugh.

"Good. I guess we can go home now and leave you two alone," Conrad said.

They left and two days later, Dash was discharged

from the hospital. Walking back into Gilbert Manor with Elle by his side, he realized that he finally had his family back and had come home.

Epilogue

Dash heard the whispers pass through the winter ballroom in Gilbert Manor. They called him charming and said he was lucky. For the first time in his life, he actually felt it. Those feelings had nothing to do with being a Gilbert and everything to do with the woman at his side.

His wife. Dr. Elle Monroe Gilbert. Their wedding had been a small intimate affair with only their immediate family in attendance. But Elle had thought the town of Gilbert Corners would enjoy a Christmas Ball and she'd been right.

There was a big Christmas tree in one corner of the ballroom and presents for every child in town under the tree. There was a DJ playing a mix of holiday classics and Top 40 music.

The food had been prepared by students from the local high school under Conrad's supervision and the decorations had been overseen by Indy and Rory.

Dash couldn't help but remember all those lonely Christmases he'd spent waiting for Rory to wake up, Conrad to come home and Elle to be back in his life. He just hadn't realized he'd been waiting.

"This is the best Christmas ever," Elle said.

"You're the best Christmas present ever, and I can't wait to unwrap you later," Dash said, pulling her into his arms and kissing her deeply.

There was a round of applause for them and he knew he'd always be grateful to Elle for breaking the Gilbert Curse and giving him his heart back.

* * * * *

Cynthia St. Aubin wrote her first play at age eight and made her brothers perform it for the admission price of gum wrappers. When she was tall enough to reach the top drawer of her parents' dresser, she began pilfering her mother's secret stash of romance novels and has been in love with love ever since. A confirmed cheese addict, she lives in Texas with a handsome musician.

Books by Cynthia St. Aubin

Harlequin Desire

The Kane Heirs

Corner Office Confessions
Secret Lives After Hours
Bad Boy with Benefits

The Renaud Brothers

Blueblood Meets Blue Collar
Trapped with Temptation

Visit the Author Profile page
at Harlequin.com for more titles.

You can also find Cynthia St. Aubin on Facebook,
along with other Harlequin Desire authors,
at Facebook.com/HarlequinDesireAuthors!

Dear Reader,

Confession time. As both a writer *and* a reader of romance, I am 100 percent guilty of playing favorites. I'm talking tropes, and for me, the One Trope to Rule Them All has got to be forced proximity. And when that forced proximity includes only one bed? *Chef's kiss*

What better way for notoriously tempestuous—and famously reclusive—artist Bastien Renaud to get to know art gallery co-owner and Silicon Valley heiress Shelby Llewellyn? Forced to hunker down at his home in the woods of Maine when her car slides into a ditch, Shelby finally has Bastien's undivided attention after months of his refusing to take her calls. But just because a nor'easter forces them to play house doesn't mean Bastien has any intention of playing nice. Their chemistry heats up as the temperature drops, and Bastien finds himself tempted to agree to her proposition, and perhaps make one of his own...

I hope you enjoy book two in The Renaud Brothers series and would love it if you come find me on Facebook, Instagram or even TikTok if you're brave!

Cheers!

Cynthia

One

Why her?

Sebastien Renaud—Bastien, to the handful people who didn't run to the other side of the street when they saw him—knew this to be a pointless question, but he asked it, anyway.

The bottle of nonalcoholic beer was clammy in his hand and for the first time in ten years, he felt the old ache for numbness. Relief from reality.

The woman two barstools down from him stared at her phone, *pretending* to be engaged in whatever it was she read while she waited for him to notice her.

He'd been noticing her all day.

First, in a rental car in the parking lot of the coffee hut that made the only decent Americano in the town of Bar Harbor, Maine. Next, browsing in Got

Wood, his two-story Main Street storefront specializing in the hand-carved wooden bowls, wind chimes, and other tourist bait he replenished on his monthly trips into town.

Now, she was at his bar.

Unlike the store, the bar didn't technically belong to him, but at two o'clock in the afternoon on a Tuesday deep into a hard winter, he typically had the place to himself.

Which was exactly how he liked it.

"Another one?" Sergei, a burly, black-bearded man, wiped the backs of his hairy hands with a towel and leaned against the polished wood bar that Bastien had helped him refinish before the "summer people" descended earlier this year.

Though Bastien had always prized this spot for its rare combination of ice-cold beverages and minimal conversation, its proprietor had been awfully attentive to *her* since she'd arrived.

In all his years living in a town flooded with outsiders on a seasonal basis, he'd never seen anyone try so hard to look like a tourist.

A pink knit hat emblazoned with Arcadia National Park. Showroom-shiny hiking boots with a mostly decorative tread. A snow-white cashmere turtleneck sweater beneath a heather gray fleece vest. Athleisure leggings that hugged her curvy thighs and ass to his advantage, but that wouldn't combat the weather outside the many boutiques where they were sold.

Clearing her throat, she propped her hand on her fist

and batted her lashes as Sergei. "You don't happen to carry 4 Thieves whiskey, do you?"

Hearing the name of his brothers' distillery spoken so casually by a voice he'd only ever heard via his phone's voice messages proved unsettling. In the audio clips, its sweetness had been lessened considerably.

"Absolutely," the bartender practically crooned. "How would you like that?"

"Neat," she said. "I heard 4 Thieves is best at room temperature."

This was his cue.

Or what *she* hoped would be his cue.

Because Bastien was one of the thieves in question, as she well knew.

As the entire damn world well knew since *Bad Boys of Booze* had become a VidFlix streaming sensation.

Though he'd appeared in only a few episodes, and even then, under extreme duress, his quiet life had been invaded by a soul-sucking parade of producers, directors, tabloid news reporters, and assorted media leeches.

And *her.*

Shelby Llewellyn.

Co-owner of an art gallery in San Francisco's Mission District and daughter of gazillionaire Gerald Llewellyn, a Silicon Valley tech magnate. In addition to classic cars, private jets, and Lamborghini yachts, works of art—and the artists who created them—were part of Llewellyn's extensive collections.

Which was, Bastien supposed, why his daughter had been calling at exactly 11:00 a.m. every Thursday for the last year. The verbiage was always exactly the same, though her overall delivery ranged from bubbly to brusque.

Father saw one of your sculptures on BBoB. Huge fan of your work. Wondering if you'd have any interest in putting together an exhibition at our gallery. Call back at your earliest convenience.

Which had turned out to be never.

Feeling her eyes boring into the side of his face, Bastien lifted his beer and swigged what remained of the lukewarm liquid while preparing for the inevitable pitch.

"I'm sorry," she began, ducking her head. "I know this is superweird, but aren't you—"

"Very tired of listening to questions people already know the answer to, Miss Llewellyn."

She straightened in her chair and swiveled to face him.

When their eyes locked, Bastien felt a stab of gratitude that he'd also helped bolt the stools to the floor in addition to refinishing the bar.

Shelby Llewellyn was an angel.

But not one of the glowing, ethereal beings featured in paintings of the Nativity.

An *earth* angel.

Rosebud lips, wide fawn-brown eyes, and a halo of golden curls. As far from the sleek, severe-looking picture of her on the gallery's website as he could possibly imagine.

"You want to get this over with?" he asked. "Or do

I need to call Sheriff Dawkins to have you arrested for stalking?"

"Sheriff Dawkins wouldn't piss you out if you were on fire," Sergei said, setting a generous pour of amber liquid down in front of Shelby. "Much less believe that a pretty lady would willingly follow you around."

Bastien's grip on his bottle tightened. "I don't recall inviting you into this conversation."

The bartender held up his hands and backed away. Wise.

"I guess there's no point in trying to pretend this was a happy coincidence." Shelby lifted the glass to her lips, took a sip, and coughed. Her cheeks reddening, she patted her chest and reached for her water.

"Or to pretend that you actually like whiskey," he added.

"I do," she insisted in a scratchy voice. "I don't usually drink it straight but didn't want a whiskey-neophyte error to hurt my chances." Having recovered, she held the drink out to him in a silent offer.

Bastien shook his head. "Don't touch the stuff."

She arched an eyebrow at him. "How do your brothers feel about that?"

Even now, he couldn't help but think of his brothers in terms of the roles they'd each played in the "missions" that had made them such effective thieves in the first place. Wearing names that were better suited to a French dauphin, they crept into scrapyards and junkyards, retrieving the items their father, Charles "Zap" Renaud, needed to build his illegal moonshine stills or sell for cash.

Laurent—Law—the youngest and eventually the tallest, was the eyes. Always on the lookout for opportunity or danger.

Rainier—Remy—a couple of years older than Law, had been the hands. No lock he couldn't pick or engine he couldn't rig.

Augustin—a mere ten months younger than Bastien—had been the mouth. Capable of talking his way into or out of any trouble depending on what was called for.

And Bastien. The brains and brawn in one formidable package.

"I expect my brothers have more important things to worry about," he said, feeling an unexpected surge of pride.

Law's twins had just begun to try out their chubby legs, shepherded by their heiress mother, Marlowe Kane, and a never-ending rotation of adoring distillery staff. Whereas Remy was presently using the gigantic wad of cash he'd received from selling his share of the distillery to Marlowe's brother to take his ten-year-old daughter and fiancée on a private cruise of the Mediterranean.

Augustin, it was best not to think about.

"I just saw that they've been renewed for another season." Sergei had added ice and sour mix to Shelby's whiskey and she managed it with far less difficulty. "That's got to be good for business."

Bastien tore his eyes away as she pulled an atomic red maraschino cherry from her drink and bit it from the stem.

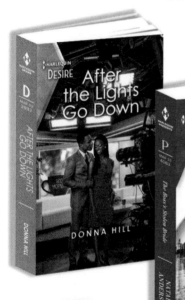

LOYAL READER
FREE BOOKS VOUCHER

YES! I Love Reading, please send me up to 4 FREE BOOKS and a Free Mystery Gift from the series I select.

Just write in "YES" on the dotted line below then return this card today and we'll send your free books & gift asap!

➡ _YES_ ⬅

Which do you prefer?

☐ **Harlequin Desire®**
225/326 HDL GRTA

☐ **Harlequin Presents® Larger-Print**
176/376 HDL GRTA

☐ **BOTH**
225/326 & 176/376
HDL GRTZ

FIRST NAME

LAST NAME

ADDRESS

APT.#

CITY

STATE/PROV.

ZIP/POSTAL CODE

EMAIL ☐ Please check this box if you would like to receive newsletters and promotional emails from Harlequin Enterprises ULC and its affiliates.

HD/HP-622-LR_MMM22

▲ If offer card is missing write to: Harlequin Reader Service, P.O. Box 1341, Buffalo, NY 14240-8531 or visit www.ReaderService.com ▲

BUSINESS REPLY MAIL
FIRST-CLASS MAIL   PERMIT NO. 717   BUFFALO, NY

POSTAGE WILL BE PAID BY ADDRESSEE

HARLEQUIN READER SERVICE
PO BOX 1341
BUFFALO NY 14240-8571

NO POSTAGE
NECESSARY
IF MAILED
IN THE
UNITED STATES

"You want to get on with yours?"

She set aside her drink and relocated one stool closer, sending a delicious current of vanilla and lavender his way. "I want to do a solo show of your work at the Llewellyn Gallery in San Francisco."

He turned to fully face her. "You came all this way just to say the exact same thing that's in all your voice mails?"

She cocked her head and studied him from beneath half-lowered lids. "You mean you actually listened to them?"

"Sometimes," he lied.

Most of them, several times over.

"But you just decided to ignore them, anyway?"

"Not answering isn't the same thing as ignoring." He swung his knees back toward the bar to give her his profile.

Shelby responded by moving to the stool directly next to his. "Do I get an answer now?"

Bastien's brain ticked like a bomb, his senses so full of her he could scarcely manage an intelligent thought. "No."

"No, I don't get an answer, or no, you won't do the gallery show?" Her knee brushed the outside of his thigh at precisely the same moment her voice dipped into a sultry register. His head swam, light and hollow as a balloon. A sure sign that blood was rushing to regions below the belt.

He had to get out.

"Take your pick." Bastien rose from his seat and

tossed two twenties down on the bar. "That's for hers and mine," he said to Sergei's wide, sloping back.

The sound of a cowbell clucked his departure. An icy blast of wind broke against his face like the waves on a ship's prow as he stepped onto the nearly deserted sidewalk.

He would never tire of this feeling.

As a boy in Terrebonne Parish, he'd thought of the bayou as a living thing—its hot, damp breath always making his shirt stick to his back. Dribbling salt into his eyes. The first time he'd ever felt real cold had bordered on an almost religious experience. It had seemed to reach all the way down into his lungs, hardening him like a diamond. When he exhaled a white cloud, he felt purged and pure.

"Mr. Renaud!"

His name sounded like a seagull cry echoing off the quaint old brick buildings of the main drag. Bastien glanced over his shoulder to find Shelby hurrying up the sidewalk, her parka draped over her arm. She hit a patch of gray, hard-packed snow and he watched as, almost in slow motion, she windmilled her arms for balance, her brand-new boots skidding frantically.

He lunged without thinking, catching her upper arm as her feet shot from under her, and nearly taking his own out in the process.

There was a brief, violent dance, accompanied by a colorful stream of curses before he arrested their momentum by hauling her up against him.

Their breath mingled in feathery puffs as he looked down into her eyes, still startled wide from her slip.

Her knuckles pressed into his chest where she'd panic-gripped his coat, her breasts molding to his rib cage, and the warmth of her thigh alarmingly close to the part of him thickening with every second spent close enough to lower his mouth to hers.

And he wanted to.

He wanted to feel the snowflakes melt on her lips and taste the silky sweetness of her tongue. Wanted to feed the howling hunger created by the loneliness of his self-imposed isolation.

Isolation that had been necessary to protect the ones he loved.

That one thought proved the perfect catalyst to end this moment the only way it could end. With her on her way back to her hotel, and him, alone.

"What the hell were you thinking, running on an icy sidewalk with boots like that?"

Bastien took two steps back and snatched her parka from the sidewalk, where it had landed. "And would you put this on?"

He held the coat open, grateful his hands were occupied and unable to capture one of the silky coils that had worked its way loose from her bun. It looked so soft against the pale skin of her neck.

She stuck out her arms and allowed him to slide the sleeves over them. "Won't you even consider it?"

Bastien captured the zipper and slid it over the swell of her breasts. "What makes you think I haven't?"

The flakes were falling faster now, trimming her lashes.

"If you've considered it, then there's at least some part of you that's interested," she pointed out.

Oh, there was. And the longer he stood there staring at the single freckle just next to her lips, the more interested that part got.

"Where the hell is your scarf?" he asked.

"I didn't bring one," she said. "I hadn't planned on spending very much time outside."

Bastien whipped his own scarf from beneath the collar of his coat and looped it around her neck, then tucked the ends inside. His knuckle grazed her collarbone in the process, the contact glowing there even after he jammed his hand back into his pocket.

Her eyes softened as her ungloved fingers floated up to touch the knots of dark blue and gray wool. "You can't give me this. It looks handmade."

"It is and I'm not." He turned and began to walk toward his truck. "You can mail it to me when you get back."

"Won't I need your home address for that?" she called after him.

Bastien smiled in spite of his irritation. She was resourceful. He had to give her that.

"Mail it here," he said, pointing to Got Wood's storefront. "Laney will see that I get it."

The frozen hinges of his truck door complained loudly as he swung it open, levered himself into the cab, and then turned the engine over. He took his time calibrating the defroster, wanting to make sure she was safely inside the shop before he shifted into Drive and proceeded up the hill that would take him out of town.

What was normally a thirty-minute trip took him the better part of an hour as the storm began its work in earnest. And though he felt relieved when he arrived at the mouth of the road that wound into his property, he couldn't shake his sense of unease.

It only increased when he pulled his truck into the garage he'd completed just in time for winter. Walking through his usual rituals once inside the house did nothing to quiet his mind. Not kicking off his boots in the mudroom. Not placing his keys on the hook by the front door. Not lighting a fire in the antique iron woodstove or replenishing the neat stack of logs beside it. Not turning on his record player or making himself an espresso.

After all of this, he attempted to sink into his chair to read and sprang up out of it after only five minutes.

He began to pace.

Something he hadn't done since before his release from prison. Then and now, the feeling was the same. Like his skin was suddenly two sizes too small.

Bastien grabbed his phone from the table next to the chair and glared at its screen, empty of notifications.

If he could at least confirm she'd made it back to her hotel safely, then he'd be able to relax. Which would be easy enough for him to find out if she was staying anywhere in town.

Especially a town like Bar Harbor during the off-season.

Fortunately, he knew exactly where to start.

"It's a good day to get wood, this is Laney." Just that one line was enough to conjure his store manager into his mind. Short, puckish, and possibly some kind of forest sprite, she had shown up one day and basically refused to leave. Asking him question after question until he finally offered her a job just to have a moment's peace. The arrangement had worked even better than he'd hoped, and, as he felt less motivated to be around people, she took more and more of the day-to-day responsibilities of running the retail side of things.

"What have I told you about answering the phone like that?"

A harried sigh issued from the other end of the line. "I can see your name on the caller ID, Batman."

Bastien pinched the bridge of his nose. "For the thousandth time, can you please *not* call me that?"

"Nope," she chirped.

"What are you still doing down there, anyway? I told you to close up early and go home before the storm hit."

"Considering home is exactly one floor above where I'm currently standing, I feel like my odds of making it there are pretty good." In the background, he heard a double beep followed by the mechanized announcement of the alarm system arming. "What's up?"

Bastien tried to keep his tone casual. "Did anyone stop into the shop after I left?"

"If you're talking about the blonde who looked like she stepped out of a J.Crew catalog then yes—yes, she did."

"Did you two talk at all?"

"I talk to everyone that comes into the store. My customer service skills are exceptional, which you would know if you actually spent more than ten minutes a month here."

"Did she happen to mention where in town she was staying?" he asked, choosing to ignore her barb.

"The Skylark Inn."

Bastien's shoulders relaxed away from his ears. Warm, cozy, and run by Bar Harbor's self-appointed town aunt, the Skylark was within walking distance of his shop even in weather as ugly as this.

"Anything else?" he asked.

"She bought that Frankenstein of a salad bowl I've been trying to offload forever and asked for directions to your house."

"Right," Bastien said, walking back to his chair to retrieve his untouched espresso.

"She really did."

With dawning horror, he realized that Laney was completely serious. "You told her no, I'm assuming."

"I mean, I tried to, but she insisted that it would work perfectly as a planter if she drilled a couple holes in the bottom."

"About the directions," he added.

"Give me a little credit, Batman."

Again, the roller coaster of his anxiety cruised into a dip. "Good."

"If she actually follows the instructions I gave her, she'll end up at the Kreb's blueberry farm, turn on her GPS and head back to town."

"Shit." Dark liquid sloshed over the rim of the demitasse as he planted it on the bookshelf and pounded toward the door.

"What?" Laney asked.

"Kreb's is smack in the middle of a ten-mile dead zone. Once she gets there, she won't be *able* to turn on her GPS."

"Since when do you care if I mess with reporters?"

"She's not a reporter! And even if she was, you don't send someone out to the middle of nowhere with a nor'easter howling down on us. For Christ's sake, *think*, Laney."

It came out harsher than he'd meant it to, and Bastien winced at her audible in-drawn breath. "I appreciate the creativity," he said quickly as he exited his home, "but if you could perhaps stick to general mischief?"

Her laugh eased a measure of his tension. "Sure thing, Bruce."

Bastien slammed his truck door closed, then started the engine. "Bruce?"

"Batman without the cape," she said, and hung up.

He backed out of his drive a hair faster than was advisable under the current conditions and clipped his fence, then executed a tight turn onto the narrow driveway.

Glancing at the display on the truck's console, he did some quick mental math. He'd left Shelby on the sidewalk exactly an hour and eleven minutes earlier and it would take him a solid hour and a half to get to her, depending on how far out of town she'd made it. *If* the miniature SUV some ass-hat had rented her at the Bangor airport actually had four-wheel drive.

Where the end of his private drive met the county

road, Bastien glanced to his left and stepped on the gas, but something in his peripheral vision brought him up short.

It was no more than a flicker at first. A gray phantom, there and gone again between flurries.

Only when he rolled down the passenger side window and leaned across the seat did he realize how close he'd come to running over Shelby Llewellyn.

Two

Shelby Llewelyn squinted at the wall of howling whiteness as miniature ice chips pecked her eyes and cheeks.

Somewhere behind her, the SUV sat idle, the rear tire on the driver's side sunk in the ditch beside the disappearing road.

She'd done everything right.

Everything that everyone, especially her father and brother, had explained about driving on snowy roads when they'd tried to talk her out of this trip.

Don't panic. Don't stomp on your brakes. Turn into the slide.

She'd breathed. She'd tapped. She'd turned.

And slid into the ditch, anyway.

Where she'd remained calmly stationary, as also instructed.

Until.

Until the battery in her phone—perpetually used until she wrung every minute out of four percent—died.

Before it had, her one last glance at the charge-guzzling map revealed she was a quarter mile away from Bastien Renaud's twenty-acre property.

That his actual home would be so deeply buried within, she hadn't counted on. Got Wood's store manager may have all but spelled out the land's location in her zeal for gossip, but Shelby had begun to suspect she'd had never actually set foot in Bastien's home.

Had Shelby known, she wouldn't have chugged what remained of her coffee before stashing the essentials on her person and body-slamming her door open. She buried her face in the borrowed scarf and breathed the intoxicating scent of Bastien Renaud into her lungs.

At two minutes into her walk, the numbness became annoying.

At five, slightly vexing. At ten, rage-inducing.

At seventeen, a large, dark shape bloomed out of the ether, making sounds that Shelby eventually recognized as words.

"What?" she shouted. Or *thought* she shouted. Her lips and tongue seemed to be moving slowly and only with great effort.

The road disappeared from beneath her boots as something collided with her. She stared up and saw the white dome of the sky and thought for a minute she might have fallen down a snowbank.

Except the snowbank was moving.

And swearing.

Shifting her glazed eyes, she caught the underside of a jaw and a nose and a mouth that chugged steam in time with the foulest combination of words she'd ever almost heard.

Her weight shifted abruptly, and she was hoisted upward into a completely different universe. This one was warm, and bright, and filled with a scent that reminded her of clean laundry.

Then she heard a loud bang followed by muffled panting in ears still ringing and stinging from the bitter cold.

As a dedicated student of art history, she felt uniquely qualified in her assessment that Sebastien Renaud was not a man who could be reduced to the two-dimensional realm. He had to be *experienced*. The hulking form. The piercing eyes. The brute strength. All of which she'd had the advantage of observing when she'd nearly wiped out trying to chase him down the sidewalk. Her humiliation burned anew at the memory of him effortlessly hauling her up one-handed. Zipping her into her coat. Wrapping her in his scarf. Gazing down into her eyes with a potent mix of protective fury and smoldering—

"What the hell were you thinking?"

Yes, she thought. *That, exactly.*

Preempting seemed like the thing to do here. Or image management? Surely there had been something in her recently acquired MBA that applied to this situation.

"I'm f-f-fine," she stuttered, not quite suppressing a full body shiver.

"You're f-f-fucking crazy." He was suddenly very loud, and very angry. "You could have *died* out there."

She aimed what she hoped was a disarming smile at him. "N-now do you believe that I really want to host your gallery show?"

Shelby had heard of laughing through tears but had no idea that laughing through a scowl was a thing.

Or that it would act as a defibrillator that quickly restored the feeling to the still-chilled surface of her face.

He was so close, she could see the tiny orbs of melted snow glowing around the crown of his head. Close enough to taste coffee and spice on his breath. Gingerbread men. And possibly magic of some kind.

"I hit my head. Not hard," she added quickly, when his brow folded and his mouth flattened. "My coat was stuck in the door, and I bent down to open it and I couldn't see very well because of the snow."

"Why aren't you back at your hotel?"

As her weather-induced shock began to fade, additional details about her surroundings surfaced. The ticking sound of his hazard lights. The dull roar of wind, snowflakes shivering across the windshield of his truck like sequins.

"That was my plan until you left me standing there on the street. Then it was just a matter of pride." The tips of her fingers tingled as she squeezed her hands into fists. "I remembered Sergei mentioning that Sheriff Dawkins didn't like you, so thought he was probably my best bet at finding out where you live."

"Son of a bitch," he grumbled.

"He didn't give it to me. I was in the parking lot trying to guess which way I thought you might live when you drove by."

Her peripheral vision must be coming back because she could clearly see his knuckles whitening as he gripped the steering wheel. After throwing the vehicle into gear, he stopped abruptly, buckled her seatbelt, then resumed driving.

"I f-followed you," she said, teeth chattering. "By the time I stopped at your—"

"There's nothing wrong with being cautious." His jaw hardened as they both looked at the speedometer nudging ten miles an hour.

"I *am* cautious. It's just…my car in San Francisco is electric and I was so busy watching the road, I forgot to watch the gas gauge."

"*Not* talking is a perfectly acceptable reaction to shock."

"I'm not in sh-shock," she insisted. "And I would have been at your house twenty minutes ago if I hadn't run out of gas. So don't act like this is a rescue because really all you're doing is carrying the baton over the f-finish line."

He slowed for a sharp turn in the road and scrutinized her profile.

"What?" she asked.

"Just looking for possible head trauma."

A fresh wave of heat hit her stinging face and she noticed that he'd cranked all the vents in her direction and had them on max despite the fine film of sweat gleaming at his hairline.

They crested a final rise and the rough road smoothed out into a ribbon of black asphalt where the snow wasn't sticking.

"Heated," he said. "Should get as far as the main road in spring."

They pulled into a garage, and he turned off the engine. "Stay," he said, pointing a finger at her.

Though she didn't appreciate being addressed in such demanding and simplistic terms, she was too grateful for the warmth and dazed from the storm to argue.

Bastien swung out of his seat and slammed his door closed, then came around to open hers. He unbuckled her belt and offered her a hand.

Shelby took it. His grip was warm, sure, steady, and rough as sandpaper. Strong enough to hold the world to its orbit.

Bastien flinched at her icy fingers and muttered more curses under his breath as he helped her down from the truck's cab.

"I can walk," she said when he hovered there with his eyes fixed on her pathetically undersuited "hiking" boots.

When one of those boots crossed the threshold into Bastien Renaud's home, she decided the version of him she'd constructed before meeting him in person needed serious revisions. When she'd heard the words "converted shipping container" fall from Laney's burgundy lips, Shelby had been expecting something in the way of a bunker. A dark, quiet burrow for a dark, quiet bachelor.

This home was anything but.

Not one shipping container, but many, stacked and cooperatively modulated with the hillside in a spatially symbiotic relationship that would have turned Frank Lloyd Wright puce with envy.

"Nine." He hung his keys on a rack near the door.

"I'm sorry?" she said.

"How many containers it took me to build this. Give me your phone so I can plug it in."

Shelby handed it over, eyes hungrily moving over every detail of the space. The two-story wall of windows, the spiral staircase, the hammock suspended in a conservatory off the open kitchen. The ludicrous backdrop of towering trees behind the whipping curtains of snow. Peppered throughout, his art.

Furniture constructed from repurposed wood as well as the whimsical carvings and assemblages of recycled items he'd tried not to become famous for.

"Oh, wow," she whispered, aware that she was floating toward an antique brass stove in one corner of the room.

"Not yet," Bastien said. "You could have frostbite. You never expose frostbite to direct heat."

She heard a scraping sound and felt something nudge the backs of her knees.

"Sit," he urged.

She sat.

He tugged on her sleeve, and she glanced up to find

him wadding a handful of her puffy coat in his hand. "It's Prada," she said.

"It's useless. They didn't even waterproof the fabric."

Shelby's cheeks stung as they flooded with blood. It had taken her such a long time to feel at home in the wildly privileged world where she now operated. Apparently, she'd now become so comfortable with it, she was incapable of identifying her own ridiculousness in a situation like this.

"You'll need to take it off," he said. "And the boots. We need to get you warmed up slowly."

Bastien disappeared into the kitchen and returned with a tumbler of amber-brown liquid.

Having shrugged out of her jacket and pulled the sodden wool hat off her head, Shelby was attempting her shoelaces with limited success, her numb fingers fumbling with the various eyelets and zippers.

"Let me." He handed her the glass and kneeled. *Had his shoulders been this broad in the bar?*

Smoky fumes wafted up from the drink. "I thought you didn't imbibe," she said.

His large hands proved surprisingly nimble as they undid her quadruple knot, then shucked the boot from her foot. "I don't," he said. "But ever since that damn show, every distillery from here to Saskatchewan has been sending me booze."

That damn show.

Shelby didn't need to ask. After all, it was the reason she had come to Maine in the first place. The reason she had proposed to her father that they host a showing of Bastien Renaud's kinetic sculptures.

Bad Boys of Booze had been where she'd first seen his work. After a particularly grueling day at the gallery, she'd ended up crying into the beautiful curry their chef had left for her and watching the episode where his brothers rebuilt the onsite restaurant, following the fire at the end of season one. Bastien had shown up to give them a chandelier-type hanging mobile for the brand-new cathedral ceiling.

After reattaching her jaw when Bastien first appeared on screen, Shelby had taken one look at the piece and known her father—an avid collector of sculptures of all types—would love it.

She'd been right. Just as he'd loved the idea of the gallery doing a showing of Bastien's work.

If she'd known how difficult this idea would be to bring to fruition, she would have promptly flipped the channel to one of her favorite cooking shows and gone about with the rest of her night.

Shelby lifted the glass to her lips. "We've established that I'm not good at drinking this straight."

"Small sips," he said, peeling off one of her thick socks. "Go slow."

This time, she did.

Allowing the tiniest trickle of the liquid through her lips, she held very still as the warmth spread down her throat and into her chest. An answering heat rose from the soles of her bare feet as Bastien gently inspected them. A golden spike drove straight down her middle as she tried not squirm.

For his part, Bastien seemed to be intensely focused on the task at hand. First, cupping her heels, then sliding up the arches and out over the balls of her feet before the pad of his thumb gently grazed the underside of each toe.

"So soft." His voice was distracted. Perhaps not even meant for her to hear.

The moment was killed by her leg's involuntary jerk as she suppressed a giggle. "Sorry," she said. "That tickles."

He cleared his throat and rocked back on his heels. "Any numbness or tingling?" he asked in a far more clinical manner.

"A little," she admitted.

The furrow in his brow deepened. "How about burning?"

"My calves, mostly."

"Do you have anything on under those?" His eyes flicked to her legs.

Shelby blinked at him. "Excuse me?"

"The leggings," he prompted. "Do you have anything on under them? Like thermals."

"Oh. You meant *layers*." Her lacy thong felt like an imaginary brand glowing beneath the stretchy fabric. "Um, no. Just the usual…underthings."

"Hurry and take them off." He planted a hand on the arm of her chair to push himself up. "I'll bring you a robe."

"Can't I just dry them in front of the fire?" she asked, hearing the panic lacing her own voice. "They're not even that—"

"Off." The single syllable echoed through the airy space as he stalked down a hallway.

The task proved easier said than done.

The buttery faux-leather pants that had slid on so easily in her cavernous California closet didn't want to yield their grip on her clammy calves and ankles.

"All good?" he called from the hallway.

"Not exactly," she called back. "I might need a little help."

A beat of silence. "What *kind* of help?"

Her phone chose that precise moment to begin tinkling out the iconic violin-heavy score of the Wicked Witch's flight in *The Wizard of Oz*.

"Shit." She penguin-waddled toward the table where he'd plugged in her phone. "Sloan," she said, hoping she sounded breezy as opposed to out of breath. "How's it going?"

"Oh thank goodness. Your father said he's been trying to reach you for hours. We've been *so* worried."

Shelby rolled her eyes at the melodramatic assertion and lifted her coat from where Bastien had hung it to dry. Holding it at her waist, she shuffled backward and gracelessly dropped into a chair.

Bastien's emergence a mere nanosecond later left her wondering if he'd glimpsed part of her humiliating spectacle.

"I'm sorry to have worried you both," she said, speaking into the phone. "The storm hit pretty hard, and reception has been spotty."

They locked eyes as he held a plush robe of the deepest midnight blue out to her. When she took it, he mimed taking off his shirt and pointed to her, then performed an operation that looked remarkably like taking off a pair of pantyhose, then pointed to himself.

Then he turned his back to give her privacy.

"Can you hold on for just a second?" She set down the phone without waiting for an answer and quickly stripped away her sweater. She was already reaching for the front clasp of her bra when she paused.

Should she leave her bra on? He hadn't made any motions that might suggest she remove it. But would he really have mimed removing ladies' lingerie?

Shelby chewed the inside of her cheek and watched as the broad planes of Bastien's back expanded on in inhale.

Strange undercurrents of heat moved over her as she imagined him turning around to see her standing there in nothing but her scrap of a thong and matching bra in the palest shade of pink.

"Shelby? Are you still there?" Sloan's soap-opera voice demanded from her phone.

She quickly shrugged into the robe and snapped her fingers to give him the all clear.

"I'm here," she said, sandwiching the phone to her face.

"Where exactly *is* here?" She could tell by the gun-shot-like echoes that Sloan was currently marching across the gallery, designer heels subtly scarring the old wood with every step.

"Bar Harbor, Maine."

The sigh from the other end expertly combined

equal parts pity and exasperation. "I meant, are you in your car? At your hotel?"

Shelby swallowed against the hard knot at the base of her throat as Bastien pulled up an ottoman and seated himself in front of her.

"Neither," she said.

His index and middle fingers brushed her right ankle on either side as he worked the stubborn cuffs over her heels and off her feet. He rose and disappeared into the kitchen with the pants.

"The reason I ask is that I told the wedding planner that you would arrange a catch-up meeting when you're back in town, but *he* said he needed to get ahold of you before his flight to Milan."

Ahh.

So, it hadn't been concern for Shelby's well-being that prompted Sloan to inquire about her whereabouts. She was irritated that this trip had interfered with the planning for Sloan's wedding to Shelby's father.

Bastien had returned with a large tub of water that he set on the floor beside her chair. She watched in fascination as he dipped a washcloth, wrung it out, and gently wrapped it around her foot. Her eyes widened as an army of pins and needles marched beneath the damp cloth. He repeated the process with her other foot before slowly working his way up her ankle and calf.

"What was that sound?" Sloan asked.

"It's wine," Shelby lied, earning her a curious look from Bastien. "Actually, I just sat down to dinner. I better let you go."

"Can you at least give Fernando a call?" Sloan asked, her voice rising by several octaves.

"Sure thing."

Enduring Sloan's syrupy sweet standard sign-off set Shelby's teeth on edge. She disconnected and tossed her phone at the couch, disgusted.

"Friend of yours?"

Beneath the robe, she noticed the fine film of sweat had begun to glue her thighs together as Bastien's hands moved closer to her knees.

"Depends on the time of day," she answered.

"I don't follow."

"From nine a.m. to seven p.m., she's my boss. The rest of the time she's my father's fiancée and a royal pain in the ass."

"I'm guessing you don't approve of the match?" he teased.

Her head seemed twice as heavy, and she tried to lift it from the back of the chair.

"It isn't that I don't approve," she said, glancing down at the remarkable sight of his work-roughened fingers against the impossibly white flesh of her kneecap. "I would just prefer he was with someone a little closer to his own age than to mine."

"I see," he said.

She had always had trouble with social cues, but with Bastien, she found it even harder. His expressions were so minimal, his words so quiet, it was like trying to decipher Morse code.

Shelby took another sip from the glass in her hand,

noticing how it made her joints feel loose and her muscles wavy.

He patted her legs dry with a towel and gave her ankles a final squeeze. "Give it half an hour and then you can sit in front of the fire."

"How long will I need to stay here, exactly?"

He turned to look out the window and she followed his gaze, both of them noting the wedge of snow already piling up against the windows.

"That car isn't going anywhere anytime soon," he said. "And neither are you."

Three

Bastien had long ago told himself that one of the many reasons he didn't like being around people was because he didn't like being around their problems.

Kneeling before Shelby Llewellyn, he had to adjust that theory. It wasn't just that he didn't like being around other people's problems. He couldn't stop himself from noticing how those problems affected them.

Whether a flat tire or news of a horrific accident, his sensory abilities launched into overdrive. The slightest modulation in the tone of voice, the tiniest shift in expression, the most minute change in body language all beamed straight into his skull like a radio station he couldn't tune out of.

The change that had taken over Shelby the second

her phone began to ring was painfully obvious. Due in part, he guessed, to her complete lack of a filter.

Watching the rapid shifts in her facial expressions while his hands had moved over her skin had been a welcome distraction. Helping keep his mind out of the gutter and his blood above the belt.

Because as much as he might try to convince himself otherwise, he had liked touching her. Her smooth, pale, nearly poreless skin reminded him of the first time he'd seen a Vermeer painting in one of the textbooks in his high school art teacher's classroom.

At sixteen, he'd been so enamored of the luminous woman standing in light streaming in from the window, he'd covertly torn out and pocketed the page.

An act that had proved tragically prophetic.

Banishing the memory, Bastien refocused his attention on his immediate vicinity. In the four years he'd occupied this house, a woman hadn't crossed the threshold. And now, here Shelby was, wandering around his living room and chattering away like a bird in a space that had only, ever, been his.

He quickly noticed her tendency to touch everything that caught her attention and wondered if this had been a liability for her in the art world, where tactile experiences with the objects were typically discouraged.

"And this one reminds me of the *Venus of Willendorf*," she said.

She stood before bookshelves tall enough to require a rolling library ladder. One bare foot perched on the rung second from the bottom, she hooked an arm through to balance herself as she held out the small hand-carved sculpture she was referring to. For a brief moment, the robe gapped, revealing an enticing sliver of thigh.

Tearing his gaze away, Bastien busied himself at the sink, taking an extralong time to soap and then rinse her glass before setting it in the dish rack.

"What about this one?" she asked, holding up another miniature. "Did you make this before or after the chandelier in episode five?"

"I thought I told you to stay put," he said, crossing the room to take the carving and return it to its home on the shelf. "You really shouldn't be walking around this much."

Shelby glanced around as if moderately surprised to find herself on the ladder. She seemed almost oblivious as she pinged through his house like a pinball. Unaware of the movement of her body.

Unaware of how she was affecting him.

And being affected by Shelby Llewellyn was a problem.

Even if he hadn't been aware of her name and its connections, he was painfully aware of her age. Twenty-seven to his thirty-nine. A gap of years that made him feel inexplicably weary.

At last, she stepped down from the ladder, relieving him of the mental image of her breasts being exactly at his mouth level, and poorly hidden by a robe that seemed determined to cooperate in his accidental seduction.

She had made it only two feet toward the couch before discovering the antique record player and the cabinet holding the neat row of albums beside it. "You have Brahms? I love Brahms! Would you mind if I played it?"

"Does Brahms help you sit still?" he asked.

Her smile was sheepish as she put the record on the player and, at last, settled herself on the couch.

"When's the last time you ate?" he asked.

"I had some of those spiced nuts at Sergei's bar," she mused. "Before that it was a muffin and coffee at the airport."

"Well, alright then." He retreated to the kitchen, glad to have a task that required both action and attention. "I didn't have anything fancy planned. How does spaghetti Bolognese sound?"

He should have known better than to ask.

She appeared behind him as if by magic, peering under his arm as he opened the cupboard and took out a jar of the homemade pasta sauce he'd canned when his tomato plants had gotten a little overambitious the previous summer.

"Did you can all this yourself?" she asked.

"Not all of it," he admitted.

Much of the collection had come to him through the kindness of Law's wife, Marlowe. The few times he'd visited for the TV episodes he'd grudgingly participated in, he found the bed of his truck filled with neatly packed cardboard boxes of homemade jams, pickles, and preserves.

They were, he had been dismayed to admit, pretty damn delicious. A statement that Marlowe had threatened to make the products' tagline.

"Can I help?" Shelby asked.

"How did I know you were gonna ask that?" he murmured.

"Because deep down, you know I'm the kind of caring, conscientious soul whose gallery you should definitely allow to host your first private show?" She batted her lashes at him in a comically obvious manner.

"Nice try," he said. "The way you could help most is by taking a seat at that bar counter and staying there."

"I'm not saying I'm an amazing cook," she said, migrating to the other side of the bar, "but I am saying that before I got my MBA, I spent a month at Le Cordon Bleu school in Paris."

Bastien moved the large cutting block to the counter in front of her. "I'll be expecting top-notch knife skills then."

She held out a hand for the yellow onion that Bastien had pulled from the basket on the counter. "Put me to work."

"If you insist." He handed it over before moving to the magnetic plate affixed to the wall to select a chopping knife, then presented it to her handle first.

Her eyebrows lifted as she tested its weight in her hand. "Nice," she said. "How long have you lived out here?"

"Are you just making conversation, or do you really not know?" Bastien turned on the gas burner, then set a cast-iron skillet over the flames. After drizzling in the olive oil, he added the onion that Shelby had chopped.

"Has anyone ever told you that you're the tiniest bit paranoid?" she asked.

"They wouldn't dare." He smirked at her over his shoulder.

"How about this?" she asked. "I tell you everything I know about you, and then you don't have to wonder."

"That depends on whether I believe you," he said, using a wooden spatula to stir the onions.

"I can see we have our work cut out for us," she said. "Would it help if you got to ask me things first?"

Exhausting as this back and forth felt, Bastien had to admit he was intrigued by the prospect.

"Why do you *really* want to do a show of my work at your father's gallery?"

"Because my father loves your work, and his fiancée told him you'd never agree to do it."

And that's when Bastien knew he liked her.

This simple, vulnerable answer to his somewhat intrusive question.

"Fair enough," he conceded, surprised he'd not looked at the clock for the better part of an hour.

By this point in any interaction, he was usually counting the minutes, his brain feverishly churning out excuses that would allow him to leave. While he was out of practice, talking to Shelby came with an ease there was no precedence for.

Even if her physical presence made him aware of the gnawing ache in his navel. Returning to his fridge, he opened a pack of beef from the local butcher shop and added it to the pan.

Maybe his body would be willing to accept heartier fare in lieu of the other craving that had woken after a long hibernation.

He heard the chair scrape back and felt the air change in the kitchen. She cleared her throat and rattled the jar of red lentils that she'd plucked from the pantry.

"What are you doing?" he asked.

"Shoo." She motioned for him to scoot out of the way and stole the spatula from his hand.

Bastien stood there, speechless at having just been evicted from his own kitchen.

"You'll thank me, I promise."

He watched as she shook in lentils, dried oregano, a few dashes of Worcestershire sauce, and a generous pinch of brown sugar, then tasted the sauce.

"What do you need?" She stared at the saucepan, bringing her hand up to tap her lip…and accidentally flashing him a side glimpse of her bare breast.

Images flickered through his mind in alarmingly vivid detail. Walking into the kitchen. Standing behind her. Filling his hands with her hips. Loosening the robe's tie. Letting his fingers slide beneath the edge. Tracing the lacy thong panties he'd accidentally caught a glimpse of. Trailing his fingers up her belly to her breasts. Feeling her nipples go hard beneath his palms.

The ache in his groin threatening to become a problem, he focused his attention on finding another task.

"How about some wine?" he asked.

Shelby gave him a querulous look. "I thought you didn't drink."

"That doesn't mean you can't." He bent before the cupboard where he kept the samples he was sent, pretending to consider them for much longer than he actually needed to while he let his burgeoning arousal diminish.

"It's really okay," she said. "You don't have to open anything on my account."

"I need to add some to the sauce, anyway, so really, you'd be doing me a favor." He grabbed a Spanish Barolo and set it on the counter, then hunted for a corkscrew. After pouring her a glass, he went to the fridge and opened a nonalcoholic beer for himself.

Shelby swirled the glass and brought it to her nose before taking a sip. "That's delicious. Porter would love this."

Porter.

He felt a twinge of instant dislike.

Bastien could just imagine him. Ivy League-educated with a house in the Hamptons. Maybe a yacht. The kind of guy who used seasons like verbs.

"I'm glad you like it," he said.

A scratchy sound announced the record finishing one side.

"I'll get it," she said. After setting her wineglass on the counter, she shuffled back into the living room and reset the player.

While she did, he tasted her sauce.

"Tell me that's not better than what you usually have."

It was. "I suppose," he allowed.

"It's the lentils," she called. "They add almost a root-vegetable sweetness."

"Consider me a convert," he said, using her absence to regain control of his kitchen.

When dinner was finished, she insisted on helping

him with the dishes before returning to the living room. There they sat, listening to the wind howl beneath the mellow music. Her with her second glass of wine and Bastien with his second bottle of nonalcoholic beer.

"Shoot!" Shelby sat up suddenly and reached for her phone. "I can't believe I almost forgot."

"Everything okay?" he asked.

"I'm just sending the name of this wine to Porter. He's going to school to be a sommelier."

Though he knew it was ridiculous, he felt a stab of jealousy when she grinned down at her screen.

"How long have you guys been together?" he asked when she had set her phone aside.

"About twenty years," she said.

"How is that even remotely possible?"

"Because he's my brother?" Her perplexed look informed him exactly how much he'd given away.

He felt relief and chagrin in equal measure. "Older or younger?"

"Neither."

Bastien felt like he was the one two glasses of wine in. "Twins?"

"Oh, no," she laughed. "Porter and I were both adopted after the Llewellyns' two biological children had already left for college. Kind of a reboot."

"How old were you? If you don't mind my asking."

For the first time since he noticed her following him around town earlier that day, Bastien saw a shadow pass behind her eyes.

"Seven." The lamp beside her flickered and she glanced around. "We're not going to lose power, are we?"

The vein of fear in her voice cut through his curiosity. "If we do, I have a generator," he said.

Shelby hugged his robe tighter around her. "I know this is silly…especially for a woman my age, but I get a little freaked out in the dark."

"Hang tight." He went to the kitchen and came back with two camping lanterns, several flashlights, a handful of candles, and a long, fire-starting lighter, all of which he set directly in front of her on the coffee table.

"Anything happens," he said, "we won't be in the dark."

Shelby swiped her hand dramatically across her forehead and mouthed an exaggeration "phew."

Just as the lights went out.

Four

Panic.

Shelby had often heard it described as a wave.

To her, it always felt like a whirlpool. The force spinning her, speeding up, and increasing in force the further it sucked her down. Her heart galloped. Her breath sped, causing her lungs to struggle to absorb oxygen before it was already being exhaled again.

She screamed at herself inside her head to break her paralysis and reach for one of the flashlights on the table. But before she could move her stiff limbs, a cool blue glow seeped in under tightly fastened eyes.

She opened her eyes to find Bastien sitting next to her, holding one of the camping lanterns.

"It's alright," he said in an even tone he might use

with a spooked horse. "I'm right here. I'm going to get these candles lit, then I'll see about the generator."

When he had every available light source ignited, he turned his attention to the old iron stove and bent to toss in more kindling and another log. As the fire began to crackle, the ball of ice encasing her heart slowly thawed.

"You okay?" he asked. The candlelight danced over his features, making him look even more kingly.

Shelby nodded, though she doubted he believed her.

"The generator is in the basement," he said. "Do you want me to stay with you a little longer or should I go get it running?"

Suddenly, the idea of being separated from his big, warm, comforting presence filled her with dread.

"Can't I come with you?"

"The basement isn't completely finished yet and right here is going to be the lightest place until I can get the backup power on," he explained.

Scolding herself for acting like a ridiculous child, Shelby assured him she'd be fine.

"Ten minutes," he said before taking only the dimmest lantern with him.

But Bastien didn't come back in ten minutes. Shelby sat there staring at her phone, watching the digital display, and trying to slow her breathing.

The panic began to creep back in, dragging unhelpful thoughts in its wake.

Has something happened? What if he's down there right now unconscious?

She glanced again at her phone screen. With the

electricity gone, the Wi-Fi she'd been connected to vanished, and she had one small unimpressive bar of cell service.

Shelby scooted forward on the couch cushion, took a long steadying breath, and picked up a lantern by the plastic handle. Carrying it over to the stove, she found her boots warm and dry, and she slipped her feet into them.

Holding the lantern out in front of her, she proceeded in the direction she'd seen him go. The pale light revealed the dark rectangle of an open door and the first few stairs that disappeared into an inky darkness.

"Bastien?" she called from the top of the stairs.

No answer.

Her heart resumed its thrumming, beating so hard that the rushing in her ears dampened the sound of the crackling fire.

She hated basements. Hated any dark place with a door that could be closed to keep the abyss contained and her within it.

Her tongue tasted metallic, and a high-pitched buzzing filled her ears as she stepped onto the first stair.

"Bastien?" When she received no answer, she made herself put one foot in front of the other. Halfway down the stairs, a muddy bronze light flickered from the hanging bulb overhead.

She heard a whirring hum, and the light grew stronger just before Bastien appeared.

He froze in his tracks, his hand flying to his chest as he saw her standing there.

"What the hell are you doing down here?" he demanded.

To her horror, Shelby felt the telltale ache at the base of her throat. "You said ten minutes," she said. "It's been fifteen." She blinked her stinging eyes to keep the tears at bay.

She was telling him something without meaning to. By the way his expression softened, she knew.

A chill stole up her spine beneath the bathrobe and she turned on her heel to clump up the stairs, back into the warmth, without another word.

All of the lamps glowed to a slightly diminished degree, giving the living room an almost romantic look. Shelby placed the lantern on the coffee table and sat down hard on the couch, turning her face toward the stove.

Bastien didn't return to the chair where he'd been before the power went out, but sat on the couch, next to her. He didn't move to touch or comfort her. He didn't speak. But somehow the silence drew the story out of her.

"Before the Llewellyns adopted me, I was in the foster care system."

"For how long?"

"Three years." Deciding she didn't want to get into the period before that just yet, she continued, "In one of the last homes I was in, one of the older kids locked me in a closet as a joke and forgot about me. I was only in there for a couple of hours, but—"

"A couple hours?"

When she jumped at the sudden volume of his voice,

Bastien continued more quietly, but with just as much malice. "Where the hell were your foster parents when this happened?"

"Our foster father was at work. Our foster mother was out shopping. The older kids were left to take care of us whenever she had errands to run."

"And did you tell your foster mother when she got home?"

"I didn't have to. She was the one who found me." Shelby shook her head. "It really wasn't a big deal—"

"Of course, it was," he growled. "People like that have no business being trusted with vulnerable children."

"They did the best they could," Shelby replied. "And it was a lot more than some people do for kids who don't have anywhere to go. Do you know how many children out there never know what it's like to be raised inside a family?"

"There are some families it's better to be raised outside of," he muttered darkly. Flames glazed his eyes orange as he stared fiercely into the woodstove. His hands bunched into fists on his lap and only then did Shelby discover the dark smear over one of his knuckles.

"What did you do?" she asked, scooting closer to him.

Bastien blinked and seemed to arrive back from somewhere far distant. "Skinned it trying to get into a tool chest. The door to the generator room was stuck."

"Let me get you a Band-Aid."

"It's fine," he said. "It's not that deep."

"It most certainly is not fine," she said. "I bet you haven't had a tetanus shot lately. You could develop a nasty infection, and being as isolated as you are, I would hate if anything happened to your hands."

The corner of his mouth ticked upward in a smirk that made her knees feel like butter.

Her cheeks burned when she realized exactly what she'd said.

"Wait here." She got up off the couch, but then realized she had no idea where his Band-Aids were.

"In the drawer to the right of the bathroom sink," he called.

Shelby slipped her feet out of her boots and quickly scurried into the bathroom, closed the door behind her and flipped on the light. In the drawer next to the sink, she found the box of Band-Aids exactly where he said they'd be.

Returning to the living room, she plopped down on the couch next to him and moved his hand onto her thigh. It felt heavy and warm—even through the robe's thick, soft fabric.

The wound wasn't deep, but she carefully cleaned it and smeared it with translucent ointment that she'd also found in the drawer before applying a bandage.

"Good as new," she said, missing his hand's weight when he lifted it to examine her handiwork.

"Well, if you ever decide you're done with gallery work I know at least one profession where you'd excel."

"School nurse?"

"I was thinking loungewear model, but okay," he said.

"Please," she scoffed. "But speaking of, do you think I might borrow something to sleep in?"

"Of course." He pushed himself off the couch and gracefully ascended the spiral staircase to the loft above. A light came on, bathing the high ceiling in a golden glow.

Bastien returned with a small, folded pile of clothing atop a fluffy white pillow and a rolled blanket.

"The clothes are for you," he said. "The pillow and blanket are for me. I'll sleep down here and you can take the bed upstairs."

"Absolutely not," Shelby insisted. "I am not taking your bed and making you sleep on a couch."

"You're not *making* me do anything," he said. "I'm offering."

She folded her arms across her breasts. "As much as I appreciate your offer, I would prefer to sleep on the couch."

"Then I guess you'll be sleeping on top of me." Bastien draped himself across the couch. Reclining the way he was and with that seductive smirk playing about his lips, he bore the slightest resemblance to Adonis.

As much as the prospect caused tendrils of heat to unfurl in her belly, she couldn't quite bring herself to go through with it.

They considered each other, a game of chicken she was determined to win.

"If you insist." Shelby reached for the tie at the waistband of the robe and began slowly and deliberately working at the knot.

The alarm in his eyes was instant and so, so satisfying.

"What do you think you're doing?"

"Changing."

His gaze darted about. "You can't do that here."

"No?" Her thumb hooked through the last loop and pulled it free. Only her arms now held the robe closed.

"I'm not leaving," he said.

"Neither am I."

Like the silver screen duels of old, they locked gazes in unflinching concentration.

She slid her hands farther toward the center of the tie. "I'm going to do it."

"Go ahead." Bastien rolled onto his back and pillowed his hands behind his head. When she noted the smug set of his smile, she understood why he looked so untroubled.

He didn't believe her.

He didn't think she actually had the guts.

And he wasn't the first. Something about her telegraphed a mild temperament with mild goals and ambitions. Reliably un-shocking. Un-challenging. Un-troubling.

She was beyond sick of it. She wanted to be seen. To be heard. To be known.

Blood rushed in her ears as fizzy excitement lifted her stomach. Her eyes remained fixed on his as she dropped the tie and let the robe fall open, shrugging her shoulders as it pooled at her ankles.

His pupils dilated as his heavy-lidded gaze moved

from her mouth to her breasts to her belly. And lower. His breathing quickened.

In the quiet of the room, she actually heard him swallow. When he spoke, the words that came out were the very last she was expecting.

"Come here."

Five

Bastien had intended to call her bluff.

Instead, she'd called his.

He had counted on the junkyard dog visage he'd earned in one too many fights to do what it had always done: send her scampering back to the safety of a life as far away from him as possible.

Back when he'd entertained hopes of finding someone, his appearance had been something he had to work to overcome, proving by conversation and body language that he wasn't a threat.

Because for most of his life, he had been. He'd been a man who wasn't afraid to dirty his hands or bloody his knuckles when the situation called for it.

Tonight, his bloody knuckle had been bandaged. And now, Shelby Llewellyn stood before him, naked save for a scrap of lace, giving him an expectant smile as sweet and full of promise as Christmas morning.

It made not one goddamn lick of sense.

Bastien pushed himself up from the couch, no longer attempting to conceal the disparity in their heights or their sizes. His last-ditch attempt to let her run.

She didn't.

So he couldn't.

God help him, but he couldn't stop himself from drinking in the mind-bending loveliness of her from every angle. Front. Side.

Behind.

Seeing the rounded end of a charcoal pencil poking from the thick twist of hair secured at the back of her head, Bastien pulled it free, releasing a cascade of gold. No longer curly, but a wild squall of waves shaped by the wind and the weather.

"It's a mess," she said. "Don't look."

He leaned in close enough to feel the warmth radiating from her shoulder. "I thought you wanted me to look."

"I do," she said. "And…touch, if you want to."

If he wanted to? Was she out of her mind?

His hand hovered above the golden waves. His eyes closed on a pained inhale as he ran his fingers through it, loosening the tangle of silky strands. Gooseflesh rose on her forearms and spilled down to her legs, tightening her perfect, pert nipples in the process.

This was all he would allow himself. All he *could* allow himself despite the soul-deep ache of longing.

To taste her. To feel the warmth and weight of her body in his arms.

"I have an idea." Desire deepened his already raspy voice, and her subtle flinch strengthened his resolve.

"What's that?"

"I want to draw you."

"Me?" she laughed, the sound as bright as a brass bell.

"You."

"Oka-a-ay," she said.

"Just lie down there," he said, motioning toward the couch.

She did as asked. First seating herself, then swinging her legs up and stretching them along the cushions with her back propped against the pillows.

With the pencil still in his hand, Bastien walked to the large buffet cabinet and retrieved his charcoals and sketchpad. He carried both back to the living room and set them next to his chair, then went to work.

His hand swept into motion as if of its own volition, finding her shape on that always-intimidating blank white field. Though he hadn't done more than rough out an idea, he fell into a familiar kind of trance. Stroke by stroke, she emerged from the void like Aphrodite from the sea foam. In the curve of a hip. The rounded dune of her thigh. As ever, he failed to spend as much energy on the body as he did the face.

For him, the face had always been his favorite part to capture.

A habit he'd been regularly scolded for in his high school art classes.

"Where did you learn how to do this?" Shelby asked dreamily.

Bastien's charcoal halted at the uneasy feeling that she'd somehow just plucked his thoughts from the very air. "I still don't know that I can."

"But really though," she said.

"Mr. Millar." It had been the first time he'd let himself think about the kind, quirky old man in as long as he could remember. "My high school art teacher."

"Has he seen any of your sculptures?" she asked innocently. "He must be ridiculously proud of you."

Had she taken a hatchet to his chest and removed his heart, it would have been less painful. "He passed while I was in prison."

The words failed to alter the look in her sweet, sleepy eyes as he thought they might. He quickly moved on to her pillowy lower lip. The delicate delta where her earlobe fanned out under her cheek.

"Still," she said. "I bet he'd be proud of you if he could see the kinds of things you were making now."

"I doubt it," Bastien said. "I stole his car."

This, at last, produced a visible change. "You did?"

"Yep. Zap, my old man, got mad that I was spending so much time away from home. Going to his after-hours classes. Even to these special workshops Millar would host for free at his house. So one day, Zap decided I needed to prove my loyalty to him by steeling Mr. Millar's car."

Her eyes widened. "What did you do?"

"I refused at first, but my father had a way of persuading people that was difficult to resist." In this case, that had involved telling Bastien that if *he* didn't, he'd send Augustin to do it instead. A piece of the twisted tale he kept for himself. "I felt so bad about doing it that I got piss drunk before I went over. Mr. Millar tried to talk me out of it, but I—I just grabbed his keys, and I left. He didn't even try to stop me."

He had no idea why he was telling her this, but now he couldn't stop.

"I thought that maybe if I ran it into an ATM, I could just take the money and run. Get as far away as I could. Instead, I split my head open on the dashboard and knocked myself out. Which made me pretty convenient for the police to find."

Shelby was sitting up now, her hand pressed to her mouth. "Oh, Bastien," she said. "I'm so sorry."

"You're sorry?" His laugh was full of acid. "Why the hell would you be sorry?"

"I'm so sorry that you had the kind of father who would put you in that position."

Something in him broke then, and he tossed aside both the pad and the charcoal. His head fell into his hands. He jumped when he felt something warm on his knee and realized she was kneeling in front of him.

"Don't," he nearly growled at her. "Just, please. Don't."

She nodded, a patient smile fixed on her face.

As if she had just remembered she was mostly nude, she grabbed the throw blanket and wrapped it around her shoulders as she reached for the sketchpad. "Can I see?"

"I'm going to need to you remember that I haven't

done this in a very long time," he said. Sneaking a glance to gauge her reaction, he took in many details simultaneously. Her damp lashes. Her gleaming cheeks.

"It's...beautiful," she said.

"*You're* beautiful," he replied.

Shelby made a rude noise and rolled her eyes. "Look, I'm perfectly fine with being cute, or even adorable. Girl next door."

Sensing an exit ramp from the tension thickening between them, Bastien hastily took it. "Did you even have next door neighbors growing up?"

"I mean, there are six separate dwelling structures on my father's estate, so technically yes."

"He was married when you were adopted?" he asked, remembering she had referred to 'Llewellyns,' plural earlier.

Shelby nodded and rose to her feet, taking the drawing with her as she went to sit down on the couch. "Grace. My adoptive mother. She died about a year ago."

"And your father is already engaged again?" he asked.

"Correct," Shelby said. "Sloan's not a bad person, really. Just super high-strung and weirdly competitive where I'm concerned. I'm sure there's a story there."

What a rare creature she was, this woman who offered ready forgiveness to a person who had clearly made her life more difficult, all because she could see what difficulty might have caused it.

"I'll do it," he said.

She glanced up from the drawing that was still resting in her lap. "Do what?"

"The show at your father's gallery." He sagged back against the couch.

"Really?" Her voice was full of delighted disbelief. And yet, he already knew, even in this moment, he was going to regret it. He always did. Every time he accepted the occasional social invitation or agreed to a commission.

Anything that put him in close proximity to people of any number.

"Really," he confirmed.

It happened so quickly.

One minute she was there on the next cushion over, then she was practically in his lap. Hugging and thanking him with equal enthusiasm.

She drew back a hair too slowly.

In the infinitesimal delay, their faces drifted toward each other as if drawn by magnets.

He could taste the wine on her breath as she exhaled, but her nearness was so much more intoxicating. Bastien felt drunk. On the storm. On her words. On the shape of her flowing effortlessly from his pencil in graceful strokes.

The first brush of their mouths was feather-light.

The second was curious. Questing. The kind of hovering alignment used to rule out puzzle pieces.

Or in their case, to lock them home. Their mouths melded with an ease he had never known. She opened to him effortlessly. Generously. Offered herself up without hesitation. Her curves. Her warmth. A gift he hadn't had to earn, beg, steal, or borrow in order to have. All her honeyed sweetness his to explore. All her luxurious softness and living heat.

He let himself sink backward the blanket fell from her shoulders and her naked breasts pressed against his chest. He had to touch her or die.

The tips of his fingers grazed the small downy dip at the base of her spine and followed the shallow ravine upward, over her shoulders, and back down to span her rib cage and brush the hard pearls of her nipples.

She shuddered and moaned into his mouth and her tongue grew bolder. Sliding over his, delving deeper and more insistently. Bastien felt an answering fire kindling at the base of his spine and spreading to a dull ache behind his cock. Delicate fingers pressed against his straining erection, and he felt his control abandoning him. Sliding away like an avalanche.

Marshaling all his strength, he tore his mouth away from hers and sat her up. Locating the blanket, he wrapped it around her shoulders before the sight of her rosy, flushed breasts could overrule his sanity.

Hurt and confusion filled her eyes as she looked up at him. "What's wrong?"

"You win," he said. "You sleep down here by the fire. I'll sleep upstairs."

"But I don't understand—"

"I think it's better that we both just get some rest." It sounded unconvincing even to him, but she let him go without further argument.

Bastien trudged up the stairs and into his quiet bedroom.

But rest wouldn't find him.

All night, he wrestled with the sheets until he nodded off just before dawn. He woke up with a situation that drove him straight into a cold shower. As he stood under the stinging spray, the icy water pelleting him with thousands of needles, he vowed to swallow his pride and call Sheriff Dawkins to help get her car out of the ditch.

With a sense of profound regret, he remembered having agreed to the gallery show. By the time he was dressed, he reminded himself he hadn't signed anything. Perhaps by the light of day, cooler heads would prevail, and she'd realize that their meeting up again under any context wasn't a good idea.

The plan solidified in his mind, he descended the stairs determined to politely rid himself of Shelby Llewellyn.

But when he got there, she was already gone.

Six

As one of the few humans who preferred Halloween to Christmas, Shelby had always thought the term "Winter Wonderland" might be overselling the season just a tad.

Exploring Bastien Renaud's property just after sunrise, she realized just how wrong she'd been. Ice transformed the trees into crystalline sculptures of breathtaking delicacy. The pristine blanket of white made the entire world seem new and clean. The chorus of winter birdsong was so soul-lifting that she'd actually spun in an ecstatic circle when she'd accidentally startled an explosion of bright red cardinals from one of the trees.

She'd halted abruptly when she noticed she was no longer alone.

Bastien stood there like a sentinel, a scowl welded to his face and columns of breath issuing from his nostrils.

Given what had occurred between them the night before, this didn't bode well.

"You're awake," she said, trying to summon the brightest tone she could.

"After what happened yesterday, you left on your own without so much as a note?" he demanded.

"I didn't go far," she said. "I just wanted to listen to the birds. And, anyway, the snow has stopped."

Even as she said it, flakes as fat as doves' feathers floated down between them.

So much for female solidarity, Mother Nature.

"You could have fallen down a drift and I might not have found you until spring thaw. This isn't a goddamn Disney movie."

She knew he was right, and to be honest, her early constitutional hadn't just been about the birds. She'd awoken on the couch with her brain had been buzzing like a bluebottle fly. The sense of rejection. Confusion. He hadn't wanted her there, and as much as she tried to convince herself that this fact didn't bother her, it still stung.

True, it hadn't been her best idea. But sitting there with his eyes on her for all that time had proved to be a distinctly emboldening influence. All morning, she'd stoked the fires of her irritation against him. But now, she was peeved to discover that he was every bit as alluring as he'd been the night before.

"Come on," he said, herding her back toward the house. "Let's get you back inside."

Though her first instinct was to argue, a growling stomach and a dire need for coffee won the day.

"Walk in my footprints," he ordered, and she was forced to admit that this simplified the operation significantly.

She hated it when that happened.

"Do you think someone will be able to come pull me out today?" she asked. "I have a four-thirty flight back to LA and—"

Bastien halted abruptly. Had she been following him any closer she would have run nose-first into his back. He threw his arms out wide, as if to block her from oncoming traffic.

Then she saw it: a dark smudge on the field of pristine white.

And it was *moving*.

A bear. Alive and about ten yards away.

"Aren't they supposed to be hibernating?" she whispered.

"They are," he said through the side of his mouth.

"Shouldn't you be waving your arms or yelling or something?" she asked. "That's what they do on those survivalist shows."

Bastien took several steps forward. "Damn it, Ben," he shouted. "We're not doing this again."

The bear lifted its great, dark head, clouds of breath puffing from his muzzle.

"Umm, are you sure that's a good idea?" she asked.

"Weren't you the one just saying that this isn't a Disney movie?"

"Considering the fact that global warming is the reason that bears are not hibernating like they used to, I'm going to say yes. I don't remember seeing that covered in a Disney movie lately."

"Are you saying you watch them?"

He shot her a dark look. "You really think now is the time for this line of questioning?"

"Seeing as you named him, I'm going to say yes."

Bastien released an exasperated sigh. "He woke up too early last spring and got into my cabin while I was on a trip to Saskatchewan to deliver a piece. When I got home, I found him passed out on the porch."

Shelby folded her arms over his borrowed coat. "Are you absolutely certain you're not Goldilocks?"

"Goldilocks is the one who did the invading."

When Ben began rubbing his hindquarters on a birch, Bastien cut his eyes toward the house.

They both backed slowly away in a series of crunching steps until they were safe on the front porch. When they crossed over the threshold, Shelby heaved a small sigh of relief and glanced toward the door.

"I see you've done some Ben-proofing since then." She nodded toward the impressive series of locks.

"I'm all for peaceful coexistence." Bastien unlaced his boots and set them in the plastic tray near the front door, then went to the kitchen.

On the counter had to be one of the more expensive and elaborate espresso machines she'd ever seen. This was one of the many oddly endearing contradictions she'd noticed. She'd never considered that there might be such a thing as luxury minimalism, but had she been pressed, those are the words she would have chosen.

He busied himself with grinders and knobs, and before long the machine began to hiss and emit a heavenly aroma. He filled a mug, then added steamed milk and brown sugar. Shelby accepted her cup gratefully and tried to keep her eyes from rolling back in her head when she took the first sip.

"I'll make us some breakfast." Bastien kept his back to her as he cracked eggs into a bowl and begin dumping in flour, baking powder, and other ingredients she could only assume were for pancakes. "After we eat, I'm going to try to get Sheriff Dawkins to come haul you out of the ditch."

"Sounds good," she said as her heart actively dropped into her guts. Logically, she hadn't expected him to ask her to stay around any longer than necessary despite the kiss she could still taste on her lips, but she couldn't help feeling a pang of disappointment.

Apparently, whatever fever had possessed them last night, he had made a full recovery. Which was just as well. She needed to get back to San Francisco.

In addition to the birdsong, she'd been woken up by the chirping of her phone.

Her father always rose early, but Wednesdays were reserved for the church of golf. Which meant he'd risen at exactly 4:00 a.m. Pacific Time to begin his morning ablutions. She had briefly considered letting it roll to voice mail and pretending she didn't have reception, but knew the longer she avoided his calls, the more tense the conversation would be when she finally answered.

Because she did.

She always had.

The conversation hadn't been a friendly one.

He'd checked on her safety first, as always, and listened carefully while she described the series of events that had caused her to miss her original flight. The silence that followed had seemed unreasonably excessive and she knew what was coming even before she heard it.

"Sloan said that Fernando never received a call from you last night."

Shelby remembered a time when the warm, booming voice on the other end of the line had been associated with all things friendly and wonderful in her world. Like the sun's own rays warming everything within their reach.

Now it left her feeling cold and strange.

"I'm so sorry," she'd said. "Everything was crazy with the storm. I promise I'll call as soon as we hang up. I mean, when it's a decent hour there."

A prolonged pause.

"You know how much this means to me."

Her chest had tightened and her throat had ached. Never in a million years would she want to begrudge him his own happiness. It was why he'd found it with a woman like Sloan that she couldn't understand.

It had been a lengthy, awful process, the way the only mother she had ever known had died. People always described battles with cancer as brief and brave.

Given the choice, Shelby had decided that she'd much rather that had been the case. The fact that her father had met Sloan a mere three months after her mother's death, she could only blame on herself. After all, it had happened as a result of her father's wanting to purchase a gallery and make Shelby its co-owner.

Enter Sloan.

"I know," she'd said.

"Call me when you've spoken with him?" He didn't trust her.

"I will," she'd promised.

"Are you sure you don't want me to send one of the fleet to pick you up at the Bangor airport?"

"I'm sure." Though she'd flown by private jet many times before, Shelby couldn't get used to the idea of an entire plane arriving just for her.

The sound of Bastien's fridge door slamming shut dropped her out of her reverie.

"You really don't have to go to all this trouble," she said to him. "Technically I'm supposed to be watching my carbs. I know you wouldn't guess that based on my stunning performance at dinner last night, but I have a dress to fit into a couple months and somehow, I don't think a giant stack of pancakes is going to be helpful."

"I have every confidence we can burn it off," Bastien said, loading strips of bacon on a sheet tray.

Shelby froze with her coffee cup halfway to her mouth.

"Getting that car out of the ditch is going to be no walk in the park," he added, seeing the look on her face. She thought she caught the hint of a smirk tugging at one corner of his mouth.

And, oh, Lord. What that mouth had done to her.

She couldn't even rightly call it *kissing*. Mostly because it resembled what she'd experienced with Grant—the one and only long-term boyfriend her father hadn't managed to frighten away—in only the vaguest sense of the word.

No, Bastien hadn't kissed her.

He'd *consumed* her.

Burning away all previous notions she'd had and elevating the skill to an art.

Even now, she could feel his lips on hers. Taste the heat of his tongue. Conjure the delicious rasp of his wood-roughened hands on her back. Her breasts.

Her nipples hardened beneath the ghost fingers moving over their swell.

Whether out of defiance or pure, bloody-minded will, she elected not to cross her arms over her chest to conceal the small darts poking against the shirt she'd borrowed to sleep in.

A little jolt of satisfaction coursed through her as she caught his eyes slipping downward before he cleared his throat and busied himself at the griddle.

Before long, delicious aromas drifted from the stove, and by the time a plate was placed in front of her, she dove in with gusto.

An embarrassment of riches, this. Real creamery butter, maple syrup, perfectly scrambled eggs, and beautifully crisped bacon. When her plate was cleaned, Shelby sat back and sighed.

"Do you eat like this every morning?"

Bastien sipped coffee from an earthenware mug with a thick, uneven handle. "Not every morning. Sometimes I eat breakfast in town."

She dabbed at the corners of her mouth and set aside her napkin. "Must be nice to have such an enthusiastic metabolism."

His jaw tightened. "There's nothing wrong with your metabolism."

Shelby snorted. "Look at your drawing in the cold light of day and tell me that."

He set down his mug hard enough to make the silverware jump, shoved back from the table, and stalked toward the living room.

"I was kidding," she insisted, her socked feet slipping on the wood floor as she scrambled in his wake. Suddenly, the idea of watching him examine her naked body filled her with abject terror.

"Never was much good at taking a joke." He pulled his sketchpad from between the couch and the end table. And then she was in his hands, and before his eyes, and there was nothing she could do about it.

From her vantage point, she couldn't see over his shoulder, so she stepped into his peripheral vision and flushed at the naked heat in his gaze. As if in a trance, his index finger traced the curve of her hip on the page.

"Look at this."

His voice had a faraway quality. Like he wasn't really talking to her, or anyone in particular.

"What about it?" she asked tentatively.

"Look at how perfectly proportioned you are." His

finger began to move, traveling down the indent of her waste and up her rib cage, mapping the shoreline of her breast. Her pulse quickened when he lingered there, eyes hazing over with some unknowable thought. "Perfect," he whispered again.

Shelby shifted. "That's just the way you drew me. Not the way I really *am*. You were being complimentary because you know how self-conscious I am. It's the same thing those sketch artists do outside of Sacré-Coeur in Paris. Nobody would part with a single franc for a realistic depiction."

He turned to look at her, his eyes like smoldering ash beneath his long fringe of eyelashes. "Really? Is that what I did?"

She cleared her throat. "It certainly looks that way to me."

Bastien set down the drawing pad and took her by the hand. "Come with me."

The first stirrings of alarm began when she surmised they were moving toward the spiral staircase that led up to the bedroom.

"Where are we going?" she asked, knowing it was a dumb question.

"There's something I want to show you."

She reluctantly climbed the stairs at his urging, pausing at the top to take in the spare bedroom.

A bed with a tall, modern headboard of sleek gray fabric. A beautiful chest of drawers she suspected he or one of his brothers had probably made. A large wardrobe and, by far the most impressive feature, a giant skylight covered with a thick grayish white blanket of snow. The underwater light emanating through it gave the room an unreal quality. Impossible to tell whether it was day or night, or some strange interval between.

Large warm hands rested on her shoulders, angling her toward the full-length mirror in the corner. Catching only the barest glimpse of her wild hair, Shelby tried to turn away. The broad wall of his chest prevented her from returning to the spiral staircase.

"Humor me."

Warm breath tickled the back of her neck as he lifted her hair and secured it with the tie he slipped from her wrist.

"You see the way this curve echoes this one?" The pad of his index finger traced the line of her neck while he simultaneously gripped a handful of her T-shirt to tighten it against her torso.

"Mmm-hmm," she mumbled, ever so articulately.

"And here." His hand roamed over her hip, fingertips dimpling her flesh through the borrowed sweatpants.

"Umm, sure."

He wasn't satisfied with this answer, or so she gleaned by the fact that he hadn't released her. "Do you have any idea how many artists would have cheerfully murdered each other to have a chance to paint you?"

Shelby caught his eye in the mirror. "No, and frankly I'm relieved because I'd hate to have that on my conscience."

In the unnatural silence created by the snow's insulation, she feared he could hear her heart thundering away in her chest. He'd yet to let go of the handful of

shirt, his knuckles grazing the small of her back and
the thin T-shirt fabric doing the absolute bare mini-
mum to conceal her breasts.

Why hadn't she slipped into her bra after her morning clean-up session in his bathroom before her early
morning field trip outdoors?

Her uneasy swallow might as well have been a crash
of cymbals.

Last night, she'd borrowed boldness from the wine
and the wild storm. Now, in the light of day, she was
paralyzed. Incapable of so much as twitching a finger
in the direction of her desire. Every bit as consuming
as it had been the night before, but impossible to own.

"You're beautiful, Shelby," he said. "Just accept it."

"Then why didn't you want me last night?" she
blurted before she could stop herself.

There was a tug at her waist and Shelby felt herself
being shifted slightly. Something hard, thick, and long
pressed against her rib cage.

Shelby broke out in a full body shiver as his lips
brushed her ear with the hot words.

"Do I really have to spell it out for you?"

"I'd appreciate that, yes."

"I'm an ex-con from a notorious moonshining family whose dirty laundry has been thoroughly aired in
front of the entire world. The last thing I need is one
of the wealthiest men in the country thinking I took
advantage of his young, beautiful daughter while she
was at my mercy because of a blizzard."

"If you don't want me, that's one thing, but I'd rather
be rejected on my own merits or lack thereof rather

than ruled out because you think I belong to Gerald Llewellyn."

His fingertips tightened over her hip, gently drawing her backward until that steely part of him was firmly nestled against her back.

"Of course, I want you." His voice was gravel and smoke. Rough, low, and strangely lovely.

"But...you left. You said we should get some rest—"

His chest expanded against her on deepening breaths. "I didn't want you to do anything you might regret."

Bastien's fingers splayed across her belly beneath the hem of the shirt.

He was waiting.

He had made this hers to decide. In no uncertain terms. With no reservations or repercussions. One word, and he'd back away and let her be. Finish the breakfast dishes and call the sheriff to help her out of the ditch. She could be on her way back to San Francisco in a matter of hours.

He'd still come out for the gallery show, she knew. After all, he'd given his word.

Unlike other men of her acquaintance, that meant something to him.

And what did it mean to her?

Everything.

This show. This chance.

Would giving in to the hunger inside her hurt that chance?

Would this be one more in the long line of indictments that the woman who stole her father's heart could level against her?

"I could never regret you, Bastien."

The rumble within his deep chest felt like a purr, turning her muscles weak as she let herself melt like butter against the heat of his body.

She might have slid down just as easily had he not anchored her to him with arm around her rib cage.

"I've got you." His lips brushed the sensitive shell of her ear.

What a revolutionary idea. That she could relinquish herself into his keeping, if only for a while.

Shelby watched as the hem of the T-shirt lifted and disappeared over her head. Bastien stripped off his thermal shirt, leaving his massive torso bared to her hungry gaze. She moved to turn, longing to touch the slopes of muscle, but his arms held her fast.

"Not yet," he said, hooking a thumb into the waistband of her sweatpants. He tugged them down and emitted a soft snicker when he saw that she had on a pair of his boxer shorts beneath.

"Did you raid my laundry room or something?"

Shelby looked at him sheepishly in the mirror. "The sweats were too big otherwise."

The pad of Bastien's thumb played over the sensitive flesh just above the elastic waist, causing her belly to jump beneath it. The slow, maddening arc seemed to glow on her skin.

"That's because you're a delicate fucking flower, Shelby Llewellyn."

"Now there's one thing I've never been accused of."

Bastien bent to gently run his stubble over her jaw as his lips brushed her neck. "That's because you're surrounded by people who have no idea how to look for beauty."

Shelby had long ago decided there was an impeccable etiquette that people born into money possessed. Her graceless snort of laughter was yet one more sign that she was an outsider.

"You're saying this to a woman who works at an art gallery. The daughter of a father who's devoted an entire wing of his estate to his private collection, worth millions of dollars."

His hands began to move downward, taking the shorts with them, and she stood before him and her reflection in nothing but the improbably lacy underwear she had laundered in the sink early this morning.

She caught the smile trying to land on Bastien's lips.

Shelby notched her chin upward. "My energy healer said that putting orange next to my root chakra would help improve my confidence."

When he spoke, his voice was full of grit that softened her knees, then warmed her blood.

"If nothing else, you're going to leave here knowing that power."

Bastien's hands skimmed upward, molding to the curve of her waist and gliding up her rib cage before sliding forward to relieve her of the weight of her breasts. She moaned as he lightly brushed each of her nipples, letting her head rest against his pectoral muscle. Her eyes fell closed to appreciate the intensity of this subtle sensation. Dizzy with a sense of newness, strangeness, giving herself over to someone unfamiliar. And yet, every part of him felt... Right.

His intoxicating scent. His instinctive understanding of her body. His ability to reduce her to little more than animated jelly and a wildly beating heart.

Through the barest crack in her eyelids, she peeked at the mirror's reflection and the intensely erotic sight of his rough, large sculptor's hands kneading her breasts.

Her breath had begun to time itself to his ministrations, catching each time he squeezed her nipples between thumb and forefinger.

"Has anyone ever made you come like this?" As if to illustrate his point, Bastien lightly pinched her nipple just enough to send a shock of electricity arcing through her. It dissipated quickly, replaced by a heaviness in her chest.

Might as well get it over with.

"There's something I should probably tell you before we go any further."

He let his hands slip down to rest at her waist, giving her his full attention. "What is it?"

"I have kind of a hard time in that, um, department."

A furrow appeared in his broad brow. "Which department?"

Her cheeks blazed an even brighter red as she cleared her throat. "*The* department," she said, hoping to telegraph with her expression what she'd prefer not to have to vocalize.

Recognition dawned slowly on his features. "Orgasms?"

She nodded. "It's not that I can't have them. Just that having them *with* anyone is…difficult."

"Difficult how?" he asked.

Her throat felt like someone had stuffed it full of cotton. "Difficult in that I've never been able to have one with an actual partner."

"*None* of your partners?" The concern etched into his brutal features struck her as irresistibly endearing.

"Well, *partner*," she amended. "I didn't really start dating until college, and my father is a little—" she paused, searching for the right word "—old-fashioned when it comes to meeting anyone who wants to take me out."

"To scare them off?"

"It's not like he *tries* to intimidate them." A sentence she'd spoken on more than one occasion and mostly believed to be true. "He just wants to make sure that I'm safe."

"From men like me?" The rasp of desire in his voice and the heated way he looked at her made Shelby's middle ripple with warmth.

"Probably," she admitted. "Anyway, I just didn't want you to feel bad if you couldn't— I mean…if *I* couldn't—"

"How about you focus on what *you're* feeling instead?"

"Currently, that would be humiliation."

Bastien's warmth radiated against her bare back. "Not here." He gently tapped her temple, then moved his hand to cover her navel. "Here."

Shelby's stomach tensed beneath his palm.

His lips warmed her earlobe. "Breathe."

And then she could. As if his saying it had some-how made it possible.

"Come with me." Lacing his hand with hers, he walked over to the bed and sat down, tugging her toward his lap. "Let's get you figured out."

There was nothing inherently romantic about those words, or the manner in which he spoke them. Which was why Shelby felt a twist of confusion when they caused a small revolution in her body. Beginning with the rush of moisture that appeared between her thighs.

Perhaps in addressing this so practically, he'd taken away all the romantic pressure.

But sadly, not her self-consciousness.

"I could lie down if that would be easier for you," she suggested.

"Is that what you'd prefer?"

She shook her head, curious about his original intentions despite her hesitance.

"All right then." With a hand on the small of her back, he guided her to straddle his lap, the outsides of his steely, hair-roughened thighs at once foreign and delicious between hers.

"Would you mind if I touched you first?" she asked. "Having sensory input helps me ground myself."

A lazy cat smile curled one corner of Bastien's mouth. He planted his hands on the mattress and leaned back. "Help yourself."

"Can you close your eyes? I know it's silly, but I've actually never done this in daylight before."

Bastien's eyes went as flat and empty as a shark's. "How long were you with this boyfriend?"

"A year," she admitted.

"A *year*, and he never got you off *or* took you in the daylight?"

Shelby nodded.

His dark eyebrows lowered. "What's his name?"

"I'm not telling you that," she said, half-laughing. "Especially not with that look on your face."

He shook his head, disgusted, but closed his eyes, anyway.

With her heart flapping in her rib cage like a manic bird, Shelby slowly reached out and set a hand on his chest.

She marveled at the smoothness of his skin, the coarseness of the sprinkling of dark chest hair that funneled into the ridge between his abdominal muscles. He tensed as she trailed her fingertips down, where the trail of hair appeared just above his navel, and trickled into the waistband of his jeans.

He grunted when she circled his belly button with the tip of her fingernail. Moving upward again, she let her palms splay flat across his pectorals, then over the great expanse of his shoulders and down the wide wings of muscle at his back.

Journeying around to the front again, she noticed the small black line peeking from the waistband of the boxer briefs beneath his jeans.

"What's this?" she asked.

"A mistake."

"Can I see?"

"I sure can't."

She shook her head at him, grateful his eyes were closed so he couldn't see the slight tremor in her hands as she unbuttoned his jeans and peeled away the denim.

"Oh, wow," she said, taking in the red-black tangle of lines and shapes, desperately trying to assemble them into something recognizable. "It's…very colorful."

"It's supposed to be a ladybug."

Given this information, she could almost make out a wing. "And what exactly made you want to get a ladybug?"

"Guilt, mostly."

"Guilt?"

"Bug is my niece Emily's nickname. It's based on a drawing she sent me after I left the distillery."

"How long ago was that?"

"Four years."

She felt the pang of irritation at herself for stumbling into what was likely a painful topic and resumed trailing her hand over his belly instead.

His breathing had quickened, his eyebrows drawing together in concentration. "Is it my turn yet?"

Heat flooded Shelby's cheeks. Her breath grew ragged with anticipation.

"Yes," she said, letting her eyes fall closed as his opened.

His breath tickled the sensitive skin of her throat before his warm lips found her jawline. He planted kisses there, working his way up toward the shell of her ear. She squirmed as he traced her earlobe, lightly flicking the tip of his tongue over it. His exhale cooled the part he had just moistened, causing her to break out in a full-body shudder.

"So far, so good," he said.

Then he was moving again. Brushing his lips across hers before working his way to the other side and repeating the process.

"Here's what we're gonna do, Shelby Llewellyn. You're going to put your hands on your knees and you're not going to move them unless I tell you to. Got it?"

Despite the fact that handcuffs had never been her thing, the thought of being at Bastien's mercy produced a delicate flutter in her navel.

She placed her hands over her knees.

"Good," he said. "Now, open your mouth."

Shelby peeked at him through one eyelid. "Excuse me?"

"Mouth open," he said. "Eyes closed."

Shelby's lips parted ever so slightly and the pad of Bastien's thumb danced over her damp lower lip before dipping inside.

He lightly stroked her tongue and applied gentle pressure to open her mouth wider. Then the thumb retreated and was replaced by his index and middle fingers. Probing in a slow sensuous exploration that made her feel like she was falling.

"Suck them," he said.

Though nervous at first, the exercise became a fascinating sensory exploration. The calluses. The creases.

Just when she was beginning to let the heady power

overtake her, he pulled his fingers from her mouth. Seconds later she felt them brush her nipple before he painted a path down her sternum, her belly button, and below the hem of her lace panties.

Then she discovered what he'd *really* been about. Already coated with slickness, they easily parted her sex, sliding against that most sensitive part of her. Making her cry out when they circled the engorged bud within.

"How does that feel?"

Shelby bit her lower lip and tried to find words that didn't want to make her jump out of her own skin.

"Good," she said lamely.

Bastien increased with the pressure ever so slightly. "Just good?"

"*Very* good?"

"You're gonna have to do better than that."

As if to inspire her, he delved lower, where a building ache made already challenging verbal exercises that much harder.

"Feels…hot," she panted.

"And?"

"Wet," she said breathlessly.

"What else?" he urged.

Shelby gasped as two fingers slipped inside of her, his thumb finding her sensitive nub and circling.

"Absolutely delicious."

Her loquaciousness was rewarded by his pushing farther inside her. She was already thinking of something else to say when he curled his two fingers and found a spot that made her feel like a harp whose strings had all been plucked at once.

"Oh, God," she cried, immediately embarrassed by the ragged sound of her own voice.

"You like that?" She heard the smile in the question.

"Love," she breathed. "I love that."

Was it foolish of her to reveal so much so soon? To put this much power in his hands? From what she could tell, it had already lived there. She lost herself to the sensation coiling around her most secret places. Places that only she had been able to reach until this moment.

"In that case…"

He quickened his pace, further stoking the coals of the fire spreading wildly within her. Shelby felt the first twinges of her release and became aware that she was mumbling. Repeating a phrase over and over like an incantation to prolong whatever magic this was.

"Don't stop. Don't stop. Please—"

"Baby, I'm not gonna stop until. I've wrung. Every last. Drop from you." He paired each phrase with a thrust of his fingers, circling the bright, hot pearl of pleasure beneath his thumb.

Wave after wave lapped at her, pulling her deeper and further out to sea. She didn't know when she'd reached up to anchor herself on his shoulders, but realized her fingernails were digging into the mounded muscles there.

The world had taken on a bluish cast, when at last she opened her eyes. Glancing downward, she saw a pink flush lighting up her chest and spilling down between her breasts. Bastien's hand found the back of her neck and gently tipped up her face until their eyes met.

"There's nothing wrong with you."

Her mouth opened to offer some kind of explanation. A justification.

"There's *nothing* wrong with you," he repeated.

More denials bubbled up her throat, but his lips were on hers before she could give them voice. Their mouths fused, tongues twining in a sensuous dance. Shelby curled her fingers into the silky hair at his nape and kissed him back. Kissed him with every ounce of relief and wonder he'd awoken inside her.

He sank backward on the bed with her astride him, his hands leaving her only to unbutton his pants and slide down his zipper.

"I want to touch you like you touched me," Shelby whispered against his lips, letting her fingers trail down the wash of his abdominal muscles.

Bastien pillowed his hands behind his head, granting her free access.

Tentatively at first, she molded her hand to him through the soft fabric of his boxer briefs, marveling at the thickness and length of what she found there.

She'd been no prude even though she'd only had one long-term relationship, but Bastien was far beyond the realm of her experience.

Tucking her fingers beneath the elastic waistband, she found the hot, silky head of his sex and he groaned as she captured the bead of moisture at its tip and slicked it downward.

Encouraged by his reaction, she leaned forward to

plant small kisses on the taut plane of his stomach, breathing the scent of clean skin and fabric softener as she did.

He reached down to hold her hair out of her face as she shimmied the boxers down his hips, freeing his erection. It lay against his stomach, as thick, long, and smooth as the finest Carrara marble. He sucked in a breath when she wrapped her hand around the base, testing the decadent texture.

A stolen glance upward revealed his face to be a mask of concentration.

Drunk on having this monumental man within her power, she lowered her lips and kissed him there, too.

His throaty grunt of pleasure became a vibration she could feel in the sensitive skin of her lips. She took her time exploring. Running her tongue over his ridged head, tasting him like something meant to be savored, then taking the tiniest fraction of him into her mouth.

His hand closed firmly over hers.

"Wait," he groaned between clenched teeth. That she could affect him so filled Shelby with a strange sense of pride.

And made her absolutely ravenous at the same time.

Bastien rolled onto his side to open the drawer in the nightstand and pulled out a foil packet, which he handed to her. Shelby tore it open with her teeth and sheathed him, rolling the condom down in one firm stroke.

As he was lying there inert, Shelby understood that he wanted *her* to choose.

She didn't know if it made her a coward, but she

lied down on her side, facing away from him, wriggling until her behind brushed the cords of his muscular thighs.

"Like this," she said. "I want you like this."

Seven

Bastien had expected that being with Shelby would make him feel his age, and he was right, but not in the way he had thought. Far from the catalog of injuries from sports, and then in fights, his body had been changed under her touch. Her mouth on him had produced an eagerness he hadn't felt since he was a much younger man. Her hands had alchemized him into something miraculously new.

By the time she had presented him her elegant back, he was half-mad with need. And as had become his custom when in a hurry, Bastien slowed down. When adrenaline took over, mistakes happened. And even though he knew sleeping with Shelby was one of them, he was determined to enjoy every second.

A man only got so many of these particular kinds of mistakes in his lifetime.

He stroked her back, letting his fingertips find the elegant indent of her spine, chart the curve of her hip to her rounded ass, and down the back of her thigh.

She wriggled against him impatiently.

Bastien lifted her knee and shifted forward to slide the head of his cock against her, but not inside her. Blond curls tumbled over her shoulder as she glanced back at him, her eyes wide.

"You didn't think I was done with you yet, did you?" Anchoring his elbow behind her knee, he lifted it higher to reveal the slick, swollen petals of her sex. "Look how beautiful you are," he murmured, letting her heat kindle his as he slid against her again and again.

"Bastien," she panted, fingers curling in the sheets. "Please."

That single word might have been the most beautiful sound he'd ever heard.

Unable to resist any longer, he positioned himself at her entrance.

"Take what you want, baby. Nice and slow."

Shelby's hips curled backward. His breath caught in his throat as he became enveloped in her silken heat. With a titanic effort of will, he kept his hips still as she buried him to the hilt by infinitesimal degrees. She paused when he reached the deepest part of her, their breathing the only sound in the room.

"You okay?" he asked. His already thundering heart sped when no answer came and plummeted in his chest when he heard a small sniffle.

Her cheek was wet beneath his palm when he turned her face to his. "What is it?" he asked. "You want to stop?"

She shook her head, dark lashes clumped with tears.

"I just—" She stopped, seemingly unable to strangle out the next word. He waited while she swallowed and tried again. "I just didn't know anything could feel like this."

Bastien thumbed away another tear as it fell.

He had forgotten.

Forgotten the intensity of the neurochemical flood and its emotional consequences.

He bent to kiss her lips, her cheek, hovering above her ear as he whispered, "It's all right, angel. Everything is alright."

Whether she began moving again or he did, he couldn't be sure. It didn't matter. They moved as one. Plumbing depths together in a slow, sweaty grind that felt like salvation.

He felt the roots of his climax sinking low, wrapping around at the base of his spine, and he could no longer hold himself back. He buried his face against the base of her neck, their fingers twining in a knot clutched against her sternum as she bucked against him. Their sounds becoming more primal and demanding, their breaths more ragged.

His entire world had distilled itself into pure sensation.

Bastien cursed as her walls clenched around him, releasing a supernova of pleasure that rolled through him like a shock wave. Endless pulses wrung him, turning him inside out.

They stayed curled together as fresh curtains of snow fell, walling them off from a world where this thing between them had no place. Powerful drowsiness overtook him then and Bastien yielded to it, following her slow steady breath into sleep.

He woke disoriented in a pewter-gray light that resembled neither day nor night. His eyelids were glued together and his tongue stuck to the roof of his mouth. He'd slept hard and had no idea for how long. Patting down the sheets failed to produce his phone, and the clock was a glowing blue smear on the other side of the room. This sense of disorientation so resembled the feelings he'd had the morning after a bender that for a moment he felt an old stab of panic. Rolling over to the nightstand, he saw the discarded foil packet and remembered.

What had he done?

Sleeping with the daughter of a Silicon Valley billionaire would be bad enough on its own. But the daughter of Gerald Llewellyn? Famously protective. Famously ruthless. Notoriously unforgiving.

For years, Bastien had managed to stay free of all entanglements. Now he'd gone and flung himself straight into a web.

He slowly rolled himself into a seated position, feeling every ounce of his exertion between yesterday and today. The sweats she'd been wearing sat in a puddle beside the bed. He hastily stepped into them and descended the stairs. Shelby wasn't in the living room. Or the kitchen. He gulped down an entire bottle of water and rested his forehead against the brushed metal door of the fridge.

Only then did he notice the anemic band of light spilling from beneath the cellar door.

His heart beat like a high hat in his ears.

If she was down there, she knew. The cement steps did not betray him with any squeak as he descended. The floor at the bottom was cool beneath his bare feet as he stood frozen by the sight before him.

Seated at his desk before the array of monitors, a blue glow bathing her in an otherworldly corona, was Shelby Llewellyn. He could see both the screen that showed small tiles of the security cameras dotted around his property and what she was looking at on the screen directly in front of her. His file on her father's gallery and on Shelby herself. Or at least everything he could find after getting the access to extended background-check information he'd been granted by an ex-military contact.

"What are you doing?"

She jumped at the sound of his voice, spinning in the chair to face him. Clad only in his T-shirt and wrapped in a blanket, her knees and calves were bare, her feet tucked beneath her.

She'd been here long enough to get comfortable.

What he read in her eyes the split second before her impeccable manners took over to rearrange her features stuck a dagger between his ribs.

Fear.

"Bastien," she said quickly with a nervous laugh. "Hi."

"What are you doing down here?" he asked.

Her eyes darted to the side. "The lights flickered again, and I didn't to wake you, so I came downstairs to—"

"Snoop?"

Her foot had begun to jiggle, the same tell he'd noticed as she sat on a barstool only yesterday, working up the nerve to make her sales pitch.

By all rights, she should be the one confronting him.

That she didn't filled him with equal parts relief and anger. Relief that he wouldn't have to answer questions she had the right to ask. Anger that she hadn't been instilled with a healthy sense of protective outrage about his intrusion.

"I didn't mean to snoop. It was dark, and I bumped the desk. The screens lit up and I thought I could at least check my email since my phone reception has been so spotty. Then I saw this file on the gallery and—"

"Is that all you looked at?" He hated how paranoid the question sounded. Hated even more that he could trace it directly to its source.

Zap Renaud.

A man with few friends, but many enemies—both real and imagined. Their house—it had never really been a home—had been like the hull of a ship. The secrets within it carefully contained in a series of locked doors and boxes. Sheds and trunks. The most dangerous of them was the reason why Bastien's prison term had been made even more miserable.

The reason why Bastien constantly kept tabs on anyone who might be looking for him, or his brothers.

"Bastien, I don't understand why you have a file about the gallery when you've never even answered any of my calls."

The buzzing of cicadas filled his head at the measured suspicion of her question.

"I don't want to talk about this."

She sat up and put her socked feet on the floor. "We kind of have to talk about this," she said. "If we're going to do this show—"

"We're not." He kept his face blank and hard, summoning the stone he'd developed in his years locked up with men who preyed on fear. "I shouldn't have agreed in the first place."

Shelby hugged the blanket tighter around her as she stood. "Look, we can talk about this. I'm not accusing you of anything. I just want to understand."

"There's nothing for you to understand," Bastien said.

"Why are you acting this way? If this is about what happened between us—"

"What happened between us is that was a biological transaction resulting in a temporary chemical bond. It'll pass. It always does."

Shelby flinched, and he had never hated himself more.

"You know what the best thing is about having been a kid in the foster care system?"

His jaw ached with the effort of keeping his teeth

clenched against the apologies that wanted to flood up his throat. He didn't answer her.

"I learned how to deal with bullies a long time ago." She took a step toward him, and it was everything he could do not to gather her against him, righteous wrath and all. "You may be able to hurt my feelings, Bastien Renaud, but you're going to have to try a lot harder than that to hurt my heart."

He stood there, wordless and rigid, as she stomped up the stairs. The acoustics of the wide-open space he'd created for himself after so much time in confinement allowed him to hear her escape plan.

"Hey, Dad. I changed my mind. Can you send the jet to Bar Harbor?" A pause. "Yes, the police station has a private landing strip." Another pause. "I love you, too, Dad."

Bastien prowled over to the computer desk and sat down hard. The cold, oily feeling that filled his stomach spread to his chest.

Against his will, Remy's earworm of an intro from the *Bad Boys of Booze* trailer invaded his head. *I've been many things in my thirty-seven years. A brother. A thief. A convict...*

Bastien had an extensive list of his own, and at the end of it, the one he resented the most.

A target.

He didn't know if he'd ever be rid of it, but Bastien knew one thing for sure.

Away from him was the safest place for Shelby to be.

Eight

"There she is!" Gerald Llewellyn's voice boomed across the cavernous foyer. "The victorious negotiator."

The familiar smell of woodsy cologne enveloped Shelby as her father pulled her in for a hug. She registered the cool glass through her sweater and felt its round shape press into her spine. Five o'clock, and her father already had a Scotch in hand.

He pulled back as if to examine her, eyelids scrunched as if analyzing her for some physical change in the last forty-eight hours.

She took advantage of the moment to analyze him as well. His handsome face was tanned, but half-moon puffs lingered below his eyes, the crinkles at the corners appearing to have deepened in her short time away. The silver branching out from his sideburns and feathering his crown seemed to be multiplying virtually by the hour. His smile, once a perfect, brilliant, dazzling white, had never been quite the same since her adoptive mother died.

Shelby pecked his warm cheek, smoky fumes floating up to her nostrils as she did so. "Hi, Dad."

He took her by the hand. His palm was clammy from the drink as he tugged her across the acres of marble in the grand entryway.

"Come with me," he said. "I have something to show you." As was his way, he talked as he walked. "When I heard that you landed the elusive Bastien Renaud—"

"About that," she interrupted, her stomach flipping.

"I just knew the gallery would never do for pieces like his," he said, seeming not to hear her. "So I asked myself, if I were going to do his work justice, what kind of space would I choose?"

"Dad," she said, trying again. "You really don't—"

"That's when it hit me. What better place to display his work than right here at Green Gables?"

He pushed open the giant double doors to the wing housing his art collection with a flourish.

"Surprise!" a chorus of voices echoed.

Dismay quickly morphed into delight as a quick sweep of the room revealed both her older siblings, as well as Porter. Behind them stood Sloan, her platinum hair twisted into a perfect chignon and her face set in a delicate grimace at the loud noise.

They lifted their champagne glasses to toast her, and, one by one, came forward to offer Shelby their congratulations.

Kendall, looking as chic as one of the models in the fashion magazines she helped edit, had just returned from a trip to Paris. She air-kissed both of Shelby's cheeks, then squeezed her shoulders and whispered, "So excited for you."

David, the perfect mix of his mother's fair good looks and his father's height, had just returned from Tokyo, where he'd landed yet another major client for Llewellyn Enterprises. He looked handsome, but a little tired as he leaned in to hug her. "Nice work, Shel."

Porter waited for last, but came to her grinning, his auburn hair still burnished brass at the ends from a recent backpacking trip through the Himalayas,.

Before he'd decided to go to school to become a sommelier, his proposed career path had included stockbroker, professional tennis player, and, most recently, co-owner of a nightclub. He gave her an enthusiastic "So proud of you, Shel," and an extra tight hug.

A pang of guilt twisted in her gut and stayed as Sloan, who had watched these proceedings with a martini in hand, placed a quick, cold peck on Shelby's cheek.

"Well, isn't this a pleasant surprise." Her ability to make a word with positive connotations sound poisonous was truly impressive. "I can't wait to hear *how* you managed it."

Shelby gave her a halfhearted smile but no explanation.

"I have to be honest," Sloan continued. "I half expected to get a tearful call the day you arrived. I've heard Bastien Renaud is known for running people out of his store if they rub him the wrong way."

Shelby nearly choked on a sip of champagne from the glass someone had pressed into her hand, the bubbles turning into acid in her throat.

The whole way home, she'd planned out exactly what she would say. How she would tell her father that the good news she'd shared over the phone early that morning had turned bad. That, after sleeping with their intended artist, she'd accidentally stumbled on an extensive file about the gallery, in addition to facts about Shelby, herself.

A chill stole over her at the memory.

Most of it had been general information. Things readily accessible to the public. Nothing that fell firmly in red-flag territory. If she was being honest, it was mostly the files' existence on his laptop when he'd clearly had no intention of agreeing to the gallery show that had initially caught her. And his admission that, despite having listened to some of her voice mails, he'd simply never bothered to reply.

But most of all, it had been his reaction to finding her down there.

His face, cold with anger. The way he'd treated her in the aftermath.

She had planned to keep these pieces to herself, but now, with Sloan eyeing her like a pet she didn't fully trust, Shelby couldn't make the correct words come to her lips.

"The store was lovely," she reported. "But it's the

sculptures at the private studio on his property that I'm really excited about."

Sloan coughed, the liquid in her condensation-fogged glass sloshing onto her dress. "You saw his *private* studio?"

"I did." With a flash of pleasure, she couldn't help but wonder what Sloan might have to say if she knew what else Shelby had seen—and done—with the reclusive artist.

"Well, aren't you the intrepid explorer." Sloan dabbed at the damp patch on her dress with the napkin that had been handed to her by TJ, their family's ever-present house manager. "Did you two happen to discuss which works you'd like to feature in the exhibition?"

A film of sweat bloomed between Shelby's shoulder blades. "Some," she lied.

Sidling up to Shelby's father, Sloan snaked an elegant arm around his waist. "We'll need to discuss transportation as soon as possible. I'd really like to have all that settled before your father and I leave on our honeymoon."

Porter snagged gazes with Shelby behind Sloan's back and mimed a gag.

"Actually," Gerald said, turning his torso toward his fiancée. "I was hoping we might be able to expedite the timeline of the exhibition."

Blocks of rouge stood out on Sloan's prominent cheekbones as she blanched. "Expedite?"

"Imagine it. Our wedding ceremony overlooking the lake. The reception in the Italian gardens. And the cocktail hour here, with an exhibition of Bastien Renaud sculptures for our guests to peruse."

Red began to climb Sloan's neck like mercury in a thermometer. "But Fernando and I have already finalized the cocktail hour for the veranda," she said.

It was meant to be a gentle reminder, but having heard Sloan assume the same tone with gallery installation crews, Shelby knew it conveyed four-alarm panic.

Gerald cocked his head, speaking to his fiancée with the mildly patronizing tone that sometimes set Shelby's teeth on edge. "Would it really be that difficult to move some tables inside?"

In her peripheral vision, Shelby saw her older siblings exchange a look. They'd all been privy to an increasing number of these minor disagreements and knew they had a tendency to swell into full-blown arguments.

"I know work has kept you too busy to be engaged with some of the more minor details of our wedding," Sloan said, expertly working a gripe into her objection, "but there's a lot more than just a few tables to be considered. There's the band, the caterer, the lighting, the floral, not to mention the vintage boats we've hired to transport guests across the lake from the ceremony to the cocktail hour."

Her father's mouth flattened. "Isn't that why we hired a wedding planner in the first place? I thought you said he was a virtuoso with those kinds of details."

"He is," Sloan insisted. "But not at the last minute."

"Last minute?" Her father's laugh was rich, warm, and, as ever, garnished with condescension. "I was under the impression we weren't getting married for three months."

"Correct, darling," Sloan said, ice edging the endearment. "But invitations have already gone out and—"

"And I'm not sure how excited Bastien would feel about the idea of his work being the entertainment while people guzzle free cocktails," Shelby interrupted.

This comment earned her a grin from Porter and a scowl from Sloan. *Her* guests would never guzzle.

"Shelby makes an excellent point." Sloan's expression vacillated between entitlement and indignation. "And, anyway, the insurance alone would add a chunk to the wedding budget. You know how those adjusters will leverage any excuse." Logic that appealed to her father's inherent suspicion of unreasonable markups.

His eyebrows drew together as he considered.

"As sought after as he is, I don't think he'd appreciate being an afterthought to our day." Sloan's manicured hand slithered up to the back of his neck, squeezing gently in a move she and Porter jokingly called "steering." The determined, steely look Gerald Llewellyn often employed in a business setting began to soften.

"It seems I'm destined to be overruled." He took another sip of his drink, pressing his lips together before swallowing. "Alright then. We'll forget about dovetailing the exhibition with the cocktail hour."

Shelby's relief was short-lived.

"Having it in place before the rehearsal dinner at the gallery makes more sense, anyway."

He was famous for this move in negotiations. Toying with his opponent. Letting them think they'd won, then hitting them with something completely out of left field.

"But we had originally talked about August," Shelby insisted. "That cuts the timeline significantly."

Sloan's red-lacquered nails toyed with the silver hair at her father's nape. "A miracle worker like you?" she purred. "I'm sure you'll have no problem whatsoever."

Any hope Shelby had of their earlier alliance buying her a show of solidarity had been wildly misplaced. "Of course," she said, her mind already spinning out scenarios that would allow her to wiggle out of this or buy herself more time.

"To Shelby." Gerald raised his nearly empty glass, catching the light from the glittering chandelier overhead. "Who clearly inherited my persuasive prowess."

They made the rounds of clinking glasses.

"Another one, darling?" Sloan asked, nodding toward Gerald's empty drink.

"Please," he said.

Had it been anyone else, Sloan would have signaled to one of the staff. For her father, Sloan insisted on making the drink herself. She started off in the direction of the bar, her runway-model body moving like water beneath the pale green silk of her sheath dress.

Kendall and David took this as their cue to begin to migrate toward the dining room.

Porter hung back, falling into step with Shelby. "You think if I slip TJ a hundred spot, he'd accidentally spill a Perrier on her?" he muttered through the side of his mouth.

"To what end?" Shelby glanced up at him.

"To see if she'll melt." He shot a roguish grin at her.

"I think we're far past the point of aquatic intervention."

"Good point," he said. "You want to tell me why you're freaking out?"

Her laugh was thin and utterly unconvincing. "What makes you think I'm freaking out?"

"Your face, mostly."

Shelby rolled her eyes at him.

"I mean it. You look like you're about to bolt."

Setting her empty glass on the silver tray at the end of the buffet as she passed, she smiled at TJ, who appeared out of the ether. Tall, lean, and Alfred-esque in a tidy black suit, he had been with them since she was a girl and had always looked about sixty years old, and always made that sixty look good.

"Thanks, TJ," Shelby said.

"My pleasure." He inclined his head as they passed.

"So?" Porter asked as soon as they were alone again.

Shoulders sagging, Shelby blew a stray curl away from her forehead. "It was an eventful trip."

Even as she said it, a rapid-fire slideshow of her passionate tangle with Bastien, ending with his arctic dismissal, flipped through her head. The memory of his broad back disappearing down the hallway still stung.

"I'm just glad you made it back in one piece. When I heard about the blizzard, I thought you'd be stuck there for at least a week."

Her brother vastly underestimated the motivational powers of a truly awkward situation. "I really lucked out," she said. "The storm broke just in time. How's the club?" she asked in an obvious bid to change the subject. To her great relief, Porter didn't resist.

"Hopelessly invaded by hipsters."

"That's what you get for naming all your drinks after famous film-noir movies."

"The launch didn't go as well as I'd hoped," Porter said. "We lost our publicist."

The "we" in question referred to Porter's best friend and business partner, Darragh McClane. Once classmates at Yale, they'd both eschewed the invitation to join their respective family businesses in favor of exploring career paths of far more creativity and, so far, less profit.

"Uh-oh," Shelby said. "Did Darragh break up with the marketing exec already?"

Tall, dark, and with possible Scottish mob ties, her brother's business partner chose significant others the way some men selected ties. Frequently, and always with an eye to accessorize his current identity.

"She broke up with *him*." Porter held open the door to the family dining room with an elbow.

Their father was already seated at the head of the table.

Shelby suffered an involuntary twitch when she noticed Sloan sat in the spot formerly occupied by their late mother. For the first few months of their whirlwind courtship, she'd at least maintained the appearance of hesitation to slide into the dead woman's shoes—and walk-in closet—out of respect.

With the precision of an army regiment, all four siblings assumed their usual seats at the twelve-foot table. For the last seventeen years, they'd gone through this ritual at least once a week. More often, when they were younger. Now that they all had careers and, in Kendall and David's case, serious relationships, it had become increasingly rare.

Over the soup course, they would each share pertinent updates that had occurred since their last dinner. Once the entrée was served, upcoming travel plans would be shared. Only over coffee were questions of a more personal nature discussed.

This evening proved no different.

"Did you get to see the inside of his...*house*?" Sloan's spoon clinked as she stirred stevia into her decaf. "I heard that he built it himself."

Shelby poured a thin stream of half-and-half into her own cup before reaching for a cube from the leggy little Spode sugar bowl TJ always put out for her. "I He did," she said, savoring the first sip. "And, yes. I did get to see inside."

"I imagine that was quite an experience." Sloan set aside her spoon.

"Not really," she said mildly.

"How *did* you manage that, anyhow? I hear he's famously protective of his private address."

Translation: *I looked but was never able to find it.*

"Goddamn, that smells good." Porter, whose gap-toothed grin she'd seen for the first time on her first visit to the Llewellyn home, leaned forward to capture the curls of steam rising from a homemade peach cobbler.

"Remind me to make sure you're not seated at the mayor's table," Sloan said from the side of her mouth.

"Just make sure I'm next to the bar and I'll be happy," Porter retorted.

The comforting sound of the coffee cup sliding discreetly into its saucer became the sound effect for the incoming announcement. "We've decided not to do a family table."

A brief but noticeable silence followed.

"With so many of our professional colleagues present, we just thought it would probably be better if we circulated."

Shelby had absolutely no doubt whose reasoning her father was providing them.

She glanced at Kendall and David but neither revealed any irritation if they felt it.

When the last hint of dinner had been cleared away, her older siblings said their goodbyes, citing early meetings. For his part, Porter had done his best to smooth over the dinner conversation. But he, too, hightailed it out of there at the first available opportunity. As the only one still living at Green Gables, Shelby wished she could do the same.

When she'd finished her MBA, her father had insisted she move back in and spend some time saving up her money while she decided where she should ultimately like to be. The answer to that was increasingly becoming wherever Sloan was not.

With this directive in mind, Shelby had made it as far as the hallway when her father called after her. "Shelby? Would you mind stopping by my study before you turn in?"

The phrasing made it seem like she had a choice as to the timing. Experience had taught her this was not the case.

Her chest tightened when she heard the question. Of the occasions she'd been asked to come to her father's office, only one of them had been good. It had been there among the sumptuous fabrics and polished wood, where Gerald Llewellyn and Grace had asked her how she might feel about coming to live with them.

Just as he had all those years ago, he motioned to the sitting area, where two overstuffed leather chairs sat in the cozy glow of an authentic Tiffany lamp.

Shelby chose one, sat, and braced herself for the inevitable.

"I'm going to ask you a question," he said, sitting forward with his hands on his knees. "No matter what, I need you to be one-hundred-percent honest with me."

"Alright," she said, trying to pretend the bottom hadn't just dropped out of her stomach.

"Do you think hosting Bastien Renaud for a gallery show is a good idea?"

Now was her chance.

She could—very politely and with great tact—explain to her father how they should postpone the show until next year. Make sure they solidified the staff and worked on their business plan before undertaking such a large venture. But the words refused to pry themselves from her tongue.

"Why do you ask?"

His posture deflated on heavy sigh. "It just seems that this idea might be creating a lot of…tension between you and Sloan."

"What gave you that idea?" she asked, already knowing the answer.

"Don't be angry, but she mentioned that you seemed to be under a lot of pressure lately and she's afraid it may be affecting your experience at the gallery." He brushed a piece of lint from his slacks. "She knows how hard you are on yourself."

Shelby's pulse rushed in her ears at the oblique reference to her recent mistake involving the sale of a major piece. An error in the wire transfer that she had corrected almost immediately after reaching out to the patron to apologize profusely. That the patron had been one of their major donors was an ironclad example of her awful luck. That it kept returning to the conversation, a testament to Sloan's masterfully passive-aggressive orchestrations.

"I'm fine, Dad. I love working at the gallery," she insisted. "It can be challenging at times, sure, but I'm still learning."

His kind blue gaze came to rest on the arm of his chair. He buffed out a scratch in the leather with his thumb. "There are a lot of galleries out there, you know. Plenty where I have contacts. I would just hate for your work relationship to make your family relationship that much harder."

Instinct and experience told her she needed to handle this conversation very carefully. The last thing she wanted to do was place her father in the position of taking sides.

Shelby was more than a little afraid that she already knew how that scenario would play out. She swallowed the lump in her throat and quickly blinked her stinging eyes.

"If Sloan feels it would be best for me not to work there—"

"No, not at all," her father insisted. "In fact, she was just saying the other day how much you reminded her of herself when she was in that phase of her career."

All of two years ago, Shelby thought to herself.

"My point is, there are so many options and I just want to make sure you know you have my support if you ever decide you want to make a change," he said.

"I appreciate that."

Gerald cleared his throat and rose from the chair, casually strolling over to the small bar cart in the corner to splash Scotch into a squat rocks glass. He held up the bottle to her in invitation.

"I'm okay," she said. "The wine at dinner was plenty for me."

If her father caught the subtle censure in her comment, it failed to change his plan.

Between courses, Shelby had followed Kendall to the restroom, trying to make her mention of his increasing consumption feel like a casual comment and hoping on some level that, as the oldest, Kendall might see a way to bring it up privately.

Her father sipped his drink and stared at the oil portrait of their family he'd commissioned when Shelby started high school. All their faces burnished into perfection by the paint's smoothing influence.

"I know this has been a lot," he said. "Before I met Sloan, I wasn't sure what kind of life I'd have without your mother. Most days, I didn't even want to get out of bed."

Shelby remembered. His unshaven face at the dinner table. Silver invading the stubble on his jaw almost overnight.

"At first, the idea of dating…felt like a betrayal," her father continued. "But then I realized that I was the one with those feelings. I was afraid I would never be who I was when I was married to your mother. But I think that's kind of the point. Moving on from grief means allowing yourself to become someone different. Accepting that you're still you."

Shelby felt chastened and selfish. However much she had resented Sloan, she couldn't deny that she'd brought her father back to life.

"I know, Dad. And I promise I'll work harder at trying to make Sloan feel at home."

His eyes misted when he turned to look at her. "On a related topic, I have a favor to ask."

"What's that?" she asked, her antennae twitching.

Her father turned to fully face her. "Sloan would really like for you to be her maid of honor, but she insists you'd just say no if she asked."

Shelby's fingernails dug into her clammy palm. "I thought she wasn't doing any of that."

Gerald returned to his seat and perched on the edge of the cushion. "She wasn't going to."

"What changed her mind?"

His eyes slipped to the side. "When Kendall's magazine did a feature on Sloan, they gifted her the bridesmaids' dresses they used in the photo shoot."

"I guess I'm just surprised that she'd want me to be her maid of honor instead of her friends or family."

Her father stared into his drink like the Delphic oracle. "She's not especially close to her family. And as hard as she works at the gallery, she doesn't really have very many close friends." He pinned her with a pleading look. "You two actually have more in common than you realize, Shelby."

A headache began to pulse at her temples. She felt a keen longing for her bathtub and her bed, and knew that agreeing was the quickest way to get there. "I'd be happy to be her maid of honor," she said. "If she still wants me."

His face brightened as he crossed the room to plant a smoky kiss on her cheek. "That's just wonderful, sweetheart. Why don't we go tell her the good news?" He was already on the way to his study door when she spoke up.

"Would you mind if I turn in, actually? I'm exhausted and I'd much rather have this conversation when I'm fresh enough to be excited."

"Of course," he said.

She couldn't help but notice that his own eyes were bloodshot as she hugged him good night.

"Shelby?" he called after her when she had stepped into the hall.

She glanced back at him.

"This trip to Maine. You going to talk to Bastien Renaud in person. I know that wasn't easy for you. But you did it, and just look what you accomplished as a result." He took a step toward her. "I'm very proud of you. I just wanted you to know that."

Her throat ached. "Thanks, Dad."

He smiled at her and dramatically shooed her away as he had when she was a child. "Get out of here, would you? And get some rest."

Shelby took the back way to her room in the east wing of the house, not wanting to risk a run-in with Sloan in the hall before she'd had a chance to process all the information she'd just received.

Only when she was safely on the other side of her bedroom door did she allow the tears to come. For her father. For herself. The shame she felt lying to her siblings as they offered undeserved congratulations.

By the time she had plunged into a steaming bath, she felt wrung out and hollow. She'd just dragged a warm washcloth over her face and sunk up to her chin when her phone pinged with a text message.

Blotting her hands on the fluffy towel she'd placed within arm's reach, she blinked her bleary eyes at the phone's screen and felt her stomach somersault.

A text from Bastien Renaud.

When she read it, she couldn't help but hear the words in his deep, scratchy voice.

We need to talk.

Nine

Bastien stared at his screen, willing an answer to his text to materialize.

Because some tech genius thought it would be helpful to know, he could tell his message had been read but not responded to.

Only nine o'clock on the West Coast. And for him it was both too late and too early.

With a sigh, he pushed himself up from the couch and began to pace. He'd made his space as open as he possibly could but had still underestimated the isolating power that a Maine winter could have on a person. He longed for spring, and the times when he could hop on his motorcycle on a whim and hit the road.

His years in prison had left him with a paralyzing

sense of claustrophobia and he knew that his desire to reach out to Shelby was a form of escape.

His phone pinged, and the searing wave of frustration he felt when he saw that it was from his brother Remy bordered on primal.

Gallery show in San Francisco???

News traveled fast. Especially with the advent of the ravenous social-media army of *Bad Boys of Booze* fans constantly posting any damn scrap of information they could find about him to the many pages and Reddit threads the show had inspired.

Which was how he would wager Remy had found out what Bastien had discovered via the search engines he had flagged for any mention of his name. It used to be a trickle that increased to a daily deluge with the wild success of the show. He'd since narrowed the parameters, which had at least cut down on the volume. Which had made the appearance of the email with his name and the Llewellyn Gallery in the subject heading that much more perplexing. Following the link, he'd been led to the gallery's website where, under the events and announcements page, an exhibition featuring his work had been announced for three months' time.

Before he could respond to Remy's text, another popped up from Law in the running thread he had with both his brothers.

Bastien voluntarily entering civilization? The hell you say.

Three bubbles appeared, indicating one of them was composing another reply.

Announcement is a mistake, he answered preemptively. Already reached out to them.

"Them" still hadn't returned his message five minutes later and, in very real danger of looking for something to break, he pulled on his coat and boots and stalked out of the main house to his studio.

Snow crunched under his boots and sparkled like a carpet of crushed diamonds in the blue moonlight. The frigid air crystallized inside his nose and bit his cheeks, and he was grateful for the physical sensation to pull him out of the cyclone of questions in his head.

One, in particular.

Why the hell would she do this?

He knew she was upset when she'd left, but announcing the show after he'd rescinded his agreement was a bizarre choice of revenge. Especially for her.

The large metal door to the outbuilding groaned its protest as he wrenched it open. He made a mental note to oil the track when they had a stretch of days above freezing. Kicking the snow off his boots, he flipped the switch for the industrial heater and scrubbed his hands together in its instant orange glow. He'd turned on all the lights and was circling his current work in progress when his phone began to ring.

Her. Finally.

"Hey," he said.

"Hello." Her greeting was polite, but cool.

"Anything you'd like to tell me?" he asked when she said nothing more.

"Not that I can think of," she said.

He waited through a full inhale and exhale, grappling with his temper.

"You publicly announce that I'm doing a show at Llewellyn Gallery after I told you I wouldn't, and you don't think it's worth mentioning to me first?"

An abrupt splash on the other line almost swallowed her reply. *"What?"*

"You heard me."

"I heard you," she confirmed. "But I have no idea what you're talking about."

Bastien hung the hammer he'd left on his worktable in its appointed place on the pegboard and held the phone away from his face. A quick refresh of the web page in his internet browser confirmed he hadn't imagined the entire thing.

"Go look at your gallery's website."

Silence cracked on the other end until it was interrupted by another splash, followed by a very emphatic curse that made him smile despite the circumstances.

"Where are you?" he asked.

"I...got your text while I was in the tub and—"

"Never mind." Bastien bit the inside of his cheek hard to keep himself from feeding the image developing in his head. "Point is, you can clearly see the show is posted on the website."

"It would appear so," she said after an extended silence.

"But you didn't put it there?"

"Absolutely not," she insisted.

"I'm confused." He picked up a set of pliers and set

them in their appointed spot. "If you didn't put this announcement out there, then who did?"

"Sloan or one of her lesser marketing minions would be my guess. And in the last half an hour, too."

"You told them I turned down the offer and she *still* put an announcement on the website?" he asked.

"Could you hold on a minute?" The ambient sounds on her end disappeared, and he knew she'd muted her line. Probably so she could get out of the tub.

This time, he was utterly unsuccessful at preventing the mental picture. Shelby, naked and wet, her smooth skin glowing a rosy pink from the warm water as she reached for a towel. A potent mix of arousal heated by his simmering anger amplified the wave of lust that rocked him backward onto the stool by his work desk.

He sat up straight when her voice reappeared on the line.

"Alright. I'm back."

He cleared his throat and fixed his attention on his work in progress, still only a framework of twisted metal. "I'm listening."

"The thing is, I had already told my father that you'd agreed to the show before we, er, you—" she hesitated "—changed your mind. I was going to tell him in person when I got home this evening, but he had all my siblings there and champagne at the ready to celebrate—"

Bastien flinched at the gasp-squeak that interrupted her sentence. "What? What is it?"

"My father's assistant. Congratulating me on landing the show and telling me he had her send a note out to the main donors about an opening night reception."

Bastien massaged his brow above a left eye that had begun to throb.

"Oh, God." From the smeared, muffled quality of her words, he guessed she had dropped her face into her hands. "What the hell am I going to do?"

An arrow of guilt pierced the wall of "not my problem" he'd been building ever since the announcement had arrived in his inbox. Hearing the genuine panic in her question, he felt his resolve softening.

"An illness? No, they'd never believe that." She spoke distractedly and at measured intervals.

"Are you pacing?" he asked.

"Why?"

"You sound like you're pacing."

"It helps me think."

Imagining her strolling back and forth in nothing but a towel had precisely the opposite effect on him. He blew out a resigned exhale. "Alright."

The line dropped into a brief silence. "Alright *what*?"

"Alright, I'll do it." Bastien's stomach hardened into a cold ball beneath his ribs. The idea of traveling across the country to face Gerald Llewellyn and a group of his assorted art cronies sounded about as appealing as recreational flaying. But, he supposed, this entire situation was at least partially his fault. Or his brothers and their ridiculous show, which was the only reason the tech magnate knew Bastien's name in the first place.

"You're serious?" The evident relief in her question made him feel about a thousand times worse.

"Yeah," he said, picking at a ball of adhesive on his

worktable. "But I'm only there for the opening night. And I'm not doing any artist talks or anything like that."

"No artist talks," she agreed. "But maybe a small-ish dinner the night before the opening?"

Bastien shook his head, but his censure was only half-hearted at best. He couldn't help but feel a grudging affection for her bottomless tenacity. "I've just agreed to do the show and you're already making another ask?"

"A smallish ask. A pre-ask, really, because I know my father is going to reach out to you and invite you to stay at Green Gables, anyway," she explained.

"I wish he had," Bastien said. "Him, I could say no to."

"Exactly." Hearing the smile in her voice created a curious, spreading warmth in his chest.

He scrubbed his face with a palm and sagged backward against the cabinet. "When am I flying out for this smallish predinner?"

The next several minutes were spent with Shelby giving him names, potential dates, and instructions.

"I promise to make this as painless as possible," she said, finally coming to the end of her efficient spiel.

"It's not the pain I'm afraid of," he said.

"What *are* you afraid of?"

He stared out a window overlooking the very spot where he'd found her the morning after their first kiss, remembering the dizzying rush of relief he'd felt knowing she was safe. Finally comprehending what it really meant.

"People," he said.

And the next two months cemented the many reasons why. His formerly quiet life exploded in a flurry of emails and calls with everyone from specialty transportation companies to insurance adjustors to Sloan Whitley, whose name Bastien had come to dread seeing in his inbox. Her missives consistently came in one of three flavors Bastien cared for not at all: patronizing, passive-aggressive, or pissed-off.

Shelby being her primary target over the course of organizing this circus of a show.

Before he knew it, his studio and several temperature-controlled storage units had been cleaned out, and eleven of his selected pieces awaited their official unveiling at Llewellyn Gallery. The night before his own pilgrimage, Shelby insisted they have one last call to run through the itinerary a final time.

Like the suit hanging from his closet door, the earpiece he wore for the many coordination calls had been a new and surprisingly welcome addition to his life. Now, it allowed him to pack while they spoke.

"And then I'll pick you up at the airport," she said casually , almost as an afterthought.

"I appreciate the offer, but I've already booked a rental car," he said, emptying his sock drawer onto the bed.

"I'm not doing it as a favor." Her voice had taken on a bossy quality he found irresistibly sexy. "There's something I'd like to talk to you about before all the madness begins."

"Something else, you mean? Because I seem to re-

member our having talked several times a week for
the last couple months. In fact," he said, pulling down
his seldom-used carry-on bag from the closet in his
bedroom loft, "it almost feels like we're talking now."

"In person," she said. "And in private."

He had a sneaking suspicion he knew about what.
Of all the topics they had covered in the time since
they'd seen each other last, there was one that they'd
strenuously avoided.

Their ill-advised night together.

Conversations had been friendly, bordering on
flirty, but had never so much as grazed being sexual.
Not that Bastien hadn't thought about it.

Thought about *her*.

"Do I need to be worried?" he asked.

"Not at all," she said. "It's just something I could
use a little help with."

This explanation produced more questions than it
answered, but if his years in prison had taught him
anything, it was patience. Waiting in line. Waiting for
hearings. Waiting for release. As much as the thought
of not having his own transportation filled him with a
humming concern, curiosity overruled it.

"Fine," he said.

Except it wasn't.

Unease gnawed at him in the early hours of the
morning when sleep failed to relieve him, gathering
strength as he called Laney to make sure she remembered that he'd be out of town for a few days.

Back from his Mediterranean cruise, Remy had invited him to come and stay at the home he now shared

with Cosima while Bastien was on the West Coast. He had declined, citing the need to return to Maine right away for vague business reasons he knew his brother was canny enough not to believe. The whole exchange made him feel oily.

He hated lying as much as he hated flying.

It wasn't claustrophobia per se. Even in a plane of the size that made cross-country flights, he would feel the same chest-compressing, throat-constricting concern after the initial liftoff. Knowing that no matter what anyone said or did, there was no getting off this plane until the wheels again touched the ground. Knowing he had zero control of the profusion of elements that needed to go perfectly in order for everyone to survive.

In Bastien's experience, everything going perfectly had been a wildly unlikely scenario. The thought of adding a second and third leg to his itinerary, even to see Remy and Emily, filled him with dread.

Almost as much dread as he felt seeing his name on the sign held by a man in an impeccably neat chauffeur's uniform after he'd survived six hours in the air. He'd come off the plane jittery and tense despite Shelby having booked him in first-class. The additional legroom had helped immensely. His seatmate had not.

Sensing his discomfort, the elderly man had provided him statistics about how much less likely he was to be killed in an airplane than in a car. All the while, Bastien's mind helpfully churned out terrible headlines of the kind he'd come to loathe.

Bad Boys of Booze Brother Burned in Freak Flight Failure!

Just when he was mentally walking through steps to acquire a rental car and spend the next week driving back to Maine, the chauffeur spotted him and waved. It shouldn't have surprised him that Shelby provided physically identifying details.

After refusing an offer of carrying his garment bag to the car, Bastien followed the man out to the parking area reserved for VIPs and their reluctant guests.

"Here we are, sir." The driver inclined his head and held a gloved hand out to a sleek mastery of chrome and glossy black paint—a Mercedes-Maybach. The smell of new leather mingled with a familiar perfume whooshed out to him as the driver stepped aside. Bastien ducked, and only when the door was closed behind him did he allow himself to look across the buttery leather console separating the two back seats.

He almost didn't recognize her. All Shelby's generous softness had been buttoned into a cream-colored suit and black blouse that concealed her curves. Her blond curls were twisted into a tight knot at the nape of her neck. Her wide honey-brown eyes were screened by a pair of stylish black-framed designer eyeglasses. He knew at once this was her gallery look.

Which made sense because, this late in the afternoon, she would have been coming from work.

"Was the Maybach really necessary?" he said quietly as their driver got into the car.

"My father insisted."

My father.

If he never heard those two words again, Bastien could die a happy man.

The car's engine purred to life and they began to glide out of the parking space.

Shelby flicked a shy glance at him before looking back at the console mounted on the headrest of the seat in front of her. "Are you too warm? Too cold? There's individual climate control, you know. Your seat also has a heater if you want." She pointed to the array of buttons just above the armrest on his door and he noticed that her own had been turned on. Two flame-like shapes glowed above the seat hieroglyph.

"I'm fine," he said. Another lie.

From the minute he'd set foot in the tiny Bangor airport, he'd begun to realize the cost of his years of self-inflicted isolation. It left him completely unprepared for the manic, invasive, relentless crush of bodies and egos. The grating impatience, short tempers, petty demands, and outsized blowups over the most minor of inconveniences.

It had left him feeling physically exhausted and mentally burned out.

And he still had to face the gauntlet of meeting Gerald Llewellyn and Sloan Whitley.

Shelby tapped the map icon on the console mounted on the chair in front of Bastien, and he could see their path from the San Francisco airport to her father's estate in the countryside beyond the city.

Forty-five minutes. With an approximate arrival time of 5:30 p.m. Maybe he'd at least have some time to rest and get his head together before this "small-ish dinner."

"So," he said, plunging ahead with the inevitable. "What was it you wanted to talk to me about?"

She sat up a little straighter and swiveled her knees to face him. Business mode. "Sloan is probably going to find a way to grill you about why you agreed to do the show and I just want to make sure that we're on the same page."

Ah.

Bastien's phone pinged, and he fished it out of his pocket to see he had a text from her with an attached document. "What's this?" he asked.

"Notes," she said.

A quick scan revealed what she'd come up with where their history was concerned in a column of neat little bullet points.

- Developed rapport via phone and email last several months.
- Began talking via video calls.
- Decided to meet up in person so I could see pieces not yet on your website.
- Hit it off during my visit and decided to move forward with the show.

"What makes you so certain that she'll ask?"

Shelby reached for a water bottle. "Because she hasn't yet, which means she's saving it for a special occasion."

Bastien slumped back against his seat. "Look, I'll be the first to admit that Sloan isn't exactly the most pleasant person to interact with. But you think you might be just the tiniest bit paranoid?"

She eyed him from behind her chic frames. "This from the guy who assembles entire files on people who so much as deliver a pizza to his place."

Fair point.

"I'm telling you, she's been entirely too solicitous lately," Shelby said. "She's planning something for this show. I just know it."

Bastien perused the list once again. "For this, you felt the need to pick me up from the airport?"

Shelby cleared her throat, worrying the hem of her jacket. "Actually, no."

He waited, bracing himself for additional revelations.

"I was also wondering if you'd like to have sex with me again while you're in town."

It was a damn good thing he hadn't been swallowing liquid when she asked this, or it might have ended up showering the smoked glass shield between them and the driver. Soundproof, he guessed, judging by some of the stories she'd told him about her father's suspicious nature.

"As we've established, I'm terrible at the whole seduction thing," she continued when he didn't answer, "and this way we can at least discuss our terms and make sure everything is clear up front. I enjoyed it, and you seemed to enjoy it, so provided your relationship status hasn't changed—"

"I 'seemed' to enjoy it?" he repeated, incredulous.

Shelby blinked rapidly. If she had rehearsed this

conversation, and he suspected that she had, it wasn't going the way she had planned. "It's also an excellent tension release, which you seem to be experiencing plenty of at the moment." Her eyes flicked to his white-knuckle grip on the door handle.

"I'm being propositioned in broad daylight in the back of a car that costs more than my entire house. Forgive me if I seem a little taken aback."

Her face turned a pink so vibrant that he was surprised her glasses didn't fog. "I'm sorry if I've made this awkward. There's no pressure either way. If you don't want to—"

"Of course, I want to," he answered without thinking. And he did. For years, he'd lived without physical contact of that nature, and having been roused from hibernation, his libido had proven to be much like Ben. Prowling around with claws and teeth, demanding satiation. "But I think there are some factors you may not have considered."

"Such as?"

"Your father."

"What I do with my body is none of his business. And, anyway, he doesn't need to know."

Something about the idea of being her dirty little secret didn't sit comfortably with him. Still, he found this new streak of independence encouraging.

"You say that now. But if he or Sloan picks up on something, that is a whole different ball game."

"What is there to pick up on?" she asked.

"There's a level of comfort with each other's bodies that's noticeable between people who are intimately involved."

Shelby shifted in her seat. "You honestly think my being too comfortable around you is going to be the main problem?"

She had a point there.

"How would you propose this rendezvous takes place?" he asked.

"The suite that we had made up for you connects to mine through a hallway no one has used in years. Once everybody has turned in for the night…" She trailed off, leaving him to imagine their shared seclusion.

"You've been very thorough," Bastien said.

She seemed to relax a little. "Thank you."

"I just have one question."

"What's that?"

Bastien looked out to a clear sky unfettered by Maine's constant border of trees, interrupted only by a long blue smudge of the bay on the horizon. He felt exposed. Vulnerable. Just as he had watching the low country sunsets of tie-dyed outrageous cadmium reds, cotton candy pinks, and ochre yellows by the oil refinery gases.

"After the opening, when I head back to Maine, what then?"

She offered him a neutral smile. "You go back to being a hermit, I go back to being a moderately miserable gallery co-owner who'll never darken your doorstep again."

He thought about the courage it must have required for her, shy but doggedly persistent Shelby Llewellyn, to approach him so brazenly. The woman he'd met almost three months ago never would have made such a request for herself. And especially never purely for her own pleasure. If he could give her nothing else, he could give her that. And then return to protecting the order and sanity of her life by being as far away from it as possible. All this, he told himself while acknowledging his motives for considering her proposition were anything but altruistic.

He wanted her.

After months of attempting—unsuccessfully—to convince himself otherwise, he was finally able to admit it. Every second that ticked by on the display screen only served to amplify that knowledge.

He wanted her, and she wanted him back, and after all the years of his solo existence he still wasn't immune to it.

Despite the twinge in his gut, Bastien held out a hand for her to shake. "Game on, Miss Llewellyn."

"Did you tell Law and Remy you'd be coming out here?" she asked, steering the conversation into less salacious waters.

"I did." He'd failed to mention the romantic connection to Shelby, despite Remy deliberately fishing for details. He didn't think of it as a lie so much as none of their damn business. Hell, a one-night stand Remy had forgotten about completely turned up nine years later and launched the show that was responsible for his current difficulties. Of course, she was also responsible for making his brother—and niece—happier than Bastien had ever seen them. But this hadn't yet served to dislodge the grudge sticking to him like tar. "They're swamped. Between the distillery, kids, the show, life, et cetera."

"That's too bad," Shelby said, returning her gaze to her phone. "With this being your first official show and all."

Bastien shrugged. "My sculptures have never really been their thing."

"Except for the one on 4 Thieves property. Which, I've been meaning to ask you about."

He felt a familiar flicker of irritation at what he knew was coming. He hated having to explain himself, to distill the entire meaning of months of creative labor and its inspiration into concise paragraphs for browsers to ignore while sipping free champagne.

This was as good a practice run as any.

"I've worked out that Law is the hawk, Remy is the coyote, and Augustin is the bobcat. I just can't figure out why you'd have chosen a wild boar for yourself."

No one, not even the keyboard horde, had picked up on this. Seeing the one figure apart from the others, they'd assumed it to be Augustin.

After all, he'd been the one to run off with Law's fiancée and a loan he'd taken out against the business.

"I didn't choose," he said. "Our mother did."

The one subject they had successfully kept from being aired on the show—their mother's story—had undergone a vast transformation in Bastien's mind once Remy had revealed she'd been killed in a car accident a week after she left. Since he'd been an angry fifteen-year-old boy, it'd been embarrassingly easy for Zap to turn him against her. Had he known then what he knew now, he and his father would have come to blows much sooner than they did. And for reasons much more sinister.

Shelby pressed him no further and neither of them felt inclined to fill the silence of the remaining half-hour drive. Highway gave way to suburbs, then to rolling hills and rising ridges of lush green trees until they came upon an old stone wall lit with flickering lanterns.

No sign designated this as the entrance to a 75-acre estate, but Bastien felt the exclusivity practically oozing from the quiet, well-maintained road. The result of old money splendor handily purchased by new money's staggering accumulation.

As was his way, he'd taken it upon himself to make a study of the grounds through the profusion of images readily available in a variety of luxury real-estate websites and magazines that had done elaborate features over the years. Various bits of the information he'd uncovered floated through his head as they wound toward the manor based on an English Cotswold country house. Authentic Roman pool. World-class gardens. Six additional homes. A large spring-fed reservoir. An equestrian center. Expansive orchards. Two private roads. Wooded trails. Breathtaking panoramic views of California's Pacific Coast range.

All of which fell staggeringly short of the actual experience.

Pulling up to the circular drive and the ivy-covered carriage-house-style garage with a mere ten bays, Bastien traded one last look with Shelby before her car door was opened by their chauffeur.

"Everyone will still be at work for a while yet," she said. "I can take you to your suite so you can unwind a bit before dinner."

Music to his ears. "Can we see yours first?"

Shelby shrugged. "If you like."

Collecting his garment bag and over-the-shoulder duffel, he followed her into the house.

Anticipation of dislike had clung to him like fog from the moment he'd awoken this morning. To have it dissipate so quickly after his arrival surprised him. Much of the artwork he'd seen in the featured articles was still present, but made more casual with plants, furniture that looked like people actually sat on it, and a host of other small but significant changes he'd not have expected to find in Gerald Llewellyn's home.

"This way," Shelby said, walking past the main living area and down a hallway to a set of stairs artfully concealed by a tall wood panel he wouldn't have recognized as a door in a million years.

"Took me the longest time to get the hang of this when I was a kid," she said, aiming a playful smirk at him over her shoulder as she climbed the stairs.

Which was when he remembered.

Shelby hadn't been born in this kind of house, either.

She'd been adopted into it.

No story that begins well ends with a child in state custody. He knew this from experience.

They pushed through a door at the top of the stairs that turned out to be a second concealed panel and stepped out into a hallway with a colonnade of arched windows spilling golden light onto a polished parquet floor.

"The main house was built in 1907," Shelby announced, apparently picking up on his appreciation of the ornate crown molding. "If you ever get lost, just remember that my suite is the third on the left after Artemis." She waved a hand toward a bronze whose classic Grecian proportions he couldn't help noticing mimicked her own.

Stopping before a door, she reached into her bag and pulled out a metallic card she flashed at a panel above the door handle. He heard a click, and she pushed through, holding it open for him to follow.

"You hold on to this one," she said, offering the key card. "Just so you can come and go as you need to."

This simple gesture pierced him.

He might be inside Gerald Llewellyn's estate, but *this* was her home. She trusted him to have access to it.

Within her suite of rooms, the shift in mood was immediately noticeable. Whereas understated elegance ruled the rest of the home, Shelby's portion was filled with a chaotic, if lively, energy. Too many plants crammed into the windowsill. Half-burned candles sat on the counter of the kitchenette. Throw blankets strewn on the couch and chaise longue. A round, fat cushion stationed on the floor before a nook bearing shelves of books, candles, and more plants.

He wouldn't characterize the place as messy by any stretch of the imagination, but he could see where horizontal surfaces tended to accumulate objects that didn't necessarily have a home. Magazines. Mail. More books. Wandering over to one, he saw it was a cookbook with a cracked spine cracked and pictures of a distinctly 1960s vintage.

"Is this where you got the idea of putting lentils into spaghetti sauce?" he asked, holding up an image of a green Jell-O mold with dubious aggregate suspended in the transparent shape.

"I collect them," she said by way of explanation. "The bathroom is through that door if you want to scope that out, too."

Of course, it wasn't a bathroom. It was a whole goddamn spa. Marble counters. A shower that was as big as his bedroom and featuring a marble bench in addition to an array of showerheads with various hoses and attachments. Within, he spotted a shelf of potions and lotions, which likely contributed to her almost-good-enough-to-eat scent.

The tub.

The tub she'd been sitting in when she'd called him after the announcement about his gallery showing. Long, deep, and big enough for both of them to fit into, which for Bastien, would be a first. At six-five, he had long ago forsaken any hope of folding himself into what passed for a standard-size tub.

The adjoining suite was every bit as luxurious as hers but completely devoid of warmth by comparison. Bastien passed through the well-appointed living room to an equally stylish master bedroom complete with an equally sumptuous master bath, though some of the finishes differed. Running a hand along the granite countertop, he couldn't help but admire the crafts-manship.

"You're free to make yourself at home," she said. "I was going to run down to the main kitchen and grab a kombucha. Is there anything I can bring you?"

"I don't suppose you have any nonalcoholic beer," he said.

She aimed a sly smile at him. "There's some in the minifridge in your kitchenette."

This indication of her forethought made his chest ache for reasons he didn't dare dig into. "Thank you," he said.

She nodded. "Back in just a bit."

He waited until the door closed behind her and then dug in his pack for the small case containing his toiletries so he could shower the travel film off him.

After a good deal of trial and error, he was able to figure out the shower. Hot water beat down on his tense muscles from four separate jets and Bastien quietly cursed his decision to go with a traditional setup when he'd installed his own bathroom.

Purely out of curiosity—or so he told himself—he picked up a curved bottle with an elegant French script on the label. After flipping the lid open, he breathed in the intoxicating herbal lavender scent he remembered filling his lungs when he'd buried his face in her hair. Scent being the most strongly tied to memory, a slide-show of images followed.

His hands on her breasts. The ample curve of her ass. The absolute peace of being inside her.

"Bastien?"

He nearly slipped when he heard her voice coming through the bathroom door he hadn't bothered to close.

"Yeah," he called back.

"Any chance you could be ready in about fifteen minutes?"

Glancing down at the problem he'd developed while indulging in the memory, he turned the knob to cold. He hissed when the icy blast hit his skin. "Fifteen? I thought we had until seven thirty."

Her answer came through muted by the shower's spray and he only caught every second word. "My father asked if we could come by the gallery before dinner. Sloan mentioned there being a spatial issue she needs your input on."

He quickly rinsed and toweled himself off before swathing the fluffy fabric around his hips and stepping out.

Shelby was stationed in the doorway, her face politely turned toward the bedroom.

"What's the dress code for this evening?" he asked.

"Slacks and a button-down. Tie optional."

"You can look at me, you know," he teased. "Nothing here you haven't seen."

"I know," she said, pretending to study a knurl in the polished wood of the bathroom door. "I'm just going to get changed. Come on through when you're ready."

It took him all of five minutes to dress, comb his wet hair, and check to make sure his freshly barbered beard was still passable. Once he had, he tucked his wallet into his pocket and slipped through the entryway that joined their suites, helping himself to a non-alcoholic beer while he waited.

Shelby emerged ten minutes later, her makeup freshened, her hair in loose waves around her shoulders, and a sleeveless cocktail dress the color of ripe raspberries clinging to her generous curves.

Bastien blinked like she might be a mirage. "You look—"

"Ridiculous," she said, finishing for him, her head cocked to one side as she poked a very large—and very real—diamond stud through the lobe of one ear. "I never should have let Kendall talk me into this."

"Will Kendall be there tonight?" he asked. "Because I'd like to thank her personally."

"She's in Milan for a fashion show," Shelby noted as she stepped into a pair of nude heels. "But I foolishly promised her I'd wear it for tonight's dinner."

He folded his arms across his chest and watched as she flitted from area to area like a manic hummingbird. "Not that I want to offer this up as an option, but if she isn't going to be there, why not just wear something else?"

"I could," she said, pawing through first one drawer, then another. "But she'll see the pictures eventually."

The band of tension around his ribs that had begun to loosen in her presence tightened once again. "Pictures?"

Turning from the kitchen area, she bent over an end table. "Nothing formal. Just a few shots for the website. *There* you are." Triumphant, she slipped a glittering bangle over her wrist and straightened, her smile melting. "What? What's the matter?"

"In the time we've been planning this show, you never mentioned there would be photos."

"I never realized they would present a problem."

He set his half-empty bottle on the counter and stared down into the sink, his stomach roiling. He'd wandered so far into the desolate carnival of his own mind that he startled them both by flinching when she placed a hand on his shoulder.

"Bastien, what is it?"

His jaw remained tight, words he couldn't bring himself to say locked behind clenched teeth.

"Please, tell me," she pleaded. "Why does having pictures of you on an art gallery webpage represent such a problem?"

He blew out a breath and waded in.

"Our father screwed over a lot of people. I ran into one of them while I was in prison. He was under the mistaken impression that what my father owed, he could make me pay."

Her hand flew to her mouth, eyes wide enough to reveal the whites around her amber irises. "Pay *how*?"

Bastien picked up his bottle, grateful for the cool liquid on his parched throat. "Helping him sell contraband. Collecting on outstanding balances." He waited, glancing at her to make sure she'd followed him.

She had.

"I just wanted to do my own time and get the hell out of there, so I declined his offer. He had a bunch of his friends make sure I understood it wasn't an offer."

Her soft pink mouth turned down at the corners and for a moment a profound sense of unreality descended over him. That he could have both been jumped in a prison yard and be standing inside a multimillion-dollar mansion within the same lifetime.

"About a week later, his cell was raided. They assumed I was the one who'd ratted them out. On the inside, it's something you just don't do."

Shelby nodded, her attention riveted.

"The next few years were some of the worst of my life." Both the simplest and most inadequate way to describe what he had endured. "After I was released, I bounced from place to place, never staying anywhere too long until Law, Remy, and Augustin were getting 4 Thieves off the ground. About a year after I moved onto the property, I start getting these strange messages. Some were threats. Others, requests for money. But they all referenced things that happened to me in prison."

"What did you do?" she asked.

"Shockingly, an ex-con receiving threatening notes from another ex-con wasn't high on the police's list of priorities." It had been long enough now that he could joke about it, which was a first.

In real time, the experience had been far more disturbing.

He'd felt like he'd opened the channel for a river of filth to flow through the closest thing to a dream either of his brothers had ever known.

Days buried under crushing, sickening guilt at the thought that he'd drawn this kind ugliness within yards of his niece, barely out of her toddlerhood at the time. Hell, he'd sided with Law against Remy when he had pitched the idea of providing ex-cons job opportunities at the distillery, and that had been years before Emily was born. After, they'd gotten even more careful in selecting their candidates. More deliberate as to where on the 27-acre property they worked and who did the supervising.

Like Remy, Bastien knew more than he'd like to about the kind of choices people made when desperate.

Because the Renaud boys always had been.

"That's when I left the distillery. I figured if I couldn't determine who was sending them or stop it from happening, I could at least make sure they would never be anywhere near someone I cared about."

"And now? Are you still getting them?"

"They stopped after I moved to Maine." He finished the last of his beer and set it on the counter. "For a few precious years, I actually thought I might be able to live out my life in peace. Then *Bad Boys of Booze* started airing, everyone and their damn dog decides to track me down, and I can't tell if the flood of hate messages I'm getting are just media trolls trying to dig up more dirt on my family or—"

"If it might be the same person who was harassing you at the distillery?" she said, finishing for him.

"Yeah," he said. "And every time a new picture of me hits the internet, I can expect a new batch."

"I had no idea." She looked so stricken that for a moment, Bastien felt confused.

"How could you know?"

Shelby's phone lit up in her hand. "Oh, shit," she said, glancing at the screen. "It's seven twenty?" She rushed over to the closet near the front door, yanking a beige trench coat from the hanger, then grabbed her purse. "I'm so sorry. Could we finish this on the road?"

"Finished a long time ago." He held the door open and was surprised when she paused before walking through. "Forget something?"

She took his free hand in both of hers and squeezed it. "Thank you for telling me that."

"Why?"

She shrugged. "Because I get the feeling it's not something you tell a lot of people."

About that, she was right.

Other than her, he'd only ever told one person about what had happened to him in prison.

His brother Augustin.

Ten

Shelby's heart felt like it might leap through her rib cage as the Maybach rolled to a stop in front of the gallery that had become the source of so much hope and heartache in her life. Through the tinted windows of the car, she could make out her father and Sloan, their backs to the large plate glass window and heads tilted toward one another as Sloan pointed toward one of Bastien's sculptures.

I can do this, Shelby told herself resolutely.

I hope, the ever-present tenuous voice in her head added.

She'd imagined this moment many times over the months they'd spent planning the show.

The introduction.

Though she knew it was ridiculous, she couldn't

help but imagine a big, blinking sign over her head—*I slept with Bastien Renaud*—winking in and out above an arrow aimed at her skull.

Would they give away some unintentional hint through body language? Looks that lingered a second too long. Smiles that revealed too much warmth or fondness.

Because she knew Sloan would be watching.

She'd been circling Shelby like a hawk throughout this whole process. Watching for any minor misstep. Second-guessing every suggestion and decision. She hadn't been satisfied with Shelby's explanation as to how she got Bastien to agree to do the show, and she'd been tugging at every detail like a spider testing its web.

Now Bastien was caught in it with her.

It had required every ounce of bravado to ask him her question after she picked him up from the airport. Certainly not the most romantic approach, but romance wasn't what she was after. Which made the growing tenderness she felt toward him all the more problematic.

Hearing his horrific story, she had wanted to wrap her arms around his torso, lay her head against his chest, and hug him hard. She wondered when the last time was that anyone had.

Their chauffeur opened her door, and Shelby glanced back at Bastien, obscenely handsome in his navy slacks and pale blue shirt.

"Ready?"

He grimaced. "As I'll ever be."

"Well, there you are." Sloan conducted a quick full-body scan of Bastien before she stepped forward to clasp Shelby's elbows and noisily air-kiss both cheeks.

"So sorry we're late," Shelby said. "Last-minute catering emergency I had to sort out before tomorrow."

The flat line of her father's mouth took its time in becoming a polite smile. "We'd begun to think you changed your mind," he said, holding out his hand to Bastien. Their clasp was brief but firm. "Gerald Llewellyn. And this is my fiancée, Sloan Bedford Whitley."

"My goodness," Sloan said as Bastien gently accepted her hand. "So rough."

"Occupational hazard." The grin he gave her was the perfect mix of warm and self-deprecating, and the tension in Shelby's shoulders eased incrementally.

"I'm sure one of the two women in my life has informed you how much I admire your work," her father said. "I appreciate you allowing us the honor of hosting your first official exhibition."

"The honor is mine," Bastien said. "This is a remarkable space you've created here."

The four of them fanned out in a line as if admiring the gallery itself like a work of art.

"Why, thank you." Sloan practically levitated with satisfaction. "I apologize for the last-minute change in plans, but I thought it would be best if you looked around tonight in case anything needs changing."

Her way of subtly suggesting that Bastien might want to evaluate Shelby's decisions for himself.

"That's very thoughtful of you, Miss Whitley," Bastien said.

Sloan wound her arm around Gerald's waist. "Please, call me Sloan."

"Me, you can call one lucky bastard." Her father planted a kiss on Sloan's chiseled cheekbone.

"When's the big day?" Bastien asked.

"April twenty-second," Sloan, her father, and Shelby said in unison.

"Wow. That's coming up quick."

"It sure is." Sloan's lips curved in a comically harried smile.

"Planning this exhibition and a wedding at the same time." Bastien's deep voice took on a playful note. "You must have had some amazing help."

"The very best," Sloan said enthusiastically. "Fernando De Burgh. His official title is wedding coordinator, but I personally believe he's an angelic being especially good at tablescapes." She laughed gaily at her own joke, joined by masculine chuckles both from Shelby's father and Bastien. "And, of course, Shelby has been a big help with the exhibition."

Always the afterthought.

"Well, I can't speak for the wedding, but this looks amazing." Bastien let his gaze fall toward the wood floor. "Are these original to the building?"

The rush of gratitude Shelby felt at his changing the subject was indescribable.

"They are." Sloan ducked her head like a schoolgirl. "That's one of the features I loved best when we were considering whether to buy the building."

"I can see why," Bastien said. "Would you mind if I took a look at the lighting over here?"

"Not at all." Sloan fell into step beside him, cheerful as a chickadee as they strolled toward the back of the gallery.

Shelby experienced an inexplicable twist of jealousy.

She understood the importance of creating a professional rapport but didn't think he needed to be *quite* so enthusiastic about ingratiating himself to her father's fiancée.

"That went better than I expected." Sensing her father's proximity with the familiar crisp scent of his expensive aftershave, Shelby glanced at him over her shoulder. "I was a little concerned there when I got your text. You know how Sloan worries about any kind of interruption to the expected schedule."

Oh, she knew.

"Speaking of, remind me when he departs again?" her father asked.

She knew there was no way he hadn't remembered, but answered, anyway. "I'm afraid he needs to leave the morning after opening night."

"So soon?"

"He also owns and runs a shop in Bar Harbor," Shelby pointed out. "It's a small town, but he does pretty swift business with online orders."

"It's just, I have a tee time scheduled on Sunday morning and thought he might like to join."

"He doesn't golf, Dad."

"It's not just about the golf." He chuckled. "We were

going to visit Silver Branch Cellars afterward. Porter mentioned they're unveiling their new Amarone."

Shelby smiled patiently. "He doesn't drink, either."

Gerald's eyebrows lowered. "Has he had trouble in that area?"

Rich irony for him to be asking this.

"Believe it or not, some people prefer sobriety as a lifestyle without needing a problem to justify it."

After having heard Bastien's story about his art teacher, she suspected this might not be true in his particular case, but didn't feel her father was owed an explanation either way.

"And what else did you learn about the artist during your night snowed in at his house?"

Shelby felt heat creeping up her neck and turned to look at Bastien and Sloan across the gallery before the flush could make its way to her cheeks. "He makes a decent Bolognese sauce. He first became interested in sculpture when a neighbor taught him how to do soap carvings. He had this house invaded by a bear last spring, and he likes lentils."

"Bastien?" her father asked. "Or the bear?"

She rolled her eyes, grateful for the terrible joke and the tension between them it released.

"Both, I think."

"Is that all?" her father asked.

It wasn't.

She had learned that Bastien was protective, resourceful and brave. That he liked Brahms and the blues. That he made her feel alive.

None of which she could share with the person she loved best in all the world.

"Pretty much," she said.

The staccato burst of Sloan's laughter bounced off the gallery's modular walls moments before they rounded the corner, one of her hands brushing Bastien's forearm as the other fluttered near her neckline.

"A tent stake? Really?" she asked, actual tears of mirth in her eyes. "You're kidding, right?"

"God's honest truth," Bastien said. "If it weren't for the hole in the back of my pants, I might have gotten away with it."

Sloan dabbed at the corners of her eyes with the tip of her index finger as she rejoined them. "Bastien was just telling me about the time a hubcap saved his life."

"That sounds like quite the ordeal." Her father held out his arm and Sloan nestled against his side effortlessly. "Are we ready to go to dinner then?"

"I thought you'd mentioned there would be a photographer getting some candid shots first." Shelby folded her arms across her chest, already wondering if she could somehow manage to keep the trench coat on for the remainder of their evening.

"Oh," Sloan said. "I'm afraid he had to cancel at the last minute, but he'll be here tomorrow night."

Bastien stiffened in her peripheral vision.

"Shall we take my car?" her father asked. "That way we can all ride together."

Shelby couldn't think of anything she wanted less.

"No offense, darling, but I don't know exactly

how well Mr. Renaud will fit in the back seat of your Porsche."

"He can ride in the front then. Give you and Shelby time to chat about any last-minute details for tomorrow."

Sloan wanted to protest, but not enough to raise objections in front of Bastien, Shelby guessed.

"Alright," she said. "Let me just get my bag and we can be on our way back to Green Gables."

"Actually, I was thinking Mr. Renaud might enjoy dinner at the Pier Club. Give him a chance to see a little more of the city since he's in town for such a short time," her father suggested.

Panic rose in Shelby's chest, high and bright as a naval flare.

She should have anticipated this. Should have seen that her father would want to shape the evening in some way.

The Pier Club was the exact opposite of where she would have taken a man like Bastien Renaud. White linen tables and place settings with a small army of utensils and crystal stemware. Menus with small portions and pretentious names. Worst of all, a reliable crowd of tech bros and the supermodels they dated, all wanting to prove they could get a table.

For the first time in perhaps their entire acquaintance, Shelby hoped Sloan would argue.

"Of course," Sloan said. "Let me just call the house and let the kitchen staff know we won't be back for dinner." She sauntered off in the direction of her office, leaving the three of them.

"I hope you don't mind the change in plans."

He did. Shelby could see it all over his face.

"Food is food to me." He shrugged.

"So Shelby tells me. She also tells me you don't golf, you don't drink, and you occasionally entertain bears." Gerald's chuckle was dry and mirthless. "If you tell me your alma mater is on the east coast, I might just have to run you out of town now."

Shelby shot her father a look that he completely ignored.

"You're in luck," Bastien said, leaning a little closer to her father. "I don't have a college degree."

"And yet you've done well enough for yourself to build your own home, start your own business, and buy a few acres. What a wonderfully inspiring story that must be for others who find themselves in your situation."

The tight feeling in her stomach had progressed to a full-on cramp. This conversation was headed downhill, and fast. *What the hell was her father doing?*

"Are you referring to the educational situation or the incarceration?" Bastien asked. "I'm just trying to figure out exactly who it is I'm supposed to be inspiring."

In another first for the evening, Shelby was relieved when Sloan reappeared before her father had a chance to answer.

The drive to the restaurant was so awkward, Shelby was ready to hurl herself from the still-moving car by the time they arrived. They were promptly ushered to a table by the wide windows overlooking the bay by a maître d' who addressed her father by name.

Slipping the belt from her waist, she quickly shrugged out of the trench coat and sat down. As predicted, Sloan's eyes lasered in on the garment.

"Is that new?" she asked. "I don't think I've ever seen you wear it before."

"Kendall brought it back from Paris after the last show," Shelby said, reaching for her water goblet.

"I do envy the French their confidence." Sloan sighed. "But then, runway couture is all about making a statement, isn't it?"

Shelby bit the inside of her cheek and kept her eyes trained on the menu. Rising to the bait would only guarantee this dinner would quickly devolve from annoying to miserable. After ordering drinks and appetizers, they sat in strained silence until the two-tier tower of oysters had arrived.

"You seem awfully quiet tonight, Shelby," Sloan observed as she unfolded her napkin over her lap.

"She's probably just nervous about the opening tomorrow," her father answered for her.

"Are you?" It was the first time Bastien had addressed her directly all evening. Seated to her left at the table, his hand rested mere inches from her elbow. She longed for its warmth and weight on her knee, for the comfort it would provide her.

Shelby cleared her throat. "Not nervous, really. I just spent so much time planning everything. Now I have to wait and see if it all goes right."

"Oh, you'll get used to that." Sloan accepted a glass of champagne from their server and gazed wistfully into the sparkling liquid. "I remember my first gallery show. It seems like forever ago now."

"This *isn't* my first," Shelby reminded her.

"Right." The marble-sized diamond on her engagement ring sparkled like a miniature disco ball as she laced her pinkie with Gerald's. "I forget about that little place you worked in SoMa."

Little.

Shelby couldn't argue that it accurately addressed the space's physical size, but it had felt friendly and safe. Her leaving it was the reason Sloan Whitley had come into her—and her father's—lives. She'd cursed her decision ever since.

"What it lacked in square footage, it more than made up for in style," her father said. "And with Shelby's charm and your sophistication, Llewellyn Gallery will be the best of both." He raised his glass in a toast and lifted it to his lips, the amber liquid already half-drained.

"Will be?" Sloan's laugh was deceptively merry. "Because before we stuck the name Llewellyn on it, my gallery was basically a shoebox with drawings tacked to the wall, right?"

Gerald began dressing an oyster, his hands working calmly while his face betrayed his irritation. "You're being a little hyperbolic, don't you think, darling?"

"Am I?"

Though they were far from her favorite, Shelby lifted a glistening shell from its bed of pebbled ice. "Are these the Kumamotos?"

"It certainly feels that way to me," her father said, ignoring the question.

"And if I made a comment about how Llewellyn Enterprises would be a world-changing technology company once my son had joined your staff?" Sloan gave him a pointed look.

"Seeing as you don't have a son, I'm not sure I understand your meaning."

"My point is, I worked to make the Bedford Whitley Gallery a profitable and elite operation long before you bought it, and before Shelby joined the management team."

"Are you suggesting the additional money I invested in the new building hasn't helped?" Gerald looked almost more amused than annoyed.

"Not at all, *darling*." Sloan extracted her hand from his and reached for her champagne glass. "Merely pointing out that yours wasn't the only offer."

Shelby's hands were cold and clammy beneath the tablecloth and her throat ached with the threat of tears she desperately didn't want to shed in front of everyone.

"Please excuse me. I need to run to the restroom." She dropped her napkin in her chair and wove through the tables, a race against the sheen already blurring her vision. She reached the restroom just in time and found it blessedly unoccupied. Shelby quickly locked the door and sank to the velvet banquette provided for nursing mothers.

She must have been out of her mind.

Thinking she could bring Bastien all the way across

the country and subject him to her world, expecting that everything would magically turn out perfectly. Of all the things she resented about herself, gleamingly irrational optimism mocked her the most. The disastrous combination of naiveté, stubbornness, and hope.

Hope was always what hurt you. When would her ridiculous, relentless heart learn this?

Hadn't the first seven years of her life been evidence enough?

She let herself have another thirty seconds and then gently dabbed her damp cheeks, careful not to smear her makeup.

A quiet knock on the door startled her. "Just a moment," she called back.

"Shelby?"

Bastien.

"I'm fine. I'll meet you back at the table in just a moment." She stared at her pink, watery eyes and took a few more breaths before forcing a smile onto her face and unlocking the door.

Bastien was there when she swung it open.

"You were supposed to go back to the table."

"And risk being stabbed with a shrimp fork?" His smirk did wonders to lift her spirits.

"Still wrangling about the gallery?" she asked.

"They've moved on to the wedding now."

Shelby felt her entire soul deflate with her exhale.

"Want to get out of here?" he asked.

"As appealing as that sounds, we can't just up and leave."

Bastien arched a dark eyebrow at her. "Why not?"

"Because that would be rude."

"Ruder than fighting in front of your daughter and a total stranger in the middle of a restaurant you didn't even ask if either wanted to come to in the first place?"

When he put it like that...

"Don't you think it'll look a little odd if we suddenly leave together?"

"You forget. I'm a temperamental and famously reclusive artist. Odd is my specialty." Mischief gave his features a distinctly boyish air.

"I'm listening," she said.

"I walk out of here and wait for you outside. You go back to the table, and when I haven't come back from the restroom after a couple minutes, you insist on coming to check if I'm okay. While you're 'checking,'" he said, making air quotes with his fingers, "you'll receive a text from me about feeling uncomfortable and heading back to the house. You'll forward it to your father and Sloan and tell them you're heading back to the house to salvage things. They feel awkward for ruining the dinner and we get out of here. It's a win-win."

Shelby had to admit, his idea was pretty solid—except for the feeling-awkward part. She wasn't sure either her father or Sloan was capable of acknowledging their fault in something they would consider a completely normal part of the family gathering.

"Shouldn't we be synchronizing our watches or something?" she asked.

Bastien lowered his face to speak close to her ear. "Believe me, Shelby. I'm already counting the minutes."

Her body responded with surprising swiftness, a

fluttering clench behind her belly button followed by damp heat gathering between her thighs.

The plan worked even better than she thought it would.

Sloan appeared genuinely upset at Bastien's departure, if only to further vex her father, who muttered something about manners below his breath.

As soon as Shelby had exited the crowded waiting area and stepped on the sidewalk, she pulled in a cool lungful of night air. When she didn't see Bastien, she ventured down the street toward the valet stand and gasped when he appeared in the shadows between the restaurant and the building next door.

"Hey!" she protested as he tugged her into the alley with him. "What do you think you're doing?"

Her answer came in the circle of his big, strong arms. "I'm sorry you have to deal with that shit," he said.

"It wasn't this bad before they got engaged," she said. "I mean, yeah, they'd snipe at each other every now and then. But nothing like this. And I want him to be happy. I really do. But he's a different person with Sloan. If you'd met him back when mom was still alive, I think you two would have actually gotten along really well."

"Have you ever told him how you feel?" he asked.

"Not in so many words," she said.

"Why not?"

"I feel like if I did that, he'd have to take sides."

"Sides?" he repeated. "You're his daughter."

Shelby placed her hands against his chest to draw

back and look up at him. "I'm his *adopted* daughter, Bastien. Every day of my life, I wake up knowing how incredibly lucky I am. I'm supposed to look at the man who saved me from that hell and tell him that the woman who lifted him out of his grief is kind of annoying?"

Only when she saw his jaw flex did she realize what she'd inadvertently revealed.

They hadn't spoken of her childhood in detail in any of their conversations. Her years in foster care or the years before it. Shelby had the sense that he already knew. He'd lived the same and worse.

"Yes," he said firmly. "Want to know why?"

"Why?" she asked.

"Because you care about him, and he knows it."

"But what if he goes through with the wedding even after I tell him how I feel? Won't that just make things worse?"

Bastien lifted his hand from her waist and brushed her hair away from her cheek. "If anyone could deliver that kind of message without making things worse, it would be you."

A swarm of butterflies took flight within her as he shaped his hand to her jaw. "Now can we please go back to your place before I'm tempted to take you right here against this brick wall."

She tossed her curls over her shoulder. "How do you know that isn't what I've been planning all along?"

"With this dress, you mean?" he asked, bunching a handful of the fabric in his fist.

"With the underwear I'm not wearing under it."

His nostrils flared and his lips set in the hard, de-termined line she'd come to associate with his being turned on.

The hand he'd fisted in the skirt released and moved downward to palm her ass, seeking, but not finding, evidence to disprove her assertion.

"God damn," he growled.

"Want me to call the driver?" she asked.

"Already on it." He glanced over her shoulder to where a standard yellow taxi waited at the curb. "Shall we?"

"Absolutely."

He opened the cab door and she slid to the opposite side so he could scoot in after her. The cabbie did a double take in the rearview mirror when she provided the address.

The ride home seemed to last no longer than a minute and yet somehow stretched forever. Delicious anticipation gathered like a coming storm, bringing awareness to every part of her body that he touched.

And he touched plenty.

Concealed in the darkness of the back seat, his rough fingertips traced slow circles on the inside of her thigh, occasionally stroking the crease at the back of her knee.

How had she lived this much of her life without knowing that even this part of her body could be an erogenous zone if touched by a man who knew the art?

She glanced over to see him watching her face.

Shelby was dying to touch him in return, but evi-dence of his arousal would be much harder to hide from any staff they might run into when they arrived at the property. Thankfully, they saw not another soul once they'd let themselves into the house and made their way to her suite.

With shaking hands, she fished her key card out of her purse and swiped it across the sensor. Bastien took his time relieving her of her purse, helping her step out of her shoes, then removing his own before setting down his wallet and phone on the entryway table.

Shelby leaned against the wall in the small foyer, watching this careful preamble. Despite having consumed only a few sips of wine, she felt like she was flying. "You know what drives me crazy about you?"

Bastien untucked his shirt and began flipping open the buttons. "Will this be a bullet-point list as well?"

"Your patience," she said.

"Only when it's something I want to make last as long as possible." He took her by the hand and led her to the master bedroom, pausing before the walk-in closet to turn on the switch.

"Turn around," he said.

She did.

Cool air kissed the back of her neck as he lifted her hair and unzipped her dress. She waited, anticipating his reaction when he discovered her little secret.

"Hey." He hooked a finger through the scant, barely there thong he'd failed to feel through the fabric. "What's this about?"

"Maybe I was just trying to tempt you into taking me against the brick wall."

Shelby rested a hand on this shoulder and stepped

out of her dress with his help, impressed when he located an empty hanger and hung it up. "You look too good in that for anything to happen to it."

He flipped off the closet light, then turned and walked her backward. "But if it's a wall you want..."

Even this he did slowly, bending down to feather kisses over at the curve of her jawline, her ear, and the base of her neck before anchoring his hand in the hair at her nape. She relaxed into his grip, exposing her throat for his careful exploration. The contrast between the seductive softness of his tongue and the scrape of his facial hair would have had her curling her toes if she wasn't afraid of melting into floor.

She moaned as he worked his way upward, sucking, licking, nipping until her breath was shallow and fast and her whole body an extension of heat kindled low in her middle. Only then did he claim her mouth in a hungry, dizzying rush.

Shelby grabbed fistfuls of his soft undershirt to hold herself steady, stretching up on tiptoe to flatten her body against his.

Bastien released her hair, his hands moving downward to cradle her ass and drag her up his body. His erection branded her belly, then her hip, then nudged the sweet ache between her thighs as Shelby wrapped her legs around his waist, hooking her ankles behind his hips. Bastien lifted her higher, the fingers cupped beneath her buttocks helping spread her as he leveraged the wall to grind against her in slow, torturous undulations.

Shelby gasped when he increased the pressure, one

of his hands moving further toward her center to slide beneath the scant scrap between her legs.

"Fuck," he groaned, finding her slick with need. "I want to taste you."

Bastien pulled back and repositioned her, carrying her past the bed and—to her surprise—into the bathroom, where he lowered her onto the marble counter. They broke the kiss long enough to strip off his undershirt and came back together as if magnetized while he made quick work of his belt, button, and zipper.

Shelby reached between them and moaned into his mouth as she shaped her grip to his erection.

Bastien wrenched himself away, panting. "You first, baby. Always."

He sank to his knees, pushing her thighs apart and running his fingers over her through her panties. "Should I take my time? Taste you." He dipped to push the flat of his tongue against her aching nub, making her entire body jump. "Torture you," he said, dragging his lips along the part of her the elastic didn't cover.

"Or…" He waited until she was gazing down at him to pull her panties to the side. "Should we see just how fast and hard I can make you come?" Bastien split her open with the pointed tip of his tongue and fluttered it around her swollen bud.

Shelby's entire body jerked, and her head fell back, her breasts heaving with her already ragged breath.

"I think we have our answer." He lifted his head and she felt something akin to grief at the loss of the delicious sensation.

"I need you to do something for me," he said.

At that moment, she would have promised to bring him the ocean, drop by drop, if it only meant she could have his mouth back.

"What?" she asked.

He was touching her again, rocking the heel of his palm against her and pressing his fingers against the indentation just above her mound. "Slide the cups of your bra down, but don't take it off."

She sat forward, shrugging her bra straps down her arms, and pulled the cups free of her breasts.

"That's perfect, baby." The warmth and gentle pressure between her legs was building. Deepening. "Now, I want to see you touch them."

Shelby's cheeks burned, but she complied, cupping her breasts in her hands, slowly kneading them as he had done.

"Does that feel good?"

"Yes," she said.

"When you feel yourself getting close, I want you to pinch your nipples. Can you do that for me?"

She nodded.

"Show me."

Rotating her hands, Shelby rolled the taut buds between her thumb and index finger and bit back a cry.

"Perfect." Bastien slid a hand up her calf until it met the back of her knee and lifted onto one of his wide shoulders. The sandpapery rasp of his beard grazed the inside of her thigh, and it was everything she could do not to whimper in anticipation.

His fingers were on her again, pressing her sex to reveal the slick, swollen nub he'd teased to aching life, and when his mouth followed, Shelby thought she might die.

She felt his warm, soft lips kiss there, as he would have done to her mouth, plying her petals apart in concert with the sensuous undulations of his tongue. Shelby concentrated on the sensation, wanting to burn it onto her memory. The way he curled, and stroked, and circled all within a handful of seconds that felt like an eternity. Just when she thought he'd changed his mind about wanting to take this slow, he sucked her bud between his lips and began fluttering the tip of his tongue against her and moaning at the same time. Had her hands not already been on her own breasts, she might have forgotten what he'd asked her to do. Rhythmic pulses of bliss shot from her breasts to her sex and a cry ripped from her lips as her torso lurched upward.

In the aftermath, she lay limp and boneless, breathing hard as she returned to earth.

"I'm sorry." Bastien gripped the counter to rise from his knees and gathered her to his chest.

"Sorry?" she murmured incredulously against his chest. "For *what*?"

He pulled back to look at her.

"*That's* what I should have done our first time."

Shelby adjusted her bra to recover her half-exposed breasts.

"If I would have even let you," she said. "I couldn't even let you look at me, remember?"

"Oh, I remember," he murmured.

Shelby was quiet and content, turning an idea over in her mind. "There is something *I* wanted to do." She sat back so she could look him in the eye. "Something I've wanted to do since the moment we met."

Bastien's dark lashes lifted from his rock-chip cheekbones. "What's that?"

Smiling through kiss-swollen lips, Shelby pressed a hand against his sternum, slid down from the countertop, and walked backward toward the tub. She sat down on the edge, crooking a finger to beckon him over.

A strangled groan filled his throat as he came to her and stood still as she stripped off his boxers. "You're killing me. You know that, right?"

Shelby wrapped her fingers around his cock and began gliding them up and down in measured strokes. "You seem pretty alive to me."

His head fell backward, his eyes closed, and with hands and lips and tongue, she learned him. Every ridge and ripple. Silk and steel. Flesh and fire. All hers to command.

The ridges of his abdominal muscles sharpened as he tensed, hissing a breath through clenched teeth when he nudged the back of her throat. She fell into a rhythm, taking him deeper and deeper still, until his fingers tangled into her hair and his hips began to move.

"Oh, God, baby," he crooned. "Your mouth feels so damn good."

She moaned around him and felt him twitch on her tongue.

"Wait." The word came out as a harsh whisper. He jerked himself back.

"I'm not finished with you yet." Shelby almost didn't recognize the throaty purr of her own voice.

Recognition flared fire into his ash-gray eyes. "You don't have to do that."

She traced the slope carved by the trenches narrowing into his groin. This part of him was more beautiful than any marble statue she'd studied in her long fascination with art. This man, so long without pleasure, who'd held her on a street so far from the home that had been his respite and his refuge. A fortress whose walls she had breached for purely selfish purposes.

"I want to."

Bastien molded a hand to her cheek and swept her lower lip with the pad of his thumb. "I've never met anyone like you, Shelby Llewellyn."

She kissed his scarred knuckle and returned it to his side. "You should get out more."

He let himself be drawn forward, surrendering at last.

Instead of resuming where she'd left off, she leaned forward and traced the sharp trough above his hip with her tongue, following it with small kisses all the way to his navel. Her lips grazed the silky head of his erection, her breath dancing over the skin she'd dampened. She did this several times, always pulling away at the last second. Teasing. Tempting. Then taking him all at once.

Bastien roared his release in a single, primal note that the acoustics of the bathroom amplified. She watched him come apart in wonder. The individual beads of sweat that crawled down the ladder of his rib cage. His bared teeth and dark hair falling in his eyes.

Hers.

All hers.

How had she never known this kind of torture could feel as sweet for the giver as it was for the recipient? That his every grunt and growl could fill her with a heady draught that obliterated any traces of fear or self-consciousness?

Or was it only the act of giving *him* pleasure that would move her this way?

The thought made shadows creep into the edges of her vision.

Because she knew how untenable any shared future was. No matter how safe the circle of his arms might feel. No matter how miraculous it seemed to have his whole, huge frame and the good heart within it quaking in her hands.

He was not hers to keep.

Eleven

"You mean to tell me, while we were sitting at Sergei's bar together, you were thinking about *that*?" Bastien twirled the bottle of nonalcoholic beer he'd been nursing, the condensation forming rivulets fed by steam from the tub. Drawing a bath had been his first order of business when his soul returned to his body.

Securing food and beverages had been his second.

"I mean, not that exact scenario, but…yes." Shelby sat between his outstretched legs, her back to him and knees hugged to her chest beneath foamy bubbles. "Does that shock you?"

"A little."

She tucked an escaped tendril back into the pile on her head before reaching for her flute of prosecco. "Don't tell me you thought that men have the corner market on fantasizing about strangers."

Maybe.

"Just out of curiosity," he said, "what *was* the scenario?"

Shelby glanced over the shining curve of her naked shoulder. "You really want to know?"

"I asked, didn't I?"

Water lapped at the edges of the gigantic tub as she turned to face him. "It was basically a rewrite of our first meeting at your shop in Bar Harbor."

"You mean, instead of my being asshole and ignoring you?"

"Oh, you were still an asshole in my scenario. But instead of pretending to browse then following you when you left, I asked you about the moving mobile piece with all the carved wooden keys and you told me it wasn't for sale." Shelby plucked a strawberry from the bowl and offered it to him before taking one for herself.

"So I was even *more* of an asshole in your fantasy?"

She shrugged. "In my fantasy, the piece also had deep sentimental meaning, if it helps."

"Not much," he said. Holding out his hand, he collected the leafy green cap of her berry and tossed them both into the small trash bin. "And then?"

"*And then* I asked whether you'd be interested in a *different* kind of payment for the sculpture and, after some tough negotiating…you agreed."

"We were alone in the shop?"

"Not at all. But we were alone in the loft," she explained. "No one could see from that angle."

"But it wouldn't keep them from hearing," he pointed out.

Shelby gave him a knowing smirk. "Which is why you had to be very, *very* quiet."

Bastien stared at her, his world having taken an abrupt leap off its axis. That all this had been happening inside her head while he sat two stools away, completely oblivious, blew his mind.

"I hope I at least said thank you." He found her ankle beneath the water and wrapped his hand around it. Every now and then, he found himself awestruck by the simple grace and perfection of the human body, painfully aware that he'd never carve or construct anything so elegant.

"You did a lot more than that," she said.

"Wrote you a note?"

She playfully splashed water at his chest. "What about you?"

"What do you mean, *what about me*?" Noticing his fingers beginning to prune, Bastien reached for a towel from the stack they'd placed next to the tub and mopped the water droplets from his face.

Shelby swiveled her knees under her and bent down to unstop the tub drain. "I mean, did you have any thoughts about me when we first met?"

He stood and stepped out as the drain began its throaty gurgle. "All kinds of them."

She looked at him expectantly. "I told you mine."

Bastien helped her step out of the tub, wrapping a

towel around her shoulders before swathing the other around his hips. "I'd rather show you."

Cheeks already glowing pink from the bath and the sparkling wine deepened a shade. "You mean you can…again? This soon?"

The thought that she had done what she'd done thoroughly *not* expecting more made him suddenly, violently angry.

And hard.

He let his towel fall to the tile and took her by the hand, leading her to the bed. After evicting a small army of throw pillows, he slid between soft, sky-blue sheets and held the comforter up for her. "You coming in or not?"

"Al-l-l-lright," she said, clearly piqued by the order of operations. Her own towel puddled to the floor, and she quickly slid in and pulled the duvet up to her chin.

"This?" she asked. "This is what you thought about the first time you saw me?"

"Almost." Bastien tugged the elastic from her hair and fanned it over the pillow in a golden cloud before finding her hip and rolling her onto her side with her back to him. He then dug one arm beneath her pillow and banded the other around her waist, drawing her toward him until their bodies met in a long, serpentine line. Her shoulder blades against his chest. Her spine against his belly. The soft curve of her buttocks against his upper thighs and cock pressed to the gentle dip of her lower back.

He had known it would be like this.

From the second he'd seen her in her painfully new

puffy vest, her tractionless boot heels hooked onto the foot rail of the barstool, he had known.

The same way he knew which piece of wood contained the shape he needed for a sculpture.

Instinct.

Animal ken buried deep in the subconscious. A finer, keener sense than words could provide.

They lay there like that until he felt her begin to relax against him. No longer waiting for what came next. Living only now. Only for this.

Bastien buried his face in the sweet silk of her hair, eyes closed, whispering near her ear.

"It's freezing outside." He felt the vibration of her giggle.

"But it's—"

"Freezing cold. Bitter. Biting. Sheets of snow are tearing through the pines. Piling up against the house as the wind howls." Beneath the covers, he began slowly stroking the curve of her hip, following it up to her waist, and slowly back down her thigh. "But in here, we're safe, and warm." His fingers trailed lower, brushing the barest edge of her sex from behind.

"There's a fire in the old woodstove. Shadows dancing on the walls."

Bastien pressed his palm against the source of her heat, gently plying her thighs apart until he could feel her still-damp down with the tips of his fingers. Her rib cage expanded as she held a breath.

"There's the scent of woodsmoke and the pages of old books from the stack next to you on the nightstand."

Like a sleeper weaving bits of nearby conversation

into a dream, he'd unintentionally pushed two rooms on the opposite sides of the country together in his mind, melding their worlds.

"Hyacinths," she murmured.

"Hmm?" He'd begun to delve deeper, feeling her, slick and silky, warm from their bath.

Shelby curled her hips into him, opening to his touch. "Hyacinths. They bloom indoors…in the winter."

"Hyacinths," he agreed. His exploration of her body took on the quality of a Sunday stroll. Allowing himself to enjoy the act of discovery without any pressing need to arrive at a final destination. Pausing to spend extra time in places that made her gasp or sigh. Circling back around to a place he'd just been purely to revisit parts of her he loved to touch. By the time he withdrew his arm from beneath the pillow to push up on his elbow, she was soaked with need, trembling at his breath on her neck.

He gazed down at her, panting and flushed, dark lashes fanned against her cheek, a look of concentration creasing her forehead.

Criminal, that she had spent so much of her adult life giving pleasure and expecting none in return. Generous to a fault. Her heart was an open larder and his had been a locked vault. And she, bright-eyed and optimistic, had simply waltzed right past every protection he'd put in place.

Noticing the lapse in motion, her eyelids fluttered open.

"I need to go grab something," he said.

"Look in the nightstand."

Bastien rolled over and pulled open the drawer, glancing back at her when he noticed the condoms were the same brand they'd used at his house in Maine. Which meant she'd bought these with the hope that he'd agree to sleep with her, knowing they'd be a reminder of the rejection if he hadn't.

The thought almost unmanned him on the spot.

He tore a foil packet and sheathed himself before rejoining her. She wriggled backward to press herself against him once more.

"I have a confession to make," he said.

Shelby angled her chin to look behind her. "Kind of a precarious time to be making confessions, don't you think?"

"I didn't think about doing this the first time we met."

"No?"

Bastien shook his head. "I'd already been thinking about it for a year by then."

Her eyebrows lowered. "How's that?"

He let his fingers trail over her navel, marveling at the way her skin broke out into gooseflesh beneath his lightest touch. "Your voice mails."

"What about them?"

"I thought you had a sexy voice."

"Me?" The smooth, slightly rounded terrain of her belly jumped beneath his fingertips when she laughed. "What did you find sexy about it?"

Unable to resist the temptation of her peaked, rosy nipple, he lightly brushed it with his thumb. "You sounded smart. Sophisticated. Kind of bossy. But my favorite ones were when you were clearly annoyed at me."

"So...all of them?" Her teeth sank into her lower lip as he circled her aureole.

"Pretty much."

"And *what*? You'd listen to them and think of me curled up naked next to you in your bed?"

"Seeing as I was usually in my bed when I listened to them, that seemed like a pretty natural extension."

How she bloomed with this kind of reassurance, a flower unfolding toward the sun.

"Did you ever...?" She trailed off, her gaze equal parts sly and shy.

"Did I ever...?" Bastien repeated with feigned ignorance, unable to resist nudging her out of her comfort zone.

"While you listened to my voice mails and imagined me in your bed. Did you ever...participate?"

"Define 'participate.'"

She gave an exasperated sigh and buried her face in the pillow. "Never mind."

Reaching under the covers, Bastien found her hand and molded it around his aching cock, sandwiching her palm beneath his as he guided it up and down.

"Did I ever do this while listening to your voice? Is that what you're asking?"

She nodded, looking at him beneath heavy lids.

"Once or twice," he admitted. "A month."

She shook her head, visibly amused. "All that time, I thought you never answered the phone or replied to my texts because I didn't matter enough to respond to."

Because *I* didn't matter enough, she'd said.

Bastien made sure her gaze was focused on him before he spoke. "I didn't answer the phone because I was afraid if I ever heard your live voice on the line, I'd say yes to your gallery show. And I never told you no by email or text, because I was afraid if I did, you'd stop calling." He released her hand and brought his above the covers to press it against the elegant curve of her jaw. "You matter, Shelby. During one of the darkest times of my entire life, you mattered more than you'll ever know."

The naked gratitude in her eyes flooded his chest with molten gold.

"Thank you for saying such beautiful things to me, Bastien." Her hand had begun to move without his help, so he busied his own.

Bastien cupped her breast and bent to her, painting lazy circles around the tawny pearl with his tongue, gently testing it with his teeth until her breath came in ragged gasps and her fingernails dug into his thigh.

"Sebastien," she sighed.

How long had it been since anyone used his full first name? On her lips, it sounded equal parts prayer and praise.

She ground against him, their bodies sliding on a film of sweat.

"That's it, baby," he murmured against her.

Shelby's back arched and she gripped him by the base, taking him to the hilt just as the first pulses of her release gripped his cock.

They cried out at the same time. Her, in ecstasy. Him, in purgatory.

Bastien didn't move until every flutter and clench

had ceased. Only then did he begin the slow undulation. Curling his hips in a wave that required every ounce of restraint. Slowing whenever the tension coiled at the base of his spine threatened to whip through him like a downed power line.

He'd arrived at just such a juncture when, in a turn of events that left him open-mouthed and stunned, Shelby rolled herself on top of him.

"Psst," she said, jerking her chin toward the end of the bed where a full-length mirror stood opposite.

At which point, he realized he could watch both angles.

"Who *are* you?" he asked.

Then she began to move, and his IQ dropped below the capability of speech.

Hesitantly at first, her hips rolled in a serpentine undulation that ended at her shoulder blades before beginning again. His gaze flicked between this and the mirror, where, reflected in a standing pool of silver, he watched her breasts rise and sway, her stomach tense, and her face contort in time with her surges.

"Fuck me, baby," he panted. "Let me feel you."

Her back arched and he felt her contract around him. Silk, heat, and insanity.

His hands floated to the generous flare of her hips, fingertips sinking into her flesh as he thrust upward with her descent. Each time, their cries increased in volume and intensity until he could no longer tell where hers began and his ended.

Those first primal pulses wrapped around the root of his cock, and like a lit fuse, he felt the fire flash through him. Bastien's torso jerked upward as he lost himself violently inside her.

"Keep going," he ordered. Catching her eye in the mirror, he found the swollen bud at the apex of her sex and rolled it beneath his thumb.

She bucked twice more, then collapsed over his legs in a quivering heap.

When he'd recovered a skeletal system, Bastien wrapped his arms about her and sank back against the pillows. Her head grew heavy against his shoulder and her breath slowed. She'd fallen asleep while they were still joined.

He would have liked to stay like this. Listening to her breathing and feeling the soft ticking of her heart. He desperately wanted to simply roll to the side, pull the covers over them, and hold her while they slept.

To do so would be madness. In the restaurant tonight, it had required every ounce of his hard-won self-restraint to keep from getting in the middle of Shelby and Sloan. Just as it had to keep his mouth shut when Gerald Llewellyn was trying to bait him.

He knew the patterns well.

Backhanded compliments. Thinly disguised criticism. Parental apathy and self-involvement.

His blood had boiled as he watched her sit in the middle of it, growing more and more distressed until she had to leave at the table. He'd stalked off without a word. Not even bothering to excuse himself. When he'd seen her large tear-filled eyes, he wanted to escort her back to the table and make them look at her.

Make them see what they'd done.

What they *would* do.

This instinct was why, once her breathing had become deep and even, he carefully shifted her sleeping form until she was lying on her side. In degrees that felt almost too small to measure, he disengaged himself from her and pulled up the covers, over her shoulders. He made sure her phone was plugged in on the nightstand beside her before turning out the lights and slipping through to the adjoining suite.

This was the last act of care he would permit himself.

Shelby Llewellyn was not his to protect.

And what would make him sure he could protect her if she was?

His track record suggested exactly the opposite.

Twelve

Shelby batted at her phone alarm, rolling onto her back when she'd quieted its shrillness. Yawning, she experienced an involuntarily full-body stretch, deliciously sore but surprisingly well-rested. Each twinge and ache served as sensory reminders of all the things they'd done—and said—the night before. She had fallen asleep in his arms and woken in a cloud.

Shelby floated out of bed and into the bathroom, where she brushed her teeth before a quick shower. Standing naked before the full-length mirror, she noticed the pink patches on her breasts. Small twin bruises on the insides of her thighs where the ridge of his lean hips had pushed against—and inside—her. She ran the tip of her finger over the small, mottled mark at the base of her throat—the only souvenir that would warrant a change to her exhibition opening outfit.

A *hickey*. Bastien Renaud had given her a hickey.

Shelby smiled at herself in the mirror, enjoying an illicit thrill at the idea of wearing this secret map of his passion beneath her clothes. After donning a robe, she hurried through her makeup routine, and gathered her hopelessly sex-tousled hair into a hastily coiled knot. She was securing the last willful tendrils with bobby pins when her phone lit up with a text from Sloan.

Shelby saw the picture and froze with the last hairpin hovering between her mouth and its intended location.

The gallery's large plate glass window bearing a basketball-size hole surrounded by a spiderweb of cracks radiating out from the central point of impact. Across the bricks of the gallery's exterior wall, a word had been spray-painted in drippy red letters.

Trash.

She wasn't sure how long she'd been standing there paralyzed when she noticed Sloan's next text below it.

Call me.

Shelby did, and listened in a numb haze as Sloan relayed the details. Only the sculpture closest to the front window had been damaged. The police had already come and gone, and Sloan had set an appointment to have the glass replaced later that morning. As for the spray paint, their property management company was doing what they could with the power washer.

Sloan had been surprisingly calm while relating all of this.

"But I don't understand," Shelby said. "If the security alarm went off and alerted the police, why didn't I get a call? When I set up the service, I could swear I listed both of our numbers. And even if they didn't, why didn't *you* call me? You said this happened at three in the morning?"

Silence crackled over the line.

"You seemed so anxious about the exhibition opening at dinner last night. Your father and I agreed it would be best not to bother you until we had a plan in place."

Shelby sat down hard on the edge of the tub. Her father already knew. He knew and had agreed it would be best if Shelby didn't.

"Given the circumstances, we both feel it would be best to postpone the opening. I've already reached out to Bastien and—"

"You *what*?" She was on her feet again, startled by the unexpected encounter with her own rage-reddened face in the mirror.

"I spoke with Bastien just before you called and—"

"You called Bastien *before* you spoke with me?"

"He *is* the artist, Shelby. With an incident like this, he'll want to reach out to his insurance company as soon as possible." That she made Shelby feel foolish for not having thought of this first only poured gasoline on the already roaring inferno of her anger.

"As the one responsible for organizing this exhibition, I should have been the one to have that conversation with him. Just as I should have been the one to speak with the police."

"They're reviewing the footage from the security cameras as we speak, and they've promised to reach out as soon as they have any information." Sloan said this in the hopeful tones of a parent trying to distract a petulant child. "Until we know who's responsible, would you really want to put his work at risk?"

Shelby's mind had already begun to gnaw on this very question.

Who might have done something like this? And, more importantly, *why*?

Could it be a crazed *Bad Boys of Booze* fan, wanting to make their mark in the most literal way possible? Surely not a former inmate, still nursing a grudge.

Four years he'd spent quietly hiding away in the wilds of Maine until she came along and convinced him to come to San Francisco, where his presence had been publicly advertised, down to the address and time.

Because she'd been too much of a coward to tell her father that he'd declined their invitation.

Guilt.

Sick, hot waves of it rushed over her. She barely had time to end the call before a dry heave doubled her over the sink. Another came, then another, until tears spilled down her cheeks and her abdominals burned.

She'd been so reckless. So thoughtless and ambitious. Now everything she had worked so hard to put together was falling apart before her eyes.

Shelby blotted her cheeks with that issue and forced

herself to stand up straight. On wobbly legs, she walked over to the door separating their suites and knocked.

"It's open" came the muffled reply.

Bastien stood before the window facing out over the sprawl of green lawn that ended in the lily pond.

"Bastien, I—"

"Take a walk with me?" He glanced at her over his shoulder, early morning light making his dress shirt appear the exact gray-blue of shadows on snow. His dark hair looked damp, neatly combed back from his brutally beautiful features.

"Now?" she asked.

"Now." The odd mix of sadness and resignation in his eyes made her agree.

"Let me just grab some shoes." In her suite, she selected a pair of comfortable leather riding boots that wouldn't look too bizarre with her navy blue cashmere turtleneck sweater-dress and returned with her keys in hand. "Ready?"

Bastien nodded. "I may need you to get us outside, but I think I can handle it from there."

Shelby led him downstairs, where Green Gables and its staff were going through their normal morning routines, seemingly oblivious to the abrupt shift that had taken place in the last ten hours. They exited through the French doors that opened onto the same part of the sprawling sculpture garden she'd naively thought he might appreciate before this trip had become a complete disaster.

Only when they were outdoors did he seem to breathe.

Gravel crunched as they connected with one of the many footpaths winding through hedges trimmed with nearly surgical precision.

"Porter and I used to come out here to play hide-and-seek," she said, needing to break the silence. "And when it wasn't hide-and-seek, it was pirates. That right there was our ship." She pointed to the old stone teahouse they had scampered around and pretended the small, thick windows were portholes.

Bastien's lips remained tight, but small grooves at the corners of his eyes hinted at a smile.

"We used to do stuff like that, too. Of course, our games usually ended with one of us needing stitches, burn salve, or a pillow to sit on."

"Really?" No stranger to the kind of roughhousing that could evolve among unsupervised children, she could only imagine what it must have been like for the Renaud boys, who, by all accounts, were wilder than most.

"Oh, yeah. We're damn lucky we all made it out alive."

The conversation had the stilted quality of small talk. Words to fill the air and ease the tension until they arrived at their intended destination, and he got down to what was really on his mind.

They arrived at the wide stone stairs leading down to the Roman pool. On the far side of it, a full-sized replica of a colonnaded aqueduct stood, its reflection making the structure look like it belonged to both the earth and sky. She had never lost her sense of awe about this place. She supposed that's why she had never fully moved away, like Porter, Kendall, and David. There was still too much magic here.

Bastien slowed when he reached the old pergola with a stone bench bearing a shiny onyx plaque bearing Grace Llewellyn's name. This had been her adoptive mother's favorite place to come and sit on summer evenings. The air here always felt cool and damp. Sweet with the promise of rain.

"I owe you an apology," Bastien said at last.

"You?" she asked. "What could you possibly have to apologize for?"

"Last night, for starters."

"What about it?" she asked, her pulse picking up.

He swiveled on the bench, so his knees were angled toward hers. "I need you to know what an amazing person you are."

Ah.

"Please, don't," she said. "I know what you're going to say, and you don't need to. I'm not some starry-eyed kid, Bastien."

It felt satisfying to say even if she knew it to be patently untrue.

Because, if she was being honest with herself, that's exactly what she was. Had he a pair of X-ray glasses, he would have seen her tripping about the room like a lovesick lunatic this morning, robe flaring out like a ball gown as she spun into her walk-in closet.

"I didn't say you were," he said.

"It's not like I thought last night would was the beginning of a sleigh ride into happily-ever-after."

No, she hadn't thought it. But after last night, she had hoped.

Hoped it meant something to him, too.

Hope.

That word again.

"I wasn't saying that, either," he said.

"Then what are you saying?"

The placid calm he'd projected up to this point began to crack. Frustration peeked through the shards of his facade.

"Everything I said last night is true, Shelby. But that doesn't mean I should have said it."

"Because?" she demanded.

He heaved an exasperated sigh and pushed himself up from the bench, stalking over to the stone railing to look out over the lake.

"What happened at the gallery this morning is always going to happen. It doesn't matter how hard I try, or what I change, or which people I try to prove myself to. I am never going to belong in this kind of world. And I'll be damned if I'll subject you or anyone else to the kind of things that happen in mine."

"You don't even know what happened at the gallery yet," she protested. "No one does. People vandalize buildings in downtown San Francisco all the time. You're just using that as an excuse to push me away again."

"Again?"

Shelby didn't remember standing, but became aware that she was crossing the space between them. "After our first time together in Maine, you flipped out. You deliberately hurt my feelings so I would leave. But then Sloan put that announcement on the gallery website, and you felt guilty, and you agreed to do the show. If you regret that now, I'm sorry. I'm sorry for the horrible things that happened to you when you were growing up. I'm sorry about what happened to you in prison. And I'm sorry if this exhibition is the reason one of them found you again. But I am not sorry for finally being able to ask for what *I* want." Shelby brought her hand to her aching heart. "I'm not sorry for wanting you. And I'm not sorry if it's inconvenient for you to know that I do." If it hadn't been for the breeze cooling her cheeks, Shelby might not have known she was crying.

Bastien's mouth hovered slightly open, his eyes wide and his face blank. "Shelby, you can't want what you don't really know. That first time you saw me on the show—"

"It wasn't the show, Bastien. It was your work. It was the fact that you could take things the world had thrown away and make them into something beautiful. For a minute, you made me feel that way, too." Her lips pulled into a pained smile. "You made me feel that there was something in me that could reach someone like you."

Bastien took a step toward her. "You did, Shelby. You *do*. I meant everything I said last night. You matter. You, your safety. Your happiness. Your dreams. Your future. They matter to me. Which is why I know I can't be part of them."

Shelby indulged in a bitter laugh and swiped a tear

away with the back of her hand. "If this is what it feels like to 'matter,' I'd prefer to be ignored."

Hugging herself tightly, she turned on her heel and stalked toward the house. Halfway up the path she broke into a run, pushing her body faster and faster until she was no longer listening for the sound of his steps behind her.

Her lungs burned and her thighs screamed as she made the final push to the double doors leading to the art wing.

Where she ran smack into Gerald Llewellyn.

She only had to glimpse the shock on his face to know how she looked. Tearstained and out of breath.

"Shelby? What on earth is going on? Sloan said you hung up on her. I've been calling for half an hour now. Are you alright?"

She nodded. "I'm fine. I just went for a walk to clear my head."

"You're most certainly not fine," he insisted, moving closer to scrutinize her eye-to-eye. "Come here. Look at me."

Knowing this tendency came from a place of protection did nothing to help the discomfiture she felt at the intense scrutiny of his keen blue eyes and the ferocious intelligence behind them.

"I'm okay," she insisted. "I'm just out of breath. That's all."

His hands closed over her upper arms to prevent her from wriggling away. "What's that beneath your chin? Is that a bruise?"

Icy fingers of panic squeezed her ribs. Had she missed a spot with her concealer?

"Nothing," she said. "Dad, it's nothing. Please, just let me go."

"Not until you—"

But then her father staggered backward, narrowly recovering his balance before he careened into a marble replica of Bernini's Baroque masterpiece *Apollo and Daphne*.

"She asked you to let her go."

But this time it wasn't her father's voice ringing through the cavernous hall.

It was Bastien's.

Bastien had forgotten how good it felt.

The adrenaline singing through his veins. The pure, sweet rush of rage. The satisfaction of watching fear find the face of a man who deserved its company.

A man like Gerald Llewellyn never allowed it to stay long.

He righted himself as quickly as a cat, brushing his suit as if Bastien's hands had left dirt on the sleeves. Beneath the shelves of his sable eyebrows, his irises flickered hot and blue as pilot lights. "What the hell do you think you're doing?"

Bastien folded his arms across his chest. "Helping you give your daughter some space."

"I meant, what are you doing in this wing of *my* home?" Gerald said.

"I brought him here," Shelby said. "I ran into him after I spoke with Sloan."

Llewellyn's posture eased slightly. "I'm...very sorry about what happened at the gallery, Shelby. I know how diligently you worked to put everything together. As soon as we can select a new date—"

"Am I included in that 'we'?" she asked.

The folds bracketing Gerald's mouth deepened with his frown. "Of course, you are. Why would you even ask that?"

"Because I certainly wasn't this morning. Not when Sloan got the call about the break-in. Not when the police arrived. Not when she made an appointment to replace the window and not when you two decided to postpone. I mean, she called Bastien to discuss rescheduling before I even knew that anything was wrong," she said.

Confusion descended over him like a fog. When he had received Sloan's phone call, she had given no indication that the decision to postpone was not a unanimous one. And he'd been too wrapped up in the details of what occurred to consider whether or not Shelby knew, or how she might feel about it.

Trash.

He'd stared so hard at the picture of the dripping letters, they appeared in white negative on the backs of his eyelids every time he blinked.

The meaning had been embedded much deeper. Whether the person who had put it there meant it to apply to him, or his work, didn't matter. They were one and the same.

"I didn't know you weren't part of the rescheduling decision," he said to Shelby.

"You would have, if you had given me a chance to talk to you while we were still in your suite," she said testily.

Gerald's cheeks had gone a blotchy red beneath his ruddy tan. "When were you in his suite?"

To her credit, Shelby looked at him, and he saw in her eyes what she intended to do, and no matter what it cost him, part of him was proud of her for wanting to do it.

"Last night after we left the restaurant," she admitted. "And this morning, after we found out about what happened at the gallery."

If the cathedral ceiling had opened up at that precise moment and a lightning bolt shot through it, Gerald Llewellyn would have looked less surprised. "What?"

The crown of Shelby's blond head rose by an inch as she squared her shoulders and looked up into her father's eyes. "I was with Bastien last night."

Gerald's lips went pale around the edges. His hands balled into fists at his sides and his nostrils flared. He turned his attention from his daughter to Bastien. "Is that true?" he demanded.

Sweat broke out between Bastien's shoulder blades and on his forehead. Though he had half a foot and at least thirty pounds of muscle on the man before him, the final outcome of a physical altercation would spell trouble.

"It's true," Shelby said. Her father didn't even turn to look at her.

"I fly you out here, all expenses paid, you come into my house, eat at my table, and sleep under my roof for an exhibition of your work that my fiancée agreed to house at my gallery, and you have the audacity to take advantage of my daughter?" Curds of foam collected at the corners of his mouth. Beneath the gleaming skin on his forehead, the fat worm of a vein rose.

"Dad, that's not—" Shelby began.

"Of course, it is." Gerald shot her scathing look. "You're kind, and trusting, and you always believe the best in people. He saw you coming from a mile away. Didn't you?" he demanded, glaring at Bastien.

Bastien clenched his jaw against denials he knew would mean nothing to the man standing before him, self-righteousness smeared all over his well-fed features.

"Do you know why you're here?" The question oozed from Gerald's mouth like an oil seep.

Bastien glanced at Shelby, who silently implored him to put an end to this.

And he could end it. *Should* end it, probably. But as it had at many inopportune moments, the steely Renaud pride rose up in him, refusing to yield.

"Why?" he asked.

Gerald approached him as a hunter might an animal caught in a trap—measured steps simultaneously triumphant and calculating. "You're here because men like me make life for men like you possible." He paused to allow Bastien to fully digest the insult before feeding him another bite. "You're born into families steeped in poverty. No skills. No options. No education until someone like me comes along and raises you up. Provides scholarships. Provides second chances. Provides opportunities you didn't earn and could never create for yourself. Men like me are the reason men like you and your brothers are able to drag yourselves out of the swamp you were born into. I'm just glad I found out what you were about before you helped yourself to my daughter's inheritance the way you did her good heart."

Bastien met his eyes. Met them for every time he'd been made to cower by men who wore their uniforms like ermine cloaks, believing they'd been ordained by some God who'd chosen them to rule and him to suffer. He held it for Augustin, who went to prison a good man, and came out a broken one. For every person who'd stared scarcity in the face and mortgaged their entire future in a moment of desperation.

"That's where you're wrong." He leaned down, partially to make sure every word would be branded in Llewellyn's brain. Partially because he wanted the billionaire to be painfully aware of the disparity in their size. "Without men like me, men like *you* would have nothing. People hard-bitten enough to work on their feet for twelve-hour shifts in your warehouses. Spend nights away from their children, living paycheck to paycheck because you pay them so much less than you can afford. And why? So you can buy this ridiculous farce of a castle and cram it full of shit like this." He waved an arm at the cavernous hall with its honor guard of marble statues.

"Shit?" Llewellyn's laugh was barbed with scorn. "Is that what you call a collection that spans thousands of years of human history?"

"Shit," Bastien repeated. "The real art is something

you can never own. It's the hands that could trans-form marble into skin and pigments into the shine on a human eye. It's in the mind that channeled an idea significant enough that centuries later, we're still talk-ing about how it changed the world. What you have is a bunch of very expensive proof that art *happened*."

Gerald's meticulously clean-shaven jaw flexed. His eyes glittered with contempt above the puffed bags over his cheekbones. "You don't know the first thing about what I have."

"Maybe not," he admitted. "But I know a hell of a lot about what you don't."

"Please, enlighten me," Gerald challenged, his head lifting at the imperious angle of a Roman emperor.

"A fiancée who has the first goddamn clue how to pay a bribe."

The color leached from the billionaire's skin, his mouth puckering like a drawstring pouch.

Shelby hovered hesitantly near the door to the gar-dens, pale as a ghost and her face. "What are you say-ing, Bastien?"

"I'm saying that the goddamn paparazzi follow me everywhere. I'm saying that one of them caught a pic-ture of us outside the restaurant last night and others were already staking out the gallery. I'm saying that one of them got pictures of someone giving an envelope to the person who vandalized the gallery last night."

Bastien reached into his pocket and pulled out his cell phone, pulling up his photo app and turning it so they both could see.

Shelby's gasp drove a shiv into his very soul. "Sloan."

"I'm sorry, Shelby. I had intended to handle this conversation with your father privately."

Turning to her father, he noted that his skin was still a waxy gray.

"I'll be turning these pictures over to the police," he said, catching Shelby's eye. "I think it's best I go now."

Her face crumpled. The pain in her stormy eyes felt like a sledgehammer to his chest. "Why?"

"It's better that way." He filled the sentiment with as much tenderness as he could, willing her to understand.

Gerald slung a protective arm around his daughter's shoulders as Bastien turned to leave.

He wanted to look back at her. To find some way to communicate an apology for the planet of regret bearing down on his shoulders.

In a sense, Gerald had been right. It was better that she found out now.

There was no happy ending with a man like him.

A principle that proved itself yet again as the small plane that had ferried him from Detroit to Bangor in the last leg of his journey home hit the tarmac.

The moment he took his phone off airplane mode, it lit up like a Christmas tree. Gaping at the double-digit number inside the red bubble over both his text messages and calls, he felt a profound sense of dread.

Well warranted, as it turned out.

Remy had called eight times. Law, six. Together, they'd contributed an impressive twenty-three texts to the thread Bastien had labeled Thieves. It took several swipes to locate the message that had initiated the avalanche, but when he did, his stomach rolled.

You and Shelby Llewellyn???

Bastien followed the link Remy had pasted into the text. The picture had been taken at an oblique angle but showed him and Shelby standing on the sidewalk outside the Pier Club. Her body pressed to his, his arms anchored around her back, their faces close and flushed.

"Shit," Bastien grunted.

His seatmate, an elderly woman who had informed him that she was on the way to Bangor to visit her grandchildren, frowned at him.

"Sorry," he mumbled. He hadn't even finished the article when an avalanche of notifications from his email inbox popped up. The subject lines provided by his Renaud-based internet flags quickly progressed from bad to mortifying.

Reclusive Renaud Canoodles California Cutie!

Love for Lonely Renaud!

Hermit to Heartthrob?

By the time he returned to the text thread, he no longer had to wonder which of the gossip sites Remy had run into.

Since when did you canoodle? You live like a god-damn hermit-monk for years and then you shack up with Silicon Valley royalty right out the gate?

Law had chimed in directly afterward with a Wait, what?

"Shit, shit, *shit*." Bastien thumped his fist down on his thigh hard. "Sorry," he apologized again.

His seatmate sniffed and made a show of unbuckling the second the fasten-seat-belts light turned off. Having already released his, Bastien quickly stepped into the aisle and pulled her carry-on down from the overhead bin. Though it felt like an entire colony of ants had taken up residence below his skin, Bastien stepped back to let her exit first.

He was out of the airport and inside his truck within ten minutes. In muffled silence, broken only by the ticking of tiny ice crystals against the windshield, he rested his forehead on the steering wheel and took a deep breath. If only the chilly leather could slow his racing thoughts.

When he composed himself enough to face the drive, he turned over the engine in his truck and aimed his tires toward home.

Only, it no longer felt like home when he arrived.

What had once been space that was his, and his alone, was now a mausoleum to the memory of her.

Bastien sank into the couch and reached for the small, slim gadget that had been the source of so much trouble in his recent life. Opening up his saved voice mails, he found the very first one he'd received from Shelby.

Back then, he hadn't saved her in his contacts under the name Shelby Llewellyn. She was only *Her*. He swiped through them, listening to each before he deleted it. One by one.

When he came to the most recent, he realized it, too, had been left while he was on the plane. For a single moment, his thumb hovered over the small trash-can icon, but in the end, he couldn't do it. Nor did he press the small play button that would fill his ears with her voice. He couldn't bear it. Not now, not tonight.

Not her.

The snow crusting the fogged windows had become transparent at the edges. Soon it would begin to shrink and be gone for another season. Bastien stood at the sink in the bathrobe that had become his daily uniform. The coffee in his hand had gone cold, but he sipped it, anyway.

Caffeine was caffeine. It helped the days go faster.

An unwelcome sound invaded his monk's cell and he glared at the small glowing rectangle of his phone on the counter. He sent the call to voice mail and felt a breath of relief.

At least it had stopped.

The sick, glad knocking in his chest every time it rang, followed by the cold, sinking feeling when he realized it wasn't *Her*.

Six weeks, and he hadn't heard a word.

Shelby's new assistant had taken over as the gallery's designated representative where communications with him were concerned, now that Sloan had departed the staff.

That nothing appeared in any media outlets about either the vandalism or the broken engagement between Llewellyn and his former fiancée was yet another testament to the hushing power of the almighty dollar. The latter he had learned about from Remy, who at some point in Bastien's absence had become an incorrigible gossip hound with connections through Cosima.

From Shelby's assistant, he learned of the rescheduled opening and declined to attend. When he received the check from the sale of his pieces, it bore Shelby's signature.

His phone's display lit up once more and, realizing this had been the third time in a row, he answered it with a gruff "Yeah?"

"Wow. You sound like shit." Laney, on the other hand, sounded unreasonably perky for an hour in the single digits on a Tuesday.

"Thanks." Leaving the mug in the sink among its comrades, he shuffled toward the couch.

"I mean it," she said. "Are you sick?"

Sick? No. He just had no appetite, no motivation, no interest in getting out of bed in the morning, and preferred sleeping for as much of the day as his brain would allow him.

"It's just, you haven't been into the shop since you got back from California and I'm pretty sure Sheriff Dawkins thinks you're dead and I've stolen your shop," Laney explained.

Bastion grunted, which had become his all-purpose response to most of life's pressing coils.

"I mean it," she insisted. "He was in here the other day doing that weird thing with his mustache and tossing around terms like 'adult protective services' and 'welfare check.'"

"You told them to get bent, I hope."

"That seems like an unfair affliction to wish on a man with so many obvious shortcomings," she said.

At this, he managed a weak snort.

"Better," she said. "Look, if you won't come into town, can I swing by your place to pick up your new pieces? I feel like he'd back off for a week or so if I could at least show him a new ugly salad bowl or something."

"There aren't any."

"Ugly salad bowls?"

"New pieces."

Silence stretched over the line between.

"You've been shut away in your house for the last month and half and you haven't made a single thing?" she asked.

"Correct."

"What the hell have you been doing with yourself?"

Bastien glanced around the living room.

He examined the corona of objects spiraling out from his station on the couch, hoping to land on something he could pass off as a raison d'être.

Piles of books. Tattered newspapers. A chessboard, where he failed daily to outwit himself.

Irony.

"Gaming, mostly."

"Gaming," she repeated with obvious disbelief.

"Yep."

"What game?"

Shit.

His eyes flicked from the chessboard to the wall of trees outside the window. "Kings of the... Forest."

"Huh," she said. "I've never heard of that one. What console?"

"PS4." He felt smug rattling this off until he realized Laney was probably where he'd heard it.

"Original, slim, or pro?"

In the end, he didn't even have the energy to maintain the lie. "Fine. I made it up."

"You know, until this moment, I actually felt bad for not lying to your brother like you asked."

"Brother?"

Bastien sat up at the precise moment his phone chimed. The app connected to his security system informed him that the exterior cameras had picked up something on the motion sensor.

"What did you do?"

The sound of an engine being killed.

"What did you do, *Laney*?"

"Even Batman needed the Justice League."

Peeling himself off the couch, he walked over to the door and peered out the glass panel to its side, the figure instantly recognizable even through the glazed glass.

"You're fired," he said, cutting off the sound of her laughter as he disconnected.

"Open up, asshole. It's freezing out here." Remy's distinctive bray rumbled through the thick wood.

Bastien disengaged his series of locks and swung the door open, leaving his brother kicking snow off his boots as he walked back to the couch.

"California has made you soft."

"If you're what hard looks like, I'm glad." Once

inside the entryway, Remy made a show of looking around. "Nice place you got here."

Bastien shrugged. "You going to tell me what the hell you're doing here?"

Remy perched on the arm of the love seat as if he might need to lurch into flight at any second, something he'd done since they were boys. "I believe an *intervention* is the technical term."

"The camera crew hiding somewhere out there?" He made no effort to keep the bitterness out of his voice.

His younger brother had the good grace to look at least mildly chagrined. "Wouldn't fit in my carry-on."

"Shame," he said. "I have to think something like this would be good for ratings, right? Riding to the rescue of your hermit older brother?" Bastien absently scratched his jaw as he pondered the chessboard.

"Rugged survivalist," Remy said, scooting forward to pick through the stack of papers on his end of the coffee table.

Bastien rotated the board on its turntable to study the other side. "What's that?"

"The beard. You need at least a couple more inches before you'd appeal to the hermit demographic."

"As much as I'm enjoying your assessment of my lapsed barbering, you think you could speed this up a little?"

"Got a date?" Remy teased.

"Yeah," Bastien said. "With this couch."

Remy drew in a deep breath and launched. "You going to tell me why you've been screening everyone's calls for over a month now?"

"Been busy."

"I can see that."

In his peripheral vision, he saw his brother push aside a sheet of tracing paper. "Wait, is that—"

Bastien was up in a flash, catching his brother by the wrist just before the sheet moved below breast level on his drawing of Shelby Llewellyn. He flung away Remy's arm, stashing both the drawing and its covering inside his leather portfolio in the corner before returning to the couch.

He'd made this exact journey many times over the last several weeks. Pulling it out in the small hours, when night felt never-ending. Returning it as the light of blue dawn crept beneath the shades he kept drawn at all hours, disgusted with himself.

"You can talk to me, you know." Remy's flannel shirt blurred into a puddle of green and blue beneath his earnest face. "About what happened in San Francisco."

"No thanks." Bastien lifted his knight just to return it to its white square. "Anything else?"

"Yeah," Remy said, flicking the piece out of its box. "Finish your move. Putting it back is against the rules."

Bastien righted it. "My opponent doesn't mind."

"You won't even think about it?"

"Letting you be the chess police?' Bastien asked.

Remy flicked the piece over again. "Telling me about Shelby."

Bastien picked up the knight, then set it down hard enough to make the pieces around it jump. "Would you knock it off?"

"Sure."

Remy's index finger flashed out and the little horsehead leaped out of place, this time, taking out several of its neighbors.

White-hot rage flashed through Bastien, and before he fully registered what was happening, the heavy block of the chessboard had been upended, sending the game pieces flying.

A familiar smirk tugged at one corner of his brother's mouth. "Better. *Now* can we talk about it?"

"What good is that going to do? What happened, happened. It's over. The end."

"Ye-e-eah," Remy said. "It's the *what* bit that I'm curious about."

Bastien sagged back against the couch, overcome by an epic wave of post adrenaline exhaustion. "Is that really why you came all this way?"

His brother glanced down and palmed a chess piece that had landed in his lap. "It sure as hell isn't your hospitality."

In the comforting limbo created by his closed eyes and his brother's familiar presence, Bastien told him everything. By the time he had finished, Remy had graduated from the arm of the couch to the actual cushion, putting them at roughly eye level.

"Well, that explains it," his brother said.

"Explains what?" Bastien asked.

"Why she's been calling me to check on you for the past month and a half."

A frisson of warmth arced through him, sitting him up. "What?"

Remy scooted forward on the couch cushion and set his phone in the center of the now-empty chessboard. "Look for yourself."

Bastien glanced down at the phone and felt gooseflesh rise on his arms.

Every Thursday. She'd been calling his brother on the same schedule.

"The first few I sent to voice mail because I didn't recognize the number," Remy continued. "But then I finally listened to one and called her back."

Bastien stood like a marionette whose strings had been jerked. "Why didn't you tell me?"

"She asked me not to."

"What did she want?"

Remy, who'd never been good at sitting for long, pushed himself up from the chair arm and migrated to the same set of shelves Shelby had on the day she'd showed up in Bar Harbor. "To see how you were. Wanted to respect your wishes but was worried you'd, well...do this." His brother waved a hand over the nest of clutter. "Wall yourself off. Shut everyone out."

Bastien had to peel his tongue from the roof of his mouth to speak. "What did you tell her?"

"I lied." Remy pinned him with a pointed look. "She thinks you're fine."

"I *am* fine."

"Is this really what passes for fine in your world, Bastien? Barricading yourself in your fancy bunker like some kind of doomsday prophet?"

He bent and began to gather the chess pieces, soul-weary. "It's just safer for everyone."

"Bullshit!" Remy spat the word with enough venom to stop him short. "It's safer for *you*. Shut up here in your little castle with your search engine flags and your No Trespassing sign, you can keep the entire world out. Especially the people who make you feel shit that you might have to do something about."

Pain shot through Bastien's clenched jaw. "You don't know what you're talking about, Remy."

"Those threats you started getting while you were at 4 Thieves? Is that it?" Remy's laugh was laced with sarcasm. "You don't think we figured out that Augustin was the one who'd been sending them?"

Bastien blinked at him, thunderstruck. "When?"

"About the time we discovered he'd been taking out lines of credit against the distillery to feed his gambling habit."

"Which he wouldn't have been able to do if I'd told you and Law what he'd been up to." Speaking these words left his chest feeling strangely light. Like he'd just set down a bag of cement.

"You were protecting him," Remy said. "Just like you did all of us. But it was never supposed to be your job. You did it, anyway, and we all survived. We *survived*. And against every single odd that ever existed, here we are. In a house in Maine, you built with money you made from investing in goddamn green tech of all things. Law is a father, Bastien. *Law.* The kid who used to put the holly berries from the bush out back in his diaper?"

"I'm aware." He glanced toward the kitchen, where

the birth announcement still clung to his fridge, held up by a magnet.

The mental image this statement resurrected made Bastien smile in spite himself. "Tried to eat them, too."

"That kid now has twin sons that are the exact same age he was when he used to do that. And you're missing it. After everything we did to get out of that place, you're missing the good part."

He sat down hard on the couch. "Is this the part where you give me the name and number of a therapist I'm supposed to call?"

"Nope. This is the part where we get this place cleaned up and you go do something about that beard. *Then* you'll be ready for the video consultation I took the liberty of setting up for you."

Bastien moved to scrub a hand over his face and remembered the chess piece clutched in his palm. Unclenching his fingers, he couldn't help but shake his head.

There, with her delicate ridged crown, was the queen.

Thirteen

Shelby stood in her father's study watching him tweak the tie of his tuxedo for about the millionth time. Noting that he was only making it worse, she crossed the plush carpet and began working to even the edges of the knot.

"You remember when you taught me to do this?" she asked, breathing in the scent of his woodsy cologne mingled with starch from the crisp white dress shirt he wore beneath his suit jacket and vest.

"Of course, I do," her father said. "You needed a little help reaching my collar in those days." His bright blue eyes flicked to the leather chair now positioned in a different corner of his study.

"I sure did."

A wave of nostalgia swept over her, accompanied

by the memory. Herself at the age of eight, standing on the leather cushion to look in this same mirror while he demonstrated the right sequence of loop and folds to produce the perfect Windsor knot. Whatever she managed to produce, he'd wear out for the day, no matter how lopsided or wonky.

This had been *their* ritual.

How had he known just how much she'd needed that? Once piece of his day that she could comfortably occupy without feeling she'd stolen it from one of his *real* children.

The tradition had lapsed once she left for college, and they hadn't rebooted it when she'd returned.

Not until this morning.

His un-wedding day.

Her father's creative solution to the problem of the gigantic chunk of deposits he would have to surrender if he canceled all the plans he and Sloan had put into place. In true Gerald Llewellyn style, he'd proceeded with the party, disinvited her half of the guests, and turned it into a celebration of his general magnificence.

The speed of his bounce back once Sloan's attempt to sabotage the exhibition opening had been revealed only served to confirm to Shelby how disastrously mismatched they'd been.

If only the same alchemy could knit the hole in her heart.

An overused sentiment, but the closest thing she could think of to describe how she felt since Bastien had left. A nonfatal wound slowly leaking vital life force with every beat.

She even knew the exact moment it had been inflicted.

Hearing the ugly words her father had spoken, and the eloquent, passionate rebuttal Bastien had offered in return, had the unfortunate effect of alienating her from the former and strengthening her attachment to the latter.

Remy had proved a patient, if narrow, channel in terms of keeping tabs on his brother, providing only the most basic of updates.

Still alive, still an asshole, being her personal most-and-least favorite.

Shelby wasn't sure which hurt more. That Bastien had simply carried on without giving her a second thought, or that so many of her own thoughts still orbited him like clingy satellites.

"Well? What do you think?" Her father's voice snapped her back to the present moment, where he turned a slow circle so she could render an opinion. "Do I look like an un-groom?"

Her throat tightened at the hopeful glow in his eyes as an emotion she couldn't quite name swelled in her chest. "Can I ask you something?"

His smile dimmed slightly due to something he must have seen in her expression. "The boutonniere is a mistake, right? I'm not trendy enough to pull off a succulent?"

"The succulent looks great." Shelby hugged her arms around her middle and began again. "You remember when we were in the atrium, and you told Bastien that the only reason men like him existed is because men like you offered the hand that pulled them out of the cesspool?"

They hadn't spoken of that day since it happened, and her father looked a little peaked at Shelby's having brought it up now. "I do."

She halfway wanted to lighten the mood by making a joke, but knew if she didn't get the words out now, they would eventually choke her. "Is that what you did?" She swallowed the aching lump at the base of her throat and lifted her gaze to meet his. "With me?"

Gerald Llewellyn's mouth went slack, and his eyebrows shot up in surprise. "Good God, Shelby. Why would you ever think that?"

All too conscious of the liquid liner that the makeup artist had applied to her eyes, Shelby bit the inside of her cheek to fight back the tears threatening to spill over her lower lids.

"What you said about him, it's true for me, too. If it weren't for you, I'd have been stuck in the foster-care system. And if it weren't for the foster-care system, I'd still be—"

"Don't," he said. "There's no reason you ever have to think about that place again."

"You don't think I've thought about it every single day?" she said. "You don't think I've asked myself why I got so lucky when kids all over the world live in that kind of suffering and end up creating even worse for themselves?"

His polished dress shoes sank into the carpet as he closed the space between them. His eyes burned with intensity as he gently took her by the bare shoulders. "You didn't get lucky, Shelby. *We* did."

We.

That one word brought the only mother she'd ever known to the room with them.

"When Grace first mentioned adopting after Kendall and David left for college, I thought it was some kind of empty-nest angst that would pass once she got used to it. For a whole year we went back and forth about it. But do you know what she said that finally changed my mind?"

Shelby shook her head. She'd never heard this story.

"'We have another daughter out there, Gerald. I can feel it. We just need to find her.' And we did. And another son, to boot."

Despite her best efforts, hot tears spilled over her lower lids and dotted the corset of the couture gown slowly crushing her ribs.

"You were always meant to be ours." He pulled the pale green silk handkerchief from his breast pocket and gently dabbed her cheeks. "I'm just sorry it took us so long to find you."

She hugged him then, careful not to smudge his suitcoat. "Thanks, Dad. For everything."

His warm palm patted her bare back before he released her. They stood side by side in the mirror, assessing any potential damage.

"You know what I'm really looking forward to?" he asked, looping his arm through hers to steer them toward the front door.

"What's that?"

"When I get to walk *you* down the aisle."

Shelby made a rude noise as they proceeded toward the waiting limousine. "I wouldn't hold my breath, if I were you."

He gave her an enigmatic smile as he slid into the car after her. "You never know."

Trouble was, she did.

She *did* know.

Because for a few brief, beautiful moments, Bastien Renaud had showed her what was possible. For her body. Her mind. Her soul.

And at only twenty-seven years old, Shelby was terrified she'd spend the rest of her life measuring all men by his impossible proportions.

A subtle ache twinged behind her sternum as if on cue.

Her silly heart, bleeding wishes.

By the time they'd made it to the un-wedding cake-cutting portion of the reception, following the un-ceremony, heartache was a distant memory.

Far more corporeal concerns had taken precedence. After close to an hour and a half of being paraded around for pictures, her body was a road map of pain. Her feet, her lower back, even her face hurt from standing, smiling.

When her father announced he intended to make a slight departure from the program that required the entire family to rise from their appointed table and follow him out to the garden, she found herself less than enthusiastic about the prospect.

"Do you know what this is about?" Porter asked in a hushed whisper.

"Not a clue." She reluctantly struggled to her feet, and they melted into the migration of guests out of the gigantic palace of a tent that had been set up for the reception. Overlooking the Roman pool and the lily pond—sporting millions of tiny lights for the occasion—it abutted the sculpture garden she'd spent so much time exploring as a girl. What her father had planned beyond the fireworks that were set to begin just prior to their departure for their Bora Bora un-honeymoon, Shelby could barely begin to conjecture.

The procession had begun to slow, and many guests turned to look back expectantly at her and Porter as their father waved them forward.

Only when they reached the front of the elegantly attired congregation did Shelby spot the large dark cloth covering an object she didn't recognize in the center of a long rectangular patch of grass.

Her father's microphone-amplified voice rolled out over the assembly.

"I just wanted to begin by thanking everyone for being here tonight. Braving journeys from places as far away as Iceland and Australia to celebrate what, for me, has been by far the most difficult time of my life."

An appreciative murmur worked its way through the crowd.

"Love," he continued, "is the most transformative force in the entire universe and I'm lucky enough to have not one, but *two* daughters, whose love transforms my life on a daily basis."

Her gaze immediately swiveled to Kendall, who grinned back at her before looking up at the cloth-covered structure behind them.

"And as both of the women in my life are as enchanted by art as I am, I thought, what better wedding gift to give our new family than a piece that reflects this shared love."

His handsome face wore a knowing smile as he nodded to a man stationed off to the side of the gathering. The man nodded back and bent to manipulate an array of silver switches within the small black box by the hedge.

Shelby watched the curtains fall away, so mesmerized by the graceful flutter of silky fabric that at first, she didn't see what had caused the audible gasp that lifted from the crowd.

Porter's boyish exclamation of surprise finally broke the spell.

She looked, and the air was vacuumed from her lungs.

It was *her*.

Shelby, in the center of a swirling cloud of crystalline snowflakes and tiny birds. The wires holding it all in orbit spread out from behind her back like whimsical wings, a crown of leaves and twigs hovering above her head like an earthy halo.

Everyone was looking at her now. Warm hands reaching forward to pat her shoulder, to graze her arms and hands.

Even if she'd seen a thousand similar treatments

of the exact same subject, she'd have known the hand that created this one.

Lifting her tear-sheened eyes to her father, she emitted a strangled cry when she saw who stood next to him.

Bastien Renaud.

Handsome as the devil himself in a black-on-black tuxedo, his hair was shorter but still shaggy, his granite jaw bearing a neatly barbered beard.

"It's my honor and pleasure to unveil the newest piece in the Llewellyn collection and to introduce you to its very talented creator, Bastien Renaud."

Thunderous applause swelled around her.

"I've invited the artist to say a few words to dedicate the piece. Mr. Renaud." He nodded deferentially to Bastien, then they clasped hands in a firm shake that ended with her father clapping him warmly on the shoulder, before he handed over the microphone.

"*Snow Angel* is a piece about accidental beauty." Bastien's deep bass voice vibrated from the speakers, and had it not been for Porter's arm banding behind her back, Shelby might have fainted on the spot.

"How the intersection of a hundred seemingly inconsequential choices made over the years of a life can leave you standing at the precise place on a sidewalk where a flurry of autumn leaves fall. Or riding your bike by a lake at the exact moment an entire flock of geese takes off. These moments where fate and consequence intersect in a single, ecstatic moment of wonder…this is grace. *This* is art, and I'm grateful to be able to share mine with a very special muse."

The applause swelled once more, and time slowed as Bastien stepped down from the podium and was quickly swarmed by the crowd. She felt a jolt of anxiety remembering his discomfort in these situations and quickly began weaving her way through the milling bodies.

By the time she'd reached him, her father and Kendall were already at his side.

In the imperfect record of her inexplicably lucky life, this would go down as one of the most surreal images in the catalog.

Seeing her approach, her father shook Bastien's hand a second time and slid his arm about Kendall's shoulders. "I think we'd better go say hello to Darragh McClane, don't you think?"

"I agree completely," Kendall said, casting a sly look back at Shelby.

She'd been in on it.

The gathering followed the couple's lead, dispersing back in the general direction of the tent. Bastien stood apart, cutting a tall, dark figure against the lights aimed up at his sculpture.

Shelby picked her way over to him, keeping her weight on her toes to keep her heels from sinking into the grass.

"Your father reached out to me," he said, answering the question she hadn't yet asked. "About two weeks ago. He asked if I might have any pieces I thought would make a fitting apology for the way he'd behaved. I told him I had just the thing."

Glancing up at the intricate components, this idea

seemed beyond all reason. "You built this in two weeks?"

Bastien turned to face her. "I started building this the day you left Maine."

She blinked up at the piece in disbelief, each second that passed revealing a new detail.

"It's absolutely beautiful."

He turned to face her. "Yes, you are."

They didn't speak.

Perhaps, she thought, because art had the power to make declarations beyond the capacity of words.

One thing she knew for absolute certain. The man who'd made this sculpture *knew* her.

Knew her heart. Saw her soul.

And in seeing how he saw her, she knew his.

"So, Bastien Renaud. How are we going to do this?"

He tucked one of the curly tendrils that had escaped her intricate updo behind her ear and brushed a tear from her cheek with the sublimely rough thumb of his artist's hand. "First, I'm going to kiss you. Then, we'll figure the rest out."

"Mind if I take these off first?" she asked, lifting the folds of her flowy champagne-colored skirt to reveal the triangular toes of her nude heels. "I want to be able to give the matter my full attention."

"Baby," he said, wrapping his arms around her waist to lift her off her feet, "you can take off anything and everything. Starting with this stupid tie."

With trembling hands, she loosened the knot and slid it from his neck, letting it flutter to the earth she no longer touched. In the moment their lips met, he spun her in a slow circle, the night air cool on her neck and the bottoms of her bare feet. She let herself melt into him, returning ardor for ardor and trust for trust.

Letting this beautiful, broken man stand between her heart, and the world.

Epilogue

"What's wrong with what you have on?" Bastien stood barefoot at the mouth of the walk-in closet Shelby had insisted was necessary when he'd added a master bedroom suite onto the home in Maine, where they now spent their summers.

Well, summer.

They were drawing to the end of their first one, as witnessed by the fiery riot of leaves dancing beyond the three walls of floor-to-ceiling windows surrounding their bed.

It was mid-October, and, like the birds Shelby so loved, they'd soon be headed south.

A fact that Laney mercilessly ribbed Bastien about by demoting him from Batman to Robin.

"It doesn't match your suit." Shelby took a step

closer to him and nodded toward the garment bag he'd hauled out of his side of the closet. "May I?"

Bastien felt a sympathetic clench low in his gut when she tugged down the bag's zipper. "You're telling me we're one of *those* couples?" he asked.

She lifted an eyebrow at him.

"Right," he said. "Silly question."

They absolutely were one of *those* couples. Had been from the night of her father's wedding.

And he secretly loved it.

He loved that she insisted on signaling to the world through color coordination that they were a pair. A matched set. That they belonged to one another.

"Just as I thought," she said, fingering the sleeve of his pale blue dress shirt on its hanger. "Unzip me?"

He complied and she padded off to change.

Bastien hung up the garment bag and turned just in time to see her bare back as she unhooked her bra and tossed it on the bed.

He shut his eyes, willing her to have moved by the time he opened them.

She had.

Only now, he saw her in three-quarter profile—the tantalizing curve of one breast and the barest fraction of auburn aureole visible beneath her forearm. Bastien really wished she had removed her glasses before undressing. The contrast between the obsessively prim spectacles and her frankly sensual nude torso had an effect on him that quickly became visible to them both when she caught him watching her in the mirror.

"You remember that we need be at the party in twenty minutes, yes?" she reminded him.

Bastien bit his lower lip and crossed the room to her, wrapping his arms around her waist. "Aren't post christening celebrations one of those occasions where it's acceptable for people to arrive and leave whenever?" he asked, nuzzling her neck.

"If the baby in question doesn't happen to be your newborn niece, maybe," she said, slapping at his hands.

"Cosima won't mind," he insisted. "She's the non-traditional sort. Why else would she be hosting the christening here instead of in Boston?"

"Because she's making a gesture to weave your stubborn ass back into the family," she said.

"It's not my ass I'm thinking about right now." He panted kisses up the curve of her neck and below the shell of her ear.

Shelby relaxed against him. "Bastien?"

"Hmm?"

"Thank you."

He caught her eye in the mirror. "For what?"

"For catching me on the sidewalk outside your shop. For rescuing me when my car got stuck in the ditch. For feeding me dinner. For drawing me. For showing me my body wasn't broken. For saving me."

He swallowed against the ache growing in his throat. "But I didn't rescue you. I only carried the baton across the finish line," he said, reminding her of her own words.

"I'd never been rescued before." Lifting his hand

from her waist, she kissed his palm and laid it against her sternum. "I wasn't sure what to say."

There were many moments in Bastien's life he dearly wished he could forget. And some he knew he would remember until the last breath had left his lungs. But only one he'd fight heaven and earth to keep: Shelby Llewellyn, smiling with his hand sover her heart.

* * * * *

Don't miss any of The Renaud Brothers!

Bad Boy with Benefits
Blue Blood Meets Blue Collar
Trapped with Temptation

HARLEQUIN
PLUS

Try the best multimedia subscription service for romance readers like you!

Read, Watch and Play.

Experience the easiest way to get the romance content you crave.

Start your **FREE TRIAL** at
<u>www.harlequinplus.com/freetrial</u>.